GLENN TRUST
SHADOW MAN

BOOKS

By Glenn Trust

Sole Justice

Sole Survivor
Road to Justice
Target Down
The Ghost
Dark Winter
Shadow Man

Vinci Books

vinci-books.com

Published by Vinci Books Ltd in 2025

1

Copyright © Glenn Trust 2023

The author has asserted their moral right to be identified as the author of this work in accordance with the Copyright, Designs and Patents Act 1988. This work is a work of fiction. Names, characters, places and incidents are the product of the author's imagination or are used fictitiously. Any resemblance to actual persons, living or dead, places and incidents is entirely coincidental.

All rights reserved. No part of this publication may be copied, reproduced, distributed, stored in any retrieval system, or transmitted in any form or by any means, including photocopying, recording, or other electronic or mechanical methods, nor used as a source for any form of machine learning including AI datasets, without the prior written permission of the publisher.

The publisher and the author have made every effort to obtain permissions for any third party material used in this book and to comply with copyright law. Any queries in this respect should be brought to the attention of the publisher and any omissions will be corrected in future editions.

A CIP catalogue record for this book is available from the British Library.

Paperback ISBN: 9781036704391

The EU GPSR authorised representative is Logos Europe, 9 rue Nicolas Poussin, 17000 La Rochelle, France
contact@logoseurope.eu

Printed and bound in Great Britain by Clays Ltd, Elcograf S.p.A.

ONE

Safe Passage

Ignacio Pacheco was a patient man. It would be a while still before the passengers assembled and were loaded, but he didn't mind. He was in no hurry. For now, he was content to lean back in the cushioned seat and wait behind the wheel of the forty-foot bus.

Once, years ago, the bus transported tourists on excursions from resort hotels along the Baja Peninsula. It had been a very comfortable bus in its day, top of the line, but now it was old, and the air conditioning only worked intermittently. Ignacio didn't mind that either. The day was pleasant, not hot and not cold. He had the driver's window open, and a light breeze ruffled the strands of gray hair that curled out from under a battered LA Dodgers ball cap. He kept the cap's visor pulled down low as he drove to help block the sun, but now, it was pushed back on his head, and he enjoyed the breeze on his face.

He breathed deeply, relaxed, enjoying the time before he would go to work. Somewhere nearby, in one of the small shacks that lined the road, someone was cooking onions and peppers and chorizo. The aroma reminded him of his wife's cooking.

He'd left that morning without breakfast. It was early, so he let her sleep while he washed and dressed.

When he leaned over the bed and kissed her cheek, her eyes fluttered open, she yawned and kissed his stubbly chin. "You need a shave."

"When I get back." He laughed. "The passengers won't mind much as long as I get them there."

"I suppose not." His wife nodded, stretched, and sat up, swinging her legs over the side of the low bed. She flipped her long gray hair back out of her face with a shake of her head and stood. "How long will you be gone?"

"A week." He shrugged. "Always hard to say. Not more than ten days, I think."

"I wish you could stay. Felipe's birthday is on Sunday … a special day. Father Andreas always mentions the children with birthdays during the week, and this time Felipe's will be on that very day."

"I know all of this, Lucia." Ignacio smiled and leaned forward to give her a quick peck on the forehead. "You'll have to tell *mi pequeño* his grandpa will bring him back something special."

"He would trade it to have his *abuelito* there with him on his special day," Lucia said.

"It can't be helped. We are fortunate that they hired me to drive the bus. Who knows how long all of this will last? Things change. Politics change, and there are many others who would give much to have my position." He smiled and patted her bottom. "And the dollars they pay me."

"I know." She stood on her tiptoes and gave him a quick kiss on the lips, then folded her arms. "Now go, be safe, and hurry back. The nights are cool, and I need your rump here to warm me up."

He laughed. They laughed a lot together. For thirty-two years, they'd been making each other laugh. "*Adiós*," He called over his shoulder and gave a flip of his hand as a goodbye wave.

Now, sitting in the bus on a tiny side street in Carmen Xhán, a half mile from the Guatemalan border crossing, his stomach growled. He tried to ignore it, leaning back in the seat, watching the activity in the square just ahead at the corner. Young men, the coyotes—smugglers of people across the northern border into the United States—took the money and organized groups of people for transport north through the entire length of Mexico.

Some would go in buses like the one Ignacio drove if they had money to pay the fee. Others would walk, caravans of people they were called in the media. They paid for that privilege as well, met and guided by the coyotes to the border. When they arrived there, other bands of coyotes would take them across the Rio Grande into Texas or through the deserts into New Mexico, Arizona, or California.

The coyotes were loosely affiliated and associated with the various cartels that ran the smuggling networks. Most got along with each other, but occasionally a dispute would erupt into a flash of gunfire. When this happened, some young man trying to make his fortune from the immigrants moving north would lie in a pool of blood in the streets until the local *policías* cleaned up the mess. Then it would be back to business as usual.

Today was peaceful, though. The coyotes organized their clients in the town square. There was much bustling about, new arrivals making their way through the streets, buying provisions in the shops, looking for a place to rest before moving on.

A boomtown atmosphere prevailed around the small town and in its counterpart, Gracias a Dios, less than a mile away in Guatemala. The two towns straddled the border between the two countries and had become a focal point for hundreds of thousands of migrants making their way north through South and Central America to the United States.

The border crossing itself was a simple marker along a two-lane road with a guard shack on each side. Residents of the two towns passed freely from one country to the other.

For migrants, this was where they met the coyotes who moved among them, recruiting business, making promises to get them across Mexico's northern border with the United States. Most would keep their promises as a matter of good business practice, but some would not, and the migrants who trusted them would pay a high price. Some would pay with their lives.

The prices charged by the coyotes varied. Some migrants paid as much as fifteen thousand dollars to get to the United States border, but that was the exception. The going rate was about five thousand U.S. dollars for a single person or seven thousand for an adult and a child. This was a popular option because showing up with a child greatly increased your chances of staying in the United States.

Still, Ignacio thought, seven thousand dollars was an enormous sum. He watched and wondered where they got the money to pay the coyotes. They did not seem to be rich people. Many must have sold all of their earthly possessions —jewelry, family heirlooms, cars if they owned one, their homes—to pay the prices the coyotes charged.

It seemed too much to him. He was happy in Carmen

Xhán, but if they wanted to go that badly, he was only too happy to drive them and take the dollars the cartel paid.

As he watched, a group of young men—the coyotes—herded fifty migrants down the side street toward the bus. Ignacio pulled the lever that opened the door and climbed out.

He pushed his way through the gathering crowd. "Here!" he called out, opening the baggage compartments under the coach. "Put your things in here, or there won't be room for you inside."

They looked at him skeptically, clinging to their backpacks and duffels and bundles tied up with string.

"Listen carefully," Ignacio said. "This bus only seats forty. There are fifty of you. That means we will all be packed in like sardines in a can. So, you put your belongings in these compartments underneath." He smiled and gave a reassuring nod. "I promise once we start moving, no one will be able to get into the compartments. Your things will be safe there, and you can get them when we stop." He shrugged. "But it's your choice. You can wait for another bus with more room if you like."

It was a lecture he'd given several dozen times since he started driving the bus. The coyotes with their guns tucked in their pants stood listening.

A woman put her bundle in the compartment, took a backpack from a child with her, and tossed it in. Ignacio smiled. "Good. That's the way to do it."

The woman climbed the steps onto the bus. Others followed her example.

Ignacio climbed back up to the driver's seat, pushing his way past those who were blocking the steps. Those behind him peered along the aisle and saw that the interior was quickly becoming crowded.

"Will there be room?" a man asked.

"Yes, yes. We'll get you all in." Ignacio grinned. "By the time we get you to the Rio Grande, you'll all be very close friends ... if you don't kill each other first."

There was a murmur of laughter along the line of migrants pushing their way onto the bus. The coyotes smiled. They liked the way old Ignacio handled things and kept people calm. Not all the drivers were as capable.

Outside, two coyotes with pistols tucked in their belts took up positions by the baggage compartments. The scowls on their faces warned thieves to stay away and gave the migrants more confidence that their meager belongings would be safe.

Other coyotes herded the crowd up the steps. They were a mixture of families—men, women, and children—along with younger men and a few single women traveling alone.

The loading took thirty minutes. When the last passengers squeezed aboard the overcrowded bus, two of the coyotes came up the steps and sat in the seats reserved for them directly behind Ignacio.

"Nacho!" one exclaimed and slapped Ignacio on the back. "Always a pleasant ride when you drive. Now let's go. *¡Vamos!*"

"Why such a hurry, Rico?" Ignacio asked and pulled the lever, closing the bus door.

"I have a date in Reynosa if we can get there in two days," Rico grinned. "She's the one for me ... this week."

Ignacio laughed.

The other coyote shook his head. "Do you ever stop thinking with your balls and dick?"

"Never!" Rico laughed. "You're just jealous, Celio. Nothing waiting for you but your right hand."

The migrants in the seats closest to the front laughed. Whispered conversations sprang up.

"These coyotes aren't so bad," they whispered to each other. *"That one looks like my little brother. Even with their guns, they're just boys."*

"Yes, boys with guns that shoot bullets."

"Exactly. Bullets that will protect us on the journey."

"But can they get us all the way to the border up north?"

"We paid our money. We have to trust them. Others have and are now in America."

"But they seem so young."

"Relax. See that driver? He's older, about my father's age. He'll get us there."

Ignacio turned the ignition, and the old bus rumbled to life. The air brakes hissed as they released, and the diesel engine belched a cloud of black smoke from the exhaust. The bus rolled forward slowly, avoiding the children, who ran in front, playfully chasing and dodging it down the street.

Ignacio left the children behind and steered the bus expertly around the narrow corners and streets until they came out onto a highway leading north. Their route would take them along the coast of the Gulf of Mexico, but Ignacio avoided the main highways, which were heavily patrolled by police. Some of the local cops were honest, but some worked for the cartels and could be trouble. It was always best to avoid them if possible.

Despite Rico's wish to get there in two days, it would take at least four. In a car, driving the main highways, it might be done in three days, driving twelve hours a day, but in the bus on the back roads, that was not possible.

Ignacio settled in behind the wheel. The passengers talked in muted voices among themselves. Most did not know each other before today and were cautious about sharing their plans at first, but after a few miles, a sense of camaraderie settled over them. For now, they were all in this together.

Two hours into the journey, Ignacio spoke his first words since leaving Carmen Xhán. "Trouble."

"Where?" Celio leaned forward to peer over his shoulder. "

"*Mierda*" Shit.

Straddling the road ahead, two trucks of the *Policía Estatal* blocked their path. Five men in uniform, armed with semi-automatic rifles, stood at the sides. The leader waved an arm, palm down, directing Ignacio to stop.

Rico stirred from a nap as the brakes hissed, and the bus slowed to a stop. "What is it?" He leaned forward beside Celio to look through the windshield. "Oh."

"Probably nothing," Ignacio suggested. "Pay them a little money, and we can be on our way."

"Maybe," Celio said. "Unusual to find them on this road."

"They must have figured out that we were avoiding the main highways." Ignacio chuckled. "And missed collecting the *taxes*."

Behind him, murmurs rose up among the passengers.
"What now?"
"Policías! This can't be good."
"I knew things were going too smoothly."
"Maybe just a delay."
"But they have guns."
"Of course, they have guns. They're policías."

A woman sobbed. Ignacio turned in his seat. "Don't worry. Only a brief delay. They will want to act very official and check things out, then we pay a little money and go on our way while they wait for the next bus to come along." He grinned. "They're just hunting pigeons with those guns, and today, we're the pigeons."

"I'll check it out," Rico stood and nodded at Ignacio. "Open up."

"Be careful," Celio called after him as Rico descended the steps.

Everyone on the bus leaned forward or to the side to see what was happening out front. Rico lifted a hand in greeting. The man who seemed to be the leader of the cops said a few words. Rico nodded and returned to the bus, and stood at the bottom of the steps.

"Well?" Celio said.

"It's as we thought … a shakedown. They want money for us to continue. We'll have to pay them a little before we move on." Rico called up into the bus. "Everybody out!"

"Why out?" Celio said, eyes narrowed. "If we pay them, why shouldn't we just drive down the road?"

"Because they're *policías*, and they have an audience." Rico shrugged and grinned. "They want to show us who's boss. Maybe make up for their tiny *pingas*." Tiny dicks.

A few passengers laughed.

"Alright then," Ignacio said and stood. "Everybody out so we can get back on the road." He waited at the bottom of the steps, helping the women and children.

When everyone had gathered in front of the bus, he went to join them. The *policías* stepped in closer, forming an arc around the group. The senior officer pointed at Ignacio. "You're the driver?"

"Yes. You must be the *comandante*." Ignacio smiled.

"Step over there, please." The officer pointed to the side of the road.

"Such games," Ignacio sighed and walked to the side of

the road, mumbling, "Play your games and let us get on our way. We have miles to …"

He turned and never finished his sentence. The senior officer raised an arm, pointed a pistol at Ignacio, and fired a single bullet through his brain.

A few passengers shrieked. Some sobbed. Celio reached for the pistol in his belt, and two *policías* sent a stream of rifle bullets through his chest, barely missing nearby passengers.

Now, all the passengers were sobbing, on their knees, and begging for their lives. The senior officer stood before them, speaking in a loud, clear voice. "Enough! We will not harm you. The money you have paid is now ours. We will provide you safe passage the rest of the way to the border. There, our people will meet you and escort you across into the United States."

He waited for the sobbing and murmurs to die down, then continued, "This is all done for you by *Los Salvajes*."

He turned to Rico, standing to the side of the group. "You understand what you are to do?"

"Yes." Rico nodded.

"Repeat it."

"I return to Carmen Xhán and pass the word that all *coyotes* are now controlled by *Los Salvajes*. No one is to drive or work for anyone else, or they will end up like him." He nodded at Ignacio's body in the dirt.

"Very good." The senior officer, Luis Ibarra, said. "Do this, and you are one of us."

"A step up," Rico said with a grin.

Three men pushed the passengers back on the bus, then boarded and drove away. Another took Rico in one of the police trucks, turning back toward Carmen Xhán.

Ibarra gave a satisfied nod. It was a good beginning.

TWO

Make Friends

As commercial lobster boats go, it wasn't large, but it was typical of those working out of the Mexican village of Puerto Nuevo. At eighteen feet in length, it bobbed along on the Pacific swells like a cork.

John Sole hadn't been on board long, a couple of hours at most, enough time to sail from the transfer point into port. The brief trip was uneventful. The boat's captain and two deckhands largely ignored him. They'd been paid and told not to ask questions or engage with their passenger in any way.

With an extra month's pay in their pockets, they were happy to comply. The *norteamericano* agents paid well to simply ferry a passenger from time to time. It was a side business their captain had arranged through a local contact, a gringo he knew only as Jay, and who promised there would be others in the future and many more dollars in their pockets.

The transfer at sea from the cabin cruiser, also provided

by Jay—John Sole's NSA contact, Jason Lovell—was the most dangerous part of the journey. Timing the rise and fall of the two boats, Sole had to jump the three feet separating them. A missed step and he would fall into the Pacific waters and face the real possibility of being crushed between the two hulls.

He made the jump safely, and as soon as his feet hit the lobster boat's deck, the anonymous skipper of the cabin cruiser throttled the engine up and pulled sharply away. Sole turned to face his new shipmates.

They went about their business without looking up. He might as well have been invisible. The deckhands coiled lines and inspected lobster traps. The captain focused on the horizon and guided his boat back to Puerto Nuevo. No one spoke to him.

When the boat's bumpers rubbed against the dock, Sole stepped off. There were no goodbyes or acknowledgment that he'd ever been on board. The second his foot hit the dock, the captain reversed engines and backed away. The U.S. dollars were a bonus, but it was time to get back to work in the lobster fields.

Sole made his way through the port area. Crews and captains worked to ready their boats to go out, or, if they'd had a successful day, unloaded their catch.

He carried no bags or weapons. Jay Lovell had promised to supply everything he required after his arrival. He cautioned Sole to avoid attracting attention. A white-skinned Georgia boy with a duffel bag might catch the eye of the local *policías* and raise questions as to his immigration status. At the very least, he would have to pay off the officer who confronted him. At the worst, he might run across one who could not be bribed, not likely but possible. So, he walked through the port and down a side street, empty-handed, trying to look like he belonged.

An hour's drive south from San Diego and across the border at Tijuana brought you to the small fishing village of Puerto Nuevo, but Lovell had insisted on using the boats. He emphasized that they wanted no record of his passage over the border or his presence in Mexico.

The village itself had been in decline until it found new life as a tourist attraction, marketing lobsters the boats brought in from the Pacific. While the locals continued to live as their ancestors had for generations, well-to-do tourists paid for excursions to eat at the new high-end restaurants and sample the local lobster dishes.

Sole was not headed to the part of town that catered to wealthy tourists. He wound his way through the back streets Lovell had made him memorize. He came to an adobe-walled building in an alley and looked up. It was a two-story affair, but so low that he could almost reach up and touch the second-story window frame. He rapped three times on the door.

A minute passed. He looked up and down the alley. It was deserted, with not a person or vehicle in sight.

A black bird on the eaves of an adjacent building let out a guttural squawk and turned its head sideways to get a better look at the newcomer. A grackle, maybe, Sole wondered. Do grackles make it down to Old Mexico?

The bird stared hard at him, and Sole muttered, "I know what you're thinking. You're not from around here, are you?" He shook his head. "Pretty easy to see, I suppose."

He rapped on the door again. The bird flew away, squawking louder, annoyed that the intruder had disturbed the serenity of his alley.

He was about to retrace his steps and figure out if he'd made a wrong turn when a door opened across the alley. Jay Lovell popped his head out. "Over here."

Sole spun around, looked up and down the alley, and wrinkled his brow. "Did I get the wrong house?"

"Nope," Lovell said. "Right house."

"Then why …"

"Just making sure you weren't followed. I was upstairs checking from the window, watching the ends of the alley."

"And?" Sole frowned and walked across the alley.

"You weren't," Lovell said. "Good job." He opened the door wider, Sole went inside, and Lovell closed the door, throwing a deadbolt lock as he did.

"What if I was?" Sole said.

"What if you were what?"

"Followed."

"Oh." Lovell smiled, ignored the question, and waved an arm around the small room. "So anyway, welcome."

Sole eyed the man who'd recruited him at the FBI field office in Pierre, South Dakota. He was dressed the same, except leather sandals replaced the athletic shoes, and instead of a Grateful Dead t-shirt, a long yellow, too large, t-shirt hung from his bony shoulders. *'Viva Zapata!'* was emblazoned across the back of the t-shirt in bright green letters, while smiling dolphins jumped through the air into blue water on the front. Sole couldn't figure out how the two concepts fit together, but he noticed that Lovell's cargo shorts appeared to be the same ones he'd worn in South Dakota almost a year earlier.

"So, this is home?" Sole asked, looking around.

"Call it home base," Lovell said. "A safe place if you need it."

"Safe from what?"

"Lots of things can go wrong down here." Lovell shrugged. "But mostly safe from the cartel."

"Which cartel?" Sole asked.

"All of them," Lovell said simply. "That's why you never come here if you suspect someone is following you."

"Alright. Don't come if someone is following." Sole nodded. "Got it. Other than that, what am I doing here? You told me you were running an operation to bring down the cartels, that you'd brief me when I got here. I'm here, so brief me. How are you … we … going to bring them down?"

"Fair enough," Lovell said and led the way into an adjacent room with a kitchen table in the middle of the floor. There were two 1960s-era vinyl and steel tubing kitchen chairs at the table and a hot plate on a shelf in the corner connected by a black hose to a propane bottle on the floor. Other than that, the room was empty.

Lovell sat in one chair and motioned Sole to the other. "Something to eat?"

Sole eyed the wrappers and bags on the table, some already open, and shook his head. "No, thanks."

"You sure?" Lovell picked up a tortilla stuffed with black beans and took a bite. "This is the real stuff, not that watered down shit you get north of the border."

"Maybe later," Sole said and sighed. It had been a long day, and his patience was wearing thin. "What am I doing here, Jay?"

"Okay, sorry. I got busy and haven't eaten since yesterday." He put the tortilla back on the table, leaned back in the flimsy chair, and said, "*Amicus meus, inimicus inimici mei.*"

"I didn't take Latin in school," Sole said.

"Ancient proverb that means, my friend, the enemy of my enemy. The Arabs say it a little differently, but the meaning is the same. The enemy of my enemy is my friend." Lovell's eyes narrowed as he stared into Sole's. "You want to bring down the *Los Salvajes* cartel?"

"You know the answer to that."

"Then we are going to make friends with some dangerous people."

"The other cartels," Sole said, and he began to understand Lovell's plan.

"Right." Lovell leaned forward and put his elbows on the table, speaking earnestly, dropping the usual old-hippie indifference that was part of his cover. "Mexican authorities can't bring them down … too much corruption in the ranks, and those who aren't corrupt have almost no power. But if … and this is a big *if* right now … if we can make the other cartels our allies and get them fighting *Los Salvajes* for us, we can put them out of business."

"And when the dust settles, another cartel takes the place of *Los Salvajes*." Sole shook his head, doubtful. "How does that help?"

"Because we'll be running things … setting them up behind the scenes … making new friends with their enemies. We repeat the cycle until the cartels are gone … until they kill each other off. Our job is to keep them at each other's throats."

"Seems like a longshot. You really think they'll be gone?" Sole asked.

"Truthfully, never completely gone, but if we do this right, we can greatly reduce their power." Lovell shook his head. "It used to be marijuana, cocaine, meth. Hell, I smoked weed back in college, even dabbled in coke a couple of times, but it's different now. The cartels are into other markets. You saw that in South Dakota."

Sole listened without speaking.

"Fentanyl," Lovell continued. "Made here in Mexico, not imported from Colombia like cocaine. The precursor drugs come in freight containers from China to Mexican ports. Cartel labs use those drugs to synthesize fentanyl, and then they ship it across the border. Every dose from a sloppy distributor can kill. Hell, it's killing our kids every day."

Lovell paused before adding his ultimate argument. "Worst of all ... human trafficking ... selling people into slavery. You saw it ... sex slavery, pedophilia, but there's more. Workers forced to labor for others while the cartel collects the fees, young men forced to fight and die for warlords in other countries."

Sole nodded. "I saw it."

"You know them, John. You have history with *Los Salvajes*. They are the strongest, and they want to control it all ... drugs, human trafficking, things we haven't even thought of yet, but they will think of them, and then they'll send them north of the border." Lovell's hand smacked down hard on the table. "The cartel's world, the one they want to create, is dystopian ... a dark, evil place without mercy or light. Our job is to get them to destroy themselves."

"By pretending to be allies of the other cartels, their friends," Sole said, thinking it over, then asked, "Why me? I'm no spy ... never been involved in this sort of thing."

"Like I said, you have history with *Los Salvajes*, and this is liable to get messy ... bloody." Lovell stared into his eyes. "We know what you've been up to these past few years, pieced a lot of it together at least, and we know you'll do what has to be done if it comes to that."

"You mean if someone ends up with blood on their hands, it'll be me," Sole said, with a cynical twist of his lips.

"I mean, when it comes to taking down *Los Salvajes*, you're motivated."

Sole couldn't deny it. He took a deep breath and nodded. "Alright, let's go make some new cartel friends."

THREE

Love, Respect, and Fear

"There is news, Seve."

"In a moment." Sixty-three-year-old Severiano 'Seve' Espinoza sat on the floor with his grandchildren. He smiled. "The children have almost finished."

His brother Miguel nodded and stood waiting patiently as he had for all of his fifty-five years. There were no sibling rivalries between them. No petty jealousies as sometimes happen between brothers when one is dominant, even favored by the parents. Miguel had always understood that his brother was the heir apparent to the family fortune, such as it was. Not understanding would have changed nothing. Besides, his brother made loyalty easy, protected Miguel, shared the wealth, kept no secrets, went to him for counsel, and treated him as an equal in every way. Their devotion to each other was unbreakable, forged not just through expediency and profit, but in blood.

Now, Seve sat cross-legged with three of the fifteen grandchildren his three daughters and a son had given him. Smiling and laughing with them, he handed them pieces of a jigsaw puzzle. They knelt on all fours, taking the pieces, giggling, and trying them in different positions to fit together on the floor between them. It was a child's puzzle, nothing too complicated. The picture of a cow jumping over a crescent moon was nearly completed.

A diminutive, dark-haired boy of five slapped a piece down and slid it into position. "There! Now the cow has a tail!" He grinned at his grandfather. "Did I do good, *Tata*?"

"Excellent, Juliano! You are very clever, little one."

"I'm not so little," the boy said quickly. "I'll be big one day." He looked at his great-uncle standing patiently behind his grandfather. "Big as *tio* Miguel, I think."

"Yes, I think you are right," Seve said and pushed himself up from the floor with a grunt. "And now, little ones, I must speak with *tio* Miguel."

He led the way from the playroom he'd constructed for his grandchildren. They crossed a wide tiled patio and entered a separate wing of the rambling house. This was no typical Spanish-influenced hacienda. Seve Espinoza's tastes ran to the modern. His home was reminiscent of Frank Lloyd Wright's Arizona residence, Taliesin West. Long, window-lined hallways surrounded gardens and an enormous swimming pool. Every room had a view of the manicured lawns, the countryside, or the distant mountains.

He led his younger brother into an expansive office lined with windows on three walls. Mexico's highest peak, Pico de Orizaba, rose in the distance through the glass. Seve eased himself into the leather chair behind the desk, sighed, leaned back, and asked, "What is this news, Miguel?"

"A bus is missing," Miguel said, with no explanation. None was needed.

"Where?" Seve sat up straight.

"North of Carmen Xhán."

"Do we know who did this?"

"Brother, there could only be one group who would dare," Miguel said.

"Yes," Seve said, nodding. "I had hoped this time might not come."

"It has come just the same."

"Do we know how it happened? Were our people off the main highways, as we instructed?"

"Yes." Miguel nodded. The implication was clear. This was not a chance event. To know where the bus would be could only mean one thing. There was a traitor among them … an informant feeding information to *Los Salvajes*, giving them the route the bus would follow.

Seve's eyes narrowed. "Our people … are there any survivors?"

"That is not certain. The driver and one guard are dead in a ditch by the road. Two *policías* that we pay found them and reported it."

"Only one guard and the driver?" Seve asked. "And the other guard? There should have been a second."

"There were two. The second is missing." Miguel shrugged. "Our *policías* were very nervous when they made the report. I doubt they stayed around to investigate for long. The hijackers may have taken our guard with them to torture for information or to exchange him as part of some arrangement with us." He shrugged. "Or they may have killed him, and our two *policías* have not yet found the body."

"Or, we may know who our traitor is," Seve said. "In any event, we need our own people there to sort things out,"

"Yes." Miguel nodded.

"Have the helicopter brought around from the airstrip. Take some men to investigate. I want to know for certain who made the attack … *Los Salvajes*, yes, but who exactly and how they carried it out and where they took the bus with our cargo."

"Yes." Miguel turned and left the office.

Seve Espinoza sat gazing out the window. It was a tranquil scene—green manicured lawns, birds flitting from flower to flower or singing in the trees. His grandchildren had moved out to the pool now and were playing, laughing, and splashing the way all children do. He had worked all his life to provide a life of comfort for his family, and seeing them at play made him smile.

That the comfort they enjoyed had been purchased with the pain, blood, and suffering of others was of no concern. If the weakness of those others allowed him to profit by trafficking drugs and people, so be it. It was merely the way of the world as it had always been and, in his estimation, would always be. Who was he to change it?

Espinoza had always pictured himself as a man of refinement, a thinking man. He lived an elegant life without the showy ostentatiousness often associated with great wealth.

After obtaining a degree in architecture from the National Autonomous University in Mexico City, young Seve Espinoza returned to his family's small ranch in the state of Veracruz. He brought Elena, whom he'd met and married while at the university without his parents' permission or blessing. It seemed to them that Seve always did what he could to avoid the appearance of living a traditional life. Showing up with a new wife, without mentioning it or asking for their blessing, was just the sort of thing they expected of him.

When his aging father turned the ranch operations over to him, Seve took things in a new direction. The ranch became a sideline while Seve focused his efforts on a new business—trafficking drugs, and later people, into and out of the United States.

His university studies gave him an eye for detail. His personality made him ruthless in achieving his business goals. The family tradition was that they descended from the conquistadors who had established Veracruz as a jumping-off point to conquer the Mexican natives of the era. It seemed likely. Behind the benevolent, aristocratic, and refined façade, Seve built a cartel that ran with well-oiled efficiency and dwarfed all the others, except for one—*Los Salvajes*.

He picked up his phone and dialed two numbers. When the calls were answered, he said, "We must meet."

The voices on the other end asked no questions and simply replied, "*Sí, Don* Espinoza."

Seve Espinoza was a man of many faces. His grandchildren loved their *abuelito*. His wife of thirty-six years, Elena, loved him. His brother Miguel loved him.

As for business, his counterparts in other cartels rarely uttered a word of disagreement. If on occasion they did disagree about some issue of mutual concern, they proffered their thoughts politely and with the respect one showed to a man of his stature and abilities.

But when complications arose that might disrupt his carefully constructed plans, Seve Espinoza became brutal in eliminating the problem. For this reason, his enemies feared him.

FOUR

Much More

Reynaldo Gutierrez entered the hacienda office and stepped to the side to take up position on Juana Elizondo's right. Luis Ibarra followed him in and stood directly in front of Elizondo's desk.

"Your report," Juana said without preliminaries.

"All went as we planned," Ibarra responded.

"Be more specific," Juana said, scowling.

"Yes, of course," Ibarra said quickly. "The information we had from their man was correct. The bus arrived when and where he said it would. They were taken completely by surprise."

"Very good." Juana nodded. "You have other informants?"

"At the moment, no."

"Find others," she said. "You will need them as soon as Espinoza and the others realize what is happening."

"We may have to pay them more." Ibarra spoke softly, his head tilted to the side in a mild-mannered, respectful way, looking down at the desk and avoiding Juana's stare.

He had learned through experience that it was always good to be respectful around the Elizondo family. He explained, "It is dangerous work. Others may be reluctant in the future when …" Ibarra shrugged. "When things begin to happen."

"Pay whatever is necessary." Juana leaned forward, her eyes narrowed. "We began this. Now we will finish it."

"*Sí, jefa.*" Ibarra nodded.

"How many dead?" Juana asked.

"Only two. The driver and a guard." Ibarra smiled. "Our man was very cooperative and helped us set things up nicely."

"Where is he now?"

"In Carmen Xhán, spreading the word that all transports of migrants to the border must happen through us. No one drives the buses, no one takes their money, no one provides security except *Los Salvajes*." Ibarra shrugged. "My man drove him back, and that was the last I saw of him."

"I'm sure it was," Juana said, twirling the ends of her long brown hair between her fingertips, looking for a moment like a schoolgirl thinking, then the hardness was back in her eyes. "Alright. Have your people recruit other informants and begin setting up the next operation. We start taking control of all coyote transports this week. Send the message."

"*Sí, jefa.* I will see to it." Ibarra nodded and raised his eyes from the desk to hers, hoping to receive some acknowledgment or a simple nod of approval. There was none, and he retreated from the office.

When he was gone, Juana turned to Reynaldo standing to the side, silent, hands clasped behind his back, the posture of a soldier on parade, waiting for his orders. "You do not approve."

"I have never said such a thing," Reynaldo replied quietly, his gaze meeting hers.

"It's on your face ... in your eyes." Her brow furrowed. "I need you to speak freely, Reynaldo. My father had Garza as his confidante. You are mine ... the only one I can speak with to discuss ideas and make plans."

"I am not Garza," Reynaldo said, shaking his head.

"You could be," Juana shot back, frowning.

"Yet, I know nothing of these matters ... planning and strategy. I was kept far away from the decisions when your father ruled *Los Salvajes* and Garza counseled him."

"They are gone!" Juana smacked her hand down on the desk. "Those days are gone! You have it in you to be my Garza, to counsel and defend, but also to disagree when necessary."

"Alright," Reynaldo said and gave a solemn nod.

"Alright, what?" Juana scowled.

"I'll try."

"Good!" Now Juana smiled. "So, tell me your thoughts. Your disapproval is written all over your face."

"Not disapproval, *jefa*." Reynaldo shook his head. "Concern."

"About what?"

"That perhaps we are moving too quickly ... taking on more than we can handle."

"Explain."

"If *Los Salvajes* moves to control all of the coyotes and migrants, we will face enemies on all fronts. Every cartel traffics in people ... smuggling, buying, selling. Take that away, and they will unite against us ... against you."

"True." Juana nodded and looked into his eyes. "My father had a vision that *Los Salvajes* would one day control all the others. The cartels would unite with us, or ..."

She shrugged without finishing. There was only one *'or'*. Come under the control of *Los Salvajes* or Bebé Elizondo would crush them.

"I understand," Reynaldo said and then hesitated, uncertain that his counsel would be welcome.

"Speak," Juana snapped.

"You are not your father," he ventured, then added quickly, "No disrespect intended, *jefa*."

Juana's eyes narrowed for an instant, then she leaned back in the leather executive chair and laughed. "You are right, Reynaldo. I am not my father. But I think you will find I am much more!"

As he watched, she lifted a hand and traced a line with her fingertips from her neck down the center of her chest between the open buttons of her blouse. Her skin glistened. She took a deep breath, and her breasts rose. Reynaldo stared, transfixed.

"You see how much more I am than my father." Juana lowered her hand and sat up straight in the chair. "But I understand your concerns. You will be my filter ... my safety brake. You are to tell Ibarra that he now reports to you in all matters, and you, like Garza before you, will report to the *jefa* ... to me so that we can discuss your concerns."

"*Sí, jefa*." Reynaldo nodded.

"We are going to do a great thing, Reynaldo, and once we rule the other cartels as my father intended, you will find his killer and bring him to me." She leaned back in the chair again, this time crossing her legs so that the short black skirt she wore slid up her thigh. "We will discuss this tonight ... in my room when the others have gone to bed. Come to me then."

Reynaldo nodded, his eyes fastened on her form reclining in the chair, the curve of her thighs, her breasts rising under the partially open blouse. His heart pounded in his chest. His breath quickened. He managed to croak, "*Sí, jefa.*"

FIVE

Insurance

He began the day as he had every day since his arrival in Puerto Nuevo. John Sole walked the back alleys, making his way toward the beach. It was a short walk.

Wedged on a strip of land between the *Autopista Tijuana-Ensenada* and the Pacific Ocean, the village comprised a few square blocks of small cottages that housed the one hundred and thirty-five residents, plus a few hotels to accommodate tourists. More villages dotted the coastline to the north and south and in the hills behind.

Sole had become intimate with the layout, walked it every day, killing time while Jay Lovell 'set things up', the term Lovell had used to explain his disappearance.

It was an expression that led to a heated discussion between them and nearly ended their mission before it had begun. In true clandestine operative fashion, Lovell played everything close to the vest, sharing information only on a need-to-know basis. For Sole, that translated into very little information and a lot of time to kill.

Lovell had disappeared from the safe house the day after

Sole arrived. Sole dragged himself up off the cot in the upstairs room that served as his bedroom and found a note on the table in the kitchen downstairs. It read simply—*Be back soon.*

It became clear that Sole's notion of *soon* and Lovell's were vastly different. At first, he went with the flow. There was food in the fridge and a stash of money in a cupboard, so Sole didn't worry too much about his mysterious recruiter's sudden disappearance. The day wore on into the afternoon, and then another day, and he began to wonder if something had happened to Lovell, and if so, what the hell was he supposed to do now?

He spent the days scuffing around the village in sandals, shorts, and a t-shirt, alternately sitting on the beach staring at the blue Pacific or wandering the alleys. Locals began to recognize and acknowledge him with pleasant nods and smiles but made no effort to interact with him. There did not seem to be any money to be made from the new gringo in town. He didn't look or act like one of the wealthy tourists who came to the village to sample their lobsters or spend money on the typical trinkets available for purchase in every village along the Baja coast. The scruffy North American was just another *vagabundo*—a bum—hiding out below the border.

On the morning of the third day, Sole began to wonder if they had set him up. Had Lovell played him as part of some cloak-and-dagger bullshit game? He claimed to work for the NSA—National Security Agency—but Sole had been around long enough to know that the NSA was primarily responsible for signals intelligence. Field operations were left to the CIA, but, according to Lovell, the NSA had them conducting a clandestine operation in a foreign country because of the public backlash in Mexico when it was learned that the DEA and CIA had operated there for years. Instead, they worked under the auspices of a special operations division of the NSA—very secret, very informal, and off the record. The legality was questionable, but Lovel said the mission had been authorized at the highest levels. Sole could only guess what that meant.

For now, with Lovell missing and no one to bounce ideas off, his imagination began to take over. His head was on a swivel, constantly checking his back, flanks, and ahead. Was that chubby man reading a newspaper on a park bench, in reality, a cartel assassin in disguise? Those three gang-age young men on the corner, staring at him and whispering among themselves, could be planning a kidnapping— maybe to toss him in the back of a car and cart him off to some deserted spot to rob him and then eliminate him as a witness.

He thought of retreating to the safe house to spend his days there and wait for some contact from Lovell, but hiding in confinement was not Sole's way of dealing with threats. He preferred the open, the ability to move about, see what was coming, improvise and defend himself if a threat arose. But none did.

On the third day alone, he was sipping a *cerveza* at Bobby's Place, a side street bar owned by an American ex-pat. It had become his routine. Wander the streets and beaches during the day, grab food from street vendors when he got hungry, then finish the day at Bobby's, watching the sun setting over the Pacific. That's when Lovell finally called him on the burner cell phone he'd left him.

"What are you doing?" Lovell said as if he'd just stepped around the corner to pick up a loaf of bread.

"Having a beer. Where the hell are you?" Sole snapped back.

"Omaha."

"What? Where?"

"Omaha," Lovell repeated with a chuckle that Sole did not find amusing.

"Start explaining, or I hang up and hitch a ride back across the border, and you find someone else to play your games."

"Lighten up," Lovell said, but the chuckle was gone. "I've been getting everything set up."

"Set up? I thought everything was already set. The cartels are down here. That was the next step … get them to take each other out."

"Almost the next step," Lovell said. "First, I had to get the funding approved."

"What! You're losing me, Jay. I thought this operation was already in the works … a go from above."

"It was … it is … now."

"What the fuck does that mean?" Sole's voice rose a few decibels, and heads turned his way. He lowered his voice and leaned forward over the tiny bar table, the phone pressed hard against his ear. "Start talking."

"There was agreement in principle that we need to do this … bring down the cartels, starting with *Los Salvajes*, but agreeing to a concept and actually throwing dollars at it are two very different things. You know how it is, politicians and bureaucrats, worried about their asses if everything goes to hell in a handbasket."

"You led me to believe this operation was approved and going forward."

"It was … to a point."

"What the hell does that mean?" Sole's voice was increasing in volume again.

"Just that I came here to meet with some people to make sure the dollars are there when we need them."

"And you couldn't let me know?" Sole seethed, working to control the anger boiling up inside.

"I was afraid you might not have come along if you thought it wasn't already funded and approved."

"I might not have," Sole said.

"Well, that's why I said nothing, but I will tell you that having you already in place was the piece of the pie that turned the table in our favor."

"Having me in place?" Sole was feeling used, and that pissed him off even more.

"That's right. When I explained that you were on board ... your history with *Los Salvajes*, just sitting there in Mexico waiting for this to kick off ... the people I report to agreed to give it a go." Lovell chuckled again. "They didn't have much choice since I had you stashed at our safe house, ready to go kick some cartel ass."

"Goddammit, Jay! I don't like being used."

"Not used," Lovell said defensively. "You were just leverage. That's all."

"Same thing," Sole shot back. "And what if they'd decided that the op wasn't a go ... that I knew too much about your safe house ... about what you were up to? What then? You or somebody shows up some night while I'm sleeping on that shitty little cot and puts a bullet through my brain?"

"That didn't happen," Lovell said. "I wouldn't let that happen. I've been playing this game for a long time. I know how it works, and I would not have put you in that sort of compromising position. Trust me on this."

"My trust is running a little low right now." Sole took a

deep breath and sat quietly for a minute as the anger subsided. Lovell was smart enough to wait and say nothing.

"Alright, you got the funding," Sole finally said. "When do we start working with all the cartels?"

"Not all of them. There are too many," Lovell said, glad the conversation was back on the mission. "We'll focus on a few ... the most powerful ... the ones who can take on *Los Salvajes*."

"When?"

"In a few days. I have meetings tomorrow."

"What now?" Sole was tiring of the runaround. "You got the funding. What else do you need? Need me to *leverage* you a new car ... vacation time ... corner office?"

"That's good," Lovell said, laughing, then added simply, "Tactics."

"Tactics," Sole repeated, considering what that word might mean in the context of Lovell's world of secrecy and safe houses. "Clarify, please."

"I mean, I want it clear just how far we are authorized to go before we start leaving bodies around Mexico. You know, get them to sign off on the op ... unofficially, of course, but signed off, so our asses are covered."

"You want to make sure the op is sanctioned," Sole said.

"You read too many spy novels," Lovell laughed. "But in a way, yes. I want to make sure that we have the authorization to take out who we need to, in whatever manner is necessary to bring down the cartels and end, or at least slow, the trafficking of drugs and human beings." Lovell shrugged. "Call it sanctioned if that word works for you. I call it insurance."

"What kind of Insurance?"

"Life insurance ... so that we do what we have to and

come back alive and stay out of prison. It'll take a couple of days, and then I'll be back, and we get to work."

"Alright," Sole sighed. "But one condition."

"What's that?"

"From now on, no secrets, no disappearing in the middle of the night, no using me as leverage without my say-so because the next time you do, you'll need insurance to protect you from me."

"Understood," Lovell said, his tone sober. Sole might not be a spy, but he was a force to be reckoned with and would be an unpleasant enemy, which was the very reason Lovell had recruited him.

"What do I do now?" Sole asked.

"Relax, get some sun, swim in the ocean, drink *cervezas*. Have yourself a little vacation. It will be your last one for a while."

The call ended. Sole sat sipping his beer, looking out the fly-specked window at the people passing in the alley. The problem with insurance, he thought, was that a policy is only as good as the company that writes it, and he was not feeling reassured by the underwriting protocols of the unofficial NSA division backing Lovell.

SIX

Forgiven

The Bell 212 helicopter's rotor kicked up a dust storm as it circled, the pilots and security team on board scanning the terrain below for threats. Satisfied that the area was safe for their passenger, they landed in a field a hundred yards from the road. The rotor blades were still spinning overhead when seven men stepped out holding semi-automatic rifles.

They began systematically moving out and away, forming a security perimeter, working together with military efficiency. Alert, attentive to their surroundings, and communicating with hand signals, they adhered in every way to the training that had been drilled into them.

An assortment of U.S. law enforcement agencies had provided that training, along with an additional two months of conditioning and operational drills at a camp run by former U.S. Army Rangers. It was all part of a program for select Mexican law enforcement officers and security agents assigned to protect government officials trying to bring change to the historically corrupt Mexican government.

The men from the helicopter had once been assigned to

the security detail of a high-ranking cabinet official. Not long after returning from their training in the United States, they left government service and went to work for the Espinoza cartel at a salary many times what any Mexican government agency could afford.

When they had extended their perimeter to the road, one turned and gave a hand signal toward the chopper. Miguel Espinoza stepped out, his hands empty, but a holstered pistol strapped to his waist. He stood, hands on hips for a minute, surveying the surrounding countryside.

In the distance, a small village nestled against some low, green hills. The road he stood on was empty, but a distant speck and muted sound of an engine signaled the approach of a vehicle.

Espinoza turned and walked along the pavement, studying the ground. He found what he was looking for not far away in the roadside ditch. Two bodies, covered by dust blown up by the helicopter's rotor wash, lay side by side.

He recognized one—Ignacio Pacheco. As Seve Espinoza's right-hand man and chief confidante, Miguel often personally selected important members of their smuggling operations. The bus drivers charged with getting their cargo to the border were considered critical, and he had met with Ignacio a few months earlier. The old man's competence and frank good nature had impressed Espinoza, who thought he would be a good influence on the younger coyotes, many of whom were not much more than boys. They liked to swagger around with their guns and were all too eager to shoot someone, sometimes needlessly. He'd hoped Ignacio's maturity would have a calming effect.

Now Ignacio lay dead in a ditch with a bullet through his brain. The man beside him was one of the coyote guards, but Espinoza could not remember his name. There were many such young men in their organization, out to make a fortune from the millions the Espinoza cartel took in from smuggling illegals and drugs into the United States.

The vehicle that had been a distant speck approached and slowed. The heavy-duty, American-made pickup with dual rear wheels and an eight-foot bed stopped on the road near Espinoza. Besides the driver, there were two men inside with rifles and four more seated in the truck bed. The butts of their rifles rested on the bed floor, the muzzles pointed at the sky, like soldiers arriving for duty. They were quiet and disciplined, waiting for instructions.

Espinoza approached the driver's window and said, "They will be in that village there by the hills. Bring them to me."

The driver nodded, gunned the engine, and headed off the highway on a dusty side road toward the village. Espinoza turned to the security men with him and pointed at the bodies. "Have them taken to Carmen Xhán."

At the same time, the pickup roared into the village in a cloud of dust. Locals stopped in the streets, turned for a moment, then quickly went back to what they were doing, making a point to ignore the men piling out of the back of the pickup. It was always best to mind your own business when the cartels came into the village.

The office of the local *policías* was a small two-room building wedged in between a tiny grocery and a bar. The two officers inside had considered waiting in the bar to calm their nerves or running away but decided against it. They would need their wits about them when Espinoza began firing questions at them, and there was nowhere they could go where the cartel could not track them down.

When Espinoza's men came through the door, they were sitting in the office, one behind a small desk and one in a chair beside a door that led to a room with a single jail cell and a toilet.

One of the men from the pickup stared at them for a moment and said, "You reported the bus hijacking?"

"Yes," the officer behind the desk said.

"Come with us."

There was nothing else to do. Any resistance, any hesitation, any failure to comply immediately would only irritate the men from the pickup, and irritating the cartel men was not a healthy practice. The two officers walked out into the street and climbed into the back of the pickup, surrounded by the cartel men.

When they arrived back by the roadside ditch, everyone descended. Espinoza motioned the two officers over. "You found these men here?"

"Yes," the senior officer said, adding a solemn nod to show that he understood the serious nature of what had happened. "As soon as we discovered them."

"Your name?" Espinoza said.

"*Sargento* Cano," the senior officer said. "Felipe Cano."

"And you?" Espinoza looked at the other.

"Dominguez," the younger officer said in a voice not much more than a whisper. "José Dominguez."

Espinoza nodded at the bodies. "How did you happen to find them?"

"Well …." Cano hesitated. "We just came upon them."

"Here in this ditch?" Espinoza sneered. "What made you go looking in this ditch at this exact spot?"

Cano said nothing and stared at the ground. Dominguez looked as if his knees might give way and send him toppling over.

"Fine. I'll answer for you," Espinoza snapped. "You saw the others, heard the gunshots, and when they were gone, and it was safe, you came to see what happened and found the bodies." He paused a second and asked, "Does that sound like what happened?"

Cano nodded. "Yes, something like that, I suppose."

"You suppose!" Espinoza leaned forward. "Look at me!"

Cano and Dominguez raised their eyes from the ground and stared wide-eyed into Espinoza's angry face. "We pay you for protection, not to call us and tell us that our bus was taken and our men were killed. What did you do to protect our cargo?"

"Please understand, *señor*." Cano raised his hands in supplication the way he might have in church, praying before one of the saints. "There were many of them and only two of us."

"How many?"

"Well, I think …"

Espinoza turned to Dominguez. "You answer. How many?"

"F-five, *señor*, in two vehicles." His eyes were pleading. "I think they would have killed us if we had tried to stop them."

"No doubt," Espinoza smirked. "What did they look like?"

"Like us, *señor*," Dominguez said.

"Like you?" Espinoza glared at them. "Explain."

"*Policías*," Cano said. "Not from around here, but *policías* in uniform."

"That means nothing. Uniforms are easy to come by," Espinoza said.

"Yes, but they had vehicles … two of them. Official cars of the *Policías Estatal*.

I think they must have been actual officers," Cano said and added quickly, "But not from here."

"From where, then?"

"Michoacán," Cano said, happy to provide some information that might be considered useful. "We could see the markings on the vehicles clearly."

"So, you were close enough to see the markings but not close enough to stop the attack on our people." Espinoza glared at the two trembling police officers. "How is that?"

"We had the binoculars, *Jefe*," Cano said, looking at the ground again. "Please, you must understand. There were five of them, and only two of us, and the country is open, so we could not approach without being seen by them. If we had tried ..." He stopped and shrugged.

Espinoza looked from the two officers to the bodies in the ditch. No doubt there would be four there if the officers had tried to intervene, and they would not have known of the hijacking until the bus was overdue at the border.

"Alright." Espinoza nodded, calming himself. "You let us know what happened. That is good. It would have been better if you had stopped it from happening, but at least you notified us."

The two police officers breathed a sigh of relief. Cano allowed himself a smile. "Thank you, *Jefe*. We are glad you understand ..."

"Shut up," Espinoza snapped. "I understand you are happy to take the money we pay you as long as it suits you, and there is no danger." He leaned forward. "So, let me make this clear. You should have called us and then intervened. You could have helped the guards on the bus to resist .. surprised the others by shooting one or two so our men could react."

"I don't see how we could ..." Cano began.

Espinoza shook his head, and Cano's mouth closed. "This one time, you are forgiven, but only this one time."

He nodded at the bodies in the ditch. "Next time, it would be better for you to be there in the ditch with them." Espinoza waited for them to respond and, when they did not, leaned toward them and asked, saying each syllable distinctly, making the implied threat plain, "*¿Lo en – ti – en – des?*" Do – you – under – stand?

The terrified police officers nodded. Dominguez looked as if he might faint and fall over. Cano wondered if he had saved enough from his cartel pay to run away somewhere with his wife ... or without her, if need be.

SEVEN

Anticipation

The bus slowed and entered the districts of a large city. Heads turned, necks craned, and those who were standing in the aisle bent over, all trying to catch a glimpse of a sign, some indicator that would tell them they had arrived at their destination.

Murmurs rose, and questions were passed back and forth among the passengers on the bus.

"Where is this place?"

"Are we there?"

"Is this where we cross the border?"

"The river ... the Rio Grande should be here somewhere. Can you see it?"

"No, no river, but there!" one man exclaimed excitedly. *"There is a Walmart! That means we must be close to the border, no? Maybe even already across the border."*

"Don't be foolish. We would know if they drove us across the border. Besides, these Walmart stores are all over Mexico."

"There! There!" A woman seated beside a window pointed and

tapped on the glass. *"A sign in front of those buildings."* She read it to them. *"Instituto Tecnológico de Estudios Superiores de Monterrey. We are in Monterrey."*

The Monterrey Institute of Technology and Higher Studies sits in the far southern quadrant of the city of Monterrey, Mexico. The bus slowed and exited Highway 85, which had brought them north through central Mexico, drove past the institute, and began making its way through the side streets, bypassing the city center.

The passengers peered out at the passing suburbs and cluster of villages. After almost an hour of twists and turns, the bus moved away from the city on a dusty back road. More twists and turns, and another hour passed. They climbed into a range of low mountains and hills east of Monterrey.

The murmurs arose again.

"Where the hell are they taking us?"

"Monterrey is not on the way to the border, is it?"

"Don't be silly. There are many ways to the border. They must be taking us on a road that won't be discovered by the Border Patrol officers."

They chatted as if the events of the morning had never happened. The brutal murders of the driver, Ignacio, and the guard had terrified them. For a time, many wept and thought they would be taken into the desert to suffer a similar fate. Others tried to reason things out.

If they were to be killed, why load them back on the bus and drive away? The new guards and driver in the uniforms of *policías* said little, but they also made no threats.

As the day progressed and the new coyotes did little more than gaze out the window and chat among themselves, emotions settled down, and the migrants' fears subsided. From the sun, they could tell they were moving ever northward, and north was where the United States border awaited them. That was what they had paid for, so focus on that.

Whatever caused the murder of the driver and guard was none of their business. Better to not ask questions or cause a problem. The main thing was to get to the United States.

"It must have been some dispute between the cartels," some whispered among themselves.

"They don't seem interested in hurting us."

"I liked our other drive, Ignacio. He seemed a pleasant man."

"Yes, this new one doesn't speak, but he drives well."

The driver turned onto an uneven dirt trail, barely wide enough to accommodate the width of the bus. The top-heavy vehicle rocked as if it might turn over on its side, then righted as the engine roared and pushed it forward.

To the left, the hillside rose from the edge of the dirt trail. To the right, the hill dropped away for several hundred feet. A woman in a window seat on the downward side covered her eyes and muttered a prayer.

Then the driver made another turn, left this time between an opening in the hillside. They continued for a hundred yards through a narrow passage with rock walls towering on both sides, then all at once came out into a clearing covered with green grass. A stream flowed along one side. Birds flitted among the surrounding trees.

"¿Esto es Estados Unidos?" a voice asked. Is this the United States?

"No, not yet. We haven't come far enough, I think."

The door opened, and the guards went out, calling back inside, "Everyone out."

The passengers came down the steps, helping the older and less nimble to make it safely to the ground. Once outside, they stood in a circle, taking in their surroundings.

Large canvas tents lined the perimeter. Crates of supplies holding food and water were stacked between the tents. There were more men, coyotes like the ones who had driven them on the bus, except these did not wear the uniforms of the *policías*.

These were dressed in designer jeans and expensive athletic shoes, but like the men in uniform, they were all armed with pistols. A few had rifles.

The migrants stood huddled together in the clearing. A few of the more timid were trembling, wondering what would happen next, but most looked around with expressions of expectant curiosity.

One of their guards called out to the passengers. "Tonight, you will rest here. There is food and water and shelter in the tents. Tomorrow will be the last day of the journey. You will be met and taken across the border."

"You see," a man said, leaning over to whisper to his wife. "They are taking us across, just as we paid them to. It's only good business."

One of the men who had been waiting for them in the clearing approached and walked around them. He was slightly older and seemed in charge of the others. The migrants stood quietly as he walked around, assessing them in an uncomfortable way.

A migrant who had worked on a cattle ranch in Honduras whispered, "He looks like a buyer at auction, examining the steers."

"Careful," another chuckled back. "He may want to see your teeth or check your *polla*."

The first man grinned, grabbed his groin, and said, "Come and get it, just be gentle."

Laughter rose up among the adults. The little ones tugged at their parents to have them explain what the men said that was so funny and more laughter erupted.

The man in charge ignored the laughter. Once he had looked at each of the migrants, he turned to face them all and began giving instructions.

"You people here." He pointed at three small family groups on one side. "Go to that tent there."

"You," His finger indicated five young men standing together. "To that tent."

"But that is our son," one of the older men called out, pointing at one of the young men. "He should come with us."

"No," the man in charge shook his head. "The young men go to that tent."

"Don't worry," the young man called out to his parents. "I'll see you in the morning." Then he went running after the others, smacking one on the shoulders so that they all laughed like boys on some grand adventure.

"You, you, you ..." The man in charge began pointing at different people and sending them off to various tents.

"Why are you sending our daughters away to the other tents?" a mother called out.

The man in charge turned to face her. "Because, *Señora*, we have learned it is bad practice to have the boys and the young girls in the same tents. You were young once. I'm sure you understand that. What happens once you get across the border is your business, but for now, there won't be any *cuchi-cuchi* here." Laughter broke out among the migrants, and some of the guards joined in.

"Don't worry, *mamacitàs," he continued.* "We put guards

out at night to make sure the boys stay in their tent and away from your daughters."

There was more laughter now. The man in charge, who'd been so serious to this point, even let his mouth widen into a smile, but the mother who had questioned him noticed there was no smile in his eyes.

When the tent assignments were completed, the groups wandered off to make themselves ready for the night. They ate, drank water, and talked excitedly. Tomorrow was the day. The border to the United States waited for them.

They'd been schooled on what to expect. Many would simply turn themselves over to the Border Patrol officers. Entering the United States illegally was not a great concern. Friends who had gone before them reported back that the officers were very official in the way they handled things but also very kind as long as you cooperated. Some even rescued the illegals when they had problems crossing the Rio Grande or wandered lost in the deserts.

They all agreed that there was no reason to cause a problem and not cooperate and then possibly create problems for others. They would take the food and water they were offered, and when it was their turn, they would claim asylum for some cause, real or fabricated. Then, holding a Notice to Appear before an immigration judge at a future date, they would accept a ride on a bus or a plane to some city in the interior. Only about ten percent of the illegals would actually show up for their hearing. After all, why take a chance that the judge would be unsympathetic to their case and send them back? It was much easier simply to vanish.

Here and there, laughter rang out from the tents. Families gathered and prayed. Others played cards and gambled, told jokes, sang songs, or sat outside under the stars for a while before retiring to their cots inside.

They were very close now to their journey's end. For some, the trip had lasted for months, making their way north from the southern regions of South America or even farther from across the ocean. Night settled over the clearing between the hills and, along with it, a sense of restless anticipation.

EIGHT

Friends

The motorcade of pickups roared through town and into the countryside. A helicopter circled overhead while the men in the beds of the pickups surrounded and took over a local farmer's sugarcane field.

The men, armed with pistols and rifles, spread out across the field, trampling down the canes while the farmer looked on helplessly. They spread out, forming a security perimeter from tree line to tree line as the pickups moved back and forth, flattening what remained of the cane crop to create a tidy landing zone for the helicopter.

It could have been the president of some great international power arriving in this backwater region of Mexico. In truth, presidents, kings, and prime ministers would have been less intimidating to the residents of Carmen Xhán than the man circling overhead, watching the activity on the ground.

The helicopter descended out of a blue sky. The rotor blades slowed, and more security men hopped out. One pickup approached the side of the helicopter. A moment later, Miguel Espinoza emerged, looked around at the security men positioned around the field, and walked to the pickup. He paused before getting in and motioned to the man in charge of the security teams in the pickups.

"Jorge, is that the one who owns this field?" Espinoza asked, nodding toward a man standing at the far edge of the field.

"He is, *jefe*." Jorge Barros had worked for the Espinoza cartel for a dozen years and risen through the ranks to become the primary organizer of the migrant smuggling business at the Guatemalan border.

"Is he a friend?" Espinoza asked.

"He is neutral," Barros said with a shrug. "He takes no sides with the cartels … one of those who try to pretend things are not changing."

"We could use more neutrality," Espinoza said, watching the man who stood at the edge of the field, shoulders slumped in despair, powerless to stop the men with the guns from destroying his livelihood and condemning him and his family to a season of hunger, if not outright starvation.

"Pay him for his crop," Espinoza said and added, "Find out what he would have earned at market and pay him double."

"Double? Are you sure, *jefe*?" Barros turned, gazing at the field. "The entire crop is not destroyed, and that seems like much to pay for a little sugarcane."

"I imagine for that man standing over there, it is much." Espinoza nodded. "Too many are taking sides just now. Perhaps we can ensure that he remains neutral, or even becomes a friend. Pay him and offer my respects. Handle it personally while I go into town."

"As you wish, *jefe*," Barros said.

"Good." Espinoza turned and climbed into the pickup.

The helicopter security team accompanied him, and several of the pickups left their positions around the flattened cane field to follow them toward Carmen Xhán.

Glauco Capilla watched them drive away, his hands clenched helplessly at his side, eyes red with the tears he would fight back so as not to alarm his wife and children. His family had farmed their five hectares of land for generations, always refusing to sell out to the large conglomerates that made offers to buy every year. It was a matter of family pride that they maintained their independence, but now it would be gone.

A farmer's existence was always a fragile thing, a balancing act between nature, market prices, and creditors. Now, with half his crop gone, he had no hope of paying all his bills and feeding his family. They would go deeper into debt. To cover the debt, he would be forced to sell some of the land, leaving him even less from which to scrape out a living. Then, he would sell more land, and once the land was gone, the farm equipment and tools would go to cover their living expenses, but that would only last them for a year or so. After that, he could only hope he found a job in a city somewhere.

He squinted under the frayed brim of his ball cap. A single pickup truck came across the field to where he stood. The men inside had guns. Maybe they would kill him. He didn't know why they would, but lately, it seemed people didn't need much reason to kill. An imagined insult, prying eyes, an unwanted witness, or no reason at all, and some poor son of a bitch ended up dead.

Glauco waited and thought it might be better for him if they did. A bullet through the head would be preferable to a lingering death that might last years as he watched his wife and children waste away, or worse, turn to crime and prostitution to support themselves. But he knew the pain his death would cause his family and hoped the men would not kill him.

The pickup truck stopped a few feet from Glauco. He tensed, waiting for what would happen.

Jorge Barros got out and walked to Glauco. "Do you know who I am?"

"Yes." Glauco nodded. "Barros, the one who works for the Espinoza brothers. Everyone in Carmen Xhán knows who you are."

"Good. Then you know I speak for them."

"Yes." Glauco nodded and stared at the ground, waiting for the inevitable bad news the gods were about to send his way.

"You had a good crop here," Barros said, turning to scan the flattened field.

"Yes, it was."

"How much would it fetch at market?"

Glauco raised his eyes. "How much?"

"Yes," Barros said. "In U.S dollars, if you could harvest this season and went to market."

The reason for this question was far more than Glauco's half-stunned and half-frightened brain could conceive, so he focused on the question itself, his brow wrinkled in concentration. His farm of five hectares—a little over twelve acres—would produce about three hundred-fifty metric tons of cane, with a price of about thirty U.S. dollars per ton.

"About ten thousand five hundred U.S. dollars," he said to Barros and shrugged. "It has been a good year. Plenty of rain, and last year's stalks were still good, so we did not have to replant this season."

Barros nodded. "*Señor* Espinoza has authorized me to

pay you twice that amount for the trouble his arrival has caused you today."

"But …" Glauco's mind whirled, trying to find the hidden catch, the twist that would snatch this sudden bounty from his hands. All he could say was, "But my farm is not for sale."

Barros laughed. "Trust me. He does not want to buy your farm."

"Then, I don't understand."

"His arrival has damaged your crop. He wishes to compensate you and will pay you for the crop," Barros explained. "Come to town this afternoon. Do you know the Cantina Maricela … off the plaza?"

"Yes." Glauco nodded.

"You'll find me there. Come after the helicopter leaves, and I will pay you." Barros smiled, knowing the effect his next words would have. "Twenty-one thousand U.S. dollars."

"But wait," Glauco said, worry on his face. The last thing he wanted to do was to be accused of cheating an Espinoza. "The whole crop is not destroyed, only about two or three hectares."

"It's fine. *Señor* Espinoza has authorized me to pay you for the entire crop."

Glauco Capilla stood swaying back and forth on wobbly legs as if he might faint. Barros reached out a hand to steady him and patted him on the shoulder. "Miguel Espinoza understands the struggles of a working man."

Barros turned, climbed back in the pickup, and left Glauco standing in his destroyed sugar cane field, staring open-mouthed. Small as the sum was by western standards, after a season of toil in the fields, ten thousand dollars represented a decent living wage in rural Mexico, and by local standards, the Capilla family was well off. Doubling that amount in dollars would make them among the wealthiest people in the region ... except for the cartels.

In Carmen Xhán, the motorcade of pickups pulled down a narrow street and stopped before a tiny house. Miguel Espinoza approached the door while his security team took up positions at each end of the street. He held a small duffel in one hand and, with the other, gave a rap on the door.

A woman opened the door, her long gray hair pulled behind and tied with a ribbon the way a schoolgirl might wear it. Her brow wrinkled in surprise, then confusion, then fear. She shook her head back and forth. "No ... no ... no."

"Lucia Pacheco?" Miguel said.

She nodded without speaking.

"May I come in?" Espinoza spoke in the quiet tones of a priest, about to deliver bad news.

Lucia nodded and stepped aside.

Espinoza entered and said, "Please sit, *Señora*."

Lucia collapsed onto a chair by the door. Espinoza sat across from her on a small sofa.

"I have news," he said.

Before he could say more, Lucia burst into tears and put her face in her hands. Her shoulders shook with her sobs. "Not my Ignacio. Please, not Ignacio."

"I'm sorry, *Señora*. There was trouble on the road." There was no reason to hide the truth from her. Just the opposite. Her grief could be useful. "Your husband was murdered, shot along with another of our men."

"Nooo!" Lucia wailed, although she had known what he would say. "I told him this was not good for him to do. He was too old ... too kind a man ... not cut out for this sort of work. He said it was nothing, just driving a bus, but it was ..." She raised her eyes, angry and staring at Espinoza. "For you! And for the damned cartels!"

"I understand you are angry," Espinoza said mildly. "You have a right to be. The job we hired Ignacio to do was a simple one and should have been without danger to him or you. Please believe me, that we grieve with you." He lifted the duffel and opened it, and leaned forward, placing it on the floor at her feet. "I know this cannot replace the loss of your husband, but this money will be more than enough to give you a new life and see to your needs for years to come ... and to make sure Ignacio receives a proper burial in the church."

She stared down at the dollars stacked in bundles inside the duffel. "This is supposed to replace my husband ... my friend ... my love?"

"No, *Señora*." Espinoza shook his head. "Only to let you know that we take care of our own. Ignacio was one of us, and now you are one of us ... always."

"I won't be part of what you do," Lucia said.

"We are not asking you to be. This money is to provide for you regardless of what you choose to do in the future. *Sin condiciones*." No strings attached.

"Like an insurance policy," Espinoza added.

"An insurance policy." Lucia stared red-eyed at him. "Ignacio was my insurance, and now he is dead."

"I understand." Espinoza nodded. "And he is dead because there was a traitor among us. Someone told of the route the bus would take."

"A traitor?"

"Yes, and if by some chance you should hear word of who it might be, we would be grateful for that information." He nodded at the bag. "Very grateful."

"You think you can buy me over something like this?" She frowned. "No, I will see what I can hear about this traitor you speak of, but not for money. The money means nothing, but if there is one who took my Ignacio from me, I want him to pay for the harm he has caused. That is only just."

"You are correct. That is justice." Espinoza nodded at the duffel. "In any event, we will be grateful for the chance to deliver that justice. Find out who betrayed us, and you and your children and grandchildren will never want for anything. They will remember Ignacio as the father who provided for his family long after he was taken from them."

"He should be remembered," Lucia sobbed. "Ignacio was a good man."

"Yes, he was, and a good friend, and now, you are also our friend." Espinoza stood. "I understand that now is a time for tears, but there is something you can do for us when all your tears have been wept. Find the traitor for us ... for Ignacio."

He gave a polite bow and left through the door.

Later, after the security men and the pickup trucks, and the helicopter were gone from his farm, Glauco Capilla said goodbye to his wife. "I have to go into town to see the man, Barros."

"The cartel man?" she said, concerned. "Is that really necessary?"

"Yes. It's about paying us for the crop they destroyed with their trucks and helicopter."

"When will you be back?"

"Soon," Glauco said. "But if I am not here by nightfall,

take the children and leave in the car. Don't go to family. Go somewhere where no one knows you."

"Where can I go?"

I don't know," he said. "But it may not be safe for you here if I do not return, so take no chances and leave."

He left her wide-eyed, standing by the door of their house. The drive into Carmen Xhán was a short one, only a few minutes. He knew the Cantina Maricela well, but only as a place to avoid because it was a known gathering place for the cartels.

Leaving his car on a side street, he went inside. There was nothing else to do. Yes, he wanted the money Barros promised, but he would also have been glad to just return to farming and make the best of the remainder of his crop. But Barros had promised him an enormous sum of money, a great gift from the Espinozas. Not showing up to collect it, or running away, might make him appear afraid or guilty of some treason against the cartel, and true or not, he knew they had a reputation for repaying even the suspicion of treason.

He walked through the door and saw Barros at a table in the rear, surrounded by several other younger men. Barros waved him over. "I'm glad you came."

"Of course." Glauco nodded.

"This is for you," Barros said, reaching under the table to retrieve a small suitcase like the ones Glauco had seen people carry onto airplanes. "Open it."

Glauco opened it, his hands shaking as he unzipped the bag. Inside, he saw forty-two neatly wrapped bundles of twenty-dollar bills—twenty-five bills in each bundle for a total of twenty-one thousand dollars. He looked up, startled at the realization that Barros had been telling the truth about the money. "I - I don't know what to say."

"Twenty-one thousand U.S. dollars as promised. *Señor* Espinoza wanted to make things right between the two of you because he would like to have you as a friend." Barros smiled. "There is nothing for you to say, except perhaps, that you are his friend."

"Yes." Glauco nodded emphatically. "Now and forever, my family and I are his friends."

"Excellent!" Barros beamed.

NINE

A Good Morning's Work

"I'm not sure I understand what it is you want us to say." Assistant Secretary for Homeland Security, Harold Carter, looked around the conference table. Seven others sat there sipping coffee from china cups, munching pastries catered by an expensive boutique bakery, and listening to the discussion. Carter focused on the man seated at the far end. His counterparts from an assortment of other federal agencies put down their coffee cups, followed his gaze, and turned toward Jay Lovell.

Lovell hated these games, but it was the way Washington worked. Plausible deniability, a get-out-of-jail-free card in case the shit hit the fan. It was tiresome, but you played according to their rules, or you didn't play.

Lovell sighed, loosened the collar and tie that he was unaccustomed to wearing, and said, "The operation we are proposing will require us to …" He shrugged. "For want of better terms … to handle things in a direct manner."

"Direct?" Carter frowned.

Lovell sighed. God, how he hated the bullshit, and these

people seemed to wallow in it every day. "You might say hands-on."

"Hands on?" Carter's eyes narrowed over the frown. "Whose hands?"

"Ours," Lovell said. "And they will get dirty.

"How dirty?" The question came from the Department of Justice's mouthpiece at the table.

Lovell took a deep breath. He was tired, and with every passing second, he was becoming more tired. After the meeting in Omaha to arrange financing and technical support, he'd taken a red-eye to Washington, D.C. and checked into a hotel after midnight. If he got what he wanted from this meeting, he could catch another flight and get the hell away from Washington and back to the operation. At the moment, looking at the hard-eyed stares of the faces at the table, that was a big if.

"Very dirty. This is a rough game," Lovell said honestly. There was no reason to lie, and if he did and the shit hit the fan, he and Sole would be the ones left with their asses hanging out. "But no rougher than the one the cartels play," he added.

"You mean people will be killed." The representative from the State Department looked down at the notepad in front of him on the table and shook his head. "Put aside for the moment, the serious moral objections to what you are proposing, the U.S. government sanctioning the murder of people in a foreign country hardly seems in our best interests."

"Killing people when we are at war hardly seems like murder," Lovell shot back. "And make no mistake, we are at war. If a foreign power was sending poison across our borders, enslaving people, and selling them into bondage to the highest bidder, what would we do?"

"What do you say?" the State Department representative said to the man seated beside Lovell.

Carl Shank, head of the NSA division overseeing Lovell's activities, would have to approve every aspect of the operation. Shank nodded, cleared his throat, and said, "I don't wish to use my position to influence the decision of this panel. I will abstain from any vote but will support the majority opinion here today." He turned to face Lovell's disgusted gaze without flinching. "Continue, Agent Lovell."

There it was. Lovell was on his own. That it surprised him indicated how out of his element he was in a roomful of Washington bureaucrats. It seemed it didn't matter which agency employed them; like swamp rats scurrying for high ground when the floods came, they had a natural instinct for survival.

"Fine." Lovell nodded. "Let me put it this way. The people we will be dealing with will not hesitate to kill. It doesn't matter who. Hell, they've proven it ... police officers, government officials, newspaper editors, anyone who gets in their way, and trust me, we will get in their way. The assets I have in place are putting their life on the line to bring down the cartels. If they are discovered, they won't be lined up against a wall and executed." He opened a folder on the table in front of him. "Take a look."

He took photos one by one from the folder and passed them around. Eyebrows raised, lips twisted in revulsion, a few of the faces paled. Some held the photos and studied them for a few seconds. Others pushed them along the tabletop with their fingertips, trying to avoid contact with them as much as possible.

"These are people who ran afoul of the cartels ... horribly tortured, some dismembered ... disemboweled, and their guts pulled out while they were alive. All suffered terrible deaths." He waited for the photos to make their way around the table, then said, "If you tell us we can't operate on their terms, then you are sentencing people to die, and this is how they will die."

Carter looked at him from the opposite end of the table and shook his head. "Agent Lovell, as I said, we cannot possibly sanction murder ... excuse me, I mean killing ... of foreign nationals in their own country."

Murmurs of agreement echoed in the room.

"Yes, we can." Sylvia Lostrum, Special Assistant to the President, spoke for the first time. The murmurs ceased, and heads at the table turned in her direction. "The president wants the cartels brought down. Fentanyl is killing our youth, cartels are trafficking people as sex slaves, even supplying children to pedophile rings." She shook her head. "He feels it's time to take off the gloves and take the fight to them."

She didn't have to mention that next year was an election year. His party's majority in Congress, as well as his own re-election, were uncertain. Some pundits were already predicting a resounding defeat for the current administration.

Lostrum smiled and continued, "I'm sure you all understand what is at stake here. Yes, there is risk, but the administration feels the risk is worth taking to bring down the cartels."

Everyone at the table understood. She didn't have to add that the headlines the president would get as the crusader leading the fight against the cartels would be a popular issue for voters at both ends of the political spectrum.

Once again, the murmurs made their way around the

table. Heads bobbed up and down, signaling their agreement. Just like that, their moral considerations evaporated.

"Yes." Carter nodded from the end of the table. "I see your point, Sylvia." He looked at the bureaucrats staring back at him, their faces washed with relief that someone else had made the decision. "Are there any objections to authorizing Agent Lovell and his team to take any measures necessary, including the use of deadly force when and where they feel it is required and, regardless of location or nationality, to ensure the success of the mission?"

There were no objections. Political appointees, reliant on the president's reelection and goodwill to retain their jobs and pensions, they were more than happy to let Lostrum take the lead ... and the fall, if it came to that.

Lovell nodded and stood, gathered up the photos, and stuffed them back in the folder. "I want this in writing before the mission begins." He looked down at Carl Shank, the only person at the table in his direct reporting line. "From your office ... with your signature. Otherwise, the mission is off."

Shank raised his eyes and sputtered, "Who do you think..."

"You'll have the written authorization today," Lostrum said and smiled at Shank. "Won't he, Carl?"

"Yes," Shank mumbled and stared down at the table.

"Excellent!" Carter beamed. "Thank you all. This has been a good morning's work, and we will ..."

Lovell didn't hear the rest. He walked from the room and was on the elevator before they stood to congratulate each other on the daring stance they had taken as they sipped coffee around the conference table.

TEN

Change of Plans

They came in the middle of the night, sometime between two AM and sunrise, the period of deepest sleep for most of those in the tents. Moving quickly, with business-like efficiency, all of it well planned and nothing left to chance, they backed trucks up and began waking the occupants of the selected tents.

Noise erupted from one tent. Several families had been housed there, fathers and mothers but without their children.

"What the hell is going on?" a man called out as the men came in and shook them awake.

He and the others sat up, rubbing their eyes with the back of their hands and trying to shake the sleep from their heads.

"Get up," someone ordered., He was one of the young coyotes with a rifle.

"Now? In the middle of the night?" the man slid his legs off the side of the cot but remained seated.

"What is it, Hector?" his wife asked from the cot beside

him, then saw the men in the tent with rifles and sat up, her wide eyes reflecting the light from the flashlights they carried.

"I don't know, Marita," Hector said and looked at the man standing over him. "What is going on?"

"No!" a woman cried from the other side of the tent as rough hands shook her awake.

There were more cries and shouts from the sleeping migrants. Some were surprised, some fearful. All were fatigued by the journey that had brought them this far. When they were all awake, a man stood in the center of the tent, a clipboard in hand, and looked around as if he were counting heads.

"Calm down." The man with the clipboard looked up, turning to look at their faces, and said quietly, but firmly, "There is a truck outside. Take your belongings. You will be leaving tonight."

"Tonight?" the man called Hector said. "But the bus … we are to leave on the bus in the morning."

"There is trouble at the border," the man with the clipboard said. "We are dividing you into smaller groups so that we can get you across safely."

"But our daughters," Marita said, panic rising in her throat. "They took them to another tent. Where are they?"

"They'll be in another truck taking those from that tent, but don't worry, you'll meet them on the other side of the border."

"I don't like this. I want to see my daughters." Marita shook her head adamantly. "Taking children from their parents when we are going to a new country, across a border … it isn't right."

Clipboard man shrugged. "As I said, there is trouble. Some groups have been stopped, turned back, even imprisoned when they were caught at the border. You should be glad we found this out from our people there and can make arrangements to get you all across safely. Once we get you there, you will be reunited with others from your group in the other tents." He gave an encouraging smile. "For now, you will have to trust us. This is what you paid us to do, so hurry and get into the truck. We want to be near the border before daylight."

They sat for a moment on their cots, trying to clear their sleepy brains and process this new information and the sudden change to their plans. There were more murmurs around the tent, but slowly, people moved and gathered up their belongings. It was just one more trial in the weeks—for some, it had been months—of trials that had brought them so close to the U.S. border. At least, this was the last trial, the last obstacle. Tomorrow they would be across the border.

Outside, they climbed into the back of a truck. Marita, mother of the missing daughters, pointed and said, "There, that tent over there. My daughters are in there. Let me go see them and explain. They will be frightened when they find we are gone in the night."

"Yes," another woman called out. "I have a daughter in there too, and a son in the tent with the other boys."

"There is no time," Clipboard man said, pushing the last of the migrants into the truck. "We must hurry so that we are at the border before the sun is up. Besides, other trucks are coming for your daughters and sons now." He pointed. "See, here they are."

And as he spoke, they saw more trucks backing up to the tents where the girls and young men had been isolated. More men with rifles went inside and began waking the occupants. Then the door was slammed, and the truck bounced away down the narrow trail between the hills and back onto the road.

"Did you feel that?" Hector said to a man from the tent he'd come to know, whose name was Paco.

"What?" Paco said.

"We came along the trail and then turned onto the main road again."

"Yes? What of it?"

"It felt like we turned to the right. If we were going back toward the border, we should have turned left, shouldn't we?"

Paco's brow wrinkled as he thought, then he nodded. "Yes, I believe left is the way toward the border, but to tell the truth, I couldn't say whether we turned right or left from inside the back of the truck where I can't see outside." He smiled. "My sense of direction is not very good. Ask my wife."

A short, stocky woman seated beside him laughed and nodded. "It's true! Paco can get lost walking to the store and back."

"That's not true, Lupe," Paco said, a good-natured smile on his face. "I only got lost walking to the store. I was able to find my way back."

Others laughed and murmured, exchanging stories and pleasantries, promising to stay in touch with each other once they crossed the border in a few more hours. Things settled down after a few miles. Some drifted off to sleep, leaning against each other for support as the truck bounced along.

Hector held Marita's hand, still trying to determine the direction they were heading from inside the bouncing truck. Trouble at the border, the man said. Hector didn't know about that, but he knew that something did not feel right about this sudden change to their plans.

In the tents where the girls and boys had been segregated, the scenes were similar. Startled awake, they tried to understand what was happening and were given the same explanations. Trouble at the border meant they had to cross in smaller groups. They would be reunited with their families once they were in the United States.

Two sisters, Gabriela, aged fifteen, and Francisca, twelve, came out of the tent and saw a truck moving across the clearing. Their parents, Marita and Hector Gomez, were inside, but the truck was closed up, and they couldn't see them, only the lights at the back as it disappeared down the trail between the hillsides.

Francisca sobbed, "Mama … Papa."

The coyote herding them onto the truck by their tent said, "Yes, they're in that truck. Now hurry so we can drive after them, and you'll see them at the border."

"Come on, Francisca." Gabriela took a step up onto the truck's bumper and put a hand out to pull her sister up. "You heard. We'll be with them soon. Mama and Papa would not have left us here unless everything was as it should be."

A similar scene was reenacted in the boys' tent. Roused from their sleep, bleary-eyed, they tried to understand what was happening and were given the same assurances. All was well, but there were problems at the border that required a change of plans.

One boy turned to face a coyote who pushed him from

behind to hurry him along. He stood up straight, glaring at the man with the rifle. "I don't like to be pushed."

"Is that so?" The coyote grinned. "Well, move your ass, and you won't be pushed."

"Come on, Manolo." The boy's brother grabbed him by the arm. "The sooner we get on the truck, the sooner we get away from these assholes."

Manolo stood his ground, nose to nose with the coyote, and for a moment, it seemed there might be a fight between them.

"That's enough." The man in charge of moving the boys out of the tent came up to separate the two. "Now, what's the problem?"

"He doesn't want to move to the truck," the coyote said.

"Is that so?" The man eyed Manolo for a few seconds and asked, "How old are you, boy?"

Manolo said nothing and continued staring at the coyote. His brother spoke up. "He's fifteen, señ*or*."

"And you are?"

"I'm Javier, his brother."

"Hmm." The man in charge nodded. "He likes to fight, your brother."

"No, *señor,*" Javier said. "Not so much. He just doesn't like to be pushed. This one here," he nodded at the coyote. "He was pushing us with his rifle."

"I see." The man in charge looked at the coyote. "No more pushing."

The coyote nodded but said nothing. The man turned back to the brothers and smiled. "He won't push you again, but you must get on the truck so we can get you to the border."

"Come on." Javier pulled his brother by the arm.

As they climbed up into the truck, the man said to the coyote, "I think they will do nicely."

In the morning, the bus pulled back into the middle of the clearing. Those in the remaining tents ate a quick breakfast of tortillas and beans and then began climbing onto the bus. Questions arose about the missing passengers. Some asked the driver what happened to them and were given the same response. Trouble at the border meant they had to change their plans and cross in smaller groups.

Whispers circulated about the fate of those who were suddenly gone. One man said, "I heard the noise in the night. When I went to see what it was, the guard said to go back to sleep, that they were taking some people early, that it was none of my business. He had a gun, so I went back to my cot and slept, but now here we are on the bus, so I'm sure everything is in order, except there aren't so many of us crammed in now."

Others nodded and agreed. "This is true."

There were seats for everyone now. No one had to stand in the aisle or sit on another's lap. It was a much more comfortable ride now as the bus bounced along the trail between the hills and then turned left toward the highway that would take them to the border.

ELEVEN

Damned If I Know

"Meet me in Nogales."

"Where?" Sole asked, surprised as much by the call as by the sudden instructions. He took a sip from a can of beer he'd brought to the beach during his morning outing in Puerto Nuevo. Actually, he'd brought a case of Mexican beer, Victoria, on ice in a styrofoam chest, along with a cheap aluminum lawn chair he'd found in a corner of the safe house. Lovell said to take a little vacation, and he'd decided to do just that.

"Nogales," Lovell repeated. "It's a city on the border."

"I know where it is. Just surprised by the call from Mr. Mysterious." He was careful not to say Lovell's name over the phone. He took another sip from the beer. "Which side of the border? Mexico or Arizona?"

"Arizona," Lovell said. "We have to meet someone. Nogales is fairly neutral territory for him, not too far to drive and away from prying eyes, so to speak."

"So, who is this person we are meeting ... so to speak?"

"Look ..." Lovell paused. "I know you said no more

secrets, but as a security precaution, we generally don't say much over phone lines. I'll fill you in on everything when we meet."

"Fair enough," Sole said, drained the beer, put the empty back in the ice chest, and stood up. "Any particular way you want me to get there, or is that up to me?"

"Under your cot. You'll find everything you need. Rent a car ... four-wheel-drive type. I'll text you the name of a hotel when I get there."

"Under my cot?"

"Just check. You'll see what you need."

"Alright. Anything else I should know?"

"The usual stuff. Keep your eyes open, watch your back, assume nothing, and don't let anyone follow you, and if they do, handle it."

"Handle it? Mind if I ask who might be following?"

"People who might not like our business arrangements," Lovell said cryptically.

"Okay, I'll handle it if someone tries to follow," Sole said, considering what that implied. "I take it your meeting was successful ... that we have the authorization to handle all of our ... business arrangements ... as required."

"We have the authorization," Lovell said and repeated, "Don't be followed ... by anyone."

Shit just got real. He'd played things pretty rough and loose in the past, but he'd never used a strong arm with Uncle Sam's approval, or at least with him looking the other way.

"Okay," Sole said. "I'll make sure no one follows."

"Good. Now get the rental and get on the road. Pack what you need. We won't be back to the safe house for a while." Lovell did not add that they might never be back. "You'll want to cross back over the border through Tijuana to San Diego, then take the interstates. It's about an eight-hour drive. I'll be flying most of the day, making connections, and won't get to Nogales until this evening. We'll meet there and then hook up with our contact tomorrow."

"Okay," Sole said. "Anything else?"

"Nope."

"See you when I get there."

Sole ended the call, looked at the ice chest full of beer, thought what the hell, and waved over two young men, probably not more than seventeen or eighteen years old. "*¿Uusted gusta la cerveza?*" Do you like beer, he managed in broken Spanish.

"*Sí.*" The boys grinned, and one said in good English, "Who doesn't like beer?"

"Here." Sole nodded at the ice chest. "Have yourself a party."

"*Gracias, señor. Muchos gracias.*" They grabbed the ice chest, one on each end, and trotted down the beach. Sole made his way back to the roadway, looked back, and saw that they had wasted no time finding a group of tourists, handing them beers in exchange for U.S. dollars.

Capitalism at work. Everybody profits, he thought with a satisfied nod, and then realized he'd given up the beers he'd planned to spend the day drinking and figured he'd come out on the short end of the transaction.

A few minutes later, he was back at the safe house. Everything he needed was under the cot, Lovell said.

Sole went up the narrow stairs and pushed the cot to the side with his leg to find ... bare floor. He shook his head, annoyed, and muttered, "Son of a bitch is testing me."

He knelt and began examining the floorboards. None were out of place or bore the marks of having been moved. He pulled out his pocketknife and probed. The fourth board he checked moved and lifted as he pried gently. Underneath, he found an empty backpack and a metal box crammed with several thousand dollars in cash, assorted credit cards, a driver's license, and a passport, all bearing his picture and the name Christopher Long.

Two handguns, A Walther PPK .380 caliber and Glock 22 in .40 caliber, lay under the backpack along with a thin black leather wallet. It was a type of wallet Sole recognized. He opened it and examined the badge and ID card bearing his name inside. It all looked very official, embossed with a U.S. government seal and the inscription, Agent of the United States Government. It was unlike any federal badge or ID he'd ever seen, but a handwritten note inside the wallet read—*You'll need these*.

Lovell must have been pretty certain that Sole would sign up for the mission even before he was on board. Sole found that annoying, although he couldn't say exactly why. It simply meant that Lovell was good at what he did, and considering the shitstorm they were about to create, that was a good thing.

He put the wallet, driver's license, and credit cards in his pocket and the weapons in the backpack. As for packing his personal belongings, there wasn't much. He'd gotten off the lobster boat empty-handed. Lovell had provided him with some clothes and personal items—shorts, blue jeans, t-shirts, sandals, sneakers, underwear, a toothbrush, and a razor.

Sole tossed them in the backpack and headed outside. The next task, renting a car, was more problematic. Puerto Nuevo was not a large enough tourist center for there to be much call for rental cars. He was forced to grab a local taxi outside his new favorite hangout, Bobby's Place, and pay for a ride to Tijuana.

The airport there had all the usual rental agencies, and

Sole used his new IDs and credit cards to rent a four-wheel-drive SUV. He would have preferred something more rugged and lower-key in appearance. The car's bright red exterior and chrome wheels were sharp, snappy, and not very discreet. But Lovell had been specific about the rental having four-wheel-drive, and the SUV was the only one on the lot.

"Where will you be going with the car?" the rental agent asked behind a wide, white smile.

"Why does that matter?" Sole asked.

"It is only that if you intend to drive across the border into the United States …" The agent shrugged and smiled wider. "There could be complications."

"What sort of complications?"

"Well, technically, international travel is only allowed on corporate rental accounts, and you are renting this car as a private person."

Sole reached into his pocket and pulled out a hundred-dollar bill. "Will this *technically* take care of the complications?"

The agent smiled, made a show of gathering up the rental documents and placing them neatly inside a folder, and handed them to Sole. "Thank you, Mr. Long. Have a pleasant journey."

Sole took the keys, found the car on the lot, and headed toward the border crossing. As it turned out, there were no complications, other than the thirty-minute wait in a line of traffic.

The Customs and Border Protection officer looked at the passport, and driver's license Lovell had provided and gave Sole a reproachful frown. No doubt, he figured he was dealing with another stupid American willing to risk kidnapping, robbery, or worse, to experience Tijuana's seamy nightlife and anything-goes, border-town atmosphere. "You're lucky to be back in the States in one piece, Mr. Long." He nodded at the backpack on the passenger seat. "Bring back any contraband in the bag?"

"No," Sole said. "Just my handguns." There was no reason to try to hide them. Officers ahead of him were using metal detectors to scan vehicles for weapons and contraband. The handguns would have been found, and now was as good a time as any to find out if Lovell's bogus IDs were worth the plastic used to print them.

The officer stepped back, hand on the butt of his pistol, and nodded at an officer standing on the opposite side of the car to indicate a possible threat. "Keep your hands away from the bag and step out of the vehicle."

"That won't be necessary," Sole said. "I'm a federal agent. Can I reach for my ID?"

The officer gave a wary nod. "Alright ... slowly."

Sole pulled the wallet out and handed it over. The officer scrutinized his badge and ID for a few seconds, then said, "Wait here."

He went into the building adjacent to the arrivals traffic lanes. His partner stood near the side of the car, watching Sole. A minute later, the officer came back from the building and up to the driver's window. He handed the wallet badge and ID back. "Alright, Agent Long. Everything checks out. Do me a favor."

"What's that?" Sole said, smiling.

"Next time, just tell us up front that you're a federal agent. We can get you on your way faster and ..." The agent shook his head. "And you won't take ten years off my life. We don't need jokers. Bad shit happens down here on the border."

"You're right," Sole said. "Sorry about that."

Sole moved forward in the line of traffic. He was sorry, but he hadn't been trying to pull a joke on the officer. He was buying time.

A sky-blue Chevy van with a rusted dent over the right front headlight had pulled over on the side of the highway just ahead. The van had been following him since he left Puerto Nuevo in the taxi. At first, he wasn't sure. Most traffic headed toward the border used the Tijuana highway, but he'd spotted the van again after leaving the rental car lot and then several car lengths back in one of the entry lanes at the border crossing.

While Sole's little prank caused him a delay, they passed the blue van through in the other lane without a problem. The van drove a short distance, then pulled over and waited on the side of the highway. When Sole exited the border crossing and passed in the rental, the driver looked down and then pulled back onto the highway behind him.

The van's driver was inexperienced, never varied the distance between their vehicles, and slowed whenever Sole slowed. There didn't seem to be any immediate threat, so Sole took his time, following Interstate 805 onto California 54, then 125 up to Interstate 8 and east.

He had to do something, but not here, not yet. The area was too heavily populated, and there was no hurry. He drove for three hours after leaving the border crossing. The van maintained its separation distance the entire way until he exited at the Sand Hills Rest Area.

Without signaling, Sole pulled the SUV onto the exit and then accelerated around a horseshoe bend to the back side of the rest area building. It was late in the day, and this deserted section of the Interstate, paralleling the Mexico border, was as good a place as any for what he had to do.

The blue van slowed on the interstate, the driver clearly

uncertain about what to do next. Sole pulled the Walther from the backpack, got out, and trotted to the rest area building to wait. A few seconds later, the van came slowly off the exit ramp, the driver searching for the red SUV. He watched it pass and park at the far end of the parking lot. The driver slouched down in the seat, conspicuously trying to be inconspicuous, no doubt assuming his target was using the restroom.

Sole moved away from the building, keeping it between him and the van until he reached a clump of trees. It was only partial concealment, but it was enough. The van's driver remained focused on the building and restrooms, waiting for him to come out.

Sole left the trees, covering the last fifty feet silently. He crept up to the van, jerked the door open, and pushed the pistol's barrel into the side of the driver's head. She let out a shriek, then moved her head back and forth, her wide and terrified eyes begging for her life.

Shit! She couldn't have been more than a teenager. Trembling, she squeezed her eyes shut, expecting any second for the pistol to send a bullet through her brain.

That had been Sole's plan. The rest area was deserted. No one would have questioned it if he had. Lovell's orders were clear—no followers—and the authorization from above gave him the freedom to do what was necessary to protect the mission. And yet ...

He'd expected to find a gangbanger behind the wheel, an armed thug ready to do to Sole what he'd planned to do to the van's driver. Instead, he found a frightened girl who reminded him of ... Stop! He shook his head. Don't go there, John-boy.

He jerked her from the van and then again up off the ground when she tumbled out. "Do you speak English?"

She nodded.

"Good. You're coming with me." Holding her close by his side, with the pistol pushed hard against her ribs, he walked her to the SUV and opened the passenger door.

Pulling one of his t-shirts from the backpack, he wedged her up against the car while he tore it into strips, then used it to tie her hands and wrists together. He pushed her onto the seat, took another strip of the torn shirt, and looped it over her wrists and around the seat frame, securing it all with a knot.

He stepped back to survey his work. It was a sorry-ass way to secure a prisoner, but it was the best he could do. Given enough time alone, she could work her way out of the knots and escape, but Sole had no intention of giving her any time alone.

He sat behind the wheel, pulled the SUV onto the ramp to the interstate, and drove. They'd gone ten miles before he asked, "What's your name?"

"Sarita," the girl whispered, fighting back a sob, "What are you going to do to me?"

He answered honestly. "Damned if I know."

TWELVE

Allies

Finding neutral ground for such a meeting in Mexico was problematic. The cartels headed by the three men at the table each had tentacles that intertwined throughout the country. Occasionally, the tentacles of one would touch another and recoil in a spasm of blood and violence. Then both would withdraw, lick their wounds and return to business as usual until the tentacles touched again.

It could be over anything. One cartel moves into another's claimed territory, infringes on the supply of drugs and people flowing through their trafficking pipelines, or bribes a *policía* that was already taking bribes from another cartel.

Seve Espinoza wanted no blood associated with this gathering. The place he picked for their meeting was neutral ground. The Nayara Gardens Resort in the Costa Rican rainforest was remote enough that intruders would stand out and be spotted by the respective security details accompanying the cartel bosses. With a reputation for maintaining the privacy of its wealthy guests, the resort asked no questions about the men who booked four suites—three for their personal use and one as a meeting place.

Each flew in on their private jets the evening before the meeting was to begin. The following morning at nine AM precisely, Espinoza entered the suite reserved for their meeting and sat at a large, round table the resort staff brought in for the occasion. His counterparts—the heads of the next two most powerful cartels—waited for him.

Jesus 'Chucho' Sanchez sat hunched over, elbows on the table, staring at Espinoza over the top of an espresso cup held between his thumb and forefinger. The tiny cup in his large-knuckled calloused hands looked comical, like an adult playing with a child's tea set, but no one laughed. Stocky of stature and dark brown in complexion, he took pride in claiming direct descent from the Mayans. Whether it was true was a matter of conjecture, but what was certain was that Chucho Sanchez eliminated enemies, including those who offended him, with a brutality that was extreme even among his cartel counterparts.

In contrast, Anselmo Cardoso leaned back in his chair with the relaxed air of a man invited to sit in on a hand of poker with his college fraternity buddies. Younger than the others, he had a reputation as a ladies' man. Youthful good looks, coupled with the immense wealth his cartel activities generated, ensured that the reputation was deserved. When Cardoso was present, there was always a woman nearby whose presence could turn heads and make the hearts of men in the room pound and their groins swell. Espinoza had emphasized that no wives or girlfriends were invited to the meeting, and Cardoso had reluctantly agreed.

"Good morning," Espinoza said as he took a seat at the table. His brother, Miguel, sat beside him, an equal if silent partner.

"Good morning, *Don* Espinoza," Cardoso said in a voice as smooth as silk, no doubt the same voice he used to charm women into his bed or to curry favor with those more powerful than he, and Espinoza was definitely more powerful.

"Good morning," Sanchez growled and shot a disgusted look at Cardoso. "Why are we here?"

"Good." Espinoza nodded and smiled. "Our gruff friend Chucho brings us directly to the point." He paused and looked at the others. "We are here because I believe we may be under attack."

"Attack?" Sanchez sat up straight, glaring. "I have no reports of any attacks."

"Even so, it is happening." Espinoza looked at their faces. "From this point on, we should take extra precautions in our movements and dealings with others."

"Enough of the damned mysteries! We always take precautions." Sanchez snapped. "You say we are under attack, so who is the attacker? Say the name, and we will end this quickly."

"Not so quickly as you might think. There is someone who looks down on us from above." Espinoza looked past them through the large glass door that led out to a patio and nodded. "Like the Arenal Volcano there in the distance."

Their eyes followed his to the snowcapped peak and then came back to the table. "*Los Salvajes*," Sanchez said, spitting the words out.

"Yes." Espinoza nodded.

"And why do you think this?" Cardoso asked, the flippant playboy air gone completely now.

"Because one of my buses was attacked, the driver and a guard killed, the bus driven away with the passengers." He paused before adding, "The attackers wore the uniforms and drove vehicles with the markings of the Michoacán *Policías Estatal*."

"Yes." Cardoso nodded. "Elizondo and *Los Salvajes* own that region."

"Exactly." Espinoza waited for Sanchez to say what was barely concealed in the sneer on his face.

"They knew the route you were taking?" Sanchez shook his head. "That's sloppy work by your men, Espinoza."

"Perhaps." Espinoza smiled and allowed the insult to pass. "Or it could be that we have a spy in our midst."

"In your midst!" Sanchez said bluntly. "Not ours."

"Are you so certain?" Espinoza asked and nodded. "If there is one lesson we have learned in this business …" He shot a hard glance in Sanchez's direction. "It is that money can buy loyalty. Allegiances move with the flow of cash. Do you honestly believe that no one in your pay would turn to another who offered more, perhaps much more?"

"It is possible," Cardoso said quietly.

Espinoza waited for Sanchez to respond. As the pause lengthened, Sanchez finally conceded with a grumbled, "Alright, it is possible."

"Good." Espinoza gave a satisfied nod. "Rest assured, I will find the spy in my organization. When I do, it may lead us to others. I suggest that you do the same."

"That's it?" Sanchez smirked. "We come all this way for you to tell us to look out for spies."

"No!" Cardoso raised his voice uncharacteristically. "*Don* Espinoza is telling us that this may be the beginning of an attack on us all."

"Correct." Espinoza nodded.

"Fucking *Los Salvajes*!" Sanchez slammed a hand down on the table. "That Elizondo bitch has been stretching her wings like a vulture on a branch, eyeing us ever since her father was killed."

"Yes, *Los Salvajes*." Espinoza leaned forward, speaking earnestly. "We know their strength. Alone, we are vulnerable, but together …" He smiled and lifted his hands, palms up, shrugging as if the answer should be obvious to all, even to Sanchez. "Together, we can unite and eliminate them as a threat … permanently."

"Such alliances have always been fragile things between the cartels," Cardoso suggested and shot a glance at Sanchez.

It was true. They had all been involved in alliances with others in the past, sometimes with each other, and they all eventually ended in bloodshed.

"This is true," Espinoza said. "But it does not have to be so now when we have a common enemy."

Espinoza waited while the others considered his proposed alliance. Sanchez was the first to speak, leaning forward, his burly arms on the tabletop, staring hard at the others.

"This alliance … who do you propose to be the head of it?" His lips twisted into a sardonic smile. "You, *Don* Espinoza?"

"No." Espinoza shook his head. He'd prepared for this question. "I propose a council of three equal partners. The men at this table sit together and decide on every action we take … or do not take." He looked hard into Sanchez's eyes and added, "We vote on every issue, and from this point forward, we agree to abide by the majority vote. If the vote is unanimous, all the better, but if we consider a matter and the vote is two to one, then the majority vote will control the outcome … that is what we will do."

"Hah, a democracy!" Sanchez put his head back and

laughed. Cartels had always been ruled by blood-soaked iron fists. Democracy was a foreign concept. "And you agree to abide by the majority if lowly Sanchez and Cardoso vote against you?"

"I consider neither of you lowly. You are men of power in your own right, and to answer your question, yes. You have my solemn oath that I will abide by the decision of this council if I am outvoted on any matter."

"Hmph. A bold promise," Sanchez shot back. "But can we believe it?"

"I did not ask you to come here to create difficulties between us," Espinoza said. "On the contrary, I was hoping we could become allies, that we could agree to use our strength to fight and end the threat from a mutual enemy."

"I agree," Cardoso interjected and nodded at Espinoza. "My organization will be part of your council. We will abide by the vote, whatever it is."

"Seriously?" Sanchez turned to him, genuine surprise on his face.

"Seriously." Cardoso nodded. "I agree, as long as this is a council of three. The lesser cartels cannot be part of this. There would be too much infighting to involve them in this war with *Los Salvajes*."

"Agreed," Espinoza said, nodding. "We three and no others."

"The first vote is taken then," Sanchez said mockingly. "I can go along or be outvoted, is that it?"

"Do as you wish," Espinoza said. "You can join us now, or we will find another to take your place."

"Another tie-breaker, right? Someone to always give you your two-to-one vote while I dangle out there like the last plump grape on the vine waiting to be plucked." Sanchez grinned as if he'd unraveled the secret, then he nodded and sighed. "Alright. I'm in. My cartel will abide by the majority vote until we end the threat from *Los Salvajes*." The grin widened, and he shrugged. "After that, we'll see."

"Excellent!" Espinoza smiled like a diplomat who had just secured an important concession for his country.

"And now what?" Cardoso asked.

"Now I make a call," Espinoza said. "There is someone who says he can help us."

"Who?" Sanchez asked. "You said this alliance was between the three of us. Another cartel?"

"In a way." Espinoza smiled. "The biggest cartel of all."

THIRTEEN

An Honest Man

The drive from Reynosa to Nogales would have been shorter and much simpler for Enrique Valera if he had simply crossed the *Puente Internacional Reynosa-Hidalgo*—the McAllen-Hidalgo International Bridge, as it was called on the Texas side of the U.S. border. He could have taken Highway 281 to San Antonio and then I-10 toward Nogales.

But *Comandante* Valera, local commander of the *Poilcía Estatal*, was well known on both sides of the border around Reynosa and McAllen. This trip required caution, so he opted for Highway 2 west through northern Mexico, following the Rio Grande. When he crossed the border over the Amistad Reservoir Dam, he was just another Mexican civilian. His official credentials would have speeded up the entry process, but he used his personal identification instead, answered the immigration officer's questions, and explained he was coming into the United States to visit family.

From the dam, he proceeded north on Highway 90 to

Fort Stockton, Texas, and picked up I-10. That was far enough for the first day. He found a cheap motel along the interstate and checked in. He'd left Reynosa almost ten hours earlier, telling his wife he had to make a trip on official business, and telling his superiors he had personal family affairs to settle with some lawyers across the border.

Too many lies, he thought as he opened the door to the motel room, dropped his overnight bag on a chair, and fell back on the bed, fatigued from the day's drive. He knew lies had a way of coming back to haunt you. *Mordiéndote en el culo* —biting you in the ass—as his north American counterparts liked to say.

It couldn't be helped. Telling his wife the truth about the reason for his 'official business' could have put her and his children in danger. Telling his superiors might have landed him in a ditch with a bullet in his head ... or worse.

Enrique Valera was one of the rare ones in the ranks of the Mexican police and government, an honest man. There were others, of course, those who could not be bribed, who wanted to end the systemic corruption that plagued their country. They did what they could, but there were limits to what personal integrity could accomplish.

It was one thing to refuse a bribe over a traffic citation or some petty crime. Others might ridicule you for not making the most of the situation, but that would be the end. Arresting criminals for more serious offenses—robbery, murder, rape—was also acceptable, as long as those serious crimes were not committed by cartel members. If they were, it was usually best to let the cartel factions sort things out amongst themselves. Interfering in cartel rivalries was always a dangerous practice that put at risk the lives of police officers and anyone close to them so the cartels could make a point.

And the point? Simple. Do not, ever, under any circumstances, interfere in cartel business, including the never-ending rivalries and wars between them.

Interference was a deadly transgression and covered a multitude of scenarios. The most serious and deadliest offense of all was to inform on cartel activities. Those, who did, suffered the worst punishments, unspeakable torture, and horrific deaths. Simply killing them was far too merciful by cartel standards. A simple bullet through the head would not suffice.

For these offenses, the cartels preferred more illustrative means of execution. Favorite methods included pulling internal organs out of their still-living victims, slicing the skin off as they screamed in agony, or tightening ropes around them until organs ruptured, genitals burst, and eyeballs fell from their sockets. Nothing was too terrible. If some perverted mind could dream up a new way to inflict maximum pain and eventually death, the cartel executioners were more than happy to give it a try.

Even so, there were courageous men and women, the rare ones like Enrique Valera, who refused to be drawn into the cartels' web of corruption and violence. They did their jobs honorably, hoping others would follow their example.

But others asked themselves, "Why take the risk when those who pay me take none?"

They went along, played the game, and took the bribe. Then they took another and another, until one day they shrugged and said, "That's life ... the way things happen here. If I don't play their game, someone else will. Why should my family and I suffer for an idea ... a dream that will never come true?"

To justify themselves, they pointed their fingers at the highest levels of government, saying, "Don't forget. Even those big shots play the game and take the cartel money. Remember that defense minister who pretended to cooperate with the U.S. government while he took bribes to protect the cartels and lead the DEA astray. The damned United States even gave him a medal for it! No, thank you very much. I'll take my tiny bribe here and there, put away a little money for the future, keep my head down, and stay out of the way."

Enrique Valera lay on the bed in the cheap motel room and closed his eyes to rest. Tomorrow, he would meet in Nogales with a man from a U.S. government agency who said he wanted to help him change things. The man said that with Valera's help, they had a chance to bring down the cartels.

Valera hoped that was true. He was one of the rare ones —an honest man who had not given up ... yet.

FOURTEEN

That Other Way

Motel Tierras Baldías. It wasn't exactly a shit hole. That would have been a step up.

If the dive motel showed up in any travel registry—an unlikely possibility—it would not have qualified for over one star ... on a good day. Sole checked the directions Lovell had sent him on his phone, sighed, and wheeled into the parking lot.

The place looked like it might have been the set for a slasher movie. An unlit, weathered wooden sign hung at an angle from a shack that must have served as the office. A neon sign in the window glowed—Vacancy. No Shit. So much for living it up on a government expense account.

Sole scanned the parking lot. There was one car parked at the end of a row of wood-framed shacks that looked like the sort of places families stayed at on cross-country trips back in the day ... way back in the day ... like back in the 1940s. It didn't appear that anyone had slapped a coat of paint on it since then.

The place may not have been much to look at, but it

had a couple of features that Sole appreciated. There were no inside corridors, which meant that anyone approaching a room would have to come from the outside and be easier to spot. Likewise, the location, in the middle of nowhere, on a two-lane road a few miles out of Nogales in the desert, meant that any vehicle coming to the motel would stand out like a sore thumb, and at night, headlights would be visible for miles. There was no way a potential threat could blend in with traffic and take them by surprise, at least not if they were watching. There also did not appear to be any security cameras in the parking lot, an unusual circumstance at motels these days, even dive motels with questionable clientele.

Sole pulled up beside the lone vehicle in front of the room at the end of the line of cottages, got out, and walked around to the passenger side. He reached in, worked the knotted t-shirt loose from the seat frame, and said, "Get out."

Sarita stepped out, her wrists still bound. Since leaving the rest area and her sky-blue van behind, she'd said nothing beyond giving him her name, and Sole had asked no questions. He had a good idea what Lovell was going to say when he showed up with her, and what he would want to do about it. While Sole might have qualms about taking a young girl out in the desert and leaving her body for the crows, he had the uneasy feeling that smiling, laid-back Jay Lovell could keep smiling as he put a bullet through her head and then sit down to his morning coffee and muffin.

Sole nodded at the motel sign. "What does that mean … the name of the motel?"

Sarita looked toward the office shack and said, "Motel Tierras Baldías, it means …" She thought for a few seconds, then said, "A bad place … no, not that … like a bad wilderness place .. a bad land where people don't go." She shrugged. "It's a strange name for a motel."

"Badlands Motel." Sole looked around and nodded. "Seems about right."

They stepped up to the motel room door, but before Sole could give it a rap, Jay Lovell yanked it open. "What the fuck are you doing?" Lovell put his head outside, scanned the parking lot, then stepped aside for them to enter.

"Are you out of your mind?" he said, closing the door behind them and throwing the deadbolt. You brought a girlfriend along? You think this is some kind of Double-O-Seven bullshit?"

"No," Sole said. "It's not like that. She followed me and …"

"Damn it!" Lovell shouted, his aging-hippie demeanor evaporating. "I told you what to do if you're followed."

"I know," Sole said. He looked at Sarita, standing between them, hands bound before her, staring down at the floor. He wondered if she understood the precariousness of her situation. He shook his head and gave an honest answer. "I couldn't … not unless there is no other way. I brought her here to see if there is another way. That's how I do things. If that's a problem, you should know it now."

"Then, if you can't do it, I will!"

"No, you won't … not yet, at least." Sole waited for the fire in Lovell's eyes to subside.

The fire remained, but he said, "Tell me what happened."

Sole recounted the day, leaving Puerto Nuevo, spotting the blue van that followed the taxi, then at the rental lot and across the border. He got to the point where he pulled her from the van at the rest area, and Lovell raised a hand.

"You had her there. You could have done it there ... or any time since then ... and we wouldn't be having this conversation."

"You know my background ... what I've done. I'll do what I have to, but ..." Sole said and shook his head. "Look at her. She's just a girl."

"A woman!" Sarita said, and now the fire was in her eyes. "I saw you at the cantina, Bobby's Place, and thought you might want a woman. I'm good, but," she sneered, "Maybe too much woman for you."

"How old are you?" Sole asked.

"Eighteen." Sarita straightened her back.

"Eighteen." Sole looked at Lovell and shook his head. "Like I said, I'll do what I have to, but only if there's no other way."

"What does that mean?" Sarita said, the fire in her eyes diminishing as she tried to put together the meaning of the words in English. "If there is no other way? You are DEA, no? I don't have any drugs. Now you read me my rights and let me make a phone call. I have a brother in Torrance, California. He'll come to get me."

"We're not DEA," Lovell sighed and turned to the girl. "What's your name, *woman*?"

"Sarita Trejo." She said, her voice subdued now. "Not DEA?"

"No," Lovell said. "And you are in serious shit here ... *mierda seria*."

"I know what shit means. I speak English pretty good." Sudden worry wrinkled her smooth young brow. "Not DEA ... then who are you?"

"We'll ask the questions," Sole interrupted, knowing that the more she interacted directly with Lovell, the deeper she dug herself into the shit hole that could become her grave. "Why did you follow me?"

"Why do you think?"

"Stop the bullshit. You asked what that meant … the other way," Sole said and leaned in close, his voice low. "It means that I am supposed to take you out in the desert and put a bullet in your brain. I still might, so start talking."

"Okay, okay," Sarita said, looking into his eyes, and her defiance morphed into fear. "For money, that's why."

"Keep talking."

"I saw you at Bobby's Place, not from around Puerto Nuevo … a gringo visiting … so I thought you might want a woman. Many men come there for that, but I never saw you with any of the other girls, so then I thought you must be DEA. The cartels pay for information about DEA if we see them around. I need money, so when I saw you at Bobby's place, I started watching you to see where you go."

She talked fast, sensing that getting it all out was the key to avoiding that 'other way' of handling things. "But you didn't go anywhere. You just walked on the beach and drank beer. I started thinking maybe you were just a crazy American, but then I saw you take a taxi at Bobby's Place like you had someplace important to go, and I thought I would follow just to make sure. If you went to the DEA place in San Diego, I would know for sure." She shrugged and shook her head. "Bobby lent me his van, and now I'm here, and Bobby's van is gone. He will be very pissed off about that."

"You know where the DEA office is in San Diego?" Lovell interrupted.

"Sure." Sarita nodded. "Everyone knows that place. Just an office in a building off the highway."

"And when I didn't go to the DEA office, you kept following," Sole said. "Why?"

"I don't know. You acted strange after just walking around Puerto Nuevo ..." She shrugged again, and with it, the fear in her eyes diminished a little. "Maybe I was a little curious, and also, I needed money, and I was already following, so I thought I follow some more and see if there's a way to tell the cartel something about you so they would pay me something."

She stopped speaking and looked at their faces, trying to read what was in their minds. "You don't need to do 'that other way' to me ... in the desert with a bullet in my head." She shook her head, pleading. "I promise. Just let me go, and I will go back to Puerto Nuevo, and I won't tell anyone about you."

Sole and Lovell listened and, when she finished, looked at each other. Sole spoke first. "She's got street smarts. Not much good at tailing in a vehicle, I picked that up pretty quick, but I never saw her watching me in Puerto Nuevo or at Bobby's Place." He shrugged. "Seems like she's telling the truth."

"I suppose." Lovell nodded.

"Yes, it is truth," Sarita said quickly and added, lowering her voice in a seductive way that she must have seen in the movies. "And I can make you happy. Whatever you want, I promise I'll do it for you."

"Shut up," Lovell said and turned to Sole. "Alright, we'll hold off on doing anything until we meet our contact tomorrow. I got you a room next door. She bunks with you." He reached in a duffel and pulled out a set of handcuffs and a room key. "You'll need these. You're on guard duty tonight."

Sole took the cuffs and key, then pushed Sarita from the

room, a hand clamped around her arm. They walked into the room, and Sarita relaxed a little. Then Sole grabbed her wrist and ratcheted the handcuff closed. "You need to use the bathroom?"

"Yes, I think," she said.

"Let's go."

"You come with me?"

"Yes." Sole guided her to the bathroom, holding onto the other handcuff.

"But I don't like it if someone watches."

"So, you'll turn tricks with strange men but don't like to let them see you pee?" Sole shook his head and laughed.

"It's not so funny," she said in a voice that sounded more like a pouting eighteen-year-old than a hardened prostitute.

Sole pushed her ahead and stood by her while she took care of business. Then he guided her to one of the beds in the room, pushed her down on it, and closed the other handcuff around the bed frame.

"You don't have to do that," Sarita protested. "I said I will do anything for you." She gave a soft smile.

"Are you flirting with me?" Sole laughed out loud.

"Why do you laugh?" Sarita asked, angry, taking his laugh as an insult. "You think I am not good enough for you?"

"Oh, I'm sure you're good enough," Sole said. "But tonight, we sleep. Tomorrow, we decide what to do with you."

"Oh." The flirtatious girl vanished, and the worry returned to her face. "Please don't do that other way to me ... with the bullet in my head."

"We'll see." Sole laid back on the bed nearest the door. "Now get some sleep."

FIFTEEN

Something to Keep In Mind

The tent city in the clearing was growing. Three buses were parked now amid the cluster of tents, supplies, and vehicles at the base of the hills. Beside each, people gathered and received their tent assignments. A number of the migrants were separated from the others. Some of these traveled alone. A few families were also separated, sons and daughters taken away from their parents and assigned separate tents. The criteria used to make these assignments were not immediately apparent to the mingling throng.

Luis Ibarra watched it all, leaning on the fender of the new Humvee, a bonus from Juana Elizondo for the successful beginning of their efforts to seize control of all human trafficking. He puffed a cigar, noting how his men reacted and handled every issue that arose.

There were the expected protests from parents being separated from children, but the organizers were becoming more practiced. With each load, they gained experience in easing concerns while applying the right amount of force to gain compliance from the migrants.

They could have simply pointed their rifles and forced the migrants to do what they ordered, but Ibarra was thinking ahead. Point too many rifles, and the word would get out to stay away from these coyotes, and that would run contrary to the long-term business plan entrusted to him by Elizondo.

Like her father, everything Juana Elizondo did was on a large scale. The profits from the cartels' burgeoning human trafficking operations were enormous, a multi-billion-dollar business that rivaled the profits from running illegal drugs into the United States. Juana Elizondo wanted it all.

Her plan had two focuses. First, consolidate all coyote operations—smuggling illegal immigrants across the U.S. border—under *Los Salvajes*.

Second, create a sustainable human trafficking business, not reliant on border control issues. Western nations preferred to believe that slavery no longer existed, or if it did, it was an anomaly, a minor problem, isolated in faraway places.

Juana Elizondo recognized an important truth. The market for slavery existed in western societies and was growing. You only had to know where to look and how to recognize buyers.

Luis Ibarra had proven himself adept at knowing where to look and developing a network of buyers. For that, Elizondo moved him up through the ranks within Los Salvajes until he oversaw all human trafficking operations for the cartel. His first order of business was to eliminate competition from the other cartels.

One of the coyotes walked across the clearing from the buses. He was older than most of the others, mature, steadier, more focused, and less prone to swagger for the girls and shoot off guns for no reason. He'd been with Ibarra when they hijacked the Espinoza bus and showed ability. Ibarra had selected him as a sort of foreman to keep things moving when he wasn't around.

"Looks like you've had a busy day," Ibarra said as the man walked up.

"Busy, yes." Rufo Serrato nodded, his brow wrinkled in concern.

Ibarra saw the look and asked, "Problem?"

"Word from one of our men in Carmen Xhán. There was a visitor."

"Really?" Ibarra blew a cloud of blue smoke into the air and watched it drift away toward the hills. "Who?"

"Miguel Espinoza," Serrato said.

"And this worries you?"

"Doesn't it worry you?" Serrato said. "After *Los Salvajes*, the Espinozas are the most powerful of the cartels."

"True." Ibarra nodded and looked at Serrato, his eyes curious and searching. "Did you think they would ignore what we are doing?"

"No, not that. I only thought …" Serrato shrugged. "I thought that there was a plan to eliminate the other cartels."

"There is," Ibarra said, puffing the cigar and watching Serrato's eyes.

The answer only deepened the look of concern on the coyote's face.

"Alright," Ibarra said without elaborating on the plan. "You've done well today. Go back and organize things. These people must be gone by tomorrow morning before the next load arrives."

Serrato nodded and walked across the clearing to the buses and tents. Ibarra watched, mulling over a different sort of concern.

Criminals, by definition, were dishonest. Most were liars, and all sought profit for themselves with as little work as possible and over the needs of others.

Loyalty only went so far, and what there was of it was based on respect and fear, lubricated by the prospect of financial gain. Ibarra wondered how far Serrato's loyalty, respect, and fear of *Los Salvajes*, would take him when things heated up between the other cartels.

It was something to keep in mind. If Serrato became shaky about things, others might as well. Ibarra would have to give some thought to providing a lesson in loyalty.

SIXTEEN

Truths

Reynaldo Gutierrez gasped and looked down at the woman beneath him, her thighs around his waist, the heels of her feet tapping rhythmically on his buttocks with each thrust. He moved faster, his breaths coming in gasps, her legs clenching tighter around him, drawing him into her.

Juana Elizondo turned her head back, her eyes half closed, her fingertips and manicured nails moving over his chest until he shuddered. She felt he was ready and drew him in deeper, gasping as he gave a last thrust and grunt. Their bodies tensed, muscles tight as steel springs with the final surge of passion.

Then, breathing hard, Reynaldo moved to the side and rolled over on his back.

"You sound like you just ran a marathon." Juana laughed. She turned on her side, draped a leg over his thigh, and rested her head on his chest. "Am I too much for you, old man?"

Reynaldo smiled. "I'm not so old."

"Really? I was just a child when my father sent you to look after me."

"He chose me because I was young, or at least close enough to your age not to attract attention from your friends."

"Oh, you attracted attention, Reynaldo, my love." Juana let out a girlish giggle. "All my friends wanted me to set them up with you."

"And you didn't?" He draped an arm around her and cupped a hand over her breast. "That seems selfish of you."

"I am selfish. You should know that by now," she said.

"Yes." He knew she was serious. "I know it's true."

She gave him a playful punch in the side. "You don't have to be so honest and agree."

"Yes, I do," he said, nodding. "I am honest, and that is why I am here with you now and not someone else."

"Also, true." She nodded. "You *are* honest, and that *is* why it's you and not someone else with his hand on my tit."

It did not hurt his feelings to hear it. He'd known her too long for that, had seen her selfishness in play, in work, and in love. It was part of her, bred into her by her father and by the business she had inherited. And in that way, it had become part of him, selfish, wanting to be the only one she turned to, the only one she came to, the only one to lie with her like this.

They lay silently for a while. The fine mist of lovemaking on their bodies glistened in the moonlight shining through the window. Soon, the afterglow of passion faded, and they slept.

It was still dark, but morning was approaching when she nudged him. "Wake now."

Reynaldo grunted and turned on his side. She shook his shoulder. "Wake up. Time for you to go."

Reynaldo rolled back and looked up at the ceiling, blinking the sleep from his eyes. "What time is it?"

"Almost five in the morning," Juana said. "Leave now. I have to get ready for the day."

Reynaldo sat up, reached for his pants on a chair beside the bed, and began pulling them on, frowning as he dressed. It was the worst part of their time together, the part where she was no longer his. It always happened so quickly.

One minute she slept in his arms, made love to him, chatted playfully, and the next, she turned to ice. She became Juana Elizondo, daughter of Bebé Elizondo, and the *jefa* of the most powerful cartel in Mexico.

He slipped into his shoes and stood, buttoning his shirt. Juana busied herself on the other side of the room for a minute, taking clothes from the closet, throwing them on the bed, then turned, waiting, pretending not to be impatient, for him to finish dressing and leave.

He walked to the door, and she came to him to give him a quick, perfunctory kiss on the lips. "Come see me in the office at ten. I want a report on Ibarra's activities."

"Ten o'clock." Reynaldo nodded.

"And don't look so damned unhappy," she snapped. "I could be sending someone else away from my room."

The unnecessary reminder stung. Reynaldo knew it was true. "Sorry. I only wonder …" He forced a smile and sighed. "When can we ever be together if you always send me away?"

Juana laughed. "Stop acting like a love-struck schoolboy. I have told you. One day we will be together, but not until our plan is successful and *Los Salvajes* controls everything."

She smiled, flirting. "I can't risk showing weakness, and having you around too much like this makes me weak."

"Makes you weak, or makes you look weak in front of others?"

"Both," she said and kissed his cheek.

He smiled.

"That's better," she said, opened the bedroom door, and stepped aside so he could leave.

He moved quietly down the hall to the stairs. Juana watched and was about to close the door when she noticed the door at the end of the hall was ajar. There was no light from inside, but she walked briskly to the door and pushed it open, knowing what she would find.

"Spying on me, mother?"

Sofia Elizondo stood in the center of the room, waiting. "Not spying. This is my house. I don't have to stay hidden away in my room."

"No, you don't. Instead, you sneak around, peeking at me from darkened rooms." Juana reached for the light switch and flipped it so she could see her mother's face. "You don't approve of my behavior. You've made that clear."

"No." Sofia shook her head. "Your father would not approve. Reynaldo is a good man. He has taken care of you over the years, but your father never intended that there would be a romance between you."

"Is that what you think this is?" Juana laughed.

"What else, then? You use him?" Sofia asked. "I can only wonder what your father would do if he were here."

"What would the great Bebé Elizondo do?" Juana shouted now. "He would do whatever he had to, and that is exactly what I am doing."

"Your father never dreamed that you would …"

"My father is not here, and he never dreamed of many things," Juana said, her voice rising. "*Los Salvajes* will be invincible. I will see to it, and Reynaldo will help me accomplish that."

"Perhaps." Sofia shook her head. "But there are things your father would never have done. He had ways of convincing others to do what was necessary."

"Yes! I know," Juana said. "The great Bebé Elizondo could smile his gentle smile, and people fell into line. But do you know why? It was because they feared what would happen when he stopped smiling." She straightened her back, smoothing the sheer nightgown over her hips. "I don't have his smile, but I have other ways."

Sofia's lip turned up in disgust at her daughter. "So, you use your body like a whore."

It happened without thinking, a reflex reaction to the insult and the truth it carried. Juana's hand flew up and struck her mother in the face. "You! You sit here happy to spend the money, living in the palace my father provided, but what do you do? Nothing! That's what." Juana pointed a finger at her mother's face. "You may not have to sleep with him anymore, but for years you did. You took the money he provided, the life he gave you. Don't pretend you didn't know what he did to others to provide all of that for you … for us. Believe me, mother, If I am a whore, you were one first."

Juana turned and left. Sofia remained standing in the center of the room, fighting back tears and the sting of truth in her daughter's words.

SEVENTEEN

Fair Enough

"Where is he?" Sole asked and pulled the motel room's frayed curtain aside to see the parking lot.

"On his way. It was a two-day trip for him." Lovell sat on the bed, scrolling through messages on his phone. "How's your guest? Secure, I hope."

"She's not going anywhere." Sole turned from the window. "Cuffed to the bedframe. I'll need to get her something to eat this morning."

"Really?" Lovell looked up. "That could be a waste of time and government expense money."

"If it isn't on our expense account, I'll pay for it myself," Sole said.

"Don't bother." Lovell got off the bed and held up his phone. "Message from our contact. He's on his way from Fort Stockton. He left at two this morning, so he should be here about ten. Not much to do until then. I'll run out and grab some fast food for us." He nodded at the wall separating them from the room next door. "Including the girl."

Lovell left. Sole checked on Sarita. She'd managed to

reach the television remote with her free arm and lay on the bed flipping through channels.

They exchanged looks but didn't speak. The question of what to do with Sarita remained, and neither wanted the answer right now.

Sole knew that Lovell still held to the practicality of disposing of her and dumping her body in the desert somewhere. It was probably standard operating procedure in whatever the hell special ops department of the NSA they worked for, and frankly, if their mission was to end the trafficking of tens of thousands of people and deaths of thousands of Americans from fentanyl overdoses, Lovell's solution might well be the greater good.

Sole wondered if it might also be the most humane. A young woman like Sarita, living on the fringes of the cartels as an informant, had a short life expectancy, and when it expired, the end would certainly be more unpleasant than simply putting a bullet through her head. Cartel savagery was well-documented, and age and gender meant little to them.

Still, it was not in him to do what Lovell wanted just yet. Sarita had lain through the night, one arm hanging off the bed, her wrist cuffed to the bedframe without making a sound, accepting her fate the way the powerless sometimes do. Half asleep on the other bed, Sole thought he heard her sob once. It occurred to him that he should offer a word of comfort, reassure her that all would be well in the morning, that they would work things out, but he wasn't at all sure that was true and couldn't bring himself to lie to her. At best, she'd received a reprieve, nothing more.

He wondered in the dark about his reluctance to deal

with her as he'd assured Lovell he would if the cartels followed him. Was it simply a matter of her gender? Or that she reminded him of the family he'd lost?

He had no answers to the questions weighing on him, but he knew that he wasn't prepared to do what Lovell wanted. Not yet, at least.

When Lovell returned from Nogales with sausage biscuits and coffee, Sole released her from the bedframe and took her into Lovell's room.

They sat around the single plastic table, eating. Sarita shoved two biscuits down, picked up a styrofoam cup of coffee, and looked at it. "No milk or sugar?" she asked.

"Nope," Lovell said.

"You have water?"

"Sure." Lovell took the cup from her, went to the bathroom sink, dumped the coffee down the drain, and filled the cup with tap water.

She took the cup from him, took a sip, and made a face. "Tastes funny."

Lovell shrugged. "Only water we have."

Sarita took another sip and put the cup on the table.

When they finished eating, Lovell looked at Sole. "Lock her up. Our contact will be here soon."

Sole took her back to the adjacent room and cuffed her to the bedframe again. As he was leaving, she said, "He still wants to do that other thing to me, doesn't he? Out in the desert with a bullet."

"Nothing's been decided," Sole said.

"No? Then why this?" She lifted her cuffed hand. "It's this contact … the person he keeps saying is coming to meet you, isn't it? He's the one who will do it?"

Sole said nothing, put the 'Do Not Disturb' sign over the handle, and closed the door.

At ten-fifteen, a car pulled into the Motel Tierras Baldías parking lot. It was a small foreign job, Japanese or Korean. They all looked the same to Sole. He turned from the window and said, "He's here."

"Right on time." Lovell looked up from his phone and went to the door.

Enrique Valera saw the two vehicles parked at the end of the lot and pulled in beside them. He checked his phone for the room number and went to the door.

Lovell opened it, smiling. "Enrique, my friend. You look tired."

"Yes, very." Valera nodded. "It's a long drive from Reynosa." He saw the man standing behind Lovell and nodded. "This is the man you spoke of."

"This is him." Lovell moved aside. "John Sole, meet Comandante Enrique Valera of the *Policía Estatal*."

"You look like someone I've seen." Valera's eyes narrowed. "I never forget a face. Have you been to Reynosa?"

"I have," Sole said. "But I don't remember crossing paths."

"No, we have not met before, but I know your face." Valera shook his head. "I have an excellent memory for faces."

"I was there briefly a few years ago," Sole said.

"Let me solve the mystery for you," Lovell said. "He went by the name Bill Myers then … had some trouble across the border from Reynosa … little hole in the wall called Creosote, Texas."

"Right, right." Valera nodded. "Cartel trouble, and some smugglers, and …" His forehead wrinkled as he concentrated. "And there was a man who saved a family from being shot crossing the Rio Grande. I remember now. The sheriff there passed a photograph to me to be on the lookout in case you crossed the border after the trouble with the cartel."

"You knew this?" Sole looked at Lovell. "What happened down in Creosote?"

Lovell shrugged and said, "Don't look so surprised and annoyed. I wasn't keeping any secrets from you. Just didn't think it would matter, or that Enrique would remember your face."

"The surprises just keep coming." Sole shook his head.

Valera brought them back to the point of the meeting. "You said you have a plan to bring down the cartels, and that I can be of help," he said to Lovell. "Explain, please."

They sat around the table while Lovell went through the plan to assist the cartels in taking out *Los Salvajes* and, in the process, set them against each other in a war of mutual destruction.

Valera nodded. "This all sounds fine, but what is it you want of me? The cartels will not trust me."

"Exactly," Lovell said. "There will be times when we need someone to take official action to keep things legal, at least on the surface. We'll need someone we can trust. That's you ... and any others from the *policías* that you trust."

"I see," Valera said, thinking. "I'll have to be careful in choosing others, but there are some I think we could rely on. We will begin there. If we are successful, the team will grow, but remember. We will not be in the United States. People in Mexico ... the police there know they must be cautious. There are traitors among the smiling faces that give you slaps on the back, even those wearing uniforms. It can be difficult to find those we can trust."

"I have one question," Sole said.

"What is it?" Lovell asked.

"I'm new to this, and I don't have history with the *Comandante* here, but …" he looked at Valera. "Why should we trust you?"

Lovell frowned. "I trust him. You don't have the …"

"I'll answer," Valera nodded and said, "It's a good question. In a land like ours, poor like ours, money speaks louder than honor and good intentions."

"There are many poor countries in the world," Sole said. "Not all are corrupt."

"Who is to say if they are corrupt. You?" Valera said, then shrugged. "I don't know about other countries, but I do know this. They do not have a giant sleeping next door, so close, with his treasure stacked high. That's what the United States is to many in my country … a giant with treasure, and they see it just yards away across the river, and they want it for themselves. They don't care that it is not their treasure. Many will steal it, or take it by selling and smuggling things the giant wants … drugs, people, weapons …" He shrugged. "So, they allow themselves to be corrupted, and when enough people do it, and do it often enough, it becomes easier. After a while, it does not seem like corruption to them. It seems like … life."

"But not you," Sole said.

"It may be hard for you to understand, but some of us see a different way … a better way for our country, and some of us don't think the giant's riches are worth having," Valera said.

"Why is that?" Sole asked.

"It's simple," Valera said. "The giant is also corrupt, in

his own way, with a sickness that makes no sense. We see it on the television, riots, politicians as corrupt as any here in Mexico, crime, people who are never satisfied with their lives."

He shook his head. "No, I like our ways here. I am Mexican, as you are American. We can be friends, but we are not the same. I have no desire to be you or like you. You asked why you should trust me, but I could ask why should I trust you?"

"Yes, you could," Sole said. "And I suppose my answer would be that I have no motive for being here except to bring down the cartels."

"There is much risk doing what we are going to do. For me, it is worth it. Why is bringing down the cartels worth it to you? Answer that question."

"Personal reasons."

"Personal? What does that mean?"

"It means I am here voluntarily with nothing to gain except ..." He'd opened the door to his personal demons by asking a foolish question, and now, he slammed it shut. Sole shook his head and repeated, "Nothing to gain."

"Nothing except to satisfy your personal reasons ... reasons you prefer not to bring out into the daylight for others to see. I wonder why," Valera said, looking hard into Sole's face for several seconds, then nodded. "Alright, I trust him."

"Excellent," Lovell said with an annoyed shake of his head. "Everyone trusts each other. Now let's get back to the mission at hand. Enrique, this will be dangerous. We will try to make it look as if you are merely acting in the course of your official duties, but in dealing with the cartels ..." He shrugged.

"I understand completely." Valera nodded. "In dealing with the cartels, there are no guarantees."

"Do you have a way to protect your family?"

"Protect?" Valera shrugged. "With the cartels, that is difficult, but I can put them someplace out of sight where they should be safe for a while. My parents have a small farm in the countryside a few hours south of Reynosa. I can send them there."

"Good. Make it sound like a vacation," Lovell said. "A holiday for the children. Send them now so that they are gone and not linked to what we are going to do."

"Right." Valera stood. "Then I suppose I should get back and get them moved and begin recruiting those among the *policías* we can trust."

"There's one more thing. Tell him," Lovell said and looked at Sole. "Enrique is the one most at risk if things turn to shit. He has a right to know and to make the decision."

Sole nodded and said simply, "I was followed."

The look on Valera's face said it all. Any leak, the smallest word about his involvement, and the cartels would take their revenge not only on him but on his family, friends, and anyone close to him.

"Who?" Valera said simply.

"Come with me." Sole led him to the next room, unlocked the door, and stepped aside.

"*Mierda*," Shit, Valera muttered and stepped into the room, glaring at Sarita. "Why were you following this man?"

"I told him," she said. "The cartel pays for information about DEA men. I thought he was DEA, but now I see he is not."

Valera turned to Sole. "As long as she lives, your mission

is in danger. We are all in danger … my family is in danger."

Sole nodded. "I know. I'll do what I have to, but only if it's necessary."

"It's necessary," Valera snapped back, angry at being placed in the position of deciding her fate.

Sole stepped forward. The decision was made, and he was committed. Sarita gasped and sobbed as he reached for her arm.

"Wait," Valera said. "Why did you save the family at the river all those years ago … the man who was shot by a gringo?"

"I don't know," Sole answered honestly and shrugged. "They were unarmed. One was shot, and that asshole with the rifle was going to shoot them all." He shook his head. "Couldn't let that happen."

Valera stared at him and then the girl for a minute and said, "The family told me what happened. A man called over to them and spoke to them. You tell me what he said." Valera's eyes narrowed, and he nodded at Sarita. "Answer honestly. Her life depends on it."

"I don't know exactly," Sole said, his brow furrowed, thinking. "Something like, go away and go to a doctor, and I wouldn't let the man shoot them anymore."

"*Vete a casa. Obtenga atención médica y no intente cruzar aquí de nuevo. Ve ahora. Nadie disparará,*" Valera said. "Except they said your Spanish wasn't so good."

He looked at Sarita and said, "This man saved your life. He probably shouldn't have, but he did. Once before, he saved a family who would have been killed. They live today because of him." Valera nodded. "For now, you will live … because of him."

Sarita exhaled and sobbed. "*Gracias* … thank you."

"Don't thank me," Valera said. "Thank him. I still think we would be better off if he had killed you rather than put us all at risk. If you give me a reason, I'll do it myself."

Valera looked at Sole. "She is safe for now, but she comes with me. I won't take chances with my wife and children having her out on the streets where she might say something."

"Fair enough," Lovell said. "Let's go to work."

EIGHTEEN

Two Reasons

Luis Ibarra was angry. It happened after one of the buses they hijacked from another cartel arrived late in the evening, delayed by engine problems.

The migrants in the tents had settled down for the night. Ibarra was impatient to get to the hotel room in Monterrey that had become his home while he organized the coyote operations. A young woman waited for him there, and not one of the migrant girls from the buses. This one had special skills that Ibarra gladly paid for.

Ibarra and his men watched as the bus sputtered into the clearing just after midnight, trailing fumes and smoke from below. It was one that Chucho Sanchez's cartel used before Ibarra's men waylaid the driver and guards a week earlier and took the bus.

Sanchez's transportation network was unreliable. Some of the buses and trucks were barely able to make the journey north to the border. This bus was no exception. As the driver brought it to a stop, oil dripped from the overheated engine, sending thick smoke billowing out from underneath and filling the interior.

Inside, a clamor of protests arose from the passengers. Voices cried out in distress.

"Let us out. We're choking to death!"

"This damned thing is on fire!"

"The smoke is killing us!"

A young voice, one of the coyotes inside, shouted, *"¡Cállense!"* Shut up!

A moment later, the coyote fired off a round through the bus's roof to calm them down. It had the opposite effect.

The packed throng inside panicked and began kicking at windows to break them out. Men tackled the three coyotes serving as guards on the bus while the driver cowered in the narrow space between his seat and the steering wheel.

There were more gunshots fired by one coyote, on his back now, trying to avoid the kicks and punches of the panicked mob frantic to get off the bus. Several of the migrants cried out in pain.

One howled, *"Me dispararon!"* They shot me! I'm dead! Then he fell from a rear window, thudded into the dirt, and lay motionless.

More migrants began falling and jumping out of the bus windows. Some of the men clambered out and reached up to take children from their wives' arms and then helped the women out. Some ran off toward the surrounding hills with no idea where they were or where to go until Ibarra's men in the clearing stopped them.

Ibarra motioned his foreman, Rufo Serrato, forward. "Take control. Bring the guards to me."

His men circled the bus. Most were regular *Los Salvajes* men. A few had defected from other cartels, deciding to break their loyalties and join *Los Salvajes* as a matter of self-preservation when the bullets started flying. All stared at the chaos on the bus in disbelief.

It was such a simple task. The migrants wanted to go to the border and were willing to pay. The cartel was willing to take their money, load them on the bus, and transport them. Why create so much trouble for themselves, Ibarra's men asked each other as they approached the bus, trying to avoid the bullets being sprayed sporadically by the coyotes inside, who now seemed completely full of bloodlust or panic, or both.

The door burst open, and a flood of people tumbled out. Ibarra's men herded them into a circle fifty feet from the bus. The three coyote guards and the old man who had driven the bus were brought to the front.

"Who's in charge?" Ibarra asked.

One of the coyotes stepped forward. "I am, *jefe*."

"How long have you been with *Los Salvajes*, making the runs?"

"Only a few weeks," the coyote said. "We worked with Sanchez, but the word came out that everyone had to join with you or …" He grinned and shrugged.

"Where did you get this piece of shit bus?" Ibarra asked.

The coyote grinned and nodded at the old man. "This piece of shit came with him."

"This is your bus?" Ibarra asked the old man.

"Not mine … not really." The old man said and looked at the ground, embarrassed. "I stole it from Sanchez. It was the best I could lay my hands on before I joined with you." He looked around at the hard-eyed men standing in a circle around the group.

"That's the best Sanchez has? I'm not surprised." Ibarra

shook his head. "We'll get you something better to drive. For now, you will stay here in the clearing and help my men organize the groups who come in."

"But, *señor*, my family will be ..." the old man began, then saw the look in Ibarra's eyes and nodded. "Yes, for now, I will stay here and help your men, *jefe*, as you say."

"Good." Ibarra nodded and turned to the coyote who said he was in charge. "And you. How do you explain shooting off guns inside the bus, putting people in danger, shooting some of them?"

The coyote looked at his companions and grinned. "These assholes started panicking over a little smoke. When we told them to sit down and shut up, they started pushing out the windows and trying to force us out of the way."

"You could have just opened the door for them," Ibarra said.

"Yes, we could have." the coyote's smug grin widened. "But we had to take control first. If you let these assholes push you around, they are nothing but trouble from then on. You know how it is when you're in charge."

"Yes." Ibarra nodded. "I know how it is." And with one swift motion, he pulled a pistol from his waistband and fired a bullet through the coyote's head. He crumpled to the ground, his rifle clattering in the dirt beside him.

Ibarra swung his extended arm toward the next man in line. The former Sanchez man shook his head and stared wide-eyed, looking a great deal like a startled rabbit about to bound away into the brush. He started to speak. "No ..."

A bullet crashed through his brain, ending his plea for mercy. He fell beside his companion, and Ibarra turned to deal with the third coyote.

The man dropped to his knees, sobbing. "Please, please.

I did nothing. I never fired my gun or hurt anyone." He shook his head, flinging tears off his smooth cheeks.

Ibarra adjusted his aim, lowering his arm so that the pistol's muzzle was inches away from the sobbing man's forehead. His finger tightened on the trigger.

"Please, *señor*. Don't hurt him." It was a woman standing nearby in the crowd from the bus. "He is telling the truth. He never hurt anyone ... treated us well on the journey. He was in the back with us, hiding under a seat when the shooting started."

"It's true, *señor*," a man beside her said. "This one is just a boy, and he did us no wrong."

"Yes," another spoke up from the crowd. "What you did to those others was right. They were bad men, but this one treated us well and did not shoot his gun when the others did."

"Look at me, boy." Ibarra raised the pistol and tucked it back in his waistband. "Do you understand you owe these people your life?"

The coyote raised his eyes. "Yes, *señor*."

"Good. Tomorrow you will go with them when they leave."

"*Señor?* Go with them?"

"Yes. I don't have any use for you here. You may not have done the shooting, but you didn't stop it, either. You are weak. There is no place for weakness here."

"But *señor*, my home is in Guadalajara. I have no reason to go over the border."

"You have two reasons." Ibarra nodded at the bodies at their feet. "You can stay here like your friends, or you can go. Understand?"

"*Si, jefe*."

"Good. What's your name?"

"Tito, *jefe*. Tito Marin."

"How old are you?"

"Sixteen. *Jefe*"

Ibarra looked into his smooth, innocent face and nodded, a decision made. "You don't seem to be much good at this work, Tito, but we may have work for someone like you at the border. Tomorrow you go."

Ibarra turned to Rufo. "Get them situated for the night. You know what to do."

"What about the bus?" Rufo nodded at the hulk, still belching exhaust and smoke from inside. "That's not going to make it to the border."

"Use trucks," Ibarra said impatiently.

"It will take time to organize trucks for the morning."

"Then you better get started," Ibarra said. I want them out of here by noon. There'll be another load arriving in the evening."

Rufo nodded. "*Si, jefe*."

He moved briskly through the clearing, giving orders, organizing the new arrivals with renewed efficiency. Ibarra watched, satisfied. He'd eliminated two troublemakers who would have only created more problems later and, simultaneously, found a way to provide the lesson in loyalty for Serrato and the other coyotes.

NINETEEN

A Vote

"Can we trust the gringos?" Miguel Espinoza asked.

"Of course not," his brother Seve replied. "Not for most things at least, but for this ..." He nodded. "Yes, we can trust them ... for today at least. Our Arab friends, the ones we smuggle over the border sometimes, have an expression. The enemy of my enemy is my friend."

"Yes, I've heard this." Miguel nodded. "And I always wonder what happens to that friend when the mutual enemy is destroyed."

"When that time comes, we must be smarter and faster than our friend and destroy him too," Seve said. "Before he destroys us."

They stood outside a small block building along an airstrip carved out of a jungle mountainside. It was a transfer point used for smuggling cocaine from Columbia. The cocaine planes still flew but had decreased over the years as the cartels diversified, seeking new business opportunities and new markets. These days, meth, fentanyl, and human trafficking augmented their revenues, reducing their reliance on the white powder.

A caravan of vehicles, four armored SUVs, approached along the airstrip's access road, their engines racing as they rolled up in a cloud of dust. Anselmo Cardoso and Chucho Sanchez exited separate vehicles, along with the security teams that accompanied them. They came to stand with the Espinoza brothers as their men spread out, forming a protective arc around the cartel bosses.

"So where is this great savior from the United States?" Sanchez said, fists balled on his hips as he turned to scan the airfield.

"He'll be here," Espinoza said calmly. "And I never said he was a savior ... only that we should hear what he has to say."

"Tell me again how we know this is not a trap?" Cardoso asked. "Catching the leaders of three of the most powerful cartels would be a success for a DEA agent."

"He's not DEA."

"Then what? You said he is an agent of the U.S. government."

"He is from an agency responsible for their national security." Espinoza smiled. "But one that prefers to remain anonymous."

"That does not fill me with confidence," Sanchez growled. "It could still be a trap."

"It could," Espinoza agreed. "That's why when he contacted me, I told him we would only meet him here, on my airstrip, my territory, where I control everything."

He nodded at the vehicles filled with guards circling the landing strip and, farther out, men with rifles patrolling the perimeter and the jungles beyond. "Whatever he comes to tell us today, we are safe here. He would need an army to take us from here, and we would hear an army approaching."

"And if what he tells us is bullshit?" Sanchez sneered.

"A fair question." Espinoza nodded. "We won't know until we hear it, and the truth is that right now, we are not strong enough to take down *Los Salvajes*. If what he says is true, we will have the power to do it."

"And if it's not true," Sanchez sneered.

"Then he will not leave here today." Espinoza shrugged. "And we will be no worse off than before."

A small plane appeared over the surrounding hills, cruising low. It circled the airstrip and lined up with the runway. The throb of its piston engine reverberated off the hills as the pilot descended, shedding altitude quickly to accommodate the short landing strip.

It bumped down, sending a puff of dirt behind the rear wheels, followed by another from the front as the nose lowered and touched down. It rolled out to the end of the landing strip, then made an abrupt one-hundred-eighty-degree turn. The pilot gunned the engine and brought the plane to within fifty feet of the waiting cartel bosses and their assorted security teams.

The security men closed in around the plane, rifles held in combat-ready position. The door pushed open, and the men tensed, not because they expected a serious threat from inside the tiny aircraft, but because their bosses were watching. Each made a show of proving they were the most alert and attentive to their leader's security.

Jay Lovell popped his head out of the door, looked around, and grinned. "All this for me?"

He climbed down from the plane and raised his arms. Miguel Espinoza led three of his men forward. Two searched Lovell for weapons, found none, and stepped back.

The third checked the plane for other occupants, then turned to Espinoza and shook his head. "It's empty."

Miguel nodded at Lovell and said, "This way." He led the way to the three cartel bosses watching from beside the block building.

Seve Espinoza spoke first. "You are?"

"Call me Peter," Lovell said.

"Your real name?"

"What do you think?"

Espinoza nodded and smiled. "Alright, Peter, or should I shorten it to Pete?"

"Doesn't really matter what you call me," Lovell said, shrugging. "The important thing is that I know who you are." He looked from face to face, identifying each. "Seve Espinoza and his stalwart brother, Miguel ... Anselmo Cardoso ... and the fiery Chucho Sanchez."

"Keep fucking around," Sanchez growled, "and you'll see how fiery I am."

Espinoza raised a hand. "No need for that ... yet." He looked at Lovell. "You wanted this meeting for a very specific purpose ... to bring down *Los Salvajes* you said."

"Yes." Lovell nodded.

"Explain how you can do that."

"Fair enough," Lovell said and smiled. "You are at war with *Los Salvajes*."

"And you know this, how?" Espinoza asked.

"Please, Seve. We aren't stupid. We watch. We listen. We hear. We put things together. It's what we do, and we are very good at it, and we see they are moving in on all of your operations."

"Alright, we are at war with *Los Salvajes*." Espinoza shrugged. "You Americans should be happy about it."

"Oh, we are," Lovell said with a grin. "Except for one thing."

"And that is?"

"You can't win."

"I say we kill him now." Sanchez was snarling now, a dog straining at the chain, barely able to control himself. Teeth clenched, he stared at Lovell. "We'll show you who can win today."

"Stop," Lovell said, his tone sharp, the friendly chatter gone. "If you thought you could win, you wouldn't be here today." He stared hard into Sanchez's eyes. "You need help ... an edge ... some way to win, because right now *Los Salvajes* is cutting you in pieces, and you haven't figured a way to stop it."

"And you have a way?" Espinoza said.

"We do." Lovell turned, surveying the security teams standing nearby and along the far edges of the airfield. "Your men are good, but not good enough to stand up to *Los Salvajes*. They need training, better tactics, and a few advantages in weaponry. We can provide all of that."

"Bullshit!" Sanchez's voice rose again. "Our people are the best, and we pay well. Some have even been trained in the United States."

"Then let me ask you a question, Chucho," Lovell said, the smile back on his face. "If your men are so good at what they do, why is it I could kill you all in about fifteen seconds?"

Miguel Espinoza pushed forward and stepped between Lovell and Seve. The security team moved close, rifle muzzles pointed at Lovell's head.

"Relax," Lovell said. "I didn't say I *was going* to kill you, just that I *could* kill you ... all of you ... in fifteen seconds."

"I say kill this motherfucker, now!" Sanchez reached for the pistol in his belt.

"Wait." Espinoza put an arm out to stop him. He looked at Lovell. "You don't seem like a man to commit suicide. Why do you antagonize us in this way when you know what we are capable of?"

"To make a point. You need our help."

"The only point you are making is that you are a fool," Cardoso said, speaking to him for the first time.

"I've been called worse." Lovell shrugged. "What if I give you a demonstration?"

"What sort of demonstration?" Espinoza asked, his eyes narrowing. "If this is a trick ..."

"No trick," Lovell said and pointed to the block walls of the small service building. "Watch that wall, and please have your men lower their weapons. We don't want any accidents during my demonstration." When they hesitated, he added, "You have me here, and I don't plan on committing suicide. I know that if anything goes wrong, you will kill me."

Still pointing at the block wall, he waited. Seve Espinoza nodded, and Miguel Espinoza ordered their men to lower their weapons. Once the rifle muzzles were pointed at the ground, Lovell lowered his arm. That was the signal.

A thousand yards away, hidden on a jungle hillside, Sole saw the signal and squeezed the trigger. The 7.62 round struck its target as he acquired the next and squeezed again, and then a final time. All three rounds impacted their intended targets in less than fifteen seconds, followed by the crack of the rifle a millisecond later.

It was time to move. Sole slung the M24 sniper rifle and moved back into the jungle. Below, Espinoza's security men roared along the airstrip in their vehicles to a point closest to the sound of the gunshots. Several fired randomly into the trees. Others began climbing the slope.

Sole made his way down the hill's reverse slope to the SUV, tossed the rifle in, and climbed behind the wheel. The paint job on the flashy rental would never be the same, but he was down a dirt trail and onto a small two-lane road before the security teams made it to the top of the hill. By the time they stood at the summit, scanning the surrounding countryside, he had disappeared into the jungle around another hill.

Below, Lovell stood with his arms raised to show he was unarmed and had nothing to do with the bullets hitting the building. He smiled at the cartel bosses.

"You think this is funny?" Sanchez shouted. "My men will find the person who shot and will kill him in front of you, and then we will kill you."

"No," Seve Espinoza said.

"No!" Sanchez roared. He looked at Cardoso. "Take a vote!"

"I say no," Cardoso said quietly. "This was a demonstration. They wanted to show us what they are capable of doing for us. Let's see if the shooters can escape our security teams."

"He'll escape," Lovell said calmly. "In fact, he's already gone."

"He?" Seve Espinoza's eyes narrowed. "There is only one who fired three shots?"

"Only one," Lovell said.

"So what?" Sanchez said. "He fired three shots at a wall. Walls don't shoot back."

"He didn't just fire three shots." Lovell motioned toward the wall. "Look closely at the blocks."

Espinoza stepped closer to the wall, stared, then turned. "Targets."

Cardoso and Sanchez followed him over and examined the faint outlines scratched into the blocks. Three ovals about the size of a man's head.

"How ..." Espinoza began.

"Last night," Lovell said. "He arrived in the night, scratched three outlines in the wall with a knife, faint so that you wouldn't notice, but deep enough for him to see through the rifle's scope."

The cartel bosses were silent for several seconds until Espinoza said, "Alright, we see the marks on the wall ... the targets, as you call them. Please make your point."

"Those targets are about the size of a man's head because we wanted you to see that he could have put those bullets ..." Lovell smiled. "Well, like I said, I could have killed you all in about fifteen seconds."

"And you did not," Espinoza said. "No more games. Explain."

"We have a common enemy," Lovell said. "With our help, working together, we can eliminate that enemy for good."

"And when the common enemy is gone, which one of us will be your enemy then?" Cardoso said what the others were thinking.

"You said no more games. I won't lie to you. It's no secret that our government wants the cartels out of business ... all of them," Lovell said, laying out the reality of their situation. "We are offering a temporary alliance, nothing more. Together we eliminate *Los Salvajes*. After that, things return to normal." He shrugged. "The way it has always been."

"Doesn't sound like much of a deal to me," Sanchez said.

"No?" Lovell shook his head. "Then you aren't paying attention. It seems pretty clear that *Los Salvajes* is at war with you and, powerful as they are, will probably destroy all of you in a year or two. You work with us against them, and we train your people to beat them. We make you stronger to fight them, and then after, we go back to the way things were."

"Fighting each other and you," Espinoza threw in.

"Yes, but without having to look over your shoulder, wondering when *Los Salvajes* is coming for you." Lovell decided it was time to wrap things up. "I need to know today if you're in or out."

Espinoza looked at the others and said, "A vote. I say we join with them until *Los Salvajes* is destroyed."

Cardoso nodded. "I agree. We join them."

Sanchez was silent for a minute, his eyes moving from face to face before he gave a nod. "Finally, a vote I agree with. We join them and destroy that fucking Juana Elizondo bitch." He grinned, and his dark eyes narrowed. "After that, we go back to the way things were."

TWENTY

Contingency Plans

"Is this necessary?" Sarita lifted her hands from her lap and extended her wrists, handcuffed together since they left the meeting with Lovell and Sole twelve hours earlier. Valera ignored her.

They were taking the long route back through Mexico. Driving across the United States with a young woman handcuffed beside him could pose problems should some enthusiastic young deputy or highway patrol officer stop him for a traffic violation. Instead of retracing his route along I-10 to Fort Stockton and crossing the border at the Amistad Reservoir, Valera picked a smaller and far less traveled crossing at Naco, on the Arizona border with Mexico.

Flashing his badge and identification for the Mexican customs officers, he told them he was bringing a suspect back for questioning in a series of burglaries. It was an unusual duty for such a high-ranking official, but the officers shrugged and waved him through. After all, who were they to delay a *Comandante de la Policía Estatal*?

The entire process took less than a minute. Sarita sat

sullen and mute without objecting to being described as a burglary suspect. What could she say that the customs officers would believe? There was no way they would take her word over that of a police comandante, and Valera had promised her that if she made any disturbance, he would invoke the 'other way' of handling her presence.

Valera smiled, returned the customs officer's salute, and drove over the border headed east on Mexico Highway 2. The sixteen-hour drive from Reynosa to Nogales was now a twenty-hour drive back, plus a few more to his parents' farm. At least they were back in Mexican territory, and Valera could relax and keep the girl cuffed securely without questions being asked.

"Did you hear what I said?" Sarita asked, annoyed.

"The cuffs stay on." Valera turned his eyes from the road, looked at Sarita's handcuffed wrists, and shook his head. "You expect me to trust you? I don't think so."

"I'm not going anywhere." Sarita looked out the window at the desert landscape. "Where would I go?"

"I don't know, and I'm not going to give you the chance," Valera shot back. "For now, the cuffs stay on."

"You don't trust me, so how is this supposed to work? You take me to this family farm, leave me with your wife and children, and you trust me there, but not here in the car?"

"Not at all," Valera laughed. "And I didn't say I was leaving you at the farm with my family."

"But …" Sarita's brow wrinkled, her eyes confused, then suddenly afraid. "Then you're going to … what they were talking about …the other men."

"No, not that." Valera cut her off. They both knew what 'that' meant. "I probably should do it. Things would be simpler ... safer ... but I promised my friends from north of the border that I wouldn't do it ... yet."

"What then?"

"We'll see how it goes with my family."

"And if it doesn't go so well?" Sarita asked.

Valera ignored the question and took out his cell phone.

Being the wife of a police officer in Mexico was not easy. For Josefina Valera, things could be particularly trying. Enrique Valera, *Comandante de la Policia Estatal* in Reynosa, was an anomaly, a completely honest man.

Even many of the good police officers who worked under her husband's command accepted a little bribe here and there. After all, what would it hurt? Taking the money solved a problem, made everyone happy, and helped pay the bills.

A little honest bribery in the interest of smoothing things over wasn't even considered corruption by most people. It was just the way things worked in Mexico. Bribes and deals on the side oiled the machinery of government bureaucracy. They maintained a sort of social equilibrium, and people just went along with it.

Except Enrique didn't go along with it. He led by example, aware of and working around the daily little corruptions, but not taking part. It was a balancing act. A good-natured refusal to take a little bribe as a thank you for looking the other way might be laughed at by some, but others were offering larger bribes, expecting bigger favors, and they would not be denied.

A few times, he had crossed paths with the cartels and even prosecuted some of their lower-level members for personal crimes unrelated to the cartels' business. Mostly, Valera walked a fine line, doing his job and avoiding cartel entanglements as much as possible.

Josefina respected her husband's honesty and self-imposed mission to do his part to end Mexico's systemic corruption. Still, while many laughed goodnaturedly at his refusal to be corrupted, others had darker feelings on the matter. There was always the unspoken threat against family and loved ones if he angered the wrong person.

At night while the children slept, they talked of what they would ever do if a threat arose. Contingency plans, Enrique called them. He even gave her a code word and explicit instructions on what to do if he ever uttered that word to her.

Josefina had been worried about her husband since he left on his unexplained business across the border. She knew that when he stopped talking to her, it was to protect her because he was about to do something dangerous. When she saw his cell number on her phone, she answered, "Hola, Enrique."

Valera smiled as he drove, relieved to hear her voice. "*Hola, mi preciosidad.*" Hello, my gorgeous one.

Josefina took a breath before responding. "I've been missing you."

"I'll be home tonight."

"Good. We can talk then."

"I have a lot to tell you."

"Drive safely."

"Always," Valera said and ended the call.

A few hundred miles away, Josefina began gathering

clothes for her family, packing the small bags they'd purchased for this possibility. Then she hurried to their school and checked them out with the excuse that their father, Comandante Valera, wanted to take them out for a treat and was busy with official work that night.

"Where are we going, Mama?" ten-year-old Benito asked.

"To visit grandma and grandpa."

"On a school day?" Benito's smooth young brow furrowed. "Where's papa?"

"He will meet us there."

"Oh." Benito considered this and still wasn't satisfied. "But why on a school day? There's no holiday, is there?"

"Just a special holiday for us. Your father wanted me to surprise you. Now, don't talk so much while I'm driving," Josefina said and looked over her shoulder at eight-year-old Natalia, her nose pressed against the window, watching the traffic go by. "Everything alright back there, *pequeña*?"

"Sure," Natalia said, untroubled by the irregularity of their departure from school. "I like holidays, and I like visiting *abu* and *papí* at the farm."

"Good." Josefina smiled.

She drove with both hands on the wheel, fast, but not too fast. Too fast could be dangerous and might attract attention. It was one of the things Enrique had talked to her about if he ever said the code word to her—*preciosidad*—gorgeous one.

She acknowledged it with, "I've been missing you," which meant she understood and was going immediately to his parents' farm.

The truth was, she didn't understand. Her heart pounded in her chest, and her palms dampened as she clenched the steering wheel. There were too many questions.

Were they being followed? How would she know? If they were following, who would it be? What should she do to evade them?

Enrique had explained to her she had the most difficult role in their contingency plan. She had to remain calm and get the children to safety, and right now, she felt anything but calm.

Valera arrived at the farm two hours after his wife and children. Josefina and his parents had been watching from the window and came outside as soon as they saw his car. Benito and Natalia ran into the yard to greet him, shouting, "Papa!", then skidded to a stop. "Who is the girl, papa?"

Valera got out, stopped in front of the car, put an arm around his son, and knelt to give Natalia a hug. "It is so good to see you two."

"The girl, papa," Benito insisted, peering through the windshield. "Who is she?"

"Just a guest."

"I want to meet her," Natalia said and started toward the passenger door.

"Not now. Maybe later." Valera said and took her by the hand to lead her and Benito away from the car and back to the house.

"I was worried about you," Josefina said. Her eyes moved to the car and the girl still sitting in the passenger seat. "It seems we have to talk."

"We do," Valera said and turned to his mother and

father. "Sorry to do this, but Josefina and the children may have to stay with you for a while."

"That is no problem," Cedro Valera said. "It only matters that you and your family are safe. You can stay as long as you like, son. You know this."

"Not me." Valera nodded at his wife and children. "But they must stay here."

"And her?" His father nodded at the girl in the car.

"I have much to explain," Valera sighed and looked at the children. "But not here."

"You can explain to me later. For now, come children." Ana Valera took Natalia by the hand. "Benito, you too. We'll go get the meal ready."

"I want to stay here with papa and …"

"Go with *abuelita*," Valera said. "We'll be in soon."

When his mother and children were in the house, Valera turned to his wife and father. "Some things are about to happen with my work. There is no threat for the moment, but I wanted you safely here in case one arises."

"And the girl," Josefina said.

Valera spent several minutes explaining his meeting with the two men from the United States without going into the details of their plan to take down the cartels. When it came to Sarita, he said simply that she had seen and heard too much and that releasing her was not an option.

He concluded, saying, "The only choice I had was to make her disappear or bring her here."

"Disappear?" Josefina's eyes narrowed. "You mean …"

"This is a dangerous business we've started with the cartels. It may require drastic action at some point."

"But you couldn't …" Josefina nodded at the girl, watching them intently through the windshield. "You wouldn't actually harm her, would you?"

"I couldn't," Valera said. "That's why she is here."

He didn't add that he still thought he probably should have and that they would all be safer if he had dumped her in a hole somewhere between there and the border.

"Alright," his father said. "She's here, and I think you did the right thing, son. A question, though. Is she a threat to any of us ... to the children?"

"Physically, no." Valera shook his head. "I don't think so, at least. As long as she doesn't leave and speak to others about our plans and who she was following, I think she is safe enough to have here." He nodded at an outbuilding twenty yards from the house. "I was thinking we could put her in the shed with some blankets and the old mattress from my room. Keep the vehicles secured. It's miles to the nearest town, and she would not get far on foot."

"We can arrange that," his father said.

Valera looked at Josefina. "I'm sorry about this. If you want me to take care of this the other way, I will."

"The other way? You mean ..." Josefina's eyes widened, and she shook her head. "No. Absolutely not. I want to meet her."

Valera led them to the car and opened the door. Sarita remained in the seat as if glued to it, waiting for what would happen next.

Josefina leaned in and looked into Sarita's eyes. "How old are you?"

"Eighteen, *señora*."

"Not much more than a child," Josefina muttered. "What would your mother think about what you are doing?"

"My mother is dead, *señora*." Sarita's eyes brightened a bit, and she added, "But I have a brother in the States, in California."

"You won't be going to the States," Josefina said. "It seems you will stay here." She leaned closer to Sarita. "Are you going to try to harm my children in any way?"

"Harm your ..." Sarita's eyes widened in shock. "No, *señora*! Never would I harm a child! I am only here because I followed a man hoping to be paid some money for information. I needed money, but I would never harm a child to get it."

Josefina listened and watched her face and then nodded. "I believe her." She turned to her husband.

"Are you certain?" Valera asked, surprised.

"Yes. A woman can see things in another woman's eyes. This girl is not going to hurt anyone." Josefina looked at Sarita. "You heard my husband say that the farm is many miles from the nearest town. If you run away, there is nowhere you can go. We will find you, and after that ..." She shot a look in her husband's direction.

"I won't run away," Sarita said meekly and shrugged. "I don't have anywhere to go except to my brother in California, and even if I could get there, he wouldn't want me around, anyway."

Josefina turned to her husband. "Remove the handcuffs from her, please."

"Are you sure that's what you want?" Valera asked, surprised.

"Yes." Josefina gave a firm nod.

"Alright." Valera took a key from his pocket, removed the handcuffs, and stepped aside. "You can get out now."

Sarita got out and stood before them without speaking, looking at the ground and avoiding their stares.

"Well," Josefina said with an appraising nod and took Sarita by the hand. "Come meet the children." She stalked away, firm and in control, with a contingency plan of her own.

TWENTY-ONE

Trust
―――

Ignacio Pacheco's funeral was an event to be remembered in Carmen Xhán. In wealth or standing in the community, he was not a prominent citizen. Before the cartels arrived and the flow of migrants to the north began, there wasn't much wealth to speak of in the town. But Ignacio was well known, a friend to all, a man who would do a good deed with no expectation of reward, and many loved him for his goodness.

The throng that followed the procession from the funeral mass at the church to the gravesite filled the streets. At the cemetery, they formed a great circle that spilled onto the street, where people stood on tiptoe to see the service.

Lucia and Ignacio's children and grandchildren circled around the open grave, tears streaming down their faces while the priest performed the burial service:

"Our brother, Ignacio Pacheco, has gone to his rest in the peace of Christ. May the Lord now welcome him to the table of God's children in heaven ...."

He followed with a scripture verse and offered a prayer

before they lowered Ignacio into the grave. Lucia let out a long sob as the coffin rested on the dirt below and the priest gave the final Rite of Committal:

"Because God has chosen to call our brother, Ignacio, from this life to himself, we commit his body to the earth, for we are dust, and unto dust, we shall return."

Lucia muttered something in a low voice that turned her children's heads, then she tossed a handful of dirt onto the coffin, and the priest concluded the rite.

The family's period of mourning in Carmen Xhán for Ignacio extended well beyond the traditional nine days. Others also mourned, remembering the smiling man who always had a pleasant word for everybody.

A week after the funeral, Lucia sat alone in their small house, closed the Bible she had been trying to read, and said loudly what she had muttered at the gravesite. "I curse you, God. You say you chose to take him from me! You took him to yourself as if there are no others you could have taken to keep you company. It was a selfish thing for you to do, to take Ignacio away from me for yourself. I will never forgive you for that!"

Lucia made no secret of her anger at God, holding Him personally responsible for her husband's death. The people of Carmen Xhán were sympathetic, but most would not have dared express their sympathies with the same heretical words for fear the priest might hear of it.

In her grief, Lucia decided that Ignacio's killers were God's instruments. The best way to take her revenge on God was to take her revenge on His helpers and see that they paid the ultimate price. While they wouldn't go so far as to blame God, some of the men in town vowed to help Lucia find those responsible for Ignacio's senseless death and make them pay. It was well-intentioned bluster born out of sympathy for Lucia, but no one seriously expected them to hunt down the dreaded *Los Salvajes*.

Everyone knew that there was a survivor from the bus hijacking, a young coyote named Rico. When asked how he managed to survive, he said that they let him go to warn others that *Los Salvajes* was threatening to kill anyone who interfered with their control of migrant smuggling. Rico disappeared after that. Some thought he had left the area to return to wherever his home was, others that he had gone into hiding.

That made sense. Miguel Espinoza was looking for the traitor who had given away the route the bus would take, and as the only survivor, Rico was the prime suspect.

Among those who vowed to find Ignacio's killers was a local sugar cane farmer, Glauco Capilla. Sympathetic to Lucia's desire for revenge, he began a search for Rico. At first, it seemed pointless. Rico had disappeared, and he would never show his face around Carmen Xhán again, knowing that the Espinozas suspected him of being the traitor.

Glauco came up with a plan to find him. It was dangerous, but if successful, he would prove his new friendship with the Espinozas, and the twenty thousand dollars he had pocketed from the destroyed sugar cane might grow even more.

He promised his wife he would be careful. Then, he contacted Espinoza's local organizer, Jorge Barros.

Barros listened, then shook his head. "I have to tell you, this is very risky for you."

"You said Espinoza wanted me as a friend. This is my way of proving my friendship for him and repaying his generosity."

"And perhaps receiving a bit more of his generosity?" Barros smiled his understanding.

Glauco shrugged without denying it.

"Alright," Barros said. "I'll make sure that none of our people interfere with you, but if you find the traitor, you must bring him to me."

"There is another," Glauco said. "The wife of the bus driver. She must be there as well when you do what you will do with him."

"Fair enough. You find the traitor, and everyone will have their pound of flesh."

The standoff between *Los Salvajes* and the other cartels looking for migrants to smuggle in Carmen Xhán was tenuous. Buses and trucks were being hijacked more frequently. Some still made it through, but with every hijacked load, *Los Salvajes* became more powerful.

So far, the cartel violence had taken place on remote roads while an uneasy truce existed in the town. No one wanted to start a street war that would frighten away their golden goose, the thousands of migrants seeking passage to the U.S. border.

Glauco left Barros and began spreading the word around town that a local sugar cane farmer wanted to see what he could do to help *Los Salvajes*. He visited the buses, speaking with some of the coyotes who worked for *Los Salvajes*, telling them he'd heard about the move *Los Salvajes* was making on the other cartels, and he wanted to be part of it.

Most laughed at him. "Go away, old man. What can a sugar cane farmer do for *Los Salvajes*?"

One gave him a warning. "This is a dangerous game you are playing. It's best that you stop asking about *Los Salvajes*."

"It's not a game. The Espinozas destroyed my cane crop," Glauco said without mentioning the twenty thousand dollars Miguel Espinoza paid him for the damage. "If I can do something for the *Los Salvajes* ... maybe something of value that will bring me some cash, maybe I can support my family through the rest of the year."

"And what do you think you can do?"

"I have land." Glauco shrugged. "Land is always useful, not just for sugar cane. Maybe a place to store your buses, or to set up a camp, or for storage, or an airstrip. I hear they build airstrips for their business. There must be many uses they can find for my land, and in return, I can support my family. If I could meet with the one who organizes things for them, I might be able to show him that my land and I can be useful."

The coyote eyed him for a few seconds, then shrugged. "Alright. It's your skin, and I don't suppose it will hurt anything. The one who organizes for us is not in Carmen Xhán. You can find him in Comitán. Write down the name of the cantina I will give you and this word."

Glauco pulled a piece of paper, an old fertilizer receipt, and a pencil from his jeans pocket. The receipt was several weeks old, and the pencil was just a nub, but it was enough for him to record the name of the cantina and the word the coyote spelled out for him.

He read it and looked at the coyote. "I don't know this word."

"It doesn't matter. The man you meet will know it. You will find him at a table where he does business for us. It's a signal. Say this word to him, and he will listen to you and make up his mind about your offer."

"Thank you," Glauco said and returned to the pickup

he'd parked on a side street several blocks away in front of the home of Lucia and Ignacio Pacheco.

He went to the door and tapped. Lucia opened immediately, her eyes red-rimmed as they always were since Ignacio's murder.

"I may know where this Rico is, or at least where to look for him," Glauco said. He explained his plan to her and showed her the scrap of paper with the name of a cantina and the code word.

Lucia looked at it, then at his face, concern in her eyes. "Glauco, I appreciate what you are doing, but this could be very dangerous for you."

"I know. That's why I am showing you this paper with the name of the bar and code word. If something happens to me, let Jorge Barros know and ask the Espinozas to take care of my family."

"I don't know, Glauco." She shook her head.

"Do this for me, Lucia, and I will find those who killed my friend and your husband."

"Alright." She nodded. "If something happens, I will let them know and ask them to care for your family."

"Good." Glauco nodded and turned to his old farm pickup.

Mind at ease now, motivated in part by his desire to help Lucia and the prospect of another big payday from the Espinozas, Glauco made the drive to Comitán, an hour away. The town was on the route most of the buses used as they began their journey north loaded with migrants.

He roamed the streets for a while, stopped and asked directions several times, and finally found the little bar on a plaza near a tree-lined park. He parked on a side street and went inside.

As the coyote had promised, there was a man sitting at a

table by the back door, conducting business of some sort. Other men, obviously some of the local coyotes working for *Los Salvajes*, were gathered around, receiving instructions, going off to carry out orders, or reporting their business to the man.

Glauco walked over, and everyone looked up, some surprised, others snickering and murmuring, "This old farmer must have lost his way … or his mind."

Chiro Cordero, Luis Ibarra's organizer in Comitán, looked up from the table and leaned back, curiosity in his eyes and a grin on his face. "¿Estás p*erdido, hombre*?" Are you lost, man?

"No." Glauco shook his head and looked into the man's eyes.

They were curious eyes, but with something else behind them, threatening and dangerous. Everyone had told him—Barros, the coyote in the street, Lucia Pacheco—all of them warned that doing this could be very dangerous for him. He wondered now why he hadn't listened.

He took a breath and reached for the slip of paper in his pocket. The men around the table reached for the pistols tucked in their belts under their shirts, and Glauco jerked his hand away from his pocket and raised it in the air.

"What's your name, old man?" Cordero asked.

"Glauco Capilla."

"I am Cordero. What is it you want, old man?"

"I wanted to speak with the one who organizes for *Los Salvajes*. Is that you?"

"Yes."

"One of your men in Carmen Xhán gave me a word to say." He looked down at his pocket. "It's on a paper in my pocket."

"Alright," Cordero nodded at his pocket. "Take it out."

Glauco reached slowly into his pocket, watching the men who watched him. They kept their hands on the butt of their pistols but did not interfere. He pulled the old receipt out, looked at it, turned it over so the writing showed, and handed it to Cordero. "Here is the word. It says j-a-n-u-s."

Cordero took the paper, read it, nodded, and looked up at Glauco. "Do you know what this means?"

"No." Glauco shook his head. "It's a word I don't know."

"Janus ... an old Roman god. It's a code word we use."

"Yes." Glauco nodded. "That is what the young man who gave it to me said and that with that word, I could speak with you."

"True. If you have something to say, I'll listen, but you should know something about this word." Cordero laid the paper on the table, and the smile was gone from his face. "Janus had two faces. For us, this means that the person who is speaking may speak out of both sides of his face ... that perhaps we can trust him ... or perhaps not." He shrugged. "Do you still want to speak with me?"

Glauco felt his knees weaken, and he swayed before the staring eyes. These men were killers. Men like these killed his friend, Ignacio. The revenge Lucia wanted and the dollars he hoped to receive from the Espinozas seemed very far away at this moment. He looked at the faces around the table and knew that he was committed now. They would never let him leave without hearing what he had to say.

"I thought that ... well, perhaps I might be of service to you ... to *Los Salvajes*."

"How could you possibly be of service to us?" Cordero said, laughing.

Glauco began his explanation, the one he had given to

the coyote in Carmen Xhán and to Jorge Barros. He had land. It might be of use in many ways. He would be happy to help them because the Espinoza helicopter had destroyed much of his sugar cane.

When he finished, Cordero nodded and said, "I see. Yes, I heard of a farm that was wrecked when Miguel Espinoza arrived."

"Yes, yes." Glauco nodded emphatically. "That was me ... my farm and crop."

"Janus," Cordero said and tapped the paper on the table. "I think you speak out of both sides of your face."

"No, no." Glauco shook his head even more emphatically from side to side. "I speak the truth."

"Only part of it," Cordero said. "Did you think we don't have ears in Carmen Xhán? I also heard of a farmer who suddenly was rich with money ... more money than his crop would have brought in an entire season. I believe that farmer is you."

"But ..." There was nothing else to say.

Cordero stood and nodded to several of the men standing around the table. "Bring him outside."

They went through the back door and stood in a narrow alley. Glauco's eyes went from face to face, searching for some sign of sympathy, but there was none in the hard, mocking eyes that stared back.

He wanted to run, but the young men surrounded him, and besides, there was nowhere to run. Panicked thoughts crowded and bumped into each other in his brain. What were you thinking? Would Lucia tell his wife where he went? Would they come for his family next? Why can't I make my legs and arms work to struggle and at least fight before they kill me? What is that shiny object in Cordero's hand?

The knife's blade flicked through the air as if Cordero was merely swatting at a fly and not slitting a throat. Glauco's eyes bulged in their sockets as he grabbed at his throat, blood pumping between his fingers and down his arms to puddle on the alley's cobblestones. He swayed for a moment as his life faded away, and then crumpled to the ground, rolling onto his back, his hands still clutching his throat.

Glauco motioned to one of the men standing nearby. "Get rid of him."

"*Sí, jefe*." It was Rico, the Espinoza traitor, who stepped forward. Since leaving Carmen Xhán, he'd spent his time running errands and staying out of sight.

He knelt to take hold of Glauco's feet to pull him to a nearby van. As he did, the knife flicked again, this time from behind.

Rico dropped on top of Glauco's still bleeding corpse and rolled on his back, his eyes terrified and confused, staring up at Cordero, his head swaying back and forth in denial that he was dying. He tried to speak, but the knife had severed his vocal cords as it cut through the carotid artery.

"This man came here because of you," Cordero said. "It's just a matter of time before others come looking for you. Besides ..." he sneered. "You're a fucking traitor. Did you think we would ever trust you?"

Rico's eyes dulled into sightless gray orbs. Cordero nodded at his men. "Get rid of this trash."

TWENTY-TWO

Coming Together

Ibarra had selected the clearing in the hills with care. Its central location provided good access to cartel markets across the border to the north as well as in South America and overseas.

Local roads led to the Gulf of Mexico coast, where the barrier islands afforded hidden anchorages for loading the migrants selected and sold as slaves for sex, labor, or as fighters throughout the Americas. When transport farther abroad was required, a network of roads could carry the cartel buses and trucks to ports along the Pacific or to the secret airfields they had constructed for their Columbian drug trade.

The surrounding hills offered good lookout points for his security team to spot unwanted visitors. Ibarra's men could warn them off from cover or eliminate them if they chose not to heed the warnings. As yet, there had been no intruders. The Mexican police studiously avoided the region controlled by *Los Salvajes*, but it was only a matter of time before the other cartels began searching for their base of operations.

The clearing, walled in by hills, was also ideal for containing the growing number of migrants hijacked from other cartels, as well as those moving through *Los Salvajes'* normal trafficking operation. This morning, Ibarra left his Monterrey hotel room early to watch the migrants loading into the buses and trucks before the afternoon arrivals began.

There were the usual protests, mothers and fathers upset that their daughters and sons were placed in separate vehicles. His men were learning and handled most of their concerns with the usual explanations—trouble at the border required them to go in smaller groups, but they would be reunited on the other side.

Those who were not separated asked no questions. Asking questions might cause the coyotes to look at them more closely and separate them as well. Happy to still be traveling together, they loaded onto the buses, knowing that by day's end, they would be at the border.

A commotion at the far edge of the clearing caught his attention. Ibarra walked over to observe how his men handled it.

"I will not leave without my daughter," said a woman, arms crossed and standing between her daughter and the coyotes.

"*Señora*, as I explained, there has been some trouble at the border. They are looking for large groups. We separate you into smaller groups so we can move you more quickly without being caught. We find that younger people like your daughter move faster than the older ones, so we take them separately so that they aren't slowed down by those who may not be as fast." The coyote spoke reasonably, calmly, and smiled.

"No!" the woman shouted. "My daughter stays with me." The woman backed up a little until she was pressed against the younger girl, her arms extending behind her to try and hold the girl as close to her rump as she could.

The coyote nodded at two others standing nearby. They moved forward to pull the girl from behind her mother. "No!" the woman shouted.

"Wait a minute," Ibarra said, walking up. He looked at the woman. "*Señora*, you heard what this man said. We can't allow the older ones to slow down those who might get across the border more easily."

"I'm telling you, I will not leave my daughter!"

Ibarra looked into her eyes for a moment, then nodded. "Alright. You stay here with her." He turned to the coyotes. "Load the buses and trucks and get them on the road, or they won't get to the border before night." He turned to the woman and her daughter. "You go in this truck with your daughter."

"*Muchas gracias, señor.*" Thank you very much, sir. The woman brushed at the tears of relief in her eyes. "*Muchas gracias.*"

When they climbed into the back of the truck with the other girls selected for this load and the door closed them in, Ibarra turned to the coyote who'd tried to reason with her. "When you get her to Mexico City, sell her to one of the gangs in the barrios. They'll use her as a prostitute."

"That old woman?" The coyote gave Ibarra a doubtful, but respectful, glance.

"The gangs aren't too picky," Ibarra said confidently. "Not like our high-priced buyers. Get what you can for her. The gangs will find people who will pay to fuck even an old mother like her. They'll make a profit on her, and when no one wants her anymore, they'll cut her loose on the streets to starve."

"*Sí, jefe*," the coyote said. He moved off to speak to the driver, and two guards packed into the truck cab. Ibarra heard them laugh as the coyote relayed his instructions and explanation word for word.

"Sorry, *jefe*," the coyote said, returning from the truck. "I was trying to do things the way you said."

"No problem. You did fine. Sending the old woman in the truck was not your decision to make."

"Thank you, *jefe*. I was worried you might think I screwed things up," the coyote said and moved away to chat with the others and no doubt report on the good work he'd just done for the boss, reminding them though that it was not their place to make a decision like sending a bitching old mother on the bus with her daughter. That decision belonged to *El Jefe*.

Ibarra gave a satisfied nod. His next report to Juana Elizondo would be even better than the last. If he kept it up, he might even push her ass-kisser, Reynaldo Gutierrez, out of the way.

TWENTY-THREE

Lies

"What language is that?" Eyes wide, a mixture of curiosity and fear on her face, twelve-year-old Francisca's head turned back and forth as she and her sister were herded off the fishing boat onto a dock. "*¿Esto es Estados Unidos?*" Is this the United States?

"I don't know the language," Gabriela, her fifteen-year-old sister, said and added with certainty, "But this is not the United States."

After leaving the clearing in the back of a truck, they had driven for two days to a small fishing village on the Gulf of Mexico coast. There they had transferred to the fishing boat, assured that they would be taken to a small port in the United States. That was only one of the many lies they'd been told for days now.

The dock where the boat landed was a busy place. People moved by them, shouting and calling to each other in a language that sounded familiar, but wasn't. A sign on a building read *Porto de Belém*.

"Belém," Francisca said. "Is that in Mexico?" She

looked at the people, workers from the boats and warehouses, and shook her head. "It doesn't feel like Mexico."

"No, not Mexico," Gabriela said, shaking her head.

"Where then?" Francisca's eyes grew wider as her confusion and fear increased.

"I don't know." Gabriela listened to the words being thrown around by the dockhands. A memory from a geography lesson in school came to her, and she said, "Brazil. They speak Portuguese in Brazil. That must be the language."

"But when are we going to be across the border with mama and papa?" Francisca asked, and now a tear trickled down her cheek.

Gabriela, as frightened and confused as her sister, did not have the heart to give her the answer that would only terrify her more—Never.

Instead, she said, "Maybe this is just a stopover, a place to rest before we go on."

Francisca looked at her with unbelieving eyes but said nothing.

Several men surrounded the group of young girls who had been separated from their parents at the clearing in Mexico. Armed with pistols in their belts, the men motioned them forward into one of the warehouse buildings near the dock.

All the girls were frightened, but after a week on the boat, sick and unable to clean themselves properly, they were happy to be on dry land again. One man, who had been on the boat with them, opened a door, pointed, and said, "In here."

At least he spoke to them in Spanish and not the other language. Inside, they were separated once again. Francisca and Gabriela, along with two other girls, were told to sit in a corner by themselves. The room was large, the air inside humid and hot, and everything smelled like rotting fish.

An hour passed, and the man from the boat led another man over to them. This man seemed very tall as he hovered over them, looking them up and down. His black hair was slick and combed straight back from his forehead, and Francisca thought he looked like a television actor she'd seen on a Mexican soap opera tall.

He looked at their faces, made them smile for him, and told them to stand so he could see their legs and bodies. Then he nodded. "Okay, they look good."

He pulled an envelope from his back pocket and handed it to the man from the boat, who opened it. Gabriela could see that there was money in the envelope.

"Come with me," the black-haired man said in accented Spanish.

He led them to a van waiting at the door to the warehouse, where another man opened it and motioned them inside. The girls climbed in and sat on the metal floor, their backs leaning against the wall.

It was a short drive from the docks through districts of low buildings and dirty streets. When the van stopped, the door opened, and the girls got out. They found themselves in an alley that smelled of garbage and decomposing flesh. Gabriela saw several dead rats near the building's door and tried to back away, but the black-haired man pointed to the wood-framed building and said, "In there."

Even more terrified now, the girls found themselves in a low-ceilinged room, hazy with tobacco smoke and filled with loud music. Men stood lining a bar, drinking and watching a low platform where several other girls about the same age as Gabriela moved about in a clumsy sort of dance. They appeared to be drugged, and none wore any clothes.

Francisca began sobbing. "What is this place?"

The black-haired man led them through the room to another in the back. The room had several low cots covered with dirty sheets. He pointed at them. "Sit down."

The girls complied. The black-haired man looked them over as if making a decision, then pointed at Francisca. "You. Come here."

"No." Francisca shook her head and turned to her sister. "I'm afraid, Gabriela."

Black-haired man reached down and jerked Francisca from the cot. Gabriela jumped up to take hold of Francisca's other arm. "Leave my sister alone!"

Black-haired man swung his arm and caught Gabriela under the chin. She fell back, and he smiled. "Don't worry. I'll be back for you soon."

He dragged Francisca to another room. There was only one cot in this one. He pushed her in, closed the door, and turned, unzipping his pants. "I always like to break the new ones in myself and make sure they're ready for tonight."

Francisca shrieked, first at seeing the man standing without pants before her, and then at what followed.

The rape was quick and painful and left Francisca bleeding. When he finished, Black-haired man jerked her from the cot into the hall and threw her back into the room with the other girls. One by one, assisted by a drug generally used to help men with erectile dysfunction, he raped the other girls, 'breaking them in' as he had Francisca.

Afterward, the four girls sat naked in the room on the cots. Black-haired man locked the door and went to the bar in the main room, where the bartender grinned and slid a tumbler of rum to him. "It'll be a good night tonight."

"Yes," Black-haired man said, gulping down the rum and holding the glass out for a refill. He eyed the men at the bar, watching the nude girls on the stage. "I think our customers are ready for some fresh entertainment."

Manolo and Javier, separated from their parents on the same day in the clearing, were also loaded onto a boat, but this one departed Mexico's Pacific coast. The trip seemed never-ending, and Javier was seasick much of the way.

Altogether, there were a dozen boys. Their treatment during the voyage was brutal. There was no reason to lie to keep them calm. Locked in the hold for most of the journey, they were only allowed on deck for a few minutes each day to relieve themselves and receive a small ration of food—rice and fish—from one of the deckhands.

On the fourth day, one boy went to the deck rail as if to urinate over the side. As Manolo, Javier, and the others watched, he unzipped and looked over his shoulder at them for a moment. It almost seemed as if he smiled, or it might have been the reflected light from the waves shimmering off his pale face. Then he was gone, leaping over the rail to disappear beneath the blue Pacific.

A great turmoil among the crew followed his suicide. The captain was furious, shouting out about losing profits and the carelessness that allowed the boy to jump to his death. The crewman responsible for herding the boys topside and watching them was reprimanded, confined to his bunk, and told that the lost profits would come from his wages.

From that point on, they treated the boys even more brutally and gave them less time on deck. All eventually became seasick, and the hold where they were confined became a filthy, wretched hell.

When they reached their destination and the boat maneuvered up to the dock, the boys were brought on deck. Javier read a sign over a nearby building,

Puerto de Antofagasta and beneath it, *República de Chile*.

He looked at his brother. They had realized as soon as the boat's crew threw them into the hold that they were not going to the United States. "Why do you think they brought us to Chile?"

"I don't know." Manolo, who never liked being pushed or forced to do anything, was being pushed to the maximum limit of his ability to resist pushing back.

"Stay calm," Javier warned. "There is nothing to do for now. Wait until we know what is happening."

They did not have long to wait. As soon as the lines were tossed to the dock and the boat secured in place, a truck roared from around a building and came to a stop in front of the boat. Several burly men descended, wearing the same sort of work clothes as the men working on the boats and docks. They did not brandish weapons publicly, but they made a point of allowing the boys to glimpse the pistols tucked in their waistbands under their shirts.

A small man—not much bigger than the smallest of the boys—got out of the truck's passenger door and approached the boat. He did a headcount and frowned, counted again, and looked at the captain of the boat. "You are one short."

"It couldn't be helped." The boat captain shrugged. "An unavoidable accident."

"We don't pay for your accidents."

"I'll deduct half the price of one passenger," the captain said and gave another indifferent shrug. "We have expenses, and that's the best I can do. Otherwise, I'll just load these back on board and go back the way we came. There are other buyers."

It was a bargaining position. The boat captain had no intention of returning to Mexico without the payment promised to *Los Salvajes* by the buyer.

"Alright," the small man said. "One-half the price of one passenger deducted from the payment."

He retrieved a duffel from the truck's cab, walked up the ramp to the boat, and followed the captain into the wheelhouse. A few minutes later, he came out on deck without the duffel and barked an order at the men from the truck. "Load them up!"

"You heard," one of the men said. "In the truck!"

They pushed Manolo, Javier, and the others into the back of the truck. When Manolo's back bowed, and he stiffened at a shove from behind, he was struck in the back of the head with a rifle butt so that he collapsed forward, falling on Javier.

"Asshole! You didn't have to do that! He just doesn't like to be shoved."

The man with the rifle grinned and slammed the door shut. A minute later, the engine roared, and they began moving.

Outside they heard traffic sounds, and for almost an hour, they bounced along through city streets. Then the city and traffic noise died away. The truck continued for another hour over a paved highway before making a jarring turn that took them onto a dirt road. The back of the truck swayed and lurched almost as badly as the boat. A couple of the boys were as sick from the motion as they had been, locked in the boat's hold.

They were gaining elevation. The boys worked their

jaws back and forth to pop and clear their ears. Then all at once, they descended rapidly for half a mile, and the truck rolled to a stop.

They sat breathless in the dim interior. Hopes of ending up in the United States with their families were long forgotten. They could only wait for the men to open the truck and reveal their fate.

A boy of about twelve years sat with his head down on his knees and whimpered, "*No puedo tomar esto. ¿Dónde están mi papá y mi mamá?*" I can't take this. Where are my papa and mama?

"Stop it!" Manolo snapped at him. "Don't let them see you like this. Don't let them see you weak!"

"I can't help it!" The boy began blubbering. "I'm-I'm afraid … I c-can't take th-this anymore."

"If they see you weak, it will be worse," Manolo said. "They might punish you for being weak. It's always best to make people think you are strong, even if you don't feel so strong inside."

"I-I c-can't help it," the boy sobbed and shook his head.

The doors opened, and the boys squinted in the late afternoon sun. "Out," one guard ordered.

They climbed out of the back of the truck. The guards, the burly men from the dock, their weapons out now, not concealed under their shirts, pushed them into a ragged line. When they were lined up, the senior guard called out over his shoulder, "They're ready."

The small man from the front of the truck came to look at them. The others called him *El Gallo* —The Rooster— and stood aside deferentially as he walked up and down the line, eyeing the boys. Most looked at the ground as he passed.

A few, like Manolo and Javier, returned his stare. *El Gallo* nodded at them. "Good."

He took a few steps away so that they could all see him. "We have given you a great honor today. You have been enlisted in *El Ejército de la Revolución Popular.*"

The Army of the People's Revolution. He paused for them to absorb what he said, then smiled and continued, "You will fight for the liberation of your brothers and sisters here in Chile! We will train you, and you will learn to kill, and after you have learned, we will send you out, and you *will* kill for your Chilean brothers and sisters and free them from the capitalists who oppress them. For this, they will honor you for generations to come." *Gallo* looked up and down the line and nodded. "Do you understand?"

No one spoke for a few seconds, then a voice called out, not too loud, but firm, "Why don't our Chilean brothers and sisters fight for themselves?"

Gallo's head snapped in the direction of the boy who spoke. He stepped forward so that his face was inches away and said, "What is your name?"

"Manolo."

"You like to ask foolish questions, do you Manolo?" *Gallo* said, then stepped aside. One of the bigger men came forward, smiled, and with a gloved hand, swung his fist into Manolo's forehead so that his knees buckled and he stumbled to the ground.

Javier knelt beside Manolo and helped him back to his feet.

"You know this one?" *Gallo* asked.

"He is my brother," Javier said, glaring at the small man who seemed to control everything in this place.

"Good. You will train together, and you will fight together, and if the time comes, you will die together, but until that time comes, if you want him to remain alive here, you will help him see the wisdom of obeying our orders and the honor of fighting in our cause." *Gallo's* eyes narrowed. "Do you understand?"

"Yes," Javier muttered and supported Manolo on his wavering legs.

The whimpering boy let out a sob. *Gallo* went to stand in front of him. "What is your problem?"

"I-I j-just want to be with my mama and papa."

"Y-your m-mama and p-papa," *Gallo* mimicked him, and the men standing around him laughed. "So, you're a gentle one ... a mama's boy ... a lover, not a fighter, is that it?"

Gallo turned to look at his men and grinned. "Take this one to your tents. Use him like the little girl that he is. A night or two of you shoving it up his ass, and he might turn into a fighter after all." *Gallo* shrugged. "If not, we can always strap a package to him and send him to *Palacio de la Moneda* in Santiago. His guts splattered over the president's home will serve the cause equally well."

The men with the guns grinned and dragged the whimpering boy away from the others. He disappeared inside a tent, and his sobs turned to shrieks.

As it turned out, Hector's sense of direction was correct the morning they left the clearing in the back of the truck. The truck's turn to the right took them away from the border. He and Marita, along with their new friends, Paco and Lupe, and several others crammed inside with them, traveled for a week in the back of the truck.

Marita was inconsolable over the disappearance of their

daughters, Gabriela and Francisca. Hector sat with his arm around her as she sobbed, trying to control his emotions and tell himself that this was all just part of the journey.

Lupe kept telling Paco that their sons, Javier and Manolo, would be fine. Eventually, they would meet them at the border, as the coyotes promised. Paco smiled his good-natured smile and nodded but said nothing.

They reached their destination, and the truck doors opened for the last time to let them out. Faces and shoulders sagging in despair, they gazed around at their surroundings, a vast cropland covering rolling hills as far as they could see. It was a coffee plantation, and they knew their worst nightmare had come true.

A four-wheel-drive vehicle came careening along a winding dirt road toward them, followed by a truck. Both vehicles slid to a stop in the dirt, and a red-faced heavyset man got out from behind the wheel of the lead car while several armed men got out of the truck behind.

Smiling broadly, the red-faced man walked over to the coyotes who had driven the migrants and handed them an envelope. The coyotes looked inside, counted the money, exchanged a word with the red-faced man, then got back in their truck and left.

Still smiling, he turned to look at the migrants. "Welcome! Welcome to you all!" He put his fat fists on his hips under the blubber that hung over his belt and spoke to them as if it was the most natural thing in the world for someone to bring him people locked in the back of a truck. "You will be my workers. I have paid for you to work, and ..." He cast a glance at the armed men from the truck. "And that is what you will do. It's hard work but good work ... honorable work. If you work hard and don't cause troubles for me, one day you may be able to pay for your freedom from the money I will pay you, and then you can return to your homes ... wherever they may be."

"You will pay us?" Hector interrupted.

Red-faced man stopped to look at him. "Why yes, of course, I will pay you. You will need to buy your food to support yourself here and a little money left for tequila ... right?" He grinned.

"How will there be enough money for us to buy our freedom, as you say?" Paco chimed in. "And why should we have to buy what is ours already?"

His usually mild tone sounded much like his son Manolo's when he was being pushed by someone.

"That ..." Red-faced man shrugged. "That is your worry. Eat less, save more. Find ways to save. It doesn't matter to me, but for now, you work for me, and make no mistake ... you will work."

"How much?" Hector asked.

"What?" Red-faced man turned toward him, a look of surprise and curiosity on his wide face.

"How much to be free?" Hector said.

"You people ..." Red-faced man shook his head, laughing so that the layers of fat hanging over his belt rippled and jiggled. He pulled a handkerchief from a back pocket, wiped his face, and blew his nose on it, then said. "You people ask too many questions."

He motioned to the armed men from the truck, "Get them settled, then put them to work."

The armed men herded the migrants into yet another truck, where they sat huddled together while they were driven to the place they would stay. Everyone knew it was a false promise, but it was all they had, so a few spoke among themselves of the possibility of buying their freedom.

"I know how we will do it. Just don't eat very much," an older woman said. "I've lived on very little my whole life."

"Yes, and for me," her husband threw in, "From now on, no tequila ... no cerveza. We save every penny until we have enough to pay to be free."

"But how much is that?" someone asked.

Another said, "And if we save the money, how do we know that fat son of a bitch won't raise the price?"

Paco looked at Hector. "I still say, why should we have to pay anything for our freedom? We are already free."

Hector shook his head and squeezed Marita's hand. "It seems we are not."

They were silent after that. They'd been living on lies for days, first from the coyotes and now from the red-faced man. No one said it, but everyone in the truck knew in their hearts they would spend the rest of their lives toiling for the red-faced man while the lies echoed in their ears.

The cartel did not reserve its lies only for the migrants. Tito Marin arrived at the Mexico-Arizona border in the back of a box truck a couple of days after leaving the clearing. Sent away by Ibarra for his failure to try and stop the shooting on the bus by the other coyotes, he sat packed in with the migrants, trying to figure out how he could get back to his family in Guadalajara.

It had seemed such a grand adventure and a chance to make more money than he could have ever dreamed. Urged by his friends, he signed on with the Sanchez cartel to help run migrants to the border. When *Los Salvajes* came and told the rival cartel coyotes that they were taking over, Tito and his friends shrugged and signed on with *Los Salvajes*. One cartel was as good as another, they said, and the money would be even better with *Los Salvajes* as they seized control of all human trafficking.

Those friends were dead now, shot as he watched Ibarra gun them down in the clearing. He had looked down at their bodies, thinking he was next. That was when Ibarra told him he could join his friends on the ground or go to the border where they would have work for him.

When the box truck's back door opened, Tito climbed down and lined up with the other migrants. They looked around and saw that they were in a small, dusty town. The air was very dry, and Tito knew they were somewhere in the desert near the border. Several armed men, coyotes, came up to them. One went up and down the line, looking at each. "Which one of you is Tito?"

"Here, *jefe*." Tito lifted a hand.

The man looked at the migrants and motioned to the other coyotes. "You others go with these men. You will cross the border tonight when it's dark." He turned to Tito. "Come with me."

Tito nodded and followed him down an alley that smelled of urine. Another truck, a smaller one, was parked at the end. The coyote opened the back door. "Get in."

Tito looked in and saw four other young men. One had a bruised and lumpy face as if he'd been in a fight. The others sat dejected, staring at the floor and avoiding eye contact with the coyote.

"But ..." Tito turned to the coyote, wide-eyed and suddenly terrified. "I was told you had work for me here. Ibarra said it himself."

"Work?" The coyote grinned and shoved him through the open door. "Sure, sure. We have lots of work for you. "

Tito fell backward onto the steel floor. The door

slammed, and a moment later, the truck bounced along the alley.

They rode for hours in the back of the truck without a stop for food or to relieve themselves. By the time the truck braked to a halt, the five-gallon slop bucket was full, and its putrid contents sloshed over the side.

The back door opened. It was night now, and they were in another stinking alley, but this one was in a large city. Tito heard distant sounds of traffic, music, people talking and laughing.

A door to a low building opened. Several men came out and pushed Tito and the others through the door into a room lit by red, green, and blue lights mounted along the walls that reminded Tito of Christmas decorations. They were led past a crowd of men lined up along a bar, drinking and laughing. Several turned and smiled at them, nodding and muttering things to the others at the bar.

They led Tito to a tiny room with a single bed. "Wait here," a coyote said.

Tito sat on the bed and waited, but not for very long. A few minutes later, the door opened, and a large, heavyset man came in and smiled. "Looks like you're mine tonight."

"Yours?" Tito said. He shook his head, understanding what was about to happen. "No. Please, no."

"You're afraid?" The man's smile widened. "That's good ... better that way."

He came close, dropping his pants as he stepped to the bed. "You know what to do."

"No," Tito sobbed. "No, I can't."

"No?" The smiling man jerked Tito up from the bed and ripped his clothes from him, then threw him face down on the stained mattress. "Then we'll do things differently." The man chuckled. "This might hurt a little."

It was a pain unlike any Tito had experienced before. He wailed and sobbed under the man's weight, and the more he did, the more force the man used, smiling and laughing all the while. "That's it, little boy. Cry for your mama! It's better that way."

He smelled of dirty armpits and onions and peppers. Tito sobbed, thinking it would have been better to tell Ibarra to just shoot him down like his friends instead of trusting his lie about work for him at the border. The man on top ignored his sobs as he grunted and tore at Tito's flesh.

TWENTY-FOUR

Tell Him

"Hope all this is going to work."

"Hope has nothing to do with it. You having second thoughts now?" Sole frowned and looked up from his new favorite weapon, the M-24 sniper rifle Lovell had procured for him from an undisclosed U.S. law enforcement agency arsenal. Their clandestine operation apparently had full access to military-grade weaponry, and Sole was taking advantage of it, updating his wish list of weapons almost daily as their plans for taking out *Los Salvajes* solidified.

"No second thoughts," Lovell said, tugging at his chin and eyeing the assortment of weapons Sole had spread out on the bed in the room they'd rented for the night. "Just pre-op jitters, I guess."

Sole nodded and went back to cleaning and checking the rifle's mechanism. Jitters were common before any military operation, and that was what this was—a military strike against a more powerful enemy.

Sole figured Lovell's sudden nervousness stemmed from the fact that he was a spy, an undercover operator, dealer, agent, or whatever term they used these days in the secret world where he made his home. Sole, on the other hand, was a cop ... and, in a former life, a Marine. Taking direct action against the enemy or bad guys was what they had trained him to do, what he had been doing for most of his life. His private little war with *Los Salvajes* was growing into something bigger but remained a series of direct engagements with an identified enemy, and that was something Sole could handle. There was purity in it, nothing hidden or secret about killing the person who wanted to kill you.

Lovell was accustomed to fighting unseen in dark corners. If it was clandestine, he was an expert. If it involved slitting the throat of an unsuspecting adversary as they slept snuggled up to their wife, husband, or significant other, Sole knew Lovell would complete the assignment and go about his business without a minute's hesitation or regret.

But this wasn't that. This was warfare, street fighting, out in the open combat, not Lovell's expertise, and far outside his comfort zone.

Sole suspected there was another reason for Lovell's pre-op jitters. Sole had already lost everything that truly mattered to him in life and, in a very real sense, had nothing else to lose. Lovell was wagering everything—his career, his future, and his family if he had one—on their success. Sole wasn't clear about the family, as Lovell kept his personal life completely out of their relationship, but he'd staked everything on bringing an unknown player—John Sole—into the official fight against the cartels. If all their planning turned to shit, Sole would be no worse off, but Lovell could lose everything he'd spent his career working for. Sole respected that.

He completed his weapons and gear check and looked up. "We're committed. It's normal to be nervous but focus on the mission. Channel the nervous energy into action when the time comes …."

"Right … action." Lovell nodded and looked at the assortment of weapons. "I need something to do."

"You mean gearing up and shooting it out with the bad guys?" Sole shook his head. "That's not your job, and you'd be liable to get someone hurt … like me. I'll handle the contact with the enemy. Your job is escape and evasion if that becomes necessary."

Sole spoke to him like a sergeant briefing his team before a military operation because that's how he had designed it. Like all good military operations, he kept it simple. *Los Salvajes* was the equivalent of a superpower, vastly stronger than any of the other cartels. Together, they might rival them in firepower but not in force cohesion and operational discipline.

The truth was that combining their forces to take out *Los Salvajes* was dangerous. Once the bullets started flying, it was as likely that Sanchez, Cardoso, and Espinoza would take each other out as they would *Los Salvajes*.

That would come later, Sole had explained to Lovell. For now, the mission was eliminating *Los Salvajes*, and the strategy was simple. Kill as many of them as possible in well-executed attacks until the superior numbers of the other cartels could overwhelm them. Borrowing tactics from insurgencies as far back as the American Revolution and forward to current partisan movements in Belarus and Russia, Sole focused on reducing *Los Salvajes*' ability to fight by eliminating its fighters.

It all sounded good when he explained it to Lovell, but working with Sanchez's men for this operation made Sole wonder if they had any chance at all. Undisciplined, arrogant, and full of machismo bullshit, they preferred strutting to learning the tactics of concealment and surprise.

Sole did the best he could with the few days he had to prepare them, and when Lovell gave him the latest intel on a convoy of trucks carrying fentanyl toward the border, he shrugged and said, "To hell with it. Sometimes the best way for a soldier to learn is to get bloodied." He figured they were about to become very bloody.

Lovell had procured a Land Rover from one of his unnamed sources for their operational use. Now, he steered it down a stretch of two-lane road that passed through a two-mile-long valley that narrowed to fifty yards across at one end. Sole had selected it carefully and explained to Sanchez's men that victory was simply a matter of leaving more of *Los Salvajes'* dead on the ground than theirs, and preferably none of Sanchez's men would be casualties.

That meant operating from cover, focusing on their assigned fields of fire, and not randomly spraying bullets. Sanchez's men laughed and strutted.

"Trust me, gringo," one said. "We know how to kill."

"We'll show you something when it comes to killing," another chimed in, grinning. "We might even teach you something."

"We'll see." Sole shrugged and went over the plan again and then again, walking through their assigned roles in it.

The man who thought they could teach him about killing objected to having his men lined up behind trees on only one side of the valley. "It is better to put men on both sides," Teacher-man said. "More bullets do more killing that way."

Sole sighed and tried to explain the concept of an L-shaped ambush, concentrating firepower from one side and the rear or front to avoid killing your own people in a crossfire.

Teacher-man laughed and said, "I'm a pretty good shot. I'll be killing those *Los Salvajes* bastards." A thin, mean smile crossed his face. "Unless someone else gets in the way."

Sole ignored it and made assignments, positioning the men along the valley. There was no time for a run-through, not that it would have made much difference, he figured.

Lovell stopped the Land Rover at the narrow end of the valley. Sole got out, scanning the hillsides for Sanchez's men. They were concealed behind low-growing trees that dotted the hillsides, and each gave a hand wave so that he could see where they were.

They seemed to be roughly in the positions he'd assigned them. "Probably as good as it's going to get," he muttered and grabbed his weapons and a large duffel. "Meet me on the far side of the hill at the rally point when the shooting stops."

"Will do." Lovell nodded and accelerated down the highway, disappearing around a turn.

Sole opened the duffel and removed two green convex rectangular objects, M-18 Claymore mines Lovell contributed to the operation. These were modified wireless versions without the usual trailing detonator wires. Sole positioned them along the side of the road, inserted the blasting caps, and retreated a hundred yards to the position he'd selected for himself, on the hillside directly above the valley's narrowest point.

A half-hour passed, and he saw movement, but not from the *Los Salvajes* convoy of drug trucks. Several of Sanchez's men were becoming impatient. He smelled cigarette smoke wafting through the air. Chatter between their concealed positions that began as a murmur rose in volume as they called to each other, made jokes, and laughed.

"*¡Silencio!*" Sole called out, and the chatter died down a bit, although he heard a few insults thrown in his direction.

Another half-hour passed, and a distant rumble of truck engines echoed down the valley. "*¡Prepararse!*" Get ready, Sole shouted.

His orders had been to wait until he opened fire on the first vehicle in line. The plan was to disable the lead vehicle and block the road so the other trucks and vehicles in the *Los Salvajes* drug convoy were blocked and became sitting targets for the men positioned on the hillside.

That was the plan, at least. As the lead vehicle, a large super-duty pickup truck with five heavily armed men in the cab and another six seated in the bed rolled along the road toward Sole's position, a shot rang out from the hillside. Then another and another. Before long, the Sanchez men were standing in their positions, raining fire down on the convoy.

The trucks and vehicles increased their speed to escape the trap. They had not yet reached the narrow point in the valley, but Sole raised the rifle, sighted on the lead pickup's driver, and squeezed the trigger. The steel-jacketed lead bullet punched a hole in the windshield and then through the driver's sternum, just below his neck.

The pickup careened out of control, and the trucks behind dodged around it to escape the firing from the hillside and make their way past the narrow valley opening. Sole's plan was coming apart, but there was still time to do some damage.

Sole raised the rifle again, sighted on the next vehicle's driver, and squeezed off a round. A spray of blood coated the inside of the truck's windshield. Several vehicles behind swerved partially off the road and raced forward as Sole reached for the Claymore detonator handles.

One truck made it through the narrow valley opening as Sole squeezed the handle three times. The first Claymore erupted in a roar of smoke and flame, the C-4 explosive inside sending 700 one-eighth-inch steel pellets into the side of the next vehicle, another super duty pickup loaded with security men.

Designed as an anti-personnel weapon, the Claymore pellets were not enough to completely disable the oversized truck, but the seriously wounded driver lost control, and it bounced nose first into the roadside ditch.

Seven wounded and dazed men climbed out of the bed and the cab. Sole squeezed the second Claymore's detonator handle. The *Los Salvajes* men were cut down before they could raise their weapons.

Sole turned his attention to the half dozen other vehicles still on the road. A heavy firefight was in progress. *Los Salvajes* men crouched beside their vehicles, firing at targets along the hillside.

The Sanchez men stood and exposed themselves to spray bullets down at the road, but most of the firing was unaimed and ineffectual. Teacher-man rose from his position and led a few others in a mad rush toward the vehicles. Sole concentrated on finding targets through the rifle scope, eliminating them one by one.

The battle raged for ten minutes before the driver of the last truck in line gunned the engine in reverse and began backing wildly down the road toward the far end of the valley. A few *Los Salvajes* men managed to yank a door open and climb in before it had picked up speed.

Sole watched and had to give the driver credit for his

driving skills. Roaring along in reverse at thirty miles per hour, the truck and its occupants were soon out of range.

The firing finally died away as a surviving *Los Salvajes* man was surrounded and cut down in a hail of bullets. Sanchez's men celebrated by firing their rifles and pistols wildly into the air.

Sole came down to the road to survey the damage. Two dozen bodies lay scattered in the dirt, or crumpled over inside the vehicles. Another five, Sanchez's men, lay dead on the hillside or on the side of the road.

Sanchez's men were walking along the road, shooting bullets into the bodies whether or not they were alive. One man noticed Sole and ran over. "A great victory, right? We told you! We showed those *Los Salvajes* bastards!"

Sole nodded down at Teacher-man's eyes, staring blankly up from the side of the road where he'd been killed rushing the vehicles. "Tell him."

TWENTY-FIVE

Possibilities

Reynaldo walked into Juana Elizondo's office and took up his customary position before her desk, waiting to be acknowledged. A minute passed before she looked up and noted his rigid posture, a sign that he was concerned over some matter, usually one of no great concern to her.

His compulsive need to protect her was annoying, but she accepted it and used it, as she did everything else about their relationship. "Is there a problem, Reynaldo?"

"There has been an attack."

"An attack? Where? On what?" Juana sat up straight. Her chair had once belonged to her father and was far too large for her comfort but was part of the trappings of her position as the *Jefa*.

"On one of our drug shipments. It happened on a back road between the lab and the border."

"Losses?"

"Everything," Reynaldo said bluntly. "It was an ambush. Two of our vehicles managed to escape with a few of our people, but the shipment and many of our men were lost."

"What happened to our security? How were they overwhelmed so easily?"

"Not so easily," Reynaldo said. "The attack was professional ... well-planned ... the place for the attack chosen by someone who knows how to kill effectively."

"Where is this place?"

"A narrow valley that prevented our people from escaping. They became targets for the attackers on the hillside."

"And why were we using that valley if it offered such an advantage to an enemy?" Juana asked, her tone that of a commanding general demanding an after-action report on a failed mission.

"We have used it for years," Reynaldo said without flinching under her stare. "The lab is remote, the one outside Arteaga. We must use the road through the valley to move our product to the highways leading to the border."

Juana nodded and said nothing for several seconds. She knew this lab. Using the location was a tradeoff. The precursor drugs necessary for the process came from China through Lázaro Cárdenas and were transported to the lab by truck drivers working for the cartel. Its remote location offered privacy and security for the cartel's chemists to manufacture fentanyl pills in the millions. The weak link in their process was transporting the drugs through the same remote areas, making them more vulnerable to attack.

There had never been a problem before. In the past, no cartel or p*olicía* would dare interfere with a *Los Salvajes* convoy. That had changed. The question was why ... and who.

"Alright," Juana said. "It seems the other cartels are fighting back. We expected as much. Espinoza would not stand by and wait for us to overpower him, and there was no way that madman, Sanchez, would do nothing. It would help to know who was behind the attack." She looked at Reynaldo. "You said some of our people escaped. What did they say?"

"They recognized a few of Sanchez's men, but as I said, the attack was well-planned ... professional. Not like something we would expect from Sanchez."

"Professional," Juana nodded. "So, you think someone is working with Sanchez? Perhaps Espinoza or one of the other cartels?"

"Possibly all of them. It would take all of them to fight us, but that is only speculation for now."

"I don't need speculation if we are going to eliminate the threat. I need facts," Juana snapped and then looked into Reynaldo's eyes and softened her tone. "Excuse the interruption. You have more to say. Tell me."

"I was going to say that there were similarities between this attack and another ... the one that took your father from us."

"My father!" Juana's face hardened into a mask that made her ugly for an instant, even to her adoring protector. "You think he's back, that John Sole has come here to attack us?"

"I said there are similarities."

"Such as?"

"A sniper rifle was used, and the shooter was an expert ... highly accurate ... taking out the targets that would have the most impact."

"Many people in the cartels are expert shots with a rifle."

"True, but the planning behind the attack, the care in choosing the terrain and positioning the attackers. These are signs of someone with a professional background, an expert, and similar to the tactics used when your father ..."

Reynaldo saw the look in her eyes and concluded simply, "I believe we should at least consider the possibility that he was behind it."

"I suppose it's possible." Juana nodded. "The sort of thing he would do."

"Yes," Reynaldo said, "and there is something else to consider. If it is him, he may have help from someone powerful."

"Powerful? You mean someone besides the other cartels?"

"Yes."

"Who?"

"During the attack, another weapon was used … a type of mine used by the United States military. Some of our people recognized it as an explosive antipersonnel device meant to kill many people at once."

"Anyone from the cartels could pick up such a device from a weapons dealer on the black market," Juana said.

"True, but the person who used it was an expert trained to cause the greatest damage … someone with military training, probably in the United States." Reynaldo shrugged. "Someone in the cartels may have this training, but we know Sole had military training."

"It seems unbelievable that he would come to Mexico, but …" Juana thought for a moment. "He has proven over the years that he has not forgotten what we took from him."

"A man like Sole does not forget such things and move on," Reynaldo said. "It's personal for him, and I think if someone gave him a chance to come here on our ground and fight us, he would."

"Someone? Who? Are you saying the United States recruited him, gave him this explosive device, and sent him here to attack us?" Juana's forehead wrinkled, considering the possibilities. "With Sanchez's men?"

"I'm saying Sanchez is not capable of organizing such an attack, not one so well-planned and successful. Someone helped them. If it is Sole, he will not just go away after this." Reynaldo looked into Juana's eyes. "If it is him, he will come here ... for you."

"You actually believe this." Juana shook her head, ignoring the concern in his eyes.

"I believe nothing. I only say that it is a possibility for you to consider."

"I have my doubts, but if it is him ..." She sank back into the chair, tugging at her chin, thinking. "This is personal for me as well."

TWENTY-SIX

Dangerous Games

The streets of Carmen Xhán were full of them. They ran, chasing each other, playing tag, kicking soccer balls between the curbs. Shouting, laughing, joking, and teasing each other, the children of the town played the way children do around the globe.

The drama unfolding in their small part of the world meant little to them. The faces of those other people, the migrants—men, women, children, some not much older than they were, some younger even—were a curiosity at most, but not truly part of their world. It was like living beside a busy train station or airport in one of the big cities. The passengers came and went, existing in a parallel world, traveling to the border, their faces forgotten, if the children remembered them at all, only to be replaced by the next group traveling through their universe.

Some of those playing and running and chasing the soccer balls in the streets were young enough that they had never known a time in the towns when migrants didn't crowd the squares and plazas. Their parents thrived because of the migrants, working for the cartels, providing services to each passing group, happy that the local economy prospered in a place that in times past was only a tiny dot on a map in a forgotten corner of the world.

The two border towns had become a crossroads and gathering point for those headed north to the United States. The anonymous faces watched the local children running down the streets and then turned to the buses and trucks that would take them north.

Mostly, the children ignored them, but a few interacted with the coyotes who herded the migrants along toward the border. Ten-year-old Naldo Barrera had lived in Carmen Xhán all his life. This wasn't so unusual for the children of the town, but Naldo had dreams of more, of one day, living in a big house in Vera Cruz or Monterrey or maybe even Mexico City. He wanted to live the way the people did when he watched the soap operas on television with his mother.

Naldo knew that such a move required money ... a lot of money. The great blessing in his life was that he was born in Carmen Xhán and not some other village in the country. There was money everywhere in Carmen Xhán. He saw it every day.

The coyotes collected it from the migrants and then flashed it around town, buying drinks in the bars, giving presents to the local girls, paying the boys like Naldo to run errands for them. The coyotes wore good clothes, better than any that could be bought around town, and when they weren't taking the migrants north, they drove around in cars, good ones that weren't covered in rust and dents.

The coyotes' money affected everyone. People had things they never had before. Naldo saw the money and what it bought and wanted it—not all of it, and not by stealing from the coyotes. That was dangerous, but at least some of it should be his, he thought, as much of it as he could lay his hands on.

Young as he was, he knew that one day the flow of migrants might end. His parents talked about that and how they should make the most of the local boom while it lasted before life went back to the way it was before, and they were once again poor. Naldo had no intention of waiting to be poor again.

So, he tried to think of ways he could get some of the money. He would have been a coyote if he could, but he was too young for that. Then one day, he met the gringo walking down an alley, far away from the central plaza. The gringo offered him a way to make money. Naldo listened. It was as if an angel from heaven had come down and opened a treasure chest and told him if you do this one thing for me, I will make you rich … or at least, not poor anymore.

Naldo grinned and said, "Señ*or*, if you pay me what you say, I will give you everything you want."

Today, Naldo trotted down the street with several friends, dribbling a soccer ball between them. He stopped at an intersection, made a few jokes, then said he had to go. He'd been doing that a lot lately, leaving them to their games while he went to wander around town.

Naldo sauntered over to the main plaza, expertly pushing the ball along from foot to foot. He listened as he passed the buses. Most of the coyotes recognized him. Some even spoke to him.

"Hey Naldo, how's it going today?" one coyote said when Naldo stopped beside the bus where he was loading migrants.

"Going good, Emilio." Naldo flashed the boyish grin

that made him a favorite among the coyotes. "Got a cigarette?"

"You're too young to be smoking," Emilio said, but reached into his pocket and pulled out a fresh pack of smokes. It was a ritual between them whenever Emilio was in town and not on a run to the border.

"Thanks, man," Naldo said, pulled a cigarette from the pack, and reached in a pocket for a lighter. He lit up and inhaled deeply.

"You smoke like an old man." Emilio watched and shook his head. "You'll be dead of cancer before you're thirty at the rate you're going."

"No." Naldo shook his head, pounded his chest, and faked a cough. "Strong lungs."

Emilio laughed and shook his head. "*Es un chico loco.*" Crazy kid.

Naldo shrugged and took a long drag from the cigarette, exhaling a plume of smoke as he turned to watch the migrants filing onto the bus. "Where you headed today?"

"North, as always," Emilio said.

"Sure, I know that, but what's it like there?"

"The border?" Emilio shrugged. "You see the television shows from the United States. It's like that, except in some places, maybe not so nice as they make it look."

"What about between here and there?"

"Through Mexico?" Emilio shrugged. "It's just Mexico."

"For you, just Mexico. For me …" Naldo smiled. "Man, I would love to see something besides this shitty little town. Tell me about where you're going."

"Like I said, to the border." Emilio stopped to help an older woman lift her bag up the steps onto the bus. "Tonight Coatzacoalcos, up in Veracruz."

"Veracruz!" Naldo exclaimed. "That's on the ocean, right?"

"Gulf of Mexico, but yeah ... it's the ocean."

"What's it like, Emilio? I'd give anything to see the ocean and a city like Coatzacoalcos." Naldo shrugged. "Or any place besides this shitty town."

"It's nice, Naldo." Emilio nodded. "The ocean is blue, and girls walk on the beach in bikinis and wade in the water." Emilio grinned. "But you're too young to be interested in anything like that."

"Too young!" Naldo grabbed his crotch. "Not so young to not know what to do with this!"

They laughed, and after a few more minutes of talking to Emilio, Naldo moved off to wander around the plaza and side streets, listening and exchanging the same type of banter with some of the coyotes. He heard everything they said, making mental notes of the important details. Naldo had an excellent memory for details. After another hour or so, he wandered away, dribbling the soccer ball along with his feet until he made his way to a back alley on the edge of town.

He found the gringo in an old garage that wasn't much more than a lean-to made of two-by-fours and warped plywood. The gringo leaned against an old Volkswagen Beetle car. It had been a taxi once, and the faded green paint still showed through the rust.

"*Hola Naldo, ¿cómo te va?*" Hey, Naldo, how's it going? The gringo spoke pretty good Spanish without too much of an accent.

"*Va bien*," Naldo said and smiled. "I hope you've got plenty of money today. I have a lot of news."

"Don't worry," Jay Lovell said, nodding. "I've got money. First, let's hear the news."

Naldo started by telling him of Emilio's bus heading up to Coatzacoalcos, then moved on to the others. Some he'd heard as he walked by, dribbling the soccer ball. Others, he'd engaged in brief conversations similar to the one with Emilio.

When he was done, Lovell nodded. "Good work, Naldo."

He reached into his pocket and counted out bills. Naldo watched, eyes wide at the wad of cash. Lovell held the money out. "Here. Remember, don't spend this around town, or someone might notice and …" Lovell shook his head, looking Naldo in the eyes. "You do not want those people to notice you are suddenly rich with cash. That would be very dangerous for you."

Naldo took the money and smiled. "I'm careful. I hide everything you give me. Even my mother doesn't know about it. This money is not for spending. It's for getting me out of Carmen Xhán."

"Alright," Lovell said. "I'll meet you here again in three days. There should be more loads going by then."

"Right." Naldo dropped the soccer ball and began trotting down the alley, the soccer ball stuttering along expertly in front of his toes.

Lovell watched the boy and shook his head. It's all just a game to him, he thought.

He took out his phone and punched in a number. When Sole answered, he said, "I've got news."

"Let's hear it," Sole said and made notes while Lovell gave him the list of *Los Salvajes* buses and trucks and their expected routes north.

He would set up operations to intercept the buses and trucks, hijack the loads, and kill every *Los Salvajes* coyote they found. That was important, Lovell had emphasized. It was the way they protected their source of information. They could leave no one alive who might remember the boy asking questions.

The call ended, and Lovell climbed into the Volkswagen to head out of town. A half mile away, Naldo met up with his friends, and they began a game of chase. Running through the streets. His pockets loaded with the cash from the gringo, he felt lighter than air, faster than a speeding car. One day he would have a speeding car and enough of the gringo's money to leave this shithole of a town. For now, he was a child, playing games ... very dangerous games.

TWENTY-SEVEN

Stay Smart

Sole walked along the road, examining the bodies. There were eight.

In response to the attacks, *Los Salvajes* had started using convoys of security to lead their buses to the border. That was to be expected, but so far, that strategy had not worked out for them.

With Sole's training and planning, the other cartels increased their attacks on *Los Salvajes*, and with each, their killing efficiency improved. Two vehicles loaded with armed escorts accompanied this load of migrants. The lead vehicle sat in the roadside ditch, blown in half by the M72 LAW shoulder-fired rocket Sole procured through Lovell's sources for this mission. Four of the bodies on the ground came from that lead vehicle, pulled from the wreckage by Espinoza's men, and lined up for Sole's inspection.

The trailing vehicle and its security team fared no better. A brief firefight ensued. Riddled by small arms fire and a fifty-caliber machine gun—also provided by Lovell—the men inside never stood a chance. Several of the bodies Sole examined were mangled beyond recognition.

In planning the ambush, Sole factored in terrain, time of day, the firepower he could bring to bear, the distance the convoy had traveled that day, and the expected fatigue factor of the coyotes sent along as security, but the wild card in every operation so far was the cartel men assigned to work with him. Like their leader, Sanchez's men tended to be hotheaded and undisciplined. Cardoso's men were usually fairly solid, but Sole often had the feeling their hearts were not truly into a war of extermination with *Los Salvajes*.

For this ambush, he'd selected Espinoza's men. More disciplined than the others, they also showed themselves to be more loyal to the cartel that employed them. Sole knew this was largely because the Espinozas were the second most powerful cartel and, with the elimination of *Los Salvajes*, would be the frontrunner to take control in Mexico.

Sole watched Espinoza's men order the migrants off the bus and line them up. The security teams in the vehicles were eliminated, but *Los Salvajes* would have men stationed on the bus as well. It didn't take long to identify them.

After seeing what happened to their counterparts in the vehicles, the three coyotes on the bus stashed their weapons under the seats and attempted to blend in with the migrants. It was a pointless effort.

Terrified by the carnage they'd witnessed, the migrants wanted nothing to do with the remaining coyotes. They quickly identified them for Espinoza's men. The three coyotes were pulled out of line and taken to the side of the road, where each immediately received a bullet through the brain.

The terrified migrants were loaded back on the bus that

had originally belonged to Espinoza before *Los Salvajes* hijacked it along with a load of migrants two weeks earlier. It was back in their hands now, and Espinoza's men celebrated, laughing as they sent three of their own men on board to drive the bus to their contacts at the border.

Sole turned back to the bodies on the ground and pulled out his cell phone. Lovell answered immediately, waiting for word about their latest operation.

"It's done," Sole said.

"Excellent," Lovell replied. "How many?"

"Eleven in all," Sole said. "Four each in the lead and trail vehicles and three on the bus."

"Damn. They're getting serious."

"We're hurting them," Sole said.

"That's the plan. Ring up the body count."

"Doing the best we can. There's something else here."

"What's that?" Lovell asked.

"Two of the bodies in the lead vehicle wore police uniforms."

"Real or impostors?"

"They look real to me, but I'm no expert on Mexican police. They're torn up pretty bad."

"Badges?"

"One has a badge still pinned on it. The other has a hole where the badge would have been."

"How about ID on them ... something official? Badges are easy to counterfeit."

"Hang on. I'll see what I can find."

Sole knelt beside the two uniformed bodies as Espinoza's men watched in disbelief and shook their heads at the crazy gringo pulling at the corpses. It was one thing to kill and maim, but digging through the bloody remains was not part of the job.

Sole rolled a headless torso over to search through the uniform's breast pocket. Nothing.

He searched through the front trouser pockets. Nothing.

He felt around to the rear and found the dead man's wallet. There it was. A laminated ID card bearing a photo, presumably of the dead man, although there was no way to match the image with what remained of the man. He scratched it with his thumbnail and nodded.

"Found an ID card ... Sargento Alberto Rivera. It's embossed with a seal and an image of a badge, along with a hologram of some sort in the plastic to prevent counterfeiting."

"The cartel could afford to pay some expert forger to counterfeit it or buy an original from a source inside the police department," Lovell said, thought for a second, and added, "But I don't think they would go to that trouble for this type of assignment, running security for a busload of illegal immigrants. They have plenty of *policías* on their payroll. Easier to just tell them to come along for the ride."

"Agreed," Sole said and stood, wiped his hands on the side of his pants, and shoved the ID card in his pocket.

Espinoza's men grimaced.

"It may be time to get our friend involved," Lovell said. "I'll give him a call. When's your next operation?"

Lovell left the planning and timing of the attacks up to Sole. He was free to pick from the intel Lovell provided on *Los Salvajes'* operations. It was a precaution in case Lovell's cover was blown, and they picked him up. *Los Salvajes* would not hesitate to torture an American. They'd done it before, but even under torture, he wouldn't be able to pinpoint the next attack or tell them where Sole was hiding out.

"Tomorrow afternoon," Sole said, without giving details

of where and with whom. "Trying to break each team in separately before we combine them for something big."

"Good. Get on the road, but check back in the morning."

"Will do."

Sole ended the call and turned to find Espinoza's men walking around the bodies, flush with their victory, full of bluster, bloodlust, and bullshit. One looked at him and grinned. "When do we do another?"

"Not today," Sole said. "I'm getting out of the area, and I suggest you do the same."

"But we beat them. Look at the bodies, and we didn't lose even one man!"

"You took them by surprise, but it's only a matter of time before *Los Salvajes* sends people looking for their missing bus, and they'll come prepared with some surprises of their own." Sole shook his head. "No, we won this one because we were smart. Stay smart, and we'll keep winning."

He nodded at the bodies. "Get stupid, and that could be you."

He turned and trotted down the road a hundred yards to a small ravine where he'd left his car. Five minutes later, he was several miles away and accelerating.

Espinoza's men had called him their *arma secreta*—secret weapon—as he readied them for the attack. Now, watching him disappear down the road, their bullshit and bluster died away.

Stay smart. The dead bodies on the roadside made it seem like a good idea, and they followed their secret weapon's advice. They left the scene of the ambush at a high rate of speed.

TWENTY-EIGHT

A Man Alone

"Yes?" Valera answered the phone on the first chime. The number was not one he recognized, but that was to be expected. For security purposes, these calls would come from disposable and untraceable phones.

"Are you ready?" Lovell asked.

"Yes. I've seen the official reports and have been expecting your call."

"And what do the official reports tell you?" Knowing what the Mexican police were saying among themselves and how they were reacting was valuable intelligence. Another reason they had included Valera in their planning.

"Mostly, they count the bodies left behind. In most cases, bodies known to be affiliated with *Los Salvajes*." Valera paused and added, "Also, sometimes the bodies of the police officers you are killing."

"I know that must be uncomfortable for you," Lovell said. "But you knew it might come to that."

"Yes, I knew," Valera said, nodding alone in his office.

"A few of the police officers I also knew. One, I have known since he was a cadet officer in training."

"I'm sorry to hear that. You did not force him to work with *Los Salvajes*."

"I did not. Still, it is difficult to hear of his death, gunned down by another cartel."

"Is this going to be too hard for you, Enrique?" Lovell asked, wondering if there was some other Mexican police contact who could replace Valera. He couldn't think of any offhand.

"No, not too difficult. Unpleasant and unfortunate but not too difficult. I can handle my end of things."

"Good," Lovell said, relieved. "You understand the police officers who died were working with *Los Salvajes*? They were not innocent bystanders."

"I understand. It is nothing for you to worry about. I am not backing away from the operation. It only saddens me to hear of men wearing the same uniform gunned down in this way."

Lovell understood. It was time to give Valera a more serious role in what they were doing, one that eased his conscience and made him part of the plan and not just an onlooker. "Have you had any success identifying who else we might use?"

"Yes. There are a few."

"How much do they know?"

"For now, nothing."

"Alright," Lovell said. "For now, keep it that way, but can you find a way to have them join you in an operation we have planned without saying too much?"

"I think so. They trust me, but join me in what way?" Valera shook his head. "I cannot ask them to ambush and kill other *policías*."

"I wouldn't ask them or you to do that," Lovell said. "We will do the killing if necessary."

"You mean the cartels will kill them. That will be just as hard for them ... to stand by while the cartels kill others wearing the uniform."

"If we do this right, we can limit the killing. I can't say that no police officer will die, but I can say that they are not our targets."

"Yet you have killed those you've encountered in your other operations. Were the police there not your targets?"

"Yes, we have killed some of your police ... corrupt police on the cartel payroll," Lovell said bluntly. "And now we want to stop killing police."

"And how is that possible if they continue to work with the cartel?"

"*Los Salvajes* is about to send a large drug convoy to their smuggling base near the border. There they break the shipment down into smaller loads, and they're smuggled across the border ... in cars, trucks, people crossing on foot with backpacks in the desert."

"I know their methods," Valera said, somewhat impatiently. "What makes this operation so special?"

"The size. Our sources tell us they are going to add extra security to one large shipment, maybe the largest they've ever sent, hoping to get it to the border without being intercepted. That tells us we've been hurting them."

"Your source? Inside the cartel?" Valera said, tugging at his chin as he thought things through. "Is this source reliable?"

"Very." Lovell did not add that the intel he received was crossmatched with intel from three independent sources—a lab chemist, one of the truck loaders, and a mechanic who worked on the cartel's vehicles. All received regular and hefty payments for their information, sent through family members outside of Mexico.

And all three independently provided information about an upcoming operation. The chemist sent details in a coded message to Lovell, listing the quantities of drugs they had been manufacturing in their labs in preparation for a large shipment. While sitting beside Lovell at a bar, the mechanic passed the word that he had been given instructions to have a large number of vehicles serviced and ready for use. In a similar meeting at a different bar, the loader told Lovell that his driver friends were bitching because they were required to stay available and ready to be called out at a moment's notice. Piecing it all together, Sole and Lovell had decided that there would soon be an opportunity to strike the hardest blow yet against *Los Salvajes*.

"So, you want me and the men I trust to be part of this operation," Valera said.

"So far, everything we have done has been in the dark. We intended it to look like a cartel war."

"And it has. How do we police fit into this cartel war?"

"To end the cartels' power in Mexico, we have to end their ability to influence and buy government officials … starting with the *policías*. It's time to put an official face on things … get the right kind of publicity … motivate the public to pressure the government to end the corruption."

"And I am this official face," Valera said, lifting the corner of his mouth in a wry smile.

"Yes." Lovell nodded. "You are the one to expose the corruption, and while you do that, we will continue killing cartel members, reducing their power and influence."

"So, while I expose corruption, you kill behind the scenes in the name of ending corruption … a cunning plan, Machiavellian even, and it sounds very bloody."

"It's already been bloody. Our next moves should limit the bloodshed, at least as much as we can, and with luck, start a movement in the country to end the corruption."

"I do not much believe in luck," Valera said doubtfully, remaining silent for several seconds. "A people's movement … an insurrection not for more bread, better housing, or higher pay, but for more honesty in government? It's a novel idea, but I fear you give me too much credit for having influence over the public's opinions."

"We need your face and your actions, Enrique. I'll arrange the publicity and influence," Lovell said. "It will come through our sources in ways that will force your government to take note and respond."

"Alright," Valera said. "I agreed to help with your plans. I suppose I am obligated to continue."

"No, you're not obligated," Lovell said. "We've known each other too long for that. You do this of your own free will or tell me you want to back out now."

"And if I do that, can I expect a visit in the night from you and a blade across my throat while I sleep to make sure I don't talk about your plans?"

It was the type of question one expected in this sort of work but not one Lovell expected from Valera. "I would never do that," he said.

"Maybe not." Valera shrugged at his response and said matter-of-factly. "In any event, it won't be necessary. Include me in your plans. I'll be there with those I trust. When will this operation take place?"

"Soon. We'll know when we get the date of the drug convoy's departure."

"Then I have time to visit my family before it begins."

"Yes."

"Good. If there is nothing more to discuss, I am going to make arrangements to travel there tonight."

"There's nothing else to discuss. I'll be in touch."

"Very well. Goodbye."

The call ended before Lovell said goodbye. He was placing a lot of pressure on Valera and felt guilty as hell about it. Lovell might feel vulnerable at times, operating alone in foreign countries for his government, but he never had the sense that he was isolated, abandoned, and truly alone. A powerful nation supported and sustained him with unimaginable resources.

There was no one Valera dared turn to for support in his government. The cartels' tentacles had spread through all levels of Mexican society. One misspoken word and Valera, his wife and children, parents, and anyone close to him would be hunted down by *Los Salvajes*. Following the standard cartel playbook for those who interfered in their business, they would kill them all.

Valera was a man alone. Lovell respected that and hoped he had not signed his death warrant by recruiting him into their plans.

TWENTY-NINE

Falling Star

The Cessna Citation business jet circled the airstrip and began its descent. Cut out of the hillsides and long enough to handle the largest private jets, including Juana Elizondo's Bombardier 8000, the airstrip was an impressive piece of engineering. Along with the assortment of aircraft hangared along the runway, it presented an ostentatious demonstration of the cartel's immense wealth. Despite that, it remained wholly ignored by Mexican law enforcement.

Normally, Luis Ibarra would have been impressed, staring from the window at the airstrip and activity below, taking in the mountainside vistas, the Port of Lázaro Cárdenas, and the blue Pacific in the distance. On this visit, he stared from the window and wondered if he would return on this same plane to Monterrey, or if he would return at all.

The call from Reynaldo Gutierrez summoning him to a meeting at the Elizondo hacienda was brusque. "Go to the airport in Monterrey. A jet is waiting to bring you here."

"Sí, jefe," Ibarra responded, trying to keep the tremor out of his voice. "How long should I pack for?"

"Don't pack," Reynaldo said and ended the call.

Ibarra had known the call would come eventually and had been dreading it, trying to find a way to make it unnecessary. Still, the attacks on the transports continued no matter how much security he added and how often he changed the routes. Since they began, one in three loads of illegal migrants heading to the border had been intercepted, the security men killed, coyotes and police alike, and the buses and trucks transporting them returned to their original cartel owners along with the migrants inside.

Word was spreading about the attacks on the *Los Salvajes* transports. Migrants were beginning to look for other ways north with other cartels.

Ibarra considered leaving, taking the money he had now, and running for his life. It was not as large a sum as he would have liked, but it was still considerable.

He didn't. First, because he clung to the hope that he could turn things around and get the takeover of the other cartels' *coyote* operations back on track.

Second, running would only make things worse. Besides, where would he run? There was nowhere that they would not find him, and the consequences would be terrible when they did.

It was better to face Juana Elizondo. At least if they killed him, it would be clean and simple. A bullet through the brain. That was the standard punishment for those who failed their assignments. Running or betraying the cartel resulted in more severe consequences.

The torture would be horrific, and it would continue until he begged them to grant him death. And then they would torture him more. When they finally let him die, his mind crazed with pain, he wouldn't even be aware enough to appreciate and welcome the end. Ibarra knew all this because he had been on the administering end of such tortures.

The jet touched down at midday. Ibarra was pushed forward in his seatbelt as the reverse thrusters slowed the aircraft. When they released, he leaned back in the seat again and looked out the window.

Three men waited beside a black SUV parked on the apron alongside the main hangar. Ibarra didn't see any weapons, but he knew they were armed.

When the ground crew had the Cessna's wheels chocked, the pilot pushed the door open and stepped aside. Heart in his throat, Ibarra descended the short stairs. The three men surrounded him and walked him to the SUV.

One opened the door for him and motioned him into the rear seat. So far, so good. They hadn't killed him on sight, or thrown a bag over his head, bound him with duct tape, and tossed him in the rear cargo compartment.

The men climbed in without speaking to him. One sat behind the wheel, one in the front passenger seat, and one beside him in the rear. They were stern and silent but not abusive, and Ibarra breathed a little easier. Whatever fate awaited him, it would not happen ... just yet.

The drive from the airstrip winding through the hills around the Elizondo estate took fifteen minutes. They emerged from a pass between two hills onto the main drive to the hacienda. The SUV pulled up in the front courtyard, and Ibarra got out and started toward the hacienda's front door.

"Not there," one of the security men said and pointed to a multi-level outbuilding nestled into the hillside near the hacienda.

Mierda. Shit. Acid churned in Ibarra's gut. His heart pounded with enough force that he found it difficult to speak. "Has the *jefa* moved her office from the hacienda?"

"You're not meeting with the *jefa*," the security man said, and the others joined him to surround Ibarra once more. He pointed at the outbuilding again. "Over there."

Ibarra knew the building. It had once been the office of Alejandro Garza, the chief lieutenant of Bebé Elizondo, Juana's father. Garza sometimes used the lower level as an execution chamber. Ibarra wondered if Reynaldo Gutierrez continued that practice, and the acid churned a little higher into his throat.

Inside, they escorted him into Reynaldo's office. It was a simple affair without the trappings of power he'd noted on his last visit to Juana Elizondo's office. A small steel desk. A few chairs. No pictures on the walls. It did not seem to be a place where Reynaldo spent much time.

Where is Juana, he wondered. Was Reynaldo now so close to her that she trusted him to make important decisions? Or was the decision already made, and Reynaldo's role was to execute the orders he'd received?

He stopped before the desk, and Reynaldo looked up from a single paper he was studying. One of the security men came up behind Ibarra and ran his hands around his waist, between his legs, down to his ankles, and around his chest, searching for concealed weapons. He found none and nodded at Reynaldo.

"Leave us," Reynaldo said, and the security men backed out of the room to take up positions outside.

"Sit down," Reynaldo said.

Ibarra sat in a thinly padded steel chair positioned directly in front of the desk. His eyes darted around the room. "Is Juana joining us?"

"No. You are here to see me. I am acting on her behalf, with her full authority."

So, the decision *was* made, Ibarra thought. Reynaldo would carry out the orders she had given.

It was a bad omen. Juana ran *Los Salvajes* with the same attention to detail as a hands-on business manager. If she turned things over to Reynaldo, it could only be because she had made a decision about his fate and was moving on to other issues.

"I know things haven't been going so well," Ibarra began.

Reynaldo raised a hand to silence him, and Ibarra's mouth clamped shut.

"I will speak. You will listen, and then you will do what we want," Reynaldo said without needing to explain the consequences if Ibarra failed.

"*Sí, jefe*," Ibarra said.

"Do you know what this is?" Reynaldo lifted the paper from the desk.

"No," Ibarra said. "I only just arrived and ..."

"It's a record of our losses ... your losses." Reynaldo dropped the paper on the desk. "It's very detailed."

"I know things haven't gone as we expected ..." Ibarra began and closed his mouth when Reynaldo lifted a hand.

"Our problems began with your operation. First, our migrant buses and trucks were hit. You failed to stop them, and with those successes, our enemies gained the courage to attack our drug smuggling operations. Somehow they have united against us ... someone has brought them together ... leading them, and we wonder what you plan to do about it."

"I am trying to." Ibarra shook his head. "But it's very difficult, and I ..."

"I said, don't speak," Reynaldo said. "

Ibarra nodded.

"You live in that five-star hotel in Monterrey, drive expensive sports cars around the city, and sleep with women who would never talk to you if it were not for the money we pay you. You have lost focus, and we are losing confidence in you."

We? He speaks as if he and Juana Elizondo are equals, partners in running *Los Salvajes*. Ibarra wondered what that meant, but said nothing.

"Since you have been unable to stop the attacks, we are planning a surprise of our own to stop them, but for our surprise to work, we require information. Acquiring that information is the way you may regain our confidence." Reynaldo paused and nodded, signaling that he expected Ibarra to respond.

"What can I do for you?" Ibarra said meekly.

"The information we require can only come from someone working with the other cartels, someone on the inside who knows their plans."

"But I don't know their plans, *jefe*. I want to give you what you want, but how can I ..."

"There are ways," Reynaldo interrupted. "And this is not optional. You will do what is necessary to get the information we require." Reynaldo leaned forward over the desk. "Do not fail us."

Again, it was *we … our … us*. Reynaldo made it clear the threat came from above.

"I won't fail you, *jefe*. What information do you need?"

Reynaldo went over the plan they had put together to strike back at the other cartels. It would escalate the war between them, but this offered an opportunity to speed up their time frame for taking control of the others. At least, Juana and Reynaldo believed it would.

Ibarra was less certain about the outcome, but he nodded. "I will get you the information, and …" He gave a deferential bow of his head. "I hope this will win back your confidence … you and the *jefa*."

"We'll see," Reynaldo said. "Go now. My men will take you back to the airstrip. I'll give you a day, then call me with your plans."

Ibarra left the room, and the waiting security men drove him to the airstrip. Ten minutes later, he was airborne, his mind whirling. The relief that he was still breathing was tempered by the thought that it might only be a temporary reprieve.

Once a rising luminary in the cartel world, Luis Ibarra had become a falling star, a meteor flaming through the atmosphere with an uncertain future.

THIRTY

Cold Feet

"How'd it go?" Lovell looked up from his laptop at the desk in the latest dingy motel room that had become their base of operations.

As a safety precaution, they'd been changing locations every few days. By this time, *Los Salvajes* had figured out that someone was helping the cartels work together to orchestrate the attacks and would undoubtedly pay an enormous sum to find out who and where they were.

"Well, they didn't kill each other today. That's a good sign, I suppose."

Sole plopped onto a thread-bare chair across from the desk and wrinkled his nose at the sour smell permeating the chair and room. Yellowed walls, stained from years of cigarette smoke, bathroom fixtures leaking sewer gasses, and moldy carpeting all added to the cocktail of odors that transferred to everything in the room, including the two men and their belongings.

"That bad, huh?" Lovell closed the laptop and turned

off the mobile hotspot on the satellite phone supplied by the NSA.

"Not good," Sole said. "Espinoza's men can be controlled and are pretty solid, but Sanchez's are a wildcard. Never quite sure if they want to shoot up *Los Salvajes* or one of the other cartels working with them."

Sole shook his head. "And Cardoso's commitment to what we are doing seems doubtful."

"Doubtful?" Lovell sat up straight at that. "How so?"

"Just a feeling I get." Sole shrugged. "A lack of enthusiasm maybe ... like they're going through the motions but aren't convinced of the outcome."

"You think Cardoso has turned on us?"

"No, not that."

Sole shook his head. "More like he's a third-string player thrown into a game to block a hole in the line, and he'd rather be sitting on the sidelines watching the others take the hits."

"Pull his team out of the op?" Lovell asked.

"Too late for that. Everything's ready, and we need the manpower. We've been drilling for a week. Cardoso's team will be in a backup position, pulling rear guard, preventing anyone from escaping. It's not a front-line spot, but it could be critical if things don't go as planned."

"What do you think the odds are of things not going as planned?"

Sole gave a wry smile. "I'd give ourselves a fifty percent chance of everyone doing exactly what they are supposed to do." He shrugged. "If that happens, we should be alright. Battle plans always change when the bullets start flying, but if someone doesn't hold their ground, everything will turn to shit."

"Fifty percent," Lovell muttered.

"Yep," Sole said and tried to change the mood by adding, "But hey, whatever happens, a bunch of bad guys are going down."

"As long as we don't go down with them," Lovell said.

"Yeah, well, there is that." Sole nodded. "So, when do we move, I don't want to wait too long, or our people might lose whatever fighting edge they have right now."

"My source says five days."

"Certain?"

"Certain as we're going to be. He's been accurate so far."

"Alright." Sole nodded. "I'll set it up with our people … five days. Now, I just need a location and time as close as your source can estimate."

"I'll get it for you. *Los Salvajes* is keeping things close to the vest, so it won't be until just before they move, but have our teams ready."

"Will do," Sole said, noting the uncharacteristic concern on Lovell's face. He nodded at the laptop on the desk and asked, "Trouble on the home front?"

"Just the usual," Lovell said. "Politicians and bureaucrats doing what they do best … passing the buck."

"Tell me."

"There seems to be some hesitancy on the part of some now." Lovell shrugged.

"Hesitancy?" Sole's eyes narrowed. "Are we being canceled?"

"No. Not yet, at least," Lovell said. "Someone always gets cold feet, but this is an election year and …"

"And our mission is sanctioned at the *highest levels*," Sole said, repeating what Lovell told him when he brought him on board. There was no need to identify the *highest levels* whose feet were becoming a little frosty.

"Right." Lovell nodded. "But the palace mice are whispering in ears, nibbling away at their confidence."

"How long do we have?" Sole asked.

"Not sure. Weeks ... days maybe."

"That means we better get things in gear." Sole stood.

"Where are you going?" Lovell asked.

"To contact the teams and let them know we are drilling tomorrow ... and every day until we pull this thing off." Sole smiled. "After that, I think I'll get drunk. Wanna join me?"

"I believe I do."

"Good. Meet me at the bar in an hour."

Lovell nodded and watched him leave. They'd become a team. Sole was a quick study when it came to spycraft, and he'd taught Lovell a good deal about battle tactics. Together they were formidable and had seriously hurt *Los Salvajes*, but like a wounded animal, that made *Los Salvajes* more dangerous.

Now was the time to take them out completely before they licked their wounds and regained their momentum and power. Somehow, he had to keep the cold feet in Washington from interfering.

THIRTY-ONE

He Was Gone

"I didn't expect you back so soon." Josefina Valera walked across the yard of the Valera farmhouse, put her arms around her husband, and kissed his cheek as he stepped from the car. "I thought perhaps your business would keep you away for a while."

"Just a short visit," Enrique Valera said. "I have to leave in the morning."

"You came all this way for one day?" Josefina's eyes narrowed. "That means …"

She closed her mouth without finishing the sentence. They both knew what it meant. He would not have returned so soon unless he had concerns about returning at all in the future. He held their embrace for a few seconds longer than normal, and she nestled her face against his shoulder.

She had been married to a police officer too long to waste time on worries. Instead, she concentrated on the present, on the now, and the time they had safe and secure together. There would be time for worry later.

Cedro Valera watched his son and daughter-in-law from the front porch. Little Natalia sat beside him on the planks with their house guest, Sarita, drawing on a piece of paper. Ana Valera came from the house and, like her husband, watched quietly while Valera and Josefina spoke in quiet voices and embraced.

When they turned and walked arm in arm toward the porch, she spoke, the smile on her face an attempt at masking the concern in her eyes. "What a surprise!" she exclaimed.

"*¡Hola mamá!*" Valera said, smiling.

"Good to see you, son," Cedro said and stood.

Natalia was already on her feet, clinging to her father's legs as he came up to the porch. A moment later, Benito came around the side of the house, kicking a soccer ball through the dust. His eyes lit up, and he ran to his father. "Papa!"

"Hello, little ones." Valera knelt to put his arms around them. He hugged each and stood.

Benito was off then, dribbling the ball across the yard and shouting over his shoulder, "Let's kick the ball, papa! I have some new moves!"

"Me too!" Natalia said, following her brother. "I want to play too! I've got moves too!"

"Hah," Benito laughed. "What moves do you have? You're just a little girl!"

"In a minute, children. I want to speak with your mama."

"Now, papa! Come on!" Natalia shouted, chasing Benito around the yard as he deftly used his feet to keep the ball away from her kicking legs.

"I'll keep them occupied," Sarita said and rose from the porch. She gave Valera a shy smile and trotted across the yard after the children, calling to Benito, "You think girls can't play, do you? I'll show you."

With that, she cut Benito off, stepped to the inside, and with one foot, swept the ball away from him. "Now, let's see if you can get it from me," she said, laughing as he chased her.

"How's she doing?" Valera asked, watching.

"Sarita?" Josefina said. "See for yourself. The children love her, and I believe she truly loves them." She took her husband's hand. "I think this is the first time she's ever had a home."

"Home?" Valera's brow wrinkled. "I told you what she does. She sells information to cartels for money. Sometimes she sells herself." He shook his head. "This can't be her home. Don't let her come to call it that."

"She survives as best she can," Josefina shot back. "I won't judge her for that."

"I'm not judging her," Valera said. "Only pointing out that she comes from a different background ... a different world. The way she has lived ..."

"Yes, on her own ... without family ... without a place like this to feel safe and secure." Josefina motioned with her arm, sweeping around the Valera house and farm. "She did what she had to, not what she would have wanted to do."

"What are you saying?"

"I'm saying that maybe bringing her here was a good thing ... for all of us ... that maybe she should stay because it was meant to be."

"Josefina," he said softly, trying to reason. "She is here for now because I had to have her out of the way." He did not mention the other solution to her presence that he and Lovell had discussed. "She can't stay. When I finish what I am working on, she must go."

"Where? Go back to the streets to sell herself to live?" Josefina crossed her arms and shook her head. "No. I won't have it. If she were our child, alone in the world, you would pray for someone to look after her. We may be the answer to her dead mother's prayers."

"But having her here could be dangerous for the children ... for you."

"You think we aren't used to the danger. Your work puts us in danger, but I respect it. Your desire to see Mexico become something else ... something better. It is your mission, and I admire you for it." She nodded at Sarita, laughing and playing with the children in the yard. "This is my mission ... one small thing we can do as a family to help Mexico become a better place. One soul saved. If there is danger, I choose to accept it."

"And the children? The danger they may be in? Do they choose it?"

Josefina took her husband's hand. "Enrique, we all live with the danger that one day you will defy someone in power and put our family at risk. I know that you do all you can to protect us. I see how you walk a fine line, doing your job and trying to keep your honor. I accept the danger because I respect what you are doing. The children may not understand it, but they accept that we are a family, and that is enough for them now. Later, they will be old enough to make their own decisions about how to live." She looked into his eyes. "Respect what I am doing, Enrique."

Seconds passed, and he nodded. "Alright. If you say she stays, she stays." He smiled. "Who am I to go up against a woman like you."

"You are *mi amor*." Josefina kissed him on the cheek.

That settled, they turned to his parents, watching and

listening in silence. "You should have some say in all this, I think," Valera said. "I brought this problem to your home."

"Our home," Cedro replied. "Is your home, and as Josefina says, Sarita is welcome here."

"More than welcome," Ana added. "I've been taking care of men for too long. It's nice to have women around the house."

They laughed, and Cedro said, "So what is it you wanted to tell us, son?"

"There's not much," Valera said with a sigh. "Only that the mission I am on will begin very soon. Watch the television, and you'll know when it does, and when it begins, you must be alert ... *vigilante*. Take note of anything out of the ordinary ... any strangers approaching. Do not take chances. If something seems different ... unusual ... don't wait. Take everyone in the big truck and leave. Go far away, and don't tell anyone where you are going."

"Not even our neighbors, so they can watch over the farm for us?" Ana said.

"Not anyone," Valera repeated. "If things go badly, they have ways of getting information, of making anyone talk. What they don't know, they can't tell."

"You mean the cartels," Cedro said and asked the question the others were thinking. "What are you saying? That the cartels may come here and torture our friends?"

Ana let out a small gasp. Josefina's eyes narrowed.

What he was saying was harsh, unlike him, but his first concern was his family. Valera took a deep breath and shook his head. "I'm saying, the best way to protect our neighbors is to say nothing and disappear. Protect our family. Get them away. Someplace in the country. Trust no one." He shook his head and added, "I have no right to place you in this position, but I've done it, and there is no turning back now."

"You've done nothing but make us proud. Raising an honorable man is nothing to be ashamed of," Cedro said and put a hand on his son's shoulder. "I will protect our family, but you come home to us."

"I will, papa," Valera promised, knowing that keeping that promise depended on many factors, most of which were out of his control. "When this is over, I'll find you wherever you are."

A somber minute passed. They stood close together on the small farmhouse porch. It was a place of memories. A place where he had played as a child. The spot where he had introduced Josefina to his parents. Where his children sat and watched sunsets with their grandparents.

Ana said with a smile, "Let's see about getting supper ready." She put a hand to her mouth and called out to the yard, "Sarita, come help with the meal."

Sarita turned and ran laughing to the porch. She leaped through the door, followed inside by the children. Valera took Josefina's hand and led her into the yard and down the gravel drive past the fields.

They walked a mile into the country before he spoke. "You know that whatever happens, I love you."

"Of course, I know it," Josefina said and put her arm around his waist as they walked. "Now, do me one favor."

"What's that?"

"Stop worrying about us. It's a distraction from what you must do, and distractions could be dangerous for you. Papa Cedro will take care of us." She smiled. "And when this is over, you had better come back to me because I love you too."

They walked back to the house to find supper ready.

The meal was full of laughter, Sarita sitting between the children, listening to them chatter and making little jokes with them. They made plans to collect fireflies when it was dark that night and talked excitedly about the things they would do the next day.

After supper, they sat in the yard watching Sarita help the children capture the fireflies in jars supplied by Ana. They ran along the edge of the fields, laughing and calling to each other.

Benito shouted, "Here! I got one here!"

"So what?" Natalia said, laughing, "I got five. Look, you can count them!"

When Sarita had run all of the energy out of them and herself, they came to sit with the adults. It was a peaceful moment, one to be cherished, and somehow they all knew it, even the children. The stars came out, and they spoke in whispers as if in church.

It was late when Josefina said, "Time for bed, children."

They didn't argue. Josefina and Sarita took them inside to clean up and tuck them in. Cedro and Ana followed to make sure they said their prayers. Valera sat alone in the yard for a while, savoring the night and the memories of the place.

When he went inside, he kissed the children goodnight. Later, he and Josefina made love in the tiny room that had been his as a boy, and in the morning, they made love again.

He cleaned up, taking a bath in the single tub in the house. Ana prepared huevos rancheros and expertly loaded them into a tortilla for him. Cedro sat at the table, sipping thick, black coffee that filled the room with its aroma. Josefina sat quietly at his side, a hand on his thigh under the table.

Sarita sat across from them and spoke the first words she had said to him directly. "Thank you for this."

"No thanks are necessary, Sarita." He smiled and nodded at the faces around the table. "This is a family. You are now part of it."

The sun was just beginning to rise when they finished breakfast, and he went in to kiss the children goodbye. They looked at him bleary-eyed, shaking their child dreams from their heads as their father leaned over, kissed each, and whispered that he loved them."

They followed him back to the kitchen, each holding a hand. "Sit here and have breakfast now."

They climbed up on chairs, and as Ana put food on their plates, he walked out to the porch with Josefina. They stood quietly for a long moment, and he was uncertain how to say goodbye, or if he should say it.

"Come back soon," Josefina said. "We'll be waiting."

"I will."

They kissed goodbye, and then he was gone.

THIRTY-TWO

Not A Reassuring Thought

"Come with me." Luis Ibarra motioned Rufo Serrato to one of the tents in the clearing.

"Is there a problem, *jefe*?" Ibarra looked troubled, and Serrato went through the day's activities in his mind to discern if he was the cause, not a position he wanted to be in.

Things had been going fairly well for several days. For some unknown reason, the attacks on their buses and trucks had subsided. Two shipments of migrants had arrived in the clearing that day, and the process of separating those selected for special delivery to customers had been completed with minimal disruption or complaints from the families of the girls marched off to the separate tent.

If Ibarra had another concern, it must be the result of his sudden departure and return on one of Elizondo's jets that morning. Serrato braced himself for whatever bad news was about to hit him in the face.

He followed Ibarra to the tent. Inside, Ibarra paced to the far end and back, staring at the ground, then whirling to speak, as if he'd suddenly made up his mind about something.

"There is something I want you to do."

"Alright," Serrato said. "What is it, *jefe*?"

"I need information," Ibarra said.

"What can I tell you?" Serrato asked, a look of relief on his face.

"It's not information you can provide."

"I don't understand."

"I want you to bring me someone who can provide the information I need."

"Alright." Serrato nodded, not quite as relieved as he was a moment earlier, but still happy that he was not the subject of the problem troubling Ibarra. "Tell me the information you require, and I may be able to find someone who can give it to you."

"No." Ibarra shook his head. "This is not something *you may be able* to do. You must find someone who can provide the information and bring him to me."

Serrato's sense of relief evaporated completely. He was being dragged deeper into Ibarra's problems, and if they weren't resolved, he would likely end up the scapegoat, and scapegoats had very short life expectancies.

Saying no was not an option, so he said, "Tell me what information I must bring to you, *jefe*."

Ibarra explained. When he finished, Serrato said, "Alright. I'll need to pick some men to go with me."

"Take them," Ibarra said. "Choose who you want."

"Without them here, it will delay the buses departing the clearing in the morning."

"I know what it means!" Ibarra snapped. "Take the men you need and do as I say, and do it quickly. I want you back by morning."

"By morning?" Serrato's brow furrowed now in real concern. "There may not be enough time to…"

"By morning!" Ibarra roared, and everyone in the clearing heard it.

"*Sí, jefe.*"

It was well after midnight when José Ruiz stumbled from the bar in a village on the outskirts of Torreón. Cardoso's men had turned it into their off-duty hangout.

Ruiz staggered down the alley, cursing under his breath, "Fucking gringo. Be back ready for more drilling at six in the morning." He pulled his phone from his pocket and tried to focus his eyes and read the time on the screen, his face lit by the phone's pale glow. "Twelve forty-five!" He shoved the phone back into his pocket. "Fucking gringo!"

It was the common expression used by the cartel men to describe Sole. He demanded that they practice … drilling he called it … for the big operation coming. José had had enough of it, but he dared not say that to Sole. Cardoso had made it clear that, for now, they were to cooperate with the gringo and the other cartels.

"Cooperate my ass," Ruiz muttered as he made his way down the alley, bouncing off walls from one side to the other. "I cooperate while that pretty boy Cardoso sleeps in a fancy hotel fucking some woman." He chuckled. "Or some man." Rumors abounded that Anselmo Cardoso liked to swing both ways.

Ruiz was still chuckling when his world went black. Someone threw a heavy, dark blanket over his head. He struggled, but strong hands held him still and wrapped a rope around the blanket until he looked like a body in a shroud. Then they lifted and carried him bouncing down the alley.

"What is this?" He shouted one time before the barrel of a pistol was pushed against the blanket and his head. Even through the heavy material, he knew what it was.

"Stay quiet, and you will live," Rufo Serrato leaned close, speaking into the place under the blanket where his ear would be. "Another sound, and I will put a bullet through your brain."

Ruiz closed his mouth as the men bounced him along, carrying him to the end of the alley. He heard a metallic door slide open, and then he was tossed into a vehicle. He landed hard on the steel floor as his captors piled in behind him, pushing their feet on top of him to keep him still.

The van left the city and soon was careening along country roads. They drove for several hours like that, and then the van rocked to a stop. The men dragged Ruiz out, carried him for a minute, and then suddenly dropped him.

The ropes were cut, the blanket lowered, and Ruiz could see again. Then he wished he could not.

Luis Ibarra stood towering over him as he lay prostrate on the ground inside a tent. He was known to Cardoso's men as a *Los Salvajes* chief, and merciless when it came to killing. Ruiz felt his bladder and bowels loosening.

Ibarra saw his discomfort, shook his head, and sneered, "If you shit or piss in here, I will kill you now."

Ruiz nodded and squeezed his legs tightly together.

"You know who I am?" Ibarra asked.

Ruiz nodded.

"Do you want to live?"

Ruiz nodded more emphatically.

"Then tell me what I want to know. If you do that, you will live." Ibarra leaned close and smiled. "I will even make you rich ... as long as you tell the truth." The smile faded, and his eyes narrowed. "I'll know if you are lying."

"I will tell you whatever you want to know," Ruiz managed to say through trembling lips.

"Good." Ibarra sat in a canvass-bottomed chair and looked down at him. "Tell me what you have been doing with the other cartels."

Ruiz started talking, and talked for an hour, describing attacks they had made on various convoys of drugs and migrants being smuggled north. It was during one of those attacks that he had been recognized by one of Ibarra's men who survived the ambush. They were second cousins, grew up less than a mile from each other, joined rival cartels, and hated each other.

That his cousin was not killed in the ambush and was able to report back that he had seen Ruiz among the attackers was Ruiz's misfortune. Serrato and his men knew where to look and abducted him from the alley outside the bar.

What he said was eye-opening. As they had expected, some of the cartels had banded together to stop *Los Salvajes*' pillaging of their businesses. What Ibarra didn't know was that the United States was behind it. He doubted that Juana Elizondo or Reynaldo were aware.

He raised a hand and stopped Ruiz in midsentence. "You say there is an American from north of the border who leads the raids."

"Yes." Ruiz gave a solemn nod.

"What's his name?"

"He said to call him Chris." Ruiz shook his head. "But I don't think that's his real name."

"Describe him," Ibarra said.

"I don't know." Ruiz shrugged. "Six feet, dark hair, in

good shape. I think he was a soldier or maybe a cop in the United States."

"Why do you think that?"

"The way he acts the way he ..." Ruiz paused and cast a wary eye around the tent, looking at the others' face ... at his cousin's face."

"Go on," Ibarra ordered.

"The way he kills your people. He has done a lot of killing, I think." Ruiz nodded. "He is very good at it."

"And you help him," Ruiz's cousin said from the back of the tent behind Ibarra.

Ibarra lifted a hand to silence him and turned back to Ruiz. "When is the next attack? Where?"

"That I don't know," Ruiz said. "I swear I would tell you if I did. I only know that the gringo has us preparing ... training for some big attack ... a mission he calls it."

"And that's why you haven't been attacking our trucks and buses lately," Ibarra said.

"Yes, I think so." Ruiz shrugged. "I mean, I only do what they tell me to do ... go where they say ... but yes, there is something big coming. We are supposed to be ready to move whenever he calls."

Ibarra thought for a moment, then picked up the cell phone Serrato had taken from Ruiz. He punched in a number and handed it to him. When you are told to move for this mission, send a text to that number."

"But, If I do that they ..."

"Shut up and listen," Ibarra said. "Text the number 8. Nothing more. That will only take a second, and if you are careful, no one will notice."

"The number 8," Ruiz repeated.

"Yes, but only when you know you are moving on this mission, the gringo speaks of."

"Right." Ruiz nodded. "I'll do it. I swear it."

"Good. If you do, you will be paid a great deal."

"How much?" Ruiz blurted out without thinking and then paled, wishing he had kept his mouth shut. It seemed they were going to let him live, and here he was, pulling the tail of the tiger who could tear him apart if he wanted.

Ibarra laughed at the look on his face, and the others in the tent joined him. "How much does Cardoso pay you in a month, José?"

Ruiz gave a number that was a substantial sum of money by Mexican standards.

Ibarra nodded and said, "Tell no one about our meeting here and text me when you are told to move for the attack, and *Los Salvajes* will pay you ten times that as a token of our gratitude."

"Ten times?" Ruiz's eyes opened wide.

"Yes," Ibarra said. "But if you speak about our meeting … if you fail to text me when the gringo's mi*ss*ion is starting …"

"I won't fail," Ruiz broke in quickly, eyeing the cousin standing in the back who knew his family and loved ones and where they lived. "I swear it. I will send the text … the number 8, right?"

"Good." Ibarra nodded. "Do this, and you are one of us. If you fail …" Ibarra shook his head.

"I won't fail," Ruiz said and looked around the tent, saw his cousin glaring at him, and added, "I am one of you now. I swear it."

Ibarra nodded and said, "Take him back."

Serrato and his men escorted Ruiz out of the tent, threw the blanket over him again, without tying it this time, put him in the van, and drove him back to Torreón. He arrived in the city as the sun was coming up over the hills and walked the last couple of miles so that no one would see him get out of the unknown van. Yawning, he joined the other Cardoso men preparing for the day of training somewhere out in the hills.

"You look like shit, José!" One called out, laughing. "Up all night with some little *chica?*"

"Something like that," Ruiz said and climbed yawning into the back of a pickup with the others. For the rest of the day, they teased him for staying out all night and not getting his sleep like a good little boy.

"Don't let that fucking gringo, Chris, catch you sleeping on the job," one said.

The others laughed. Ruiz smiled back and tried not to think of Ibarra, or the threat in his cousin's eyes, or what would happen to him and his family if he failed to do what Ibarra had ordered, or what would happen if his companions discovered who he had been with during the night.

Ibarra waited until the sun was up before he phoned. Reynaldo answered immediately. "*Dígame.*" Tell me.

"I have information," Ibarra said and hoped it would be enough.

"Let's hear it."

"The cartels involved are Espinoza, Sanchez, and Cardoso."

"We know this," Reynaldo said.

"Yes, but someone is working with them. Training and organizing them … coordinating the attacks."

"Who?"

"The only name we have is Chris, but that is almost certainly a cover." Ibarra paused before adding the important part. "He is from the United States and has a military or police background. Our source says he is experienced in killing ... expert at it."

"Stay on the line," Reynaldo said, then muted the phone on his end. A moment later, he was back. "What else?"

Ibarra went on for several minutes, outlining the attacks José Ruiz had participated in and the training they were undergoing for some big mission. He explained the text signal Ruiz would send when they were told to move, and when he finished speaking, there was a pause. He heard the muffled voice of Juana Elizondo in the background, and his heart leaped into his throat.

Then the phone was muted again. Shit! Reynaldo was with Juana, and he could only wait while they discussed his fate and the value of the information he provided.

When Reynaldo unmuted the phone, he said, "When you receive the text, call me immediately."

"I will," Ibarra said.

"Immediately, the instant you receive the text," Reynaldo emphasized.

"I understand," Ibarra said, and then the line went dead.

He allowed himself to breathe a sigh of relief. At least they had not told him to return to the hacienda. He was sure that would have been a death sentence.

Ibarra stood in the tent opening and stared numbly across the clearing. A permanent stay of execution hung on the promise of a simple text from a terrified José Ruiz. That was not a reassuring thought.

THIRTY-THREE

Day After Tomorrow

"It seems you were right, Reynaldo." Juana Elizondo looked up from the phone lying in the center of her desk. "Someone is helping the others … a professional, and the question is …."

Her brow furrowed over the bridge of her nose. Could it be possible that the attacks were coordinated by the same person who had killed her father?

Reynaldo said nothing while she thought things through. He'd learned to give Juana space, especially when she was mulling over a problem.

To say that their relationship could be complicated was an understatement. After a night of lovemaking, they resumed their usual roles. Juana had no problem moving from passion in bed to the cold-blooded business of running the cartel. Turning that switch on and off was harder for Reynaldo.

As much as he knew he should not be, he was undeniably in love with her. He was no fool and knew her feelings were not reciprocal. It was apparent that Juana usually had an ulterior, business-related motive when she granted him private time in her bedroom. She used him for her own purposes, some of which were not always clear to him, and he didn't care.

He accepted that he was not her partner in running the cartel her father had created. *Los Salvajes* was hers, and Reynaldo was merely a loyal servant, her knight protector, and when she needed it, a good lay.

None of this mattered to Reynaldo. He had been devoted to Juana since her father assigned him as her personal bodyguard. He would take the private moments she allowed and wait patiently for the next. Now, he stood patiently watching her, a soldier waiting for orders.

Juana hunched over, tapping her fingers on the desk. She picked up the phone once, scrolled absently through the list of calls she had taken that morning, then put it down again. She wasn't even aware that her hands had picked up the phone. It was just nervous energy making its way through her fingers to allow her brain to focus.

Could Chris, the gringo Ibarra spoke of, be John Sole? It seemed impossible that he would come to them. Her men had pursued him across the United States in the cat-and-mouse chase he had organized for several years. Once or twice, they had come close, but they were always a step behind. Like chasing a shadow, she had never quite been able to reach out and put her hands on him. Then he had disappeared.

What did it mean for her if he was in Mexico now, helping the other cartels? More than anything, she wanted revenge on the man who had taken her father from her, broken her mother's heart, and destroyed their family. Bebé Elizondo might have led the bloodiest and most savage cartel in Mexico, but to Juana, he was *papi*. As long as she breathed, she would never stop hunting John Sole. Her need for revenge would not be satisfied until he was …

Her eyes opened wide, and the truth came to her. She was not alone in seeking revenge. Sole was hunting her, looking for a way to get close enough to her to satisfy his similar desire for revenge.

She looked at Reynaldo, who had watched the thoughts and emotions play across her face. He was her protector. He would know what she wanted. He would find a way.

"Do you have a plan?" she asked.

"Yes, *jefa*."

"Tell me."

Reynaldo explained the trap he planned to lay for their enemies. When he finished, Juana nodded. "It's a good plan. When will it happen?"

Reynaldo thought for a moment and said, "If my suspicions are correct, in two days. That should be enough time to arrange everything."

"Good." Juana said, tugging at her lower lip, thinking for a moment, then added, "Just one thing."

"Yes?"

"Bring Sole to me … alive."

"But *jefa*, the trap I plan will be bloody. It may be impossible to guarantee that he is not killed in the attack."

"I think you underestimate Sole," Juana said. "He has a way of vanishing, and I am relying on you to not allow him to disappear this time."

"I will bring him to you, *jefa*," Reynaldo said with no choice but to agree to her demand.

"Alive," Juana reminded him.

"Alive." Reynaldo tried to give a confident nod, but the worry in his eyes made it clear that he was not at all optimistic about returning with a living John Sole. Killing him in an ambush was one thing, but capturing him was something else altogether. He was aware Juana must recognize the difficulty and peril she placed him in, requiring him to bring Sole back alive.

"I know you can do this for me, Reynaldo," Juana said, the sharpness gone from her voice. She smiled. "Once you send the word out and your plans are set, come to me tonight, and we can review your preparations … after you take care of something I need."

It was an invitation to spend the night making love to her, and usually, he would have returned her smile, but now, the task at hand preoccupied him. He turned to leave her office and pulled his phone from a pocket.

An hour later, Lovell's phone chimed. When he saw the number pop up on the screen, he thumbed the call button and said, "Speak."

"It's coming," the voice on the other end said. "I was just told to be ready the day after tomorrow, the biggest shipment ever … all fentanyl. Nothing else."

"Nothing else," Lovell repeated back. That meant they were hurting *Los Salvajes*, and the cartel was trying to maximize their profits to compensate for losses. He knew the lab had been moved since their last big attack on fentanyl shipments. "Where will it come from?"

The voice named a small village in central Michoacán and added, "They will take the road past Cerro Tancitaro."

"Good." Lovell ended the call and immediately made another to a bank in the Caribbean.

Raul Cortez stood beside his car, an old Chevy partly assembled in Mexico. He was stopped on the side of a dirt road that wound around the hilly slopes of Cerro Tancitaro. He opened a bank app on his phone, waited a few seconds for it to load, and smiled. The *norteamericanos* were very efficient. The dollars the man on the phone had promised for the information were already flowing into his account in a Cayman Islands bank.

Lovell punched up another number on his phone. When Sole answered, he said, "Day after tomorrow. The road past Cerro Tancitaro. It's a mountain peak in Michoacán."

"Good," Sole said. "I'll get things moving. We'll need to be in place early. Did you get the extra gear I requisitioned?"

"Got it. I'll meet you tomorrow."

He picked up the phone and made three calls, one each to the different cartel team leaders, giving them the time and location for the teams to gather, then disconnected and thought over the factors that would determine success or failure, most of which he did not control. The most worrisome was relying on the team he had trained for the attack. The men from the three cartels had become pretty good in separate attacks, but getting them to work together was an ongoing problem.

He shook his head and told himself to stop overthinking. This is the big game, and the team on the field is the only one you have. There aren't any replacements on the bench or backups in the locker room. The day after tomorrow is game day, so make it work.

THIRTY-FOUR

Asses Hanging Out

The phone chimed, and for a brief moment, Jay Lovell thought of ignoring it. The middle of a major operation was not a good time for distractions, and the man on the other end would not be calling to wish him good luck.

The secure phone issued to field operatives displayed the caller's number and coded designation. It was Carl Shank, his boss at the NSA. He stared at it, tried to think of some positive outcome from answering, and came up with nothing. Not a damned thing Shank might say would be good news for the op. This was not a time for more politics and bullshit, but he had no choice.

Shank was his boss, so he sighed and thumbed the call button to answer. "This is Lovell."

"I am officially noting the date and time of this call and what I am about to tell you, Agent Lovell," Shank said, then stated the month, day, year, and hour to the minute and second. "Acknowledge."

"Acknowledged," Lovell said and repeated back the month, day, year, and hour.

It was standard procedure when issuing a verbal order. There would be nothing in writing, but Shank was recording their conversation. Whatever he was about to say, Lovell would not be able to claim later that he never received the order in time to execute it.

"You are ordered to cancel the operation against the cartels immediately," Shank said bluntly. "Acknowledge receipt of this order."

Lovell did not acknowledge. "Cancel! What the hell are you talking about?"

"I repeat. Cancel the operation immediately. Now, acknowledge receipt of this verbal order."

"Where is this coming from?" Lovell was shouting now. "I was at the meeting ... remember? I heard Sylvia Lostrum, the Special Assistant to the President, give the go-ahead ... straight from the president. She even told you to write the goddamn letter authorizing the use of any necessary force! I have that letter Shank ... signed by you!"

"There has been a policy change," Shank replied calmly. "I am preparing another letter rescinding that authorization."

"Who changed the policy? Not you. You wouldn't have the balls."

"Watch your tone, Agent Lovell," Shank barked back, his feathers clearly ruffled.

Lovell took some satisfaction from that, but it didn't change the fact that Shank was issuing an order to cancel the operation. "I want to know who's behind this."

"I've issued the order, and I expect you to comply immediately. It's irrelevant who changed the policy."

"Not to me ... not to the people in the field at this very moment. There are lives on the line."

"The people in the field?" Shank let out a chuckle.

"Cartel thugs. If they kill each other off, it will be considered a successful operation, and you can have the credit."

"Credit? Is that what you think this is about?" It was a good thing that Shank was a couple of thousand miles away, gazing out his office window at the Washington monument. If they were in the same room, Lovell would probably have his hands around Shank's neck while a security team tried to pull him off. "I don't give a shit about credit! We have an asset in the field ... not cartel, but one of our people."

"You mean Sole?" Shank said, and even through the phone, Lovell could see the sneer on his face. "Not one of our people ... a contractor ... a hired killer ... expendable."

"Expendable! He's a United States citizen, and we recruited him for this operation. You cannot order me to abandon him."

"I can, and I do," Shank said.

"If we do this, leaving him hanging out there without support, he will be killed, and you know how the cartels kill. They'll send pieces of him back to us for weeks just to rub our noses in it until there aren't any pieces left to send, and then, if they feel merciful that day, they might let him die."

"It can't be helped," Shank said. "Acknowledge the order."

"I want to hear the order directly from Sylvia Lostrum," Lovell said. "She gave the original order."

"She's unavailable," Shank said.

"Unavailable? You mean ..."

"I mean, she no longer holds the position of Special Advisor to the President."

There it was, a palace revolt. It might have taken a while, but Shank and the other weak-kneed assholes he'd seen around the table that day found a way to move her out. Probably for reasons as petty as simple jealousy. She had the president's ear on national security matters, and they did not. Power was the ultimate aphrodisiac, and being close to the president was about as powerful as any of them could ever hope to be.

Lovell shook his head in disgust and imagined it all happening thousands of miles away. Advisors scurrying about, fighting each other for the president's attention and approval over anything and everything, jockeying for position in the king's court.

An election was approaching, and anyone with recent poll numbers would have the president's attention. A suggestion that now was not the time to make waves with their neighbor to the south could shift policy overnight. A mere drop of a percentage point, one way or another, was enough to cause an epidemic of cold feet. That would be enough reason to bury the op until after the election.

Add to that a Mexican government, always hyper-sensitive to a disturbance in their uneasy relations with the cartels, suddenly objecting to the rash of attacks on the most powerful cartel of all. Their suspicions that the attacks were led by someone from across the border might result in protests about the United States unlawfully carrying out a military-style operation within their sovereign territory. It would all be fodder for politicians on the other side of the aisle. Lovell could see them pointing fingers. Look at our heavy-handed president invading another country without congressional approval. We did not elect a dictator. Political perception could override security issues in states where the electoral call would be close.

The reason didn't matter. Shank, the career bureaucrat, would never have the nerve to countermand Lostrum's directives if she were still in a position of power.

Shank broke the silence. "Acknowledge the order now, Agent Lovell."

"Order acknowledged," Lovell said.

Shank began reciting the date and exact time that Lovell acknowledged the order. When he told Lovell to confirm the date and time of the acknowledgment, he found the line dead. Lovell had already disconnected.

For a moment, Lovell thought of keeping the new orders to himself but knew he couldn't. Sole was taking the biggest risks. He had a right to know. He picked up a different phone and punched in a number.

Sole answered, "Kind of busy right now. Make it quick."

"They pulled the plug on us," Lovell said without preliminaries.

"Pulled the plug? You mean ..."

"I mean, we're canceled ... done ... operation is no longer sanctioned and approved."

"I can't just leave now. I've got men in position. Shit's about to hit the fan. People are going to die. We have a chance to get to the top of *Los Salvajes*, and we can take them out!" He paused to take a breath and added, "I'm not leaving."

"I know," Lovell said.

"So that's it? You're just pulling out?" Sole snapped back at him.

"No. I'm letting you know that we are on our own."

"We? You mean you're disobeying orders from above?"

"I mean, we are going to see this through. What happens after that ..." Lovell said, shrugging. "Whatever happens doesn't matter. As you keep saying, we focus on the mission."

"You mean both our asses are hanging out," Sole said,

his already healthy respect for Lovell bumping up a few more notches. The man was putting his career and possibly his life on the line.

"Let's just make this work, so we can go home and not spend the rest of our lives on the run or in prison."

"Fair enough," Sole said, calmer now. "What about the gear ... the equipment I requisitioned. I'm going to need it to get to the top."

"It's all in place."

"Then I'll need you in position too."

"I'll be there."

"Good," Sole said. "Do me a favor. If you have any more bad news hold off until after the op."

"Will do," Lovell laughed and ended the call.

A few minutes later, he had gathered up his gear and loaded it all in the latest four-wheel-drive vehicle acquired for the operation. The drive toward Cerro Tancítaro took most of the day, and the farther he went into the Mexican backcountry, the more at home he felt.

Things were simple here. No politics, only the mission, and the mission ... the op, as Sole called it ... was clear.

Washington, D.C. faded away into a distant barren fantasyland populated by spineless bureaucrats and politicians. The orders from people like Carl Shank were no more substantial than the mist clinging to the Mexican hillsides before the day's sun burns it away.

THIRTY-FIVE

Only Thing To Do

The phone vibrated in his pocket. Ibarra pulled it out to look at the screen. He was almost as surprised as he was relieved that José Ruiz had followed through. The message was simple—the number 8.

Assuming Ruiz knew what the hell he was talking about and had any idea when the next attack was coming, Ibarra might survive the next few days. That assumption hung on some very precarious ifs.

If Ruiz had not been discovered by the other cartels.

If he had not been tortured and forced to send the text as a trap.

If he had not run for his life and sent the text to throw Ibarra off his trail while he escaped.

Assuming all that, Ibarra's plan to get inside information on the next attack on *Los Salvajes* might just work. He stared at the screen for a few seconds, took a deep breath, and pulled up a number on his phone.

"Yes," Reynaldo answered.

"The text arrived. They are preparing an attack."

"Good."

"Is there anything else you need, *jefe?*"

"Stay where you are. Nothing else." Reynaldo disconnected without another word.

Ibarra had long since given up praying to the God he had learned about at his mother's knee, but he offered one now. *God, please let them find the bastards and kill them.*

There was nothing for him to do now but wait. All might be forgiven if Ruiz's information was accurate and Reynaldo's plan to strike back at the other cartels succeeded.

If not … Ibarra eyed the bag he'd packed and placed on the cot in his tent at the clearing. Maybe he could get away, for a while … keep running until they found him.

After that… He shook his head, telling himself to accept the reality. There would be no, after that. They would find him eventually, and Luis Ibarra would cease to exist. Running would only make the end more painful.

He'd considered blaming his failure on one of his underlings. Shit rolls downhill, especially in the cartels, and Rufo Serrato was farther down the hill and, in most situations, would have made a good scapegoat.

But not this time. Reynaldo made it clear that Juana held him personally responsible for not resolving the problems with the other cartels. Passing the blame would have only hastened her decision to eliminate Ibarra.

He pulled a cigar from his shirt pocket, scraped the cap off with a fingernail, lit it, and puffed vigorously until the end glowed cherry red. He held the lighter in his hand for a moment, noticed his hand shaking, and shoved the lighter back in a pocket. The only thing he could do now was to wait and repeat the prayer. *God, please let them find the bastards and kill them.*

José Ruiz and the two other Cardoso men who shared a small house with him had been awakened that morning with the news that the training was finished. They were moving to the attack. The journey to the hills around Cerro Tancitaro would take the entire day and into the night. The gringo wanted them in position before sunup the following day.

José sat on the toilet behind a closed door and stared at the phone in his hand—the text, the number 8, was still on the screen. He'd gone there to send the text to Ibarra so no one would see. Now, he felt the need to empty his bowels.

It took a while for the loose discharge to stop dripping into the bowl. Neto, one of his roommates, came to the door, rapped, and shouted, "Hurry up, José. You're not the only one who has to take a shit!"

José stopped staring at the text on the screen, deleted it, cleaned his ass, and stood up, buttoning up his pants. Neto pushed past him when he opened the door, then stopped and wrinkled his nose in disgust. "*Maldito hombre. Aquí huele a burro muerto.*" Damn, man. Smells like a dead burro in here.

"Fuck you," José said, moving out of the way.

"*Y tu madre, pendejo.*" And your mother, asshole. Neto laughed and slammed the door shut.

The morning was spent gathering their gear, checking weapons, and reviewing the attack plans with their leaders. The fucking gringo called Chris was everywhere at once, it seemed. He supervised, gave orders, listened to complaints, settled the squabbling between the cartel factions—instigated mainly by the Sanchez men—and ensured everyone had the gear required for the attack. José had been told it would be the biggest one of all and, possibly, the last.

The banter between the men could have been that of soldiers in any regular military unit, except these were not soldiers. They were cartel murderers who would have happily gone off to hack apart some defenseless victim—man, woman, or child—if their *jefe* ordered it.

By noon they were loading into pickups and vans for the trip to Tancitaro. When the man in charge of José's group did a head count, he discovered they were a man short. He looked at the others and asked, "Where's Ruiz?"

"José?" Neto said, laughing. "José has the shits this morning."

The others sitting in the truck's bed laughed and said, "*Sí, un cobarde de mierda.*" A chickenshit.

"He's been in the toilet half the morning. Last we saw him, he was headed to take another shit. Said he'd be back later."

"*Cabrón.*" Asshole, the group leader said. "He knew we were leaving. We'll deal with his ass when we get back."

He considered reporting to the gringo that they were a man short but decided against it. He was in no mood to hear the jeers from Sanchez's men that one of theirs had run away from the fight. He waved the pickup forward. "Let's go!"

José had been told that after the big attack, things would get back to normal. What was normal? José had no idea anymore. He only knew that *Los Salvajes* planned some sort of trap for the attackers, and he had no intention of being caught in the middle.

If any Cardoso men survived the trap and returned, they would look for him. If they found him …

Abandoning his rifle and other gear, with only a pistol tucked under his shirt, José Ruiz jogged through the streets, trying to put as much distance between him and his departing comrades as possible. Whatever would happen in the ambush at Tancitaro would happen without him.

Luis Ibarra had promised that if all went well, there was a place for him in *Los Salvajes*, but what did 'going well' mean? That was the question, and without an answer, the only thing for him to do was disappear.

THIRTY-SIX

The Trap

Reynaldo ended the call from Ibarra and turned to the three men standing in his hillside office across from the hacienda. They would spring the trap to eliminate the other cartels and their attacks on *Los Salvajes*.

All three had once worked for a Mexican counter-terrorism agency and had been trained in special weapons and combat tactics in the United States. Now, acting as mercenaries, they contracted their skills to the highest payer, giving Reynaldo an advantage over the other cartels. With an almost bottomless pit of cash to draw from, *Los Salvajes* could recruit the best, and in the mercenary underworld, these men were among the best.

"You heard the call. Are we ready?" he asked.

"We are," one of the men replied. Known by his surname, Cuevas, he was the group leader.

"Tell me how it will all happen," Reynaldo said.

"We move our men into position tonight after dark, concealed well back over the hills away from the point where the gringo must bring the others to attack."

"Tonight? They might be discovered before the attack."

"That will not happen," Cuevas said. "We will be in place, close but not too close, concealed and undetected. Once his attack on your drug shipment is underway, we will come from behind, envelope his force, and destroy them."

"But if your place of concealment is discovered?" Reynaldo persisted.

"It won't be," Cuevas said sharply. "We have selected the place carefully, and the men in our force are disciplined and follow orders ... without exception." Cuevas allowed himself a small smile. It was a thinly veiled insult aimed at the cartel gunmen whom the mercenaries considered to be not much more than rabble ... thugs with guns. Even the *Los Salvajes* men, with all their money and power, were outmatched by the mercenaries' cold, killing efficiency.

Cuevas shrugged and added, "And they want the bonus you promised if our attack is successful."

"Alright." Reynaldo dismissed the insult to his men with a nod. After all, he intended to use his cartel people as bait in the mercenaries' trap. No doubt, many would not survive ... a cost of doing business. "How will you move from your concealment to the point of the attack?"

"We wait until their assault on your trucks is underway. Once we know they are engaged, we will leave concealment and come on them from behind."

"You seem very sure how they will carry out their attack."

"Nothing is guaranteed, of course," Cuevas conceded. "But we've studied the previous attacks. The *norteamericano's* tactics have been extremely successful, and his past success works to our advantage. He will be confident of his tactics and battle plan, so we can reasonably predict how he will position his forces."

"But if he does change tactics?" Reynaldo said.

"Not likely." Cuevas shook his head to dismiss the idea. "He will not want to teach his people new tricks … a new plan. His men are undisciplined and difficult to control. Changing the plan of attack would cause confusion among them, so he will repeat what has been successful and what they have learned in the past."

"Alright, we rely on him using the same tactics," Reynaldo said. "What else?"

"It's not complicated but requires careful timing on our part," Cuevas said. "The *norteamericano* will choose high ground favorable for his ambush, and as he has done in past attacks, he will have his attackers come down from their perches to finish off survivors. His goal has always been to completely destroy your people and vehicles. That means the attack must occur where the high ground slopes down, giving them access to the road."

"The road runs through the hill country around Tancitaro," Reynaldo said. "How do you know which hill he will choose to make his attack?"

"Excellent question," Cuevas said with a patronizing smile. "Assuming the information your man has provided is correct … that he is moving his men into position to attack your trucks …."

"It's correct," Reynaldo interrupted, hoping that the texted signal from Ibarra's informant was accurate. "They are moving into position today for a major attack. We have stopped all other shipments and movement by our people, so if he is attacking, the only target can be our drug shipment from the lab."

"Good." Cuevas nodded. "Then there is only one place where the terrain suits his tactics." He pointed to a topographic map on the office wall where he had circled three areas on the stretch of road leading from the lab. "High cliffs and bluffs line the road in this area, making it suitable for a long-distance attack, sniping at our drug convoy. They could do some damage, but from here, they could not approach and completely destroy it."

He moved his arm to point at the opposite end of the road on the map. "Here, the terrain flattens out and does not offer the advantage of concealment and superior firing positions. His force would be in the open, easily seen and exposed to return gunfire from your vehicles."

"But here …" Cuevas moved to the center section of the marked road and tapped the map. "For a kilometer, the road passes through hills that slope down to the road. From there, his men can open their attack from the high ground and then leave their firing positions at the right time and move down the slope for the final kill." Cuevas tapped the map and nodded with certainty. "Here is where he will make the attack, and we will have a surprise waiting for him."

He turned and nodded at his companions. "Once the attack on your convoy begins, Diaz here will lead his men out of concealment and descend on the attackers' left flank. Rocha will lead his men on the right, and I will take the center. Taking them by surprise from behind, we should be able to destroy them."

"And our losses?"

"There will be some." Cuevas nodded. "In your vehicles on the road, the men exposed to the opening attack will suffer the most. Once our flanking movement begins and takes the attackers by surprise, the losses will diminish, and we will have the upper hand."

Reynaldo was silent for a moment before he said,

"There is one more thing. The *norteamericano* who leads them … he must be captured alive."

"Alive?" Cuevas frowned and shook his head. "This may not be possible. In the middle of the battle …" He shook his head. "Things happen when the shooting starts. People die, and we cannot always control which people die."

"Even so," Reynaldo said. "Those are the orders. We bring him back alive."

"We?" Cuevas raised his eyebrows in surprise.

"We." Reynaldo nodded. "I will be going with you."

"I …" Cuevas paused, searching for a polite way to decline the offer. "I'm not sure your training is adequate for our planned operation, and I …."

"I understand." Reynaldo raised a hand to cut him off. "I will not interfere in your plans and will stay back from the point of attack. You are the professionals, but my orders are to capture the gringo and bring him back … alive … personally."

Cuevas did not ask who issued those orders. Reynaldo reported only to one person in the cartel.

"Alright," Cuevas said, casting a doubtful glance toward Diaz and Rocha before continuing. "The leader of the attack, the one we assume is the *norteamericano*, will likely be in the highest position with the best visibility of the road and your drug convoy. From there, he can see the battlefield and direct his men where needed."

Cuevas turned back to the map, studying it for a minute before tapping his index finger. "Here, this is the highest point … these two hills are higher than the rest. If he conducts his attack as he has in the past, he should be somewhere on these hills … concealed, of course. We will have to find him, but it is where I would be to direct the attack."

"Alright." Reynaldo nodded. While your men proceed

over the hills to surprise the attackers, I will search for the *norteamericano* on those hills."

"No," Cuevas said bluntly.

"No?" Reynaldo cast him a sharp look. It was not a word often spoken to him by anyone other than Juana Elizondo.

"He is a dangerous man ... a professional. I cannot allow you to do this alone," Cuevas said. "I will bring a couple of my men, and we will go with you to find the *norteamericano*. The rest will proceed over the hill to make the attack." He turned to Diaz. "You will command my center strike force until I return to the battle."

Diaz nodded. "*Sí, jefe.*"

"There can be no discussion on this," Cuevas said, turning back to Reynaldo. "This is a condition if you are to join us on the battlefield."

"I think you forget who is paying you," Reynaldo said, his eyes narrowed at the defiance.

"If you are killed, I suspect there will be no pay," Cuevas said, shaking his head. "And in the future, others may not want to hire the men who allowed their client ... a *Los Salvajes* chief ... to be killed. This is an absolute condition. We will accompany you and help you capture the *norteamericano*. After, you can return with him safely bound and personally deliver him ... as you were ordered."

Reynaldo thought it through and nodded. "Alright. We'll do it as you suggest."

The issue settled, Cuevas asked, "Are there any other orders we should factor into our planning,"

"No. Get your men in position. I will join you later after I take care of some business."

"Later?" Cuevas frowned. "As I explained, our trap

depends on surprise. You must be in position with us before the *norteamericano* arrives with his men."

"How long will it take you to get into position?"

"If we start now, three or four hours."

"My business won't take long." Reynaldo stood and pointed to a crossroads on the map. "I'll meet you here in three hours."

THIRTY-SEVEN

Rats

The landing area was an old field, graded level and cleared of brush and trees. The descending helicopter's rotor wash kicked up a cloud of dust, spreading outward and covering the workers tending the adjacent groves of avocados. They worked on ignoring the dust and disturbance.

It was an active orchard. The avocados were carefully tended, harvested, and shipped across Mexico and around the globe, and it was a perfect cover for the fentanyl lab nestled in the center of hundreds of acres of trees.

Reynaldo Gutierrez waited for the dust to settle, then stepped briskly out of the helicopter and into a waiting car, a large SUV. Two of his security men accompanied him from the helicopter, and two more waited in the SUV.

They sped away from the landing field, kicking up another cloud of dust. The workers in the avocado fields pulled their bandannas tighter over their faces and continued working without looking at the vehicle. The orchard and fields were their world, and they studiously avoided any interaction with gun-wielding men who came and went in helicopters.

Five minutes later, the SUV rocked to a halt in the gravel lot beside a low block-walled building. Reynaldo stepped out, flanked by the security men, all stern-eyed, all silent, and all armed with pistols in their belts and carrying MAC-11 machine pistols.

It was the usual cartel show of force, ostentatious, threatening, and completely unnecessary. No one on the property was about to threaten Reynaldo or challenge *Los Salvajes*. The lab and surrounding avocado fields were owned by a dummy corporation set up by Juana Elizondo. Still, there was a traitor in their midst, someone tipping off the other cartels about drug shipments, and it was time to emphasize who was in charge.

A hundred yards away, the farm overseer heard the SUV's noisy arrival and walked out onto the front stoop of the house the cartel provided him. He saw Reynaldo and the security men, turned around, and went back inside. His job was to grow avocados, and he was good at it. What went on inside the block building was none of his business.

The building housed one of the cartel's fentanyl labs. Inside, lab workers operated in a sort of parallel but separate universe. They never came to see or speak with him, and he never went to see what went on behind the block walls. It was a mutually beneficial arrangement, and the overseer had no intention of ruining it by asking questions.

The lab was an unimposing structure, forty feet wide at the entrance and a hundred in length. The plain block walls gave it the appearance of just another farm outbuilding that might have been used once for sorting and crating avocados for shipment. Now, it was used for preparing a different sort of shipment.

In the front section of the room, workers under bright LED lights, wearing masks and gloves, combined the precursor chemicals shipped in from China to manufacture the synthetic opioid, fentanyl. Farther along, the compound they created was pressed into tablets of varying colors to hinder identification. At the rear of the building, the pills were bagged in plastic, boxed for shipment, and taken out to a loading dock to be loaded onto the various transport vehicles the cartel used.

Two of the security men remained outside. The others followed Reynaldo through the steel front door where a balding man in his fifties, a retired chemist from a university in Mexico City, came from behind one of the workbenches to stand before Reynaldo.

"Where?" Reynaldo asked.

"This way." The chemist led the way, passing the workers at the benches who, like the orchard workers, made a point of not interacting with the visitors with the guns. The chemist stopped in a far corner by the loading dock and nodded at a door. "In here."

Reynaldo left his security men at the door, entered the room, and stopped. A bloody Raul Cortez sat bound with duct tape to a chair in the middle of a tiny room that was the shipping manager's office when it wasn't being used for torture.

Two other men were bound and bleeding in chairs facing each other on opposite walls. The space was crowded and filled with the metallic scent of fresh blood. The chemist and mechanic were dead, each having screamed their confessions, pleading for mercy before dying.

Cortez's body hung limp in the chair as if he might already be dead. His face was a bloody pulp from the beating he had endured, blood dripping from the tips of his fingers, the nails ripped out by the man who questioned him. The only signs he still lived were his shallow, gasping breaths and eyes opening wide with terror as Reynaldo walked into the room.

"No …. No … please." Cortez's head shook back and forth. "No more, please. I have told them everything."

Reynaldo took in the scene. A pair of needle nose pliers and a garden pruner sat on a table beside Cortez. His shoes had been removed, the floor around him was littered with his bloody fingernails, and two toes hacked off with the pruner.

Reynaldo nodded at the gloved man standing behind Cortez. "How did you find him?"

"It wasn't hard," the gloved man said. "As you said, the traitor had to know of shipments going out. We watched everyone …."

He glanced at the senior chemist who had been one of the suspected traitors until his younger protégé was identified. The chemist stared at the floor. The look of disgust at the horror of Cortez's tortured body was mixed with relief that he was not sitting in one of the chairs.

"When you gave the order that the shipment was to go out in two days, the trap was set. Only one person left." The gloved man nodded at Cortez. "This one. He works in the back here, loading the trucks. He was gone for an hour. He said it was to check on his wife and children in a nearby village."

"And what has he told you?" Reynaldo asked.

"Everything. He identified the other two." The gloved man nodded at Cortez's cell phone on the table beside the pliers. "Also, he called an unknown number while he was gone, and there is a link on his phone to a bank account in the Cayman Islands."

"A bank in the Caymans?" Reynaldo stared down at Cortez. "How much are they paying you?"

"Please, please ... you have to understand," Cortez said, the words gurgling out of his shattered mouth. "They threatened me ... my family ... I only took the money because I had to."

"So, you betrayed us out of fear. They must be terrible men to frighten you this way."

"Yes, that's it." Cortez managed to nod. "They are from the United States ... very powerful men ... from the government, I think."

"So, after these powerful men from the north threatened you, they paid you?"

"Yes, yes ... now you understand," Cortez murmured.

"They paid you so much money that you must hide it in a bank in the Cayman Islands," Reynaldo said and shook his head sadly. "So, you're saying their threats weren't enough to buy you. You see, this is very confusing to me. Why should they pay you if you were so afraid of these men from the United States?"

"I'm trying to explain ..." Cortez lifted his eyes to Reynaldo and knew no explanation would satisfy him. He trembled in the chair, what little strength remaining in him evaporating until his head hung down on his chest.

Reynaldo spoke mildly now. "And why didn't you come to us if they threatened you? We could have protected you ... killed those who threatened one of our own ... given you a reward for your loyalty."

"I ... it's just that they are very frightening people." Cortez knew his story had been dismantled by Reynaldo's questions, but he could think of nothing else to say.

"I'm sure they are," Reynaldo said. "But you should have feared us more."

Cortez sobbed, "Please, I beg of you ... it was so much money ... I have a family, and it was so much money."

Reynaldo looked up and nodded. It took another minute for Cortez's suffering to end. The gloved man came around the chair to stand in front of Cortez, removed a lock-blade knife from his pocket, opened it, and thrust it one time into the side of the bound man's neck.

Cortez had no time to speak before the blade sliced through flesh and cartilage. Blood poured from his severed jugular vein and spurted from the carotid artery with the last beats of his heart.

The gloved man stepped back and looked at Reynaldo. "Their families?"

"Rats breed rats. Make the usual examples," Reynaldo said and turned to leave. On the drive back to the helicopter, he took out his phone and made a call. There was one more item of business to resolve.

Seated at his table in the bar in Comitán, Chiro Cordero answered on the first ring. "*Sí, jefe.*"

"Do it."

"*Sí, jefe.*"

Reynaldo disconnected. A few minutes later, he was airborne enroute to his rendezvous with Cuevas and the mercenaries.

Chiro Cordero smiled at the boy sitting across the table from him, drinking a Coke. Naldo Barrera had worked his way through the ranks of coyotes, joking, running errands for them, and making friends. Eventually, they noticed that every time he was seen laughing with the coyotes loading migrants on a bus, that bus would be hijacked on the road.

Most of the coyotes began avoiding him, saying he was bad luck.

That did not deter Naldo's entrepreneurial spirit. The money the gringo was paying him was his ticket out of Carmen Xhán. He pressed the issue with the coyotes and tried different ways of getting close to them until, one day, his name came up when Cordero was fuming about information being leaked about their operations.

It was innocent enough. A coyote said, "I swear we don't talk to anyone about our business."

"No one?" Cordero glared at him.

"I swear, no one. No one wants to interfere with *Los Salvajes*. They wouldn't dare."

"Someone is daring!" Cordero roared.

"I swear, everyone stays away from us. The only one in town who talks to us anymore is that kid, Naldo."

"Who?"

"Naldo is the name he goes by. Just a boy ... about ten years old. He's harmless ... runs errands for us while we load the buses."

"While you load the ..." Cordero shook his head in disgust. "*¡Idiota!*" Idiot!

The coyote cowered away from Cordero.

"Bring him to me!" Cordero said. "Tell him I have a special job for him ... an important package to deliver ... that I will pay him."

Now, Naldo sat with Cordero, sipping a Coke, waiting while Cordero tended to business on the phone. When the call ended, Cordero smiled at him. "Finish your Coke. I have that job for you to do."

"Okay," Naldo said. "How much you paying me?"

"Twenty thousand pesos," Cordero said.

"No." Naldo shook his head. "Dollars ... I want it in dollars."

"Okay," Cordero grinned, admiring the boy's negotiating skills. "A thousand U.S. dollars. Now let's go."

He led the way through the bar and out the back door.

Standing in the alley, Naldo turned to look at him. "Where's the package you want me to deliver?"

"You are the package," Cordero said and added, "Sorry, Naldo."

"I am the ..." A question formed in Naldo's eyes, and then for the first time, fear. He started to turn and run, but it was too late. Cordero lifted his pistol and fired one bullet through the boy's head. Naldo crumpled to the ground before he could take two steps.

By cartel standards, it was a merciful end. Cordero looked at the young body sprawled in the dirt and muttered, "Such a waste. We could have used one like you."

He turned to the men who had followed them into the alley. "Leave his body in the square in Carmen Xhán for everyone to see. Spread the word. This is what happens to rats, even baby ones."

THIRTY-EIGHT

Restless Days

Cuevas stood stoically in the cloud of dust kicked up by the helicopter. His expression made it clear that he was unhappy about having a non-professional wading into the middle of his operation.

Reynaldo saw the look on his face as he stepped out. "Tell me where you want me. I'll stay out of the way while you organize things. I'm here for only one purpose."

"I know," Cuevas said, frowning. "To bring back the *norteamericano* ... alive."

"That's right," Reynaldo said, undeterred by Cuevas' displeasure. "Now, where should I go?"

"Over there." Cuevas pointed to a rock outcropping that offered shade from the afternoon sun. "I'll join you shortly."

Reynaldo sat in the shade and watched while Cuevas went around inspecting his men, checking equipment, and reviewing the attack plan. He had to admit that Cuevas knew what he was doing and had selected a perfect place of concealment for his men—a small ravine on the backside of a ridge of hills separated from the road by a small valley and another ridge. The second set of hills would be where the *norteamericano* positioned his men on the downward slope. The mercenaries could approach from the rear without being detected, ascend the reverse slope of the next hills, and be on the other cartels before they knew what was happening.

Cuevas returned to the rock outcrop with two men in tow. He sat near Reynaldo while his men squatted in the dirt a few feet away, eating MRE—Meals Ready to Eat—bars purchased from a company that made dehydrated emergency food storage items.

"When we begin the attack tomorrow, stay with me." He looked at Reynaldo. "This is very important. Stay with me."

Reynaldo nodded his understanding. Cuevas was not going to take a chance that they might lose their payday by allowing something to happen to the man who hired them.

"Our men will move forward when the attack on your drug shipment begins. You and I, and these two men, will be in the center, looking for the high ground where the *norteamericano* will be positioned."

Reynaldo nodded again.

"Once we have him safely in custody, I will leave these two with you to guard him while I go forward to direct the rest of the attack on the other cartels."

"Understood," Reynaldo said.

After that, Cuevas pulled MREs from his pack, tossed one to Reynaldo, and sat chewing without speaking. Silence settled over the mercenaries. There were no whispered conversations, no cookfires, or lit cigarettes. The men seemed to fade into the hillside, invisible to anyone who might venture into the ravine.

The afternoon turned to evening, then full dark. Reynaldo leaned back against the rock and closed his eyes. Cuevas shook his head and kept watch through the night.

The next day was a restless one. More MREs and more doing nothing. Reynaldo discovered that waiting for action could be more trying than the battle itself. Cuevas had wanted them in position a day before they expected the attackers to ensure his men remained undetected. Now they could only watch and kill time.

Cuevas kept his men close, not allowing them to go above the adjacent ridge for fear of being spotted. The *norteamericano* was experienced and would check the reverse slope of his attacking hill before setting his men in position above the road.

The second night in the ravine was more trying than the first for Reynaldo. While Cuevas and his men relaxed, taking turns napping and keeping watch, Reynaldo felt the restless need to pace. He moved through the rocks at the edge of the slopes, stretching his legs and trying to calm the restlessness that had settled over him.

"Stretch a little," Cuevas said. "Then come get back under cover."

"You really think he might see us hidden here?" Reynaldo said.

"Doesn't matter," Cuevas shrugged. "I'm not going to give him the chance. Now finish stretching and come back under the rocks."

Reynaldo frowned but complied. When the second night finally descended over them, it was a relief. Tomorrow would be the day of action.

THIRTY-NINE

In Position

Enrique Valera leaned against the fender of an SUV bearing the markings of the *Policía Estatal* and wondered if the GPS coordinates Lovell had sent were correct. He was as close to the middle of nowhere as he could get in a day's drive from home, and as at their last meeting, he was exhausted. This time, Lovell had selected an off-the-grid ravine in the mountains a dozen miles north of Lago Pátzcuaro, a volcanic lake more than seven thousand feet above sea level.

Lovell's directions took Valera off paved roads until he followed a dry stream bed to where it ended, and the mountains rose up on three sides. He looked up at the towering mountain slope and lit a cigarette, trying not to think about his family and the fact that if he disappeared here, no one would ever know what happened to him or even where to look for a body. He smoked two more before he heard another vehicle making its way up the rocky stream bed, the sound of its laboring engine and shifting gears echoing off the mountain walls.

When the Land Rover finally came into sight, making its way around a bend, Valera breathed a sigh of relief. Lovell sat behind the wheel, clutching it and bouncing up and down in the seat as the vehicle bumped over the rocky, rutted stream bed.

"Piece of shit," Lovell muttered as he braked to a stop, got out, and stretched his head and neck to the side to work out the kinks from the jarring ride. Then he walked over to Valera. "I didn't know you smoked."

"Only when I'm nervous," Valera said.

"Me too. Got another?"

Valera reached into his shirt pocket and handed over a crumpled pack of Faros. A picture of a dead rat was emblazoned across the paper wrapper as a graphic warning that cigarette smoking could be hazardous to your health. Lovell tapped one out, lit up, and inhaled deeply, then wondered if they ground dead rats up in the tobacco. Faros were working-class smokes, short, dense, cheap, and made for those who needed their nicotine fix in a hurry.

Lovell took a more gingerly second puff and fought back the urge to cough. They smoked in silence for a minute, neither in a hurry to leave the solitude of the hidden mountain ravine. It was a world apart from drug smuggling, human trafficking, and cartel murders.

Taking a last drag on the butt, Lovell stubbed it out on the sole of his boot, pulled the paper apart, and let the remnants scatter in the wind. He looked at Valera. "Ready?"

"Ready." Valera nodded.

They went to the Land Rover's cargo hatch and began transferring the gear Sole had requested to the back of Valera's car. They managed to get it all in and force the door shut with some effort.

Valera got behind the wheel. Lovell sat in the passenger seat.

"What about your car?" Valera asked.

Lovell shrugged. "Government write-off."

"You *norteamericanos* have too much money." Valera shook his head and steered the SUV down the stream bed.

"Uh huh," Lovell replied without mentioning that the *politicrats* in Washington had pulled the plug on the mission, and the only thing left to cover expenses was the government credit card in his pocket. They would pull the plug on that, too, as soon as they realized he had gone rogue and was keeping the operation active. If he didn't go to prison for that, he'd spend the rest of his life paying off the bill for expenses and the gear he'd requisitioned for Sole.

The bone-jarring ride down the stream bed took almost an hour. From there, they picked up a backcountry trail that wasn't much more than a path. There was no reason to hurry, and Valera drove carefully and slowly. Losing a wheel now would leave Sole on his own to deal with *Los Salvajes*.

They came out of the mountains into a valley and pulled onto a paved road near Zinciro. Valera turned the SUV away from the town. They wanted no questions from locals who might see and remember a state police vehicle from the Reynosa District cruising through. Soon they were back on another dirt road, picking their way through more mountain passes.

"Might as well slow down," Lovell said. "We don't want to get there before Sole has his people in place."

Miles away, on the road leading from the *Los Salvajes* fentanyl lab to Cerro Tancitaro, Sole scouted and selected the terrain they would use for the attack on the drug convoy.

As Cuevas had explained to Reynaldo, there was only one suitable point along the road.

Sole decided to use Sanchez's undisciplined group as the blocking force. Always eager to spray bullets, he figured they would rush from cover after a few rounds to demonstrate their machismo to the other cartels. The guards in the drug trucks would probably shoot them down at will, but he decided that was not his problem. He'd done what he could to prepare them.

Espinoza's men would be the main center attack force. Focusing on the central line of vehicles, they would take out as many as possible. If a few of Sanchez's men happened to run into their line of fire, so much the better.

Cardoso's men would assault the tailing vehicles in the line and prevent escape. Like the Espinoza men, they were more disciplined, but unlike the others, they sometimes seemed reticent during a fight, not genuinely committed to the battle until they saw their victory at hand.

Sole left his gear, including two LAW rockets—the last two Lovell was able to requisition—on the high ground he'd selected for his command post and went from position to position carrying only the M-24 rifle. Walking down the hillside, he checked fields of fire and reminded the men once again how the attack would unfold and their roles in the ambush. It was well after dark by the time they were in position. He gave a final order to maintain silence. No lights, no talking, no fires. Without knowing when the *Los Salvajes* drug convoy would pass and for the ambush to succeed, nothing could give away their presence.

Then he went to his command post and leaned the M-24 against a rock beside the LAW rocket tubes. There was nothing to do for the moment but wait.

Murmurs drifted through the air. A joke followed by laughter. Someone lit up a cigarette, then another.

In an actual combat unit, violations of an order to maintain silence in anticipation of action would have received severe punishment. Sole could only raise his head above the rocks and call out in a hoarse whisper, "*¡Silencio!*"

The whispering abated somewhat, one or two cigarettes were stubbed out, and things got about as quiet as he could expect. They would spend the night on the hillside. Lovell's source had said the lab's drug shipment would leave the day after tomorrow. In the morning, they would find out if the informant knew what he was talking about.

Sole had one more task before he settled down behind the rock to keep watch. He double-checked his GPS coordinates, pulled out the satellite phone Lovell had issued him and sent a brief message.

Lovell and Valera were still ten miles away, creeping along without lights down yet another dirt road. Mexico was crisscrossed with them, some leading to villages and settlements that dated back to the conquistadors. Some going nowhere.

Lovell's phone chimed, and the screen lit up his face as he read the message. "We're getting close."

"How far?" Valera asked.

"Another five miles before we stop." Lovell closed the phone.

"*Mierda*," Valera whispered.

"I agree," Lovell said. "Shit"

Valera drove while Lovell kept track of their position. Several times he got out to walk in front of the SUV for a mile or more at a time, checking for hazards and selecting the best route around obstacles.

The stars glittered in the black sky overhead, but in the east, a pale orange glow began to cast light above the horizon when Lovell said, "Here. This will do."

Valera stopped the SUV and killed the engine. "Now what?"

"Now," Lovell said, walking to the SUV's cargo hatch. "We unload this son of a bitch and make sure we're in position when Sole needs us."

FORTY

Everything Changed

Lovell and Valera worked for an hour, unloading and assembling the gear from the SUV. When they finished, the rising sun cast its first rays over the surrounding hills. They sat side by side in the open cargo hatch and stared at the contraption resting on a tarp on the ground.

"I have never seen anything like that," Valera said.

"Military drone … Puma 3AE unmanned aerial vehicle to be exact." Lovell took a gulp of water and then got up to walk around what looked like a miniature airplane.

"It looks like a child's toy," Valera said doubtfully. He was right. Despite a nine-foot wingspan assembled from sections, it looked a lot like a giant model airplane held together with glue.

"Not a toy. Expanded endurance batteries and long-range tracking antenna give it a range of about thirty-five miles, but we won't let her get that far away." Lovell knelt and gave the drone's composite skin a loving pat. "Has a camera with infrared capability for day and night viewing if needed and can pan three hundred-sixty degrees. This is our eye in the sky. Nothing on the ground in the open can hide from it."

"How do you make it fly?"

"That's the fun part," Lovell said, standing. "Come on, I'll show you."

Lovell spent a few minutes setting up the portable console and establishing the wireless link between the drone's flight controls and cameras. When he was satisfied, he lifted the fifteen-five-pound drone and showed Valera how to hold it for launch, shoulder height, supported front and rear, and the propeller away from his face.

"What do I do now?" Valera asked.

"Wait a minute." Lovell went to the control console and started the drone's battery-powered system. The propeller began spinning, slowly at first, then faster. He nodded at Valera. "Give her a little toss forward."

Valera had barely released his hold on the drone when the propeller speed increased, and the drone soared away, slowly at first, then rising almost soundlessly until it was above the hills. He watched, fascinated. He'd heard of these drones before but had never seen one in operation. The expense was not in the *policía estatal* budget. The drone orbited overhead as Lovell got a feel for the controls.

"How much does a machine like that cost?" Valera asked.

"A lot," Lovell said, not wanting to think about the expense. The Puma was on Sole's requisition list, and he'd gotten it approved and delivered before Shank scrapped the mission. At this point, the cost was of little consequence. He could never pay off the mission's unauthorized expenses in three lifetimes.

"Time to check in," he said and took the satellite radio phone out, checked the battery, put an earbud in one ear, and handed one to Valera. "Put this in your ear, and we'll be able to talk on the same net."

Lovell handed over an earbud, then pressed the call button that sent out a short squelch burst. Valera winced and adjusted the volume.

Five miles away, Sole tapped the earbud in his right ear and answered. "Go."

"We're airborne," Lovell said.

"Good. How do things look?"

"All quiet right now. Just bringing the drone up over the ridge to identify your position." He paused, moved the control stick a little, and said, "Got you."

The drone passed over Sole's cartel attack teams dispersed along the hillside. "I see you've got a light discipline problem," Lovell said, shaking his head. "Infrared is picking up cigarettes in the shadows."

"Yeah, been an issue all night," Sole said. His voice had the sound of a fatigued babysitter trying to control a group of unruly children, except these children had guns and liked to kill people. "With full daylight coming, it shouldn't be an issue."

"You sound tired. Hang in there, buddy."

"I'll be alright," Sole said.

"How do we look from below?" Lovell asked.

"Invisible," Sole said and scanned the sky above. A tiny movement caught his eye, and he added, "Rising sun just glinted off a wingtip, but only for a second. Someone would have to know where to look to spot you."

"How about noise?"

Sole listened for a moment and shook his head. "No sound that I can pick up."

"Good. I've got the propulsion system down to

minimum levels, cruising at about thirty knots to hold down the decibels."

Sole looked up over the rock serving as his command post. The cartel men below were becoming restless. Before long, Sanchez's men would be challenging the others to some sort of cartel version of an old west showdown over some imagined insult to their manhood. After the long night waiting on the hillside, the shaky discipline he'd tried to instill in their short training time was breaking down, and his well-timed battle plan along with it.

"I need you to get eyes on the road from the lab," he said. "Give me a heads up when the drug shipment is on the way, so I can settle my people down and get them as ready as possible."

"Will do," Lovell replied, turning the drone away from Sole's position to cruise along the road. "Talk to you as soon as I pick up the convoy."

"Roger that," Sole settled back behind his rock to wait, the sniper rifle cradled over his knee.

Not thirty minutes later, Lovell was back on the air. "Got them in sight. ETA your position about ten minutes." He paused, counting vehicles. "Looks like they added extra security. Three box trucks in the center and eight more vehicles, pickups and vans spread out to the front and rear, loaded with men."

"Must be a helluva big shipment," Sole said. "Trying to make up for their losses."

"Looks like it."

"Alright, I've got to get to work." Sole trotted down the slope and checked each of his attack teams, getting them as ready as he could, warning them to stay with the plan because shit was about to get real. Then he trotted back up the hill to his command position. The scope on the M-24 rifle gave him a good view of the lead vehicle as it came around a bend in the road.

Sole tracked the driver through the scope and waited until it was even with the Sanchez men positioned on the hillside. Taking a shot through the window glass at that range was chancy. Instead of a headshot, he centered the crosshairs on the driver's torso and squeezed the trigger. The round slammed through the upper left side of the man's chest, exited just below his right rib cage, and embedded itself in the arm of the passenger riding beside him.

The passenger howled in pain. The driver died without making a sound, but with his hands clenching the wheel as he toppled over, he pulled the crew cab pickup into a hard right skid that landed it half in the roadside ditch with its tail end in the road.

Sanchez's men began pouring fire into it as the passengers jumped out to take cover behind it and return fire. Instead of trying to drive around it, as in past attacks, the following vehicle braked and closed up with the first to help provide cover. The men inside came out, ready for a fight, searching for targets on the slopes above.

This was no ordinary effort to get fentanyl from a lab to the border. More men, armed and eager to join in the action, emerged from the three box trucks in the center of the formation that should have been loaded with drugs. Sole realized this was a planned counterattack and saw his ambush was becoming a trap.

The return fire from the column of vehicles prevented Sanchez's men from acting as recklessly as usual. Most huddled in their places of concealment, raising their weapons over rocks without aiming, firing a few rounds, and ducking back down.

Espinoza's men returned fire as best they could, but the rate of fire from the men in the box trucks was overpowering. Most hunkered down, taking an occasional shot and then ducking back down again.

Casualties were mounting, and Sole knew he had to do something. He raised the M-24 and began picking off targets. Wherever a *Los Salvajes* head raised to fire up the slope, he squeezed the trigger, and the head disappeared in a misty spray of blood.

The body count among the vehicles below was rising, and as it did, the rate of fire slowed, and Sole's people on the hill began to give a better account of themselves, firing more accurately and making hits of their own.

Sole spotted the *Los Salvajes* gunmen organizing toward the rear of the vehicle column. They had spotted the weak point in the ambush—Cardoso's men—and were organizing an attack to flank them there.

Sole lifted one of the LAW rockets he'd stashed, adjusted the raisable sights for the distance, and waited. The *Los Salvajes* men gathered behind the column's rear vehicle, a large SUV with tinted windows, preparing to rush around Cardoso's men and overpower them. As they started around the end of the SV, Sole pressed the LAW's electronic firing button.

The 66-millimeter rocket covered the hundred and fifty yards to the target in less than a second. The SUV's sides were blown apart, and the gas tank ruptured in a ball of flame.

Several bodies lay scattered in the dirt by the vehicle's rear, taken out by blast and shrapnel. One *Los Salvajes* fighter, doused in gasoline and completely engulfed in flames, came running from behind the wrecked vehicle screaming as he died. Cardoso's men put him out of his misery, sending dozens of rounds into his body.

The LAW rocket broke up the *Los Salvajes* flanking attack. Sole's cartel men took heart, increasing the intensity and accuracy of their firing. The surprise counterattack *Los Salvajes* had attempted by substituting fighters for the drug shipment was backfiring. Their losses increased until bodies were scattered by every vehicle soaking the road in blood.

The intent of this ambush was to seriously weaken *Los Salvajes* as a force among the cartels, and with the battle turning in their favor, Sole's men were succeeding. Then everything changed.

FORTY-ONE

Fuck The Orders

Cuevas was up early, readying the mercenaries for their attack. Unlike Sole, he knew precisely when the drug trucks would be leaving the lab and when to be in position to descend on Sole and the other cartels from behind.

Reynaldo watched as the men checked weapons and gear. They made their preparations quietly, without the strutting and boasting common among the usual cartel men. Killing was their business.

Cuevas gave the hand signal to move out, and the men filed into a crevice-like opening in the hillside where water cascaded down during the rainy season. It was dry now, and using the rocks as handholds, they climbed up the hillside, fanning out along the ridgetop to be in position for the assault over the next ridge.

The line of site distance to the hillside where the cartels waited for the drug shipment was only about half a mile. The actual distance down the slope, across the narrow valley, up the next hill, and then down to the point of attack was closer to two miles.

Soundlessly, the men started down the slope. Reynaldo stayed with Cuevas in the center of the formation. The sun was fully up when they reached the valley and started up the next slope.

Cuevas's timing was perfect. Halfway up the climb, they heard the firing begin on the other side of the hill. As they approached the crest, the sound reached a roaring crescendo punctuated by an explosion. The trucks from the lab were taking a beating.

They topped the ridge to find the rear SUV on the road below shattered and in flames. Bodies lay strewn around it, and more were scattered along the line of vehicles. Reynaldo's plan to use the drug convoy as bait worked. The men from the rival cartels positioned along the hillside were busily engaging the targets below, utterly unaware of the threat approaching them from behind.

Cuevas motioned his men forward, and Diaz and Rocha led their teams silently downslope. Then he began scouting the two possible rocky outcrops he'd identified as the potential command post the *norteamericano* would select.

His eyes on the video feed from the drone orbiting above the action, Lovell spotted the large group of armed men fanning out as they reached the top of the ridge. Sole had just laid down the expended LAW rocket tube when the words crackled in his ear. "You've got company."

"Where?" he said, turning to look up and down the firing line he'd established with his cartel men.

"On your six o'clock. Just starting down from the ridge top."

Sole spun around and immediately picked up the movement, men making their way down, using the brush and rocks as cover to come as close as possible undetected.

Shit! The trap was obvious now. The fake drug convoy was the bait, and Sole had fallen for it. The cartel men below continued to engage the convoy, unaware of the new threat. He had to do something to slow down the men coming down the hill. "Can you see their point of command?"

"Wait one," Lovell said, working the drone's controls, looking for someone who might be in command.

Whoever they were, they were professionals, wearing jungle camo, armed with military-style small arms, and far more disciplined than any of the cartel fighters. The Mexican army, Sole wondered? They'd been known to work with the cartels more than once, but taking sides in a full-scale battle between the cartels was something else.

Mercenaries maybe? That made more sense. He adjusted positions, peering through the scope to find their leader.

Below on the slope, the threat from the trucks on the road had nearly been eliminated. Most of the *Los Salvajes* men were down, dead, or wounded. The survivors were cowering behind their vehicles now, the fight gone from them.

Sanchez's men stood and dashed for the front of the column of vehicles to finish off any survivors. They were cut down as the mercenaries descending the slope behind them opened fire.

Espinoza's men turned to try and engage the men in camo coming down at them from behind. They were the most disciplined of Sole's cartel fighters, but they were no match for the mercenaries. Moving in squad formations, the mercenaries outflanked each cartel position one by one, killing everyone within range.

Cardoso's men saw they were under attack from behind and decided it was time to leave. Most began making their way down the slope toward the road. They were still a few *Los Salvajes* people there able to fight, but the threat from behind was far greater. Making their way to the road, they used the convoy vehicles for cover as they ran toward the next bend around the hillside and where they'd hidden their vehicles. Most were gunned down as they ran. The few who weren't disappeared around the bend and out of the fight.

Lovell was back online. "In the center of their line of advance, a group of four, slightly back at about your eight o'clock. One is giving hand signals to the men along the line. Looks like he might be in charge."

"Roger," Sole said and swung the rifle around, peering through the scope.

It took a moment to identify the leader giving the signals. As Sole sighted the rifle on him, he found the man scanning in his direction with binoculars. The man dropped and pulled another down with him just as Sole squeezed the trigger. The round from the M-24 slammed into a camo-dressed mercenary standing behind. It was a hit, but not the target Sole wanted.

Cuevas had just raised his binoculars to examine the rock outcrop when he dropped to the ground, grabbing Reynaldo by the arm. The heavy crack of a large caliber rifle was followed by a thud and the sound of one of the two men Cuevas brought with him toppling to the ground. The other dove down beside Reynaldo.

Cuevas knew his attack was working. Except for the man with the sniper rifle hidden in the rocks, the mission was nearly completed. "We should end this now," he said to Reynaldo. "Turn all our firepower from every direction onto those rocks, and he will not survive."

They lay in a shallow depression behind a pile of rocks to avoid another round from the sniper rifle. Reynaldo shook his head. "No. He must be captured. This order came from …."

"*¡A la mierda las órdenes!*" Cuevas hissed through gritted teeth. Fuck the orders! "I will not have my men commit suicide so that your *jefa* can torture a man to death. We will kill him, and he will be just as dead. We'll even help you carry his body back to her, but this ends now!"

"No," Reynaldo said and crawled away along the depression, searching for a way to approach the rocky outcrop without being seen.

FORTY-TWO

Failed

Lovell's voice crackled in Sole's ear. "Get out of there, now."

"I can't," Sole said and took a quick glance over his shoulder. "My men are being flanked and killed."

"They're not your goddammed men!" Lovell shouted. "They're killers, and you brought them here to kill and be killed, nothing more. That was the fucking mission!"

It was contrary to everything he'd ever been taught, and to the code he had always lived by. You never leave a comrade on the field. "I put them into this fight, and I'm responsible for …."

"You are not responsible," Lovell said. "I am. Now, get moving!"

Sole ignored him and peered through the rifle scope, searching for the mercenary commander. He could just make out movement in the depression behind the rocks, but not enough to identify a target.

Another voice spoke in his ear. "You must leave now," Valera said calmly, reasoning with him. "I understand your feelings. It is a matter of honor among professionals, but these men have no honor. They are killers."

Sole peered through the scope, searching for a target without replying. Down the slope behind him, the last of his cartel fighters were being systematically eliminated or were running away. In a few minutes, he would be alone on the hill.

"The battle is finished now. We see it all very clearly from the drone," Valera continued. "The men you want to protect have no loyalty to you. They run away, leaving you to die. But there is something else you should remember."

Valera paused, looked at Lovell hunched over the video display, and decided it was time to be blunt. "Men like these killed your family. If they were given the order today, they would murder again ... your family or mine, it makes no difference to them. That you led them in this battle would mean nothing to them. They are not worthy of your sacrifice. Leave now, and we can save lives in the future."

Sole hesitated, lowering his head to the ground. Valera was right. He looked up and said, "One more thing to do."

He reached for the last of the LAW rockets, aimed for the rocks and depression where the mercenary commander had taken cover and depressed the firing trigger. The hill below erupted in a roaring flash and pillar of black smoke.

Sole dropped the LAW rocket tube, picked up the M-24, and retreated along the ridge. The mercenaries below were engaging the last of his cartel fighters. A few, startled by the explosion above them, fired a few rounds in his direction, but it was ineffectual, and Sole scampered over the ridge crest out of range.

He made his way around and down the hill until he came to the small ravine where he and the cartel men had parked their vehicles. He threw the rifle on the SUV's passenger seat, climbed in, and sped down the ravine. A minute later, he fishtailed out onto the main road. He heard the last of the firing echoing around the bend and headed in the opposite direction.

Relieved, Lovell piloted the drone five miles back to their small valley and brought it to a gentle landing between the hills. Without speaking, he and Valera disassembled it and stowed it in its carrying case in the police vehicle.

Valera got behind the wheel and retraced their path to the dirt road they'd followed the day before. He wondered what the unexpected counterattack by the mercenaries meant for the rest of the plan Lovell and Sole had put together.

"Does this end now, or do we finish what you started?" he asked.

"End? You mean give up?" Lovell shook his head. "Hell, no. We finish this ... one way or another."

Stunned by the rocket explosion, Reynaldo lay for several minutes, trying to clear his head and stop the ringing in his ears. Blood dripped into his eyes from cuts made by the rock splinters, and his left knee was dislocated from the blast that tossed him into the air.

He was fortunate. Cuevas and the man with him had taken a direct hit from the rocket. They lay dead, their bodies torn and blackened by the explosion.

The fighting along the road below ended, and the last of the cartel men were either dead or running for their lives. The mercenaries gathered around their fallen leader. Several laid what was left of Cuevas on a rain tarp and carried him up the slope.

Cuevas's second in command, Diaz, stood over Reynaldo and put a hand out. "Here, I'll help you up."

After that, Reynaldo was on his own, following behind, up the hill, down the slope, and up the next, until they reached where they had started that morning. When he got to the vehicles, Cuevas's body had been placed in the back of a truck. The mercenaries stood waiting expectantly.

He knew what they wanted, but Diaz made it clear anyway. "The second half of our fee was to be paid when the mission was completed."

"If it was successful," Reynaldo said. "We did not capture the one I wanted."

"It was successful. Your enemies have been killed, and our commander is dead. The capture of the man was not part of the original contract, yet Cuevas died trying to help you," Diaz said, the look in his eyes a warning that they would have their payment one way or another.

He was outnumbered, outgunned, and the truth was, Diaz was right. The trap had been successful, and only Juana Elizondo's last-minute insistence that he bring Sole to her alive made this anything but a complete success.

Reynaldo nodded, took out his phone, and called a bank in Mexico City. He spoke quietly for a minute, then disconnected and turned to Diaz. "The money is being wired to your bank in Nicaragua. You can check it now."

Diaz took out his phone and punched in a number to access the bank account. It took a few minutes to receive verification that the transfer was being processed, then he nodded and stared hard into Reynaldo's eyes. "You understand that if anything delays or stops the transfer of funds, we will return and collect the money we are owed."

Reynaldo nodded. He understood completely.

"Good." Diaz looked at his men. "*Vamos.* Our work is done."

Reynaldo was left alone, the dust from their trucks settling around him. He thought of what he would say to Juana, how to explain what had happened, then remembered the look in her eye when she told him to bring Sole to her … alive.

Cuevas's trap had nearly exterminated their cartel enemies, but he knew how she would take the news that he had not captured Sole. He had failed.

FORTY-THREE

A Sobering Thought

"There is news." Miguel Espinoza said as he stepped into the tiled, glass-windowed room overlooking the garden.

His brother, Seve, looked up from the book in his lap—a signed first edition of Octavio Paz's *Labyrinth of Solitude*—closed it and said, "I can see by the look on your face that it is not good news."

"It is not," Miguel said. "We have lost people."

"Lost?" Seve frowned and nodded to his housekeeper. "Camila, please take the children to play outside while I speak with my brother."

"*Sí*." The grandmotherly woman, who had been with the household for almost thirty years, called to the children scampering around the room, playing a robust game of *robar el sombrero*—stealing the sombrero. "*Niños*, let's play in the garden."

Camila opened the door and waved her arm as if sweeping them out of the room. The children laughed and ran out. The last to go was Seve's youngest granddaughter, who came to him and kissed his cheek before leaving. Seve smiled and gave the little one a pat on the head, and Camila closed the door gently as the girl followed her siblings out to the garden.

Seve looked at his brother, and the smile faded. "Tell me your news."

"There was an attack."

"Yes, I know," Seve said. "You mean the grand attack the *norteamericano* planned to deal a death blow to *Los Salvajes*."

"Not exactly," Miguel said. "It seems it was a trap. During the attack, our men were surprised taken from behind, and many ... most were killed."

"Tell me everything ... all the details."

Miguel spent several minutes explaining how the surprise attack unfolded. When he finished, Seve's brow furrowed. "They took our men from behind? That means they knew that we would attack their drug shipment that day, and they were ready for us, concealed somewhere nearby."

"It seems so." Miguel nodded.

"Then, there is a traitor among us."

"Yes, but I don't think it was one of ours," Miguel said. "Our men are all accounted for ... a few survivors and the others all dead."

"One of Sanchez's or Cardoso's, then," Seve said quietly, staring out the window, considering what this news might mean. Finally, he nodded and turned to Miguel. "It may be time to bring things to an end."

"In what way?"

"You say those who attacked our men looked like they might be from the army."

"They wore the type of clothes that resembled army

uniforms." Miguel shook his head. "But the army has never openly taken sides in a battle among the cartels."

"Paid for by *Los Salvajes* ... a private army of some sort."

"Yes," Miguel said. "But not part of the cartel ... mercenaries. They acted independently of the *Los Salvajes* men and vehicles, under different leadership, and took no care to avoid shooting into the drug convoy as they attacked our people from behind. Our survivors say they were killing everyone."

"*Los Salvajes* baited us with their own people, sacrificed them to kill ours." Seve shook his head. "It seems a very cold plan even for Juana Elizondo."

He thought for a minute and added, "This may work to our advantage in the long run. They are weak now. That's why they brought in the mercenaries."

"It's true. We have been hurting them." Miguel shrugged. "But money buys men and loyalty, and it won't take them long to recover."

"That's why we can't give them time to recover, and at the same time, we must prepare for what is to come when they are no longer a threat."

"The other cartels?" Miguel said.

"Yes." Seve nodded. "They are no doubt making plans, forming alliances at this moment to move against us when they no longer need us to fight *Los Salvajes*."

They were quiet for a moment, Seve thinking, Miguel watching and waiting. Seve looked up and, almost as an afterthought, asked, "And the *norteamericano*?"

"Missing." Miguel shook his head. "His body was not recovered."

"Missing? Could he have been part of the *Los Salvajes* plan?"

"It is possible but doesn't seem likely. Our survivors say

that he was personally attacked by these mercenaries and had to defend himself with a rocket."

"Then where is he?"

Several hundred miles away, in the hills of Michoacán, an out-of-place, bright red SUV pulled through the weeds and brush to the front of a deserted farmhouse almost entirely covered by overgrown trees and vines. Lovell and Valera came outside as Sole climbed out, stretched, and dusted himself off.

"Beginning to get worried about you," Lovell said.

"Me too," Sole nodded. "It was close today. I thought they had us."

"Too close," Lovell agreed. "But it may have worked to our advantage."

"Advantage?" Sole grimaced. "Those mercenaries cut our people down. They never had a chance."

"I know from your perspective … in the middle of the battle … it must seem like a setback," Lovell said. "The truth is once we dealt with *Los Salvajes*, we were going to turn the cartels on each other anyway. Those mercenaries just accelerated our timetable, that's all."

"Could you see from above if there were any survivors?" Sole asked, nodding at Valera's SUV, where the drone was safely stored away.

"A few … mostly Cardoso's men, and some from Sanchez's group in the front. Espinoza's people in the center were hit hard by the counterattack." Lovell shrugged. "A couple got away … we think."

"So, where are we in the mission?" Sole asked. "You still committed?"

"More than ever," Lovell said. "*Los Salvajes* lost a lot of people today, and they're weak ... for a while at least. Now is the time to wrap it up before they recover."

"Good." Sole nodded. "Now I have a question."

"Shoot."

"Got any food?"

"Yep. Enrique here whipped us up a batch of canned frijoles heated over a Sterno can." He grinned. "We were waiting on dinner for you."

"Sounds good. Haven't eaten anything since yesterday."

They went into the farmhouse and sat on the floor eating beans from cans while they debriefed each other on what they saw during the battle on the hillside. When the meal and after-action reports were taken in and digested. Sole looked at Lovell and nodded at Valera. "Does he know?"

"Not yet," Lovell said. "There wasn't time before."

"Tell him," Sole said. "He has a right to know before we finish this."

"Our mission was canceled," Lovell said frankly. He turned to Valera and reviewed the details from Carl Shank's call. "You have a right to know, Enrique, before you get involved in the next part of the mission."

Valera listened quietly, then looked at their faces in the glow of the Sterno flames and said, "Thank you for telling me this. It seems you have staked everything on this mission." He nodded. "I can do no less."

That was the end of the discussion.

The truth was that Valera was risking far more than either of them. Sole and Lovell might lose their careers, future, and possibly, their lives. Valera could lose all of that and his family as well, but he was committed to their plan, willing to risk everything precisely because he loved his family and wanted a different future for them. It was a sobering thought.

FORTY-FOUR

Bad News

The mercenaries had been gone for more than an hour by the time Reynaldo Gutierrez made his way out of the ravine to open ground where the helicopter could land. Diaz and Rocha had loaded Cuevas's body and their men into the trucks that brought them and departed without a salute or word of thanks. The contract fulfilled, and their business arrangement with *Los Salvajes* completed; there was nothing further to discuss.

Gritting through the pain from his injured knee, Reynaldo climbed a good distance up a hillside slope to get a signal on his phone and call for the helicopter to return. After that, he waited alone without the customary security men surrounding him, and now, minus the mercenaries, he was completely vulnerable. Had the other cartels known, they would have gone to great lengths to find and kill Juana Elizondo's chief lieutenant. Fortunately for Reynaldo, those who had survived the mercenaries' attack were running for their lives.

In any event, he wasn't alone for long. The helicopter

arrived, and several armed men jumped out, forming a protective circle around their *jefe*. Stunned by his physical appearance, they exchanged stares as he hobbled aboard the helicopter, then climbed in behind. A minute later, the helicopter lifted off.

The flight back to the Elizondo estate's airfield was short. Within an hour, he had been driven back to the hacienda and stood in his customary place before Juana Elizondo's desk.

She began without preliminaries. "I take it from your appearance that your plan was unsuccessful."

His face scarred, covered in dried blood from the close rocket blast, and swaying on his injured leg to maintain his balance, Reynaldo nodded. "It was not completely successful."

"Explain," Juana snapped.

"We killed many of their men. They attacked our drug shipment as expected and were surprised by the mercenaries from behind."

"And John Sole?"

"He managed to escape." Reynaldo shook his head. "We spotted his position on the hillside and were approaching it, but he must have seen us coming and fired a rocket at us. Cuevas was killed, and, with their leader gone, the mercenaries ended the attack."

"Ended?" Juana frowned. "You did nothing else to capture him?"

"I tried." Reynaldo looked at the floor, avoiding the disappointment in her eyes, and something else … anger. "I was injured by the rocket's explosion and could not reach his position before he escaped."

"Our losses?" she asked without inquiring about his injuries.

"The truck convoy was hit hard by their attack. Nearly all of our men there were killed or wounded."

"You told me that was expected," Juana threw in. "But we would still have the mercenaries. That was your plan. With them, we would move on what remains of the other cartels."

Reynaldo raised his head, prepared to take the full brunt of her ire. Looking into her eyes, he shook his head and said, "With Cuevas dead, they are gone."

"Gone." Juana's voice rose. "How can that be? We paid them!"

"Yes, but they believe they fulfilled their contract." He shook his head. "Now they have moved on."

"That was not the plan!"

"No, but …"

"But what?" Juana was shouting now. "Speak frankly!"

"They feel that the order to capture John Sole alive was a last-minute change, not part of the contract, and that was why they lost Cuevas." Reynaldo gave a weary shrug, knowing his explanation would not satisfy her. "That is their belief, at least."

"So, they are blaming us … me … for his death?" Juana was incredulous. "They fight for money … kill people for money … and when they lose one of their own, they quit?"

"Not just one of their own," Reynaldo said, trying to explain. "Cuevas, their leader, the man they trusted and followed."

"They were paid to follow us!"

There was no point arguing. Reynaldo shrugged. "In any event, they are gone."

"Where does that leave us?" she asked.

"Weak. Most of our best fighters were on the road in the

trucks. A few were left behind for security here, but not many."

Juana leaned back in her chair, trying to take in the enormity of the bad news. Sinking into the oversized leather cushions, she looked for a moment like the little girl Reynaldo had been assigned to protect so many years earlier. Then she leaned forward, and she was no longer the little girl.

Her face a stone mask, Juana said, "You say we hurt the other cartels badly."

"Yes." Reynaldo nodded.

"Then we must recruit now while they are weak." She slammed a fist down on the desk. "We will strike again soon before they have time to recover." She looked at Reynaldo. "Start now. Find us men ... fighters ... killers. Pay whatever we have to, but start now rebuilding our strength."

"*Sí, jefa,*" Reynaldo said and turned to leave, knowing that this time there would be no invitation to visit her that night or any other.

FORTY-FIVE

A New War

"We should meet." Anselmo Cardoso held the phone away from his ear and braced himself for the response he knew would come.

"Fuck you and your meetings!" Chucho Sanchez shouted into the phone. "Your men ran from the attack while mine stayed and fought ... and died."

"Mine died as well," Cardoso said. "If I had more survivors, it is because the gringo placed them at the other end of the line of vehicles. They had more time to see what was happening and to escape to fight another day."

"Hah! Fight?" Sanchez sneered. "They ran like frightened girls. My men told me ... the ones who got away."

"You are angry," Cardoso persisted. "That's understandable. I am also angry, but there are things we must discuss and plans to make, and it should be done face-to-face."

"To hell with your face-to-face bullshit. If we meet, it will be *mano a mano*, hand to hand, like two matadors in the ring, except I am no bullfighter. I am the bull, and after I run my horns through your gut, I'll trample you and shit on your face."

The imagery was classic Sanchez, coarse and full of bluster, anger, and insecurity wrapped up in his machismo façade. Cardoso waited for him to pause and take a breath, then said simply, "We must meet and discuss what we should do next … together … or we will be dead in a month."

"You threaten me!" Sanchez's voice rose a couple of decibels.

"Were you listening?" Cardoso asked. "I said *WE* will be dead."

"And how is this great massacre going to happen?" Sanchez sneered. "*Los Salvajes* was hurt worse than either of us in the attack."

"Chucho, do you believe that Espinoza is going to wait for us to become stronger before he decides to eliminate us?"

Sanchez made no response. Cardoso imagined the puzzled look on his face as he tried to get his feeble brainpower around what he was proposing.

"It was what we all knew would happen once *Los Salvajes* was finished," Cardoso prompted.

"You mean a new war," Sanchez said without shouting this time.

"Yes," Cardoso said. "And a different enemy."

"Espinoza," Sanchez muttered.

"Yes, Espinoza. We form an alliance … a permanent business arrangement. Together we eliminate him before he does the same to us one at a time."

"And *Los Salvajes*?" Sanchez asked.

"They are weak now. Despite our losses, we hurt them badly in the attack on their drug shipment."

"They still have the army helping them," Sanchez said. "My men who survived saw them."

"Not army. I have a contact with the Mexican army, and no army units were engaged with *Los Salvajes* against our people."

"You trust your contact over what my men saw with their own eyes," Sanchez snarled.

"My men saw them too," Cardoso said patiently. "They were mercenaries."

"Mercenaries? And you know this, how?" Sanchez asked. "Because your contact sitting in an office in Mexico City said so?"

"No, because I have spoken to the mercenaries myself."

"You spoke with them?" Sanchez paused, trying to put it all together in his mind. "You're full of shit. If they are paid by that bitch Juana Elizondo to fight for *Los Salvajes*, why would they speak to you?"

"They *were* paid by Elizondo," Cardoso said and wanted to add, dumbass. "They work for whoever is willing to pay now, and I told them we would be willing to pay."

A few seconds passed before Sanchez said, "Alright. We should meet."

"Good!" Cardoso beamed. "I knew we could reason together. Where would you like to meet? It should be soon before Espinoza makes plans of his own."

"Tomorrow at my ranch in Guadalajara. I'll be there all day."

"Excellent! I'll fly in and see you tomorrow. Then, we can finalize our move against Espinoza. I'll bring the mercenary commander with me so you can meet him and see that I am not full of shit."

The call ended, and Cardoso turned to the two men seated in chairs across from his desk. "You heard?"

"Yes." Diaz, the new mercenary commander, nodded.

"Good. He will be there all day. I'll give you the location of his ranch. I want you there tomorrow."

"We'll be there," Diaz said.

Cardoso's source with the Mexican army knew the military had not participated in the attack on behalf of *Los Salvajes* because he supplemented his army income working as a broker for a certain mercenary group. When their leader was killed, his second-in-command took their pay and looked for other work. Bitter about the loss of Cuevas, the new mercenary leader made it clear that if the work involved eliminating Juana Elizondo, all the better.

His source put Cardoso in contact with Diaz, who listened to his proposal, stipulating that eliminating Juana Elizondo be included in his plans. Cardoso had smiled and agreed without hesitation.

Now, he looked at Diaz and said, "Sanchez is the first. Cut the head off of that snake. Eliminate him and everyone at his ranch."

"Everyone?" Diaz's brow furrowed.

"Everyone," Cardoso said. "Does this trouble you?"

"Trouble?" Diaz shook his head. "No. I only want to be sure about what is expected."

"Then I'll make it clearer. I want them all dead," Cardoso said. "No baby snakes left behind to grow up and bite me in the ass later when I'm not looking."

"As you wish," Diaz said, nodding and added, "And then we go after Elizondo." It was clear from the look in his eyes that taking her out was at the top of his list of people to eliminate.

"Yes, but first, while she and *Los Salvajes* remain weakened, we take out the more immediate threat ... Espinoza.." Cardoso caught the frown that flashed across the mercenary's face and added, "Trust me, you will get your pound of flesh from Elizondo. I want her gone as much ... more even ... than you, but it is only good military tactics to eliminate threats from behind before we face the enemy in front." He smiled. "You and your men taught me that recently. Do we have an agreement then?"

Diaz nodded. "Agreed."

FORTY-SIX

Things Became Desperate

"I was careless," Sole said, reviewing the previous day's attack on the drug convoy. "I can't let that happen again."

"No plan is perfect," Lovell said. "What is it you military types say? A battle plan is only good until the bullets start flying."

"Actually, the quote is, no plan survives contact with the enemy." Sole replied and added with a wry smirk, "Erwin Rommel said it … a German general. They lost the war."

"Things worked out to our advantage," Valera said.

Sole laughed. "I admire your sense of having the advantage."

After a night on the floor in sleeping bags, followed by another meal of canned beans, they were ready to see things through to the end. They stood around the hood of Sole's car, reviewing the next stage of the plan to bring down *Los Salvajes*. Each had a role to play, but the final act would be Valera's, and if they succeeded, the other cartels would fall like a row of dominoes.

"Are your people ready?" Lovell asked.

"Ready," Valera said with a somber nod.

"Then let's do it," Sole said. "The longer we wait, the more time they have to recover, and the harder this will be."

He and Lovell transferred the drone and assorted gear from Valera's police SUV to Sole's car. When they finished, they exchanged a final handshake with Valera, wished him luck, and left the deserted farmhouse.

Valera was alone for the time being. Lovell rode with Sole. When they reached the main highway to the west, they separated. The drive across the Mexican state of Michoacán to Lázaro Cárdenas would take Valera almost four hours. Taking backroads to avoid being spotted with Valera, Sole and Lovell would be on the road a good six hours. They were scheduled to go into action in the late afternoon.

After reporting the bad news to Juana Elizondo, Reynaldo spent the night and the next day in the small office in the building on the hillside making calls, reaching out to all of his sources, offering exorbitant sums of money for fighters … for killers. Juana made it clear she was determined to move against the other cartels before they could recover and do the same to *Los Salvajes*.

He finished a call to a contact in Tijuana and disconnected, frowning. He was offering bonus money to Mexican ex-pats living in the United States if they would come to Lázaro Cárdenas and become part of his rejuvenated fighting force, but the takers were few and far between. Competition for fighters was stiff. The other cartels were already recruiting men to fill their losses.

It was midafternoon when there was a tap at the door. He looked up, "Yes?"

A nurse had come to cover his face with an assortment of mismatched and odd-sized band-aids and gauze patches to protect the shrapnel wounds he'd sustained from the rocket. The result was almost cartoonish, something from a comic book, but the man at his door did not laugh.

"She wants to see you." He was barely a man, not more than eighteen carrying an old Czech military surplus AK-47.

"Alright." Reynaldo nodded. There was no need to ask who 'she' was. There was only one who would give him an order. He stood and winced as he put weight on his injured knee. The brace the nurse had given him helped, but just barely.

Reynaldo followed the young man out and across the lawn toward the residence. He was one of five men kept back to provide security at the hacienda, all of them the youngest and least experienced. A dozen others were off scouring surrounding towns and cities for recruits.

When they reached the stairs to the hacienda's veranda, the security man took up position on the grass. He held his rifle in a way that he thought made him look professional and combat-ready and put a stern scowl on his face to show that he was entrusted with the security of *La Jefa*. Reynaldo mounted the veranda stairs carefully and went through the side door directly into Juana's office.

She looked up as he entered and asked bluntly, "How many have you recruited?"

"A few," Reynaldo said.

"A few?" Juana snapped. "We will require more than a few."

"It's a beginning, *jefa*. More will come over to us."

"When?"

"I am working on that." He hesitated, not willing just yet to give her the truly bad news that most of the possible recruits were signing on with other cartels against *Los Salvajes*.

"That does not answer my question." She watched his face for a few moments, standing speechless in front of her, then shook her head in disgust. "Get out. Thanks to you, I have to make preparations to get my family safely away."

"And you?" Reynaldo said, a look of concern on his face. "You should leave as well. I will stay behind and see to the …."

"You? See to what?" Juana sneered. "You have not shown much ability to see to anything. All that your great planning has done is put us all at risk. Now get out."

Reynaldo turned and left without looking back. He had lost her trust and wondered if he had ever had it.

Juana watched him leave without speaking, feeling no regret for abusing the man who had been at her side since her childhood. There was no time for regret. Besides, Reynaldo was nothing more than a bodyguard her father had assigned her to keep the boys away.

She knew that was the difference. Her father had Alejandro Garza beside him, a strong man, fearsome to his enemies, and loyal to the Elizondo family. She needed someone like the man she had called Uncle Alejandro, but he was dead, killed by this same man, John Sole, who had helped the cartels fight them.

Instead, she had Reynaldo, but she required more. She had picked him as her lieutenant because there were no others like Garza and because his feelings for her made him easy to control. It was a lesson learned.

Once this crisis was behind them, there would be time

to replace Reynaldo. For now, she had to get her mother and siblings safely away from the hacienda and make sure she had an escape route if things became desperate.

She lifted the phone to call the pilots standing by at the airstrip when the first shot echoed over the hacienda lawn, and things did become desperate.

FORTY-SEVEN

Redemption
_____

While Sole and Lovell took the back roads, Enrique Valera wound his police SUV through the small streets and alleys in a village on the outskirts of Lázaro Cárdenas. Locals regarded the police vehicle from Reynosa in the state of Tamaulipas with a mixture of curiosity and caution.

Reynosa, on the border with the United States, was a sixteen-hour drive away from Mexico's southwest Pacific coast. Seeing a state police vehicle so far out of its jurisdiction naturally aroused their interest and drew stares, but only for a moment before caution veiled their eyes, and they turned their heads away. The cartels paid police from many parts of the country for protection. It was better for everyone to just turn away and not ask questions.

Valera pulled the SUV to a stop beside a van in a back alley and got out. Six men dressed in black BDUs—battle dress uniforms—and tactical vests stood waiting for him. All were armed with pistols and Mexican FX-05 assault rifles. The word *Policíca* was embroidered on the back of their BDUs.

Valera had carefully chosen them to be part of the plan's final phase to take down *Los Salvajes*. Out of the hundreds of police officers he knew, he had narrowed his selections down to these six.

It was not that all of the others were corrupt. Many were honest, but what he asked of them was highly dangerous, had a chance of backfiring completely, and could put their families at risk if their identities were ever discovered. Only the most dedicated could be trusted to see it through.

Valera walked up, and a muscular lieutenant with a steel-like grip shook his hand. He was known by the other officers as *El Brazo*—The Arm. Valera took his hand, winced as Brazo squeezed, and then gave each of the others a formal shake and word of thanks for coming.

"So, when does this grand show begin?" Brazo said, grinning.

"Soon, my friend, soon." Valera looked up the line of men willing to risk so much. "Do you have any questions or doubts about what we are doing? Do you understand what we are going to do?"

He asked the questions as a formality, their last chance to withdraw with honor. They nodded without speaking, and it was enough to show they understood and were committed. They'd been fully briefed. The time for questions and doubts had passed.

"Good. Then we should be going. From this moment on, we are operational." He pointed to the hoods tucked into their belts. "All faces must be covered so no one can identify you."

"Seems such a shame to cover a face as fine as mine," Brazo said, his gap-toothed grin spreading wide.

The others laughed but pulled the hoods over their faces

so that only their eyes and mouths showed. Brazo stood smiling at Valera.

"You too," Valera said.

"I see that you wear no mask," Brazo said. "Why should I? What if I want these assholes to see my face as I take them down?"

"I wear no mask because my role in this is different. We discussed this already." Valera nodded at the mask still tucked under his belt. "Put it on or stay here."

"As you wish *mi Comandante*." Brazo pulled the mask over his large head and added, "But I do this under protest."

"So noted," Valera said, smiling. "Now, let's move. We have to meet others with a special interest in this operation."

"Your friends from north of the border?" Brazo asked.

"No. This is our operation now. The *norteamericanos* will be in a support role only," Valera said. "But there are *paisanos*, our countrymen, who have a vested interest in what we are about to do."

"*Paisanos*, huh?" Brazo nodded. "Can they shoot?"

"In a manner of speaking, yes." Valera motioned to their van. "Enough talking here. Load up, and you'll meet them soon enough."

With Valera leading the way in the SUV, they wound through the village streets and back to the main highway into Lázaro Cárdenas.

"How we looking?" Sole said just loud enough for the earbud's microphone to pick him up.

"Looking good," Lovell replied instantly, huddled over the video display while adjusting the drone's controls to gain more altitude and keep the cameras focused on the target below—the Elizondo hacienda grounds.

"Any activity?"

"All quiet. I count four bad guys in view. Two front and two rear. Probably more inside the main house and the outbuilding."

"Roger." Concealed in a clump of low brush on an adjacent hillside, Sole peered through the M-24's scope and began identifying targets. "Status from Valera?" he whispered.

"He was on his way with our visitors thirty ago," Lovell said. "Should be here any time now."

Valera's voice crackled over the communications net. "Coming up with you now. Standing by around a bend three hundred meters from the entrance."

"Alright, then," Lovell said softly. "Let the show begin."

Peering through the scope, Sole searched for his first target. A man exited the main building, descended the steps, and began limping across the grounds toward the outbuilding on the hillside. One of the guards in the yard armed with an assault rifle joined him as he walked.

Valera's SUV and the police van roared around the bend and onto the hacienda grounds. The startled young guard beside the limping man turned and raised his rifle.

"Target identified," Sole said quietly, then took a breath, released it slowly, and squeezed the trigger. The rifle thundered, and the guard crumpled in his tracks less than a second later. "Target down," Sole said and swung the M-24 to find another target.

The man limping across the lawn began a hobbling trot back to the hacienda. He appeared unarmed, and Sole let him go, searching for a more threatening target.

Another man ran around the side of the main house,

raising his rifle. A second later, he lay sprawled on the ground fifty yards from the first. "Two down," Sole said.

"Standby while my men approach the residence," Valera called out.

"We've got more targets unaccounted for," Lovell shot back. "You should hold your position until we have a chance to eliminate them.

"No," Valera said firmly. "This is our operation now. You have done your part. Let us know of any threats, but it is time for us to act officially."

"He's right," Sole said. "It's his show." He stood and began making his way down the hillside.

Lovell picked the movement up on the video and asked, "Where the hell are you going?"

"Backup," Sole said. "They might need it, and once they get inside, I'm no help from out here."

"Shit," Lovell growled. "My ass is already hanging out on this op. If anything happens to you …."

"We started this," Sole said, moving down the hillside toward the hacienda. "Let's finish it."

At the sound of the first shot, Juana Elizondo dropped the phone on her desk and ran to the veranda window. She'd been about to arrange a flight to send her family away to safety, but she'd waited too long. One man was sprawled on the ground in a pool of blood. Reynaldo was coming back toward her as fast as his injured leg would allow.

Another shot cracked in the distance. Reynaldo made it onto the veranda and rushed inside, pushing her back from the windows.

"Come with me!" he shouted, pulling her by the arm.

"My mother ... the children! Protect them!" She tried to pull her arm free, but Reynaldo held tight, disobeying an order for the first time.

"The people outside are coming for you, not your family. Send your mother to the safe room with the children. The walls are armored and will protect them, but you must leave now before it is too late."

One of the young guards stationed in the back came running through from the courtyard and shouted the obvious in a state of panic, "*Jefe*, we are under attack!"

"Take the family to the safe room and stay inside with them. No one comes in. Understand?"

"*Sí, jefe.*" The guard ran through the house shouting for Juana's mother and siblings to follow him to the safe room.

"I'll go to the safe room with them," Juana said as Reynaldo pulled her through the house.

"No." He shook his head without breaking stride.

She dug in her heels, trying to pull away, and he grabbed her by the shoulder, spinning her around. "If the other cartels find you, they will kill you. I will not let that happen. I may have failed in many ways, but not that."

"I'm not leaving my family."

He looked into her eyes, speaking earnestly. "You must get away from here to someplace safe ... someplace where you can lead us, direct what is happening, fight back. You can't do that if you're helpless, locked inside the safe room."

A second passed, and she blinked without moving.

"Juana, it is what your father would have wanted," Reynaldo said, his eyes pleading with her to let him save her.

She nodded. "Alright."

Reynaldo moved toward the doors leading to the rear garden, a firm grip on her arm pulling her behind him.

They crossed the tiled terrace, passed the pool and gardens, and moved as rapidly as Reynaldo's injured leg allowed toward the edge of the lawn. A path there ascended into the hills.

She moved more briskly now, coming even with Reynaldo, then moving ahead. Her father had the path cut into the hill as an emergency escape route. On the other side of the crest, it descended for a little over a mile to the airstrip. If she could reach it, she would have one of the pilots take her away to someplace safe, someplace where she could reorganize and mount a counterattack against those who dared invade her home.

She looked over her shoulder. Reynaldo was dropping behind, limping badly on his injured leg.

"Go," he said. "Get to the airfield. I'll catch up if I can."

Juana required no urging. She was already putting distance between her and Reynaldo and the people attacking the hacienda.

Valera's SUV roared around the bend in the road and across the lawn directly toward the hacienda's veranda. He braked hard, digging up the turf, and bolted from the vehicle, his pistol drawn, bolting up the steps to take up position along the wall beside a window.

The van followed but went wider, staying on the drive leading to the front door. Brazo led the police officers out as it braked to a stop. They fanned out, trotting toward the house in assault formation. Exposed in the open, they moved quickly to follow Valera's example and station themselves along the exterior walls near the windows and door.

A shot rang out, and stucco and plaster flew off the side of the house. Brazo spun to find a man running, spraying bullets without aiming as he ran. Brazo and two other police officers raised their FX-05s and fired three short bursts. The man tumbled forward as he ran, his finger frozen on the trigger, spraying more bullets harmlessly into the ground as he died.

With his men in position, Valera entered the hacienda residence. Moving room to room, they searched for the occupants, finding none. They worked toward the rear of the house, where Valera peered through a window and spotted an armed man crouching behind the outdoor bar near the pool.

"I'll take care of him," Brazo said, coming up to stand behind Valera and look out the window.

"He's just a boy," Valera said. "Take him alive if you can."

"If we can." Brazo nodded.

Brazo went to a door leading to the terrace while two of his men came through French doors on the opposite side. He called out to the young guard left behind to defend the Elizondo estate, "Boy, we are the police! Throw down your weapon, and you will not be harmed."

"Police!" the young man shouted back, trying to sound brave but with a tremor in his voice. "What does that mean … police? We pay the police to kill for us. Now, someone has paid you to kill us!"

"Not this time," Brazo said. "We are here to arrest you. Throw down your weapon, and you will not be harmed. You have my word."

"Your word! You are going to kill me like the others!" He lifted the AK-47 above the bar and sprayed bullets wildly across the terrace.

Brazo nodded at his men. They opened fire on the bar sending thirty rounds each through the plaster and tile. The young man was silent after that. Brazo's men found him badly wounded, lying in a pool of blood, but alive ... barely.

Valera came up beside Brazo. "There will be a safe room somewhere. Find it, and we may find what we are looking for."

"I've got movement," Lovell said into the earbud mic.

"Where?" Sole asked, making his way down to the edge of the hacienda's lawn from his position on the hillside.

Lovell checked the video feed, spotted Sole moving out onto the grass, and said, "Your two o'clock ... behind the main residence heading across the lawn to the hills. Two people. One looks like he's limping. The other ..." He paused and peered closely at the viewer. "The other appears to be female. Could be our target."

"Roger." Sole was running now, the M-24 held down at his side.

Shots rang out as he came around the side of the hacienda, Valera's men taking out the guard by the pool. He cut across the rear lawn, focused on the two people running for the hill at the rear of the property.

They were nearly at the hillside by the time he closed the distance to fifty yards. He stopped, threw the rifle to his shoulder, and called out, "Stop ... *Alto, policía!*"

The man in the rear limped badly and was slower than the woman in front. Sole had no idea who he was, but it was the woman he wanted. He called out again, "Juana Elizondo! *Alto, policía!*"

The limping man spun, raising a pistol. Sole squeezed the trigger and sent one round through his head.

Juana saw the blood spray from the back of Reynaldo's head. Wide-eyed, she watched him topple to the ground. Her defender to the last, Reynaldo was gone, and, for once, she felt the fear that others had felt when she ordered their deaths.

Sole advanced, the rifle at his shoulder aimed squarely at her head. It was the moment. After years of playing the game of cat and mouse with *Los Salvajes*, everything had come down to this exact instant in time. She was helpless, frozen, unable to escape and outrun the bullets he would shoot into her.

He had wondered what it would be like, to pull the trigger and bring it all to an end. There was nothing to stop him. Three pounds of pressure on the trigger, and it would be over.

"What are you waiting for?" Juana said, the tremble in her voice contradicting the stoic front she was trying to show. She studied his face for a second, then her eyes widened in real fear. "You're him, the one in the shadows making war on us. You use the others like the fools they are. I know your face."

He nodded. Juana held her breath, wondering what it would be like when the bullet plowed through her brain.

Sole saw the emotions, the fear, and the anticipation flash across her face but did not squeeze the trigger. Another face floated before him, one that he had pushed deep down in his memory. Shaye smiled at him, her face as beautiful as ever, watching and waiting. Behind her, Samantha and Bobby came into view, laughing and looking on curiously, waiting to see what Dad would do.

Sole sighed in relief as if a great burden had been removed from him. He shook his head and said, "No."

No, for his wife, his children, for everyone who had ever trusted him. In a life full of pain and blood, he chose not to kill. It was a moment of redemption for John Sole.

Footsteps approached at a run from behind. Valera's voice called out as he strode past Sole, "Juana Elizondo, you are under arrest."

He began citing the list of charges while one of his men handcuffed her. It was a long list, and Sole struggled to follow in Spanish. He wandered away toward the terrace by the pool and sat on the step, drained.

"You look tired, buddy." It was Lovell's voice in his ear.

Sole looked up, trying to spot the drone but couldn't. He leaned back on the stone pavers, feeling them warm and soothing under his back. "I am tired," he said.

"Looks like Valera has everything under control," Lovell said. "I'll bring the bird in, pack it up, and come get you. We've got some other business to tend to."

"I'll be here," Sole said, and under the warm sun, as Valera's men bustled around him, he closed his eyes and slept.

FORTY-EIGHT

Same Devil...Different Day

Lovell arrived at the hacienda at the same time as Valera's *paisano* visitors. Escorted to the Elizondo estate by Valera and his men, the news crews unpacked their gear, readied their cameras, and began shooting video, documenting everything they saw. Bodies on the ground, the opulence of the hacienda, Juana Elizondo being led away in handcuffs, all of it captured and flashed within minutes over the Mexican media outlets as an exclusive breaking news report.

Arranging the media event burned more than a few favors from Lovell's media contacts made during his service in Mexico. As part of his clandestine duties, he'd been feeding stories to the media for years when it suited U.S. interests, but this was the biggest of all. Not all of them could be convinced to show up, but two of the smaller Mexican media outlets agreed to send teams to cover the event on condition that the police comandante leading the raid would protect them.

Their concerns were valid, and showing up at all with

their cameras demonstrated a significant level of personal courage. More than one Mexican news reporter had been murdered for daring to cover the cartel underpinnings of Mexican society.

It didn't hurt that Lovell also assured them their coverage would make it to television screens in the United States. For journalists who spent their lives trying to find the 'big story' in a country where corruption was rampant at all levels, the sudden promise of exposure to the mega news networks in the U.S. was irresistible.

Arranging the U.S. exposure used up more goodwill from Lovell's contacts north of the border. He figured it didn't matter. With his career already at risk, and probably gone for good, he had nothing to lose. He was all in. If his gamble didn't pay off, he was going down big.

The sun was setting as he pulled the SUV onto the hacienda grounds. Valera stood in the glare of the camera lights on the front veranda near the door into Juana Elizondo's office. Reporters from the two Mexican networks that dared show up asked him questions and took down the details of the operation.

Lovell made his way around to the back and found Sole still stretched out on the terrace. "Time to get you out of here."

"I suppose so." Sole sat up, stretching. "How are things going?"

"Pretty much like we planned." Lovell chuckled and shook his head. "The local police don't know whether to shit themselves or join the party."

More police had shown up, and Valera's team, led by *El Brazo*, stood facing them and telling them to back away. Without knowing what was happening and who was behind the raid, the local police gathered at the edge of the property, waiting for further instructions. Unfortunately, their local commanders were just as confused as they were about the raid on the home of the most powerful cartel boss in Mexico.

Who would dare do such a thing? And if they dared, who was behind it? It had to be someone powerful, so the police hunkered down without taking action, waiting for someone else to decide what to do next.

"Good." Sole nodded and stood. "Valera's okay?"

"Doing fine, and he's got a big son of a bitch in black BDUs name of Brazo watching his back. Nobody's going to fuck with him, and if we can get him enough exposure, it might make the other cartels think twice about going after him."

"That's a pretty big if," Sole said.

"It is," Lovell agreed. "I need to get working on it."

They made their way to the front and climbed into their car. Valera was still on the veranda, talking to the media. He nodded at them over a reporter's shoulder and went back to answering questions. It was Comandante Enrique Valera's show now.

They drove in silence until they reached another one of the hovels Lovell claimed was a safe house. It was after midnight when Sole dragged himself from the passenger seat, stretched, and looked at the sky. "Damn."

"Yeah," Lovell said, following his gaze up to the stars burning with an intensity people accustomed to electric lighting rarely get to experience. Even in rural areas of the United States, it was hard to find true darkness anymore. "I imagine the world was a very dark place before electricity."

"Until the stars came out," Sole said. They stood for a

minute, necks craning up at the sky, transfixed by a billion points of light shimmering in the black. Sole yawned and pulled his eyes away. "Gotta sleep."

"Me too," Lovell said and headed into the shack.

Inside, Sole looked around and shook his head. "I'm not asking for five-star accommodations, but did you ever hear of running water and electricity."

"I hear a simple life is good for the *Sole*," Lovell said, grinning.

"Funny," Sole said with a smirk.

He threw his sleeping bag on the floor, stretched out, and was asleep in seconds. Lovell followed suit, and neither woke until sunlight through the cracked window glass washed over them.

Sole sat up. "How long?"

"Did we sleep?" Lovell yawned and shrugged. "A few hours."

"I mean, how long until we know?" Sole clarified.

"Oh, that ... not sure," Lovell replied. "It's gonna have to hit the news cycle in the States. Twelve hours maybe ... more or less ... then all hell breaks loose." He shrugged. "Soon, I think."

They opened cans of beans, turned their noses up, but dug in. Along with sleep, they'd been missing regular meals for several days. Sole finished first and grabbed water bottles from their pack as Lovell's phone chimed.

"Well, at least we got to eat first," Lovell said and thumbed the phone, putting it on speaker. He mouthed, *"Here we go,"* in Sole's direction, smiled, and spoke into the phone, "Good morning, boss."

"What the fuck do you think you're doing!" Carl Shank wasn't even trying to keep his voice down.

Lovell and Sole exchanged grins. Their asses might be

dangling over a cliff, but they could at least enjoy the view before they took the plunge to the rocks below.

"It's all over the news!" Shank shouted. "Some Mexican police comandante saying he took down the *Los Salvajes* cartel boss ... that the operation was a joint effort and supported by the U.S. government."

Shank paused to take a breath and began shouting again. "You violated a direct order, and I have you on tape acknowledging that order. Goddammit, Lovell, I'll have you in prison for the rest of your life."

"No, you won't," Lovell said calmly.

"Who the fuck do you think you're talking to? I swear to God, I will hunt you down, but you're right. There won't be any trial and prison. I'll just have you shot on sight ... a traitor who turned against his country ... violated direct orders from the highest levels of the administration."

"You won't do that either," Lovell said, and before Shank could start shouting again, added, "You're a hero, boss."

Shank was silent.

Lovell continued, "You and every other bureaucratic jerk off sitting around the conference table with you are heroes, including the president ... if you play this right."

The phone went dead, and Lovell knew that someone had muted it. He could imagine the discussion taking place around the table at that moment and wondered which faces were there.

Then, the phone was unmuted, and a different voice came over the line. "Do you know who this is?"

"I do." Lovell shot a glance at Sole. He recognized the voice of Sylvia Lostrum, Special Advisor to the President, and raised his eyebrows. More political infighting? Was she back in power? Whatever came next would either be good or it might be very bad.

"Lovell, you're playing a dangerous game," Lostrum said.

"Not a game, Ma'am. Just acting in the best interests of our country and according to the mission I was originally assigned."

"Don't bullshit me, Lovell. You know you were ordered to end the mission. I've heard the tape. In fact, I have possession of it."

"As I said, you can be heroes, or …" Lovell began.

"Shut the fuck up," Lostrum shot back, not shouting impotently as Shank had. Instead, her voice was quiet, calm, and threatening. "You're right. We can take credit for working with the Mexican government to bring down the largest human trafficking and drug smuggling operation in the world, but that doesn't mean you're in the clear. The way I see it …."

She paused, and Lovell and Sole could almost see the Cheshire cat smile on her face. "We own you … I own you … you and your operative partner. Is he there with you, listening?"

"He is," Lovell said and shrugged at Sole. There didn't seem to be any reason to lie.

"Good. Then, I want to clarify that you report directly to me from this point forward. Understood?"

"Understood," Lovell said.

"And your partner? I want to hear it from him."

"I understand," Sole said.

"Outstanding, Mr. Sole." And the lilt in her voice removed any doubt that she was smiling. She was taking a victory lap in front of whoever else was seated around the conference table with Shank. Then she got down to business. "We are beginning today to work, shall we say … diplomatically … with the Mexican government. Resources, technical support, manpower, whatever it takes to keep the ball rolling and bring the cartels down. As it turns out, the timing is perfect for us." There was no need to explain that the timing was perfect for the president's upcoming bid for reelection.

"We work for you now," Lovell said. "What are your orders, Ma'am?"

"No need to be so formal, Jay. Call me Sylvia," Lostrum said. "For now, lay low. Take a day to rest, then I want you here in my office to fully debrief so we can devise a long-term plan to leverage what you started."

"Both of us?" Sole asked, his voice making it clear he had no interest in sitting and hobnobbing with bureaucrats.

"Don't sound so unhappy, John." Lostrum paused and added, "No, just your partner, Jay, for now. You stay out of sight down in Mexico but be accessible if I need you."

The call ended. Lovell looked at Sole. "Well, that went better than I thought it would."

"I suppose," Sole said, not happy about being obligated to be accessible to some Washington politicrat. "Feels like we may have just traded one devil for another."

"No." Lovell shrugged. "It's the same devil … just a different day."

FORTY-NINE

A Friend

The day's rest Sole craved ended when his phone rang.

"I need a favor from you." Valera's voice sounded drained and even more fatigued than Sole's.

"What is it, Enrique?" Sole asked.

When the call ended, Sole looked at Lovell and said, "I have to take the pickup. I'll drop you at the nearest airport."

"Right." Lovell shrugged. "So much for a day's rest. You need any help with Valera? I can call our new boss and let her know something came up … that our little get-together in Washington will have to wait a day or two."

"Somehow, I don't think she's the kind of boss who accepts 'something came up' as an excuse for not showing up." Sole shook his head and began rolling up his sleeping bag. "No, I've got it."

Cedro Valera had watched the first news reports of the *Los*

Salvajes raid, saw his son's face on the television, and called the family together. "We are leaving."

Josefina and Sarita understood and gathered the children and the suitcases they had packed and made ready for this moment. Natalia and Benito were thrilled to be going on another adventure and not back to school.

I'll get some food together," Ana Valera said and went to pack all the nonperishables they could carry.

As their son had instructed, they were gone within an hour. Packed into an old farm truck that his son had driven as a boy, Cedro drove along the backroads until he came to a small village in the high plains of central Mexico. They found a small roadside inn that was little more than a row of shacks with a place to park in front, but it had electricity and running water, and everyone was ready to sleep.

Back at their now deserted farm, a local police officer from a nearby village saw the television reports, checked on the Valera family, and found them missing. Comandante Enrique Valera was known in the area, and the police officer made several calls. By the afternoon, he was ready to make another call. It took some explaining, but eventually, he was speaking with the person at the top of the chain of command.

"You have something to report? What is it?" Luis Ibarra was now effectively the *Los Salvajes* leader until someone else challenged him for the position, the other cartels killed him, or he decided to disappear with the money he'd stashed away.

"Sir, I… uh … I mean to say …" Officer Raoul Vasquez had never spoken to someone so high up in the cartels before.

"Say what you have to say," Ibarra snapped, watching the news reports on the television in his hotel room.

"Yes, of course, it's just that ..." Vasquez was accustomed to small bribes for favors or information, but he had never been in the position of negotiating one so large with a cartel *jefe*.

"Stop wasting my time!" Ibarra shouted. "If you have something important to say, you'll be well paid."

"Yes, yes ... no disrespect intended, sir." Vasquez took a deep breath. "I was watching the television and saw the reports, and ..."

"The whole fucking country has seen the reports!" Ibarra barked. "This is not new information."

"Yes, yes, of course not," Vasquez stammered. "But I thought you might want to know that I am familiar with the Valera family and that they are gone, and their old farm truck too."

"Gone?"

"Yes, sir ... parents, wife, and children of the comandante on the television ... it seems they left their farm today."

"They left ..." Ibarra screwed the phone tight against his ear. This country cop might actually have something important to say. "And I don't suppose you happen to know where they went, do you?"

"Yes, sir. I mean, that's why I called." Vasquez took a deep breath, trying to calm himself. "I made a few calls ... you know to some of my police contacts in other villages and small towns ... you know, just in case ..."

"Just in case what? For God's sake, if you know where they are, say it!"

"Yes, sir. So, I spread the word to my police contacts in the small towns. I thought that was probably where they would go because they are farmers ... you know, country people, and probably would not go to a big city where ..."

"Where are they?" Ibarra shouted.

"In a small village near Tepeaca," Vasquez said quickly. "A police officer from there called me to say he saw them."

"And how do you know for sure it's the Valeras?"

"That was easy," Vasquez said, his voice less timid, proud to show off his investigative ability. He had the cartel *jefe's* attention. "My police friend there saw them drive through a village he patrols, and he followed and saw them check into a bungalow for the night. After they went inside, he checked the manager's records and saw the name Valera on the register. Cedro Valera ... that's the comandante's father."

Ibarra was silent for several seconds. This miracle had fallen into his lap out of nowhere. Instead of running for his life, he suddenly saw a chance to take control of *Los Salvajes* ... even of the other cartels ... if he moved quickly.

"Meet me there," Ibarra said.

"What? Me? But it is very far from here," Vasquez said, wondering what he had just gotten into.

"If you want the money, I will pay you ... five thousand U.S. dollars ... leave now and meet me there early tomorrow morning."

"Five thousand dollars?" the police officer was stunned at the size of the payoff. The largest bribe he'd ever received was two hundred dollars from a *norteamericano* tourist who didn't want to go to jail for buying cocaine, and that had seemed to him an enormous sum. "Pardon, sir, but did you say five thousand ... dollars?"

"That's what I said, but have your police friend there. Both of you will be paid ... five thousand each ... but keep your eyes on them, do not let them disappear, and don't speak of this to anyone."

"Yes, sir," the police officer said. "I am leaving now and

will meet you in the morning just as you say. And I want to say that you don't have to worry about …"

Ibarra ended the call and punched another number. "Come to the hotel with a car. We are driving to Tepeaca."

"Anything else?" Rufo Serrato said. "How many men?"

"You …" Ibarra thought for a second. Too many men and it would look as if Ibarra was afraid to take care of things himself. He wanted the message out loud and clear that he was not afraid to get his hands bloody. "You and two others should be enough for what we have to do."

"Right," Rufo said, and the call ended. He wondered if now wasn't the time to cash in and get out of the country. One more day, he thought. See what Ibarra has up his sleeve. Maybe there'll be another payoff … some way to salvage things and get back to normal.

At four-thirty in the morning, Sole drove through a village on a country road and passed the little roadside inn. Cedro' Valera's large farm truck was parked in front of one of the ancient-looking bungalows, just as his son had described.

Sole continued past, scanning both sides of the road. A quarter mile along, he found what he was looking for, a dusty tan pickup bearing the markings of the local police. There was a man behind the wheel, his face dimly lit by the red glow of a cigarette.

Sole drove by without stopping, reached for his cell phone, and punched the speed dial number.

"Are you there?" Enrique Valera asked.

"Just got here … found them right where you said they'd be."

"*Gracias a Dios*, Thank God," Valera said, relief in his voice.

"They have company," Sole said, wishing he didn't have to.

"Who? How many?" Valera asked quickly.

"Just one right now, a local cop, but he is definitely watching the inn where they are staying."

"That means more are coming." Valera's voice lowered, and Sole could imagine the worry bearing down on him.

"I know you've got your hands full, but maybe you could send some of your men this way," Sole suggested.

"There are too few still, and the only ones I am certain I can trust with my family are here with me. It would take a day for them to arrive there."

The one thing Valera had wanted to avoid was happening. He blamed himself. Caught up in the work of taking down the cartels, he wasn't specific enough in his instructions.

His father had driven his family away but stopped too soon, too close to home. After a day on the road, it must have seemed far enough. When Cedro found the little village inn, he stopped to rest them all so they could leave again early in the morning.

When he contacted his son to tell him where they stopped for the night, Valera called Sole and asked for the favor. Watch out for his family.

"Alright," Sole said. "I'll stay nearby and watch. Then when they're on the road tomorrow, I'll follow."

"They may not have that much time. If the police officer has a contact in one of the cartels, they have probably already sent men to intercept them." Valera took a breath. "I'm coming to your location."

"You said yourself there isn't enough time to get here."

"I have to do something. I can't sit here while they may be in danger."

"Alright, you head this way," Sole said. "I won't leave them."

"Thank you," Valera said. "I'll call my father and let him know you are there. They will let you in and make you comfortable."

"No," Sole said. "If you're right about others coming for them, I can do more good from outside than penned up with them in a room."

"Then I should tell them to leave quickly."

Sole thought about that for a second and said, "I don't think that's a good idea. If the cartel finds them on the road in the middle of the night, it'll be hard to protect them. Too many things can happen in a moving vehicle, especially if someone is shooting at them. If they stay where they are, I can see any threats and eliminate them."

Valera wanted to shout to his father, RUN! But as he thought about it, he knew Sole was right. They would be more vulnerable on the road at night, and his father could never outrun a pursuer in the family's old truck.

"Alright," he said. "We'll do it as you say. I'm coming there. You watch and do what is necessary, but if you see a threat, call me at once so that I can alert my father."

"Will do," Sole said, ready to end the call and get to work.

"One more thing," Valera added, fighting back the emotion in his voice. "Thank you, my friend."

"Just get here safely, Enrique."

Sole turned around and headed the SUV back toward the village. Cutting the headlights, he pulled to the shoulder and coasted to a stop out of sight a half mile from where he'd seen the police officer watching the bungalow. Grabbing the M-24 and his backpack, loaded with extra ammunition and bottles of water, he trotted up into the hills.

Inside the roadside bungalow, Cedro Valera sat in a chair keeping watch, a twelve-gauge pump shotgun propped between his knees. When his head began to bob and droop, Sarita rose from the bed she shared with Josefina.

"You rest, Papa Cedro. I'll keep watch for a while. You need your sleep if you are driving tomorrow."

"You may be right." Cedro yawned and nodded. "It's been a long day and a longer one tomorrow." He held up the shotgun. "Do you know how to use this if you need to?"

"I've fired guns before … my brother's pistols. Show me how this one works."

"Alright." Cedro held the shotgun at port arms. "It is loaded and a round in the camber. This button here is the safety. Push it this way: the gun will fire when you pull the trigger. After you fire, you pump it like this to load another shell." He pumped it once, ejected a shell to demonstrate, and then loaded the .00 buckshot round back into the magazine. "Simple, see. Can you do it if you have to?"

"Yes." Sarita nodded.

"Good." He stood and handed her the shotgun. "Wake me if you hear anything unusual."

"I will."

Sarita watched him step carefully over the children sleeping on makeshift pallets on the floor, then lie down on the second bed beside his wife. Cedro drifted off to sleep in a moment, leaving Sarita to stand guard over the family.

She sat with the shotgun between her knees as she'd seen him sitting and watched the door. A smile crossed her face as she listened to the little sounds the children made as they slept, the shifting and snores of the adults, all of it made her feel at home. In the short time since Comandante Valera left her with them, she had become part of their family. She wondered how he would feel about that, remembering how he almost wanted to dispose of her the 'other way.'

It didn't matter. The Valeras were the only real family she had ever known, and she would do what was necessary to protect them.

Sole worked his way up and over the hills until he was above the police pickup, still sitting by the road. He looked down to check his position and could make out the police officer inside, still smoking one cigarette after another and dropping the butts out the window. It was amateurish behavior for a cop on a stakeout, a dead giveaway to anyone suspecting they were being watched.

Fine, Sole thought. If he was about to go up against cartel killers, the more unprofessional they were, the better.

He moved up and down another hillside until he found a clump of trees across from the motel. Dropping the backpack to the ground, he checked the rifle's magazine loads and settled in to wait.

Sometime before the sun fully rose, in the gray early morning twilight, another police vehicle arrived. From his position, Sole saw it drive slowly past the Valera bungalow. The markings on the door were from a different police jurisdiction. Two cops meant two bad guys, professional or not. Sole suspected there would be more. If a cartel was hunting the Valera family, there was no way they would rely on these two country cops to handle things.

Not long after the second police vehicle passed, a third car showed up, a shiny black Cadillac Escalade, entirely out of place in the Mexican backcountry. The boss had arrived.

Sole hit Valera's number on his phone.

"Yes," Valera said.

"Call your father. Tell him they have company and to watch the back door. I'll cover the front."

Valera wasted no time asking questions. He disconnected to make the call. A few seconds later, Sole could hear the chime of a cell phone faintly ringing in the still night air, audible through the bungalow's thin walls even from his position fifty yards away.

Things happened quickly after that. The two police pickups cruised slowly back, pulling into the dirt lot outside the bungalow, parking at either end. The Cadillac pulled directly up to the front door.

Two men came from the rear of the Cadillac and ran to the back of the bungalow. Two others exited the front and went to the door. The two police officers stood uncomfortably by their vehicles, unsure exactly what to do. One pulled the pistol from his holster and looked at the other, who followed suit. They held their weapons with the awkward stance of people not accustomed to using them for anything except plinking at beer cans and intimidating local farmers.

Rufo Serrato looked around, saw his men disappear around back, and stepped toward the bungalow's door. Luis Ibarra followed a pace behind, a pistol in his hand, low down by his side.

Serrato waited a minute to be sure his men were in position to watch the rear and prevent anyone from escaping. Then, he lifted a leg, kicked the flimsy plank door in, and was met by a blast from the shotgun.

He stumbled back, falling into Ibarra as he toppled to the ground. Ibarra pushed him off and raised the pistol.

Watching from across the road, Sole was nearly as surprised as the man kicking in the door when the shotgun roared. He recovered quickly and sent two rounds through the back of the man behind. He fell on top of the first, the pistol clattering to the ground. Luis Ibarra's dream of taking over *Los Salvajes* died with him.

Shots rang out behind the bungalow. A few seconds later, one of the men who had gone behind came running back around. Sole was up now, moving across the road toward the bungalow. He raised the rifle and sent a round through the running man's chest. He flopped over to the ground in mid-stride.

That left the two cops. Sole lowered the rifle in his left hand and pulled the pistol from his belt. It was a better weapon for engaging multiple targets at close range, and the bumbling police officers did not seem to have much fight in them.

Sole shouted to them, "*Deja tus pistolas!*" Drop your guns!

Officer Raoul Vasquez, who had started the day before by discovering the Valera family was missing and then had driven all night for the promise of his payoff, swung to face Sole. If he had thought things through, he would never have raised the pistol, but Vasquez was not a thinker, and as the gun came up in his hand, Sole sent three rounds into his chest and spun toward the second cop, who dropped his cigarette as Sole killed his partner.

Sole repeated his command, "*Deja tu pistola!*"

Wide-eyed, the smoking cop turned toward his police pickup and fired a half dozen wild rounds over his shoulder as he tried to escape. Sole fired two more times, and smoking-cop fell, bouncing off the side of his pickup, landing face-first in the dirt.

Cedro Valera came from inside the bungalow, a Winchester .30-30 at his shoulder, pointed at Sole. "*Quién eres?*" Who are you?

"*Un amigo.*" A friend. Sole lowered the pistol and turned to face Cedro.

"It's true," Sarita said, coming from the bungalow, the shotgun in her hands. "He is a friend."

FIFTY

It Was Enough

The floodgates opened. True to her word, Sylvia Lostrum urged the current administration to get behind the takedown of the cartels. Her purposes may have been cynical and designed to boost the president's political interests, but the results were significant.

Resources poured in from north of the border—manpower, materiel, expertise, training, and advanced forensic technology. The media coverage on both sides of the border made it impossible for the Mexican government to look the other way. They could buy into the narrative that they were fully engaged in the joint operation with agents from the United States to bring down the cartels or admit that one courageous police comandante did what they had failed to do for years ... stand up to the cartels.

Valera became a national hero, interviewed extensively in Mexico and by the media in the United States. His face became one of the most recognized in Mexico.

Video footage showing the Elizondo hacienda was

replayed to the wonder of everyday Mexicans who knew of the cartels but never really understood the immense wealth and power they possessed. Images of the hooded police officers, the bodies lying on the lawn of the Elizondo estate, and Juana Elizondo in handcuffs being led away from the hacienda became the sensationalized video lead-in for almost every news update on the fight to bring down the cartels.

Charged with Mexico's equivalent of racketeering, organized crime, and drug trafficking, Juana Elizondo's trial lasted four months. Her highly paid, high-profile attorneys went to work, publicly proclaiming her innocence while privately joking that they had about as much chance of victory as the Texans at the Alamo.

Enrique Valera took on the duty of working with prosecutors to compile evidence of her crimes. A transfer from the state police and promotion to General Inspector of the *Policía Federal Ministeria*—Federal Police Ministry—allowed him to bring more resources to the investigation.

The evidence of Juana's crimes was overwhelming. Knowing that she could not avoid conviction, her defense attorneys tried to present her as a victim. They told the court that she could not help being the daughter of Bebé Elizondo and that she could not be held responsible for the crimes committed by *Los Salvajes*, which were merely the continuation of her father's cartel operations.

No one expected the strategy to work, and it didn't. She was convicted on all charges brought against her, and her sentence of thirty years began immediately after the trial.

Her prison sentence began in one of Mexico's three maximum security federal prisons known as Centers for Social Readaptation. Like virtually all Mexican prisons, it was corrupt and controlled by the cartels. More than one cartel boss had bought his freedom, and Juana immediately began bribing the prison administration in preparation for her escape from prison and flight from the country.

The only thing that could prevent it was the possibility of extradition to the United States. Her attorneys began throwing up legal roadblocks to prevent that from happening, but pressure from the U.S. government increased, and Juana was eventually extradited and transferred to a prison north of the border on the condition that she would not face the death penalty.

While her living conditions improved immensely, her possibility of escape was reduced to zero. She went to trial on charges of racketeering, drug trafficking, human trafficking, money laundering, weapons smuggling, and conspiracy to commit murder by ordering the deaths of *Los Salvajes'* enemies within the United States. She was found guilty on all counts.

Emotionally distraught and unable to stand, she sat head bowed between her attorneys as the sentence was proclaimed by the judge—life plus thirty years with no possibility of parole. The cameras in the courtroom caught the tears trickling down her face. For the first time since childhood Juana wept.

The day after the raid on *Los Salvajes* and Juana Elizondo, another cartel boss was taken down, but this one was not as well publicized. Chucho Sanchez reclined in a chaise lounge by the pool at his ranch in Guadalajara. His wife, Adriana, sat beside him, thumbing through a magazine while their children played in the pool.

At eleven AM, Adriana called the children out of the pool. "Come dry yourselves. It's time to eat."

Splashing and playing, they scampered to the shallow end and climbed out, then followed their mother inside. "Are you coming?" Adriana called over her shoulder.

"Soon," Sanchez said, then stretched his stubby, hairy, and deeply tanned body under the sun.

Anselmo Cardoso was due to arrive at any time, but Sanchez had no intention of changing his routine to suit that whining, scheming *mocoso*—punk. Cardoso could present himself at the door and then wait in the study while Sanchez dressed.

He closed his eyes behind his sunglasses, luxuriating in the warm sunlight. After a few minutes, he began to drowse and thought that perhaps he should shake himself awake, take a dip in the pool, or go inside and eat before Cardoso arrived. Then he grunted, scratched at his sweaty balls through the swimsuit, and thought, fuck Cardoso. Let him wait and understand who the real head of their new cartel alliance would be.

In a few minutes, he began to snore. The light, warm breeze, the sound of the pump circulating the water in the pool, the murmured conversations inside between Adriana and their housekeeper combined like a drug to send him deeper into his nap.

Then an odd thing happened. A small shriek pierced through his drowsy haze. At first, he thought it sounded like Adriana, startled by some prank the children played on her. Then another shriek followed by a long scream from their housekeeper and more shrieks, these from the children.

Each shriek was punctuated by a loud rapping sound. Sanchez opened his eyes and started to sit up.

Three men stood before him, the muzzle suppressors on their pistols pointed squarely at his forehead. He opened his mouth to shout an obscenity at them, although his brain never had time to decide what obscenity. Three nine-millimeter copper-jacketed bullets plowed through his head. Even with the silencers on the pistols, the clacking whoosh of the shots was loud enough to hear a hundred yards away.

The mercenary, Diaz, nodded at his men. "Find anyone else on the property."

They nodded and left. As it turned out, the only other person on the ranch that day was the stableman who cared for Sanchez's horses. He came from the barn to investigate the strange noise the silenced pistol shots made and met the same fate as Sanchez, his family, and the housekeeper. Cardoso had said to spare no one, and the mercenaries dutifully complied with the order.

Diaz had his men douse the house and outbuildings with gasoline from the cans in the barn and then set it all on fire. After that, he called Cardoso. "It's done."

"Excellent," Cardoso said, watching the ongoing news reports of the raid on Juana Elizondo. Diaz and his men would be disappointed that the police had beaten them to the target they most wanted to eliminate.

The new war between the cartels began without as much coverage as the destruction of the *Los Salvajes* cartel. The Sanchez ranch ruins smoldered for a day before the smoke on the horizon was discovered and anyone reported it.

A few media outlets featured short writeups, but no

news crews spent days wandering the grounds and digging up background information from locals. Comandante Valera's heroic work to bring down *Los Salvajes* would continue to dominate the news for months.

In the meantime, as Sole and Lovell had planned, the other cartels quietly went to war. As they shot holes in each other, Valera, for the moment a grudging favorite of his superiors, broadened the scope of his work.

"Look at that." One of the men at the table nodded at the door to the bar. "Little too old to be *una prostituta*, I'd say."

"Too old?" Chiro Cordera laughed. "Never heard of such a thing. Besides, she's not half bad looking."

The woman with a smooth lean face and long gray hair hanging to her shoulders looked to be about fifty, by local standards, a little on the high end of the age scale for prostitutes, but not unheard of. Dressed in a lime green skirt cut so short that the bottom of her panties were exposed front and rear, she had the attention of every man in the small bar in Comitán. Her halter top was cut low and wide, exposing all but the tips of the nipples on her full, round breasts.

She ordered a tequila and turned, sipping from the glass and surveying the room. Her eyes moved from face to face, flirting with the men without speaking or doing anything other than sipping the tequila. She could see the hunger in their eyes as she smoothed the sides of the miniskirt, running her long brown fingers seductively over her thighs.

She decided to give them a show. Taking a napkin from the bar, she turned and bent over as if to wipe something from the toe of one of her high heel shoes. Her breasts fell forward out of the halter top so that she had to push them back under cover with her hands as she straightened. Then she turned and repeated the process, bending over to wipe at her shoe with the napkin, but this time with her bottom in the air so that the tiny thong panties she wore left nothing to the imagination.

When she straightened, the eyes staring at her from the sweating faces were hungry. She smiled and lifted the glass of tequila in a sort of toast to the men staring at her. "*Paciencia hombres. Todos tendrán su turno.*" Patience men. You'll all get your turn.

She eyed the faces as if picking her mark out of the crowd. Then, making up her mind, she took a final sip of tequila and set the glass down with a thump on the bar top.

Walking through the crowded bar, she brushed against men sitting at the tables. A few dared to reach out to touch her legs or rump as she passed, but she ignored them. Her eyes were locked on those of the man at the table in the back by the door to the alley.

"Aye, this one is something special," Cordero said and smiled as she came up before him.

The two men seated with him gaped without speaking at the woman whose nipples now were clearly visible through the almost completely open halter top.

She looked down at Cordero like one might imagine Cleopatra staring down at a horny Mark Antony, desperate to get Caesar out of the way and have her to himself. She said, "I think you should be first."

"You chose right, woman." Cordero nodded. "First and last and in between tonight."

"That will cost you quite a bit," the woman said.

"I got quite a bit," Cordero replied, gave his crotch a tug, and grinned.

The men at the table laughed.

"I'll bet you have." The woman gave a seductive smile and put out her hand. "We should go then."

Cordero took her hand and let her lead him through the back door to the alley. They walked a few paces, and she turned, coming close, putting a hand on his hip, pulling their bodies together.

"Ah, woman. I want you now," he said, pushing his lips and stubbled face against hers.

Her hands went to his waist and loosened his belt so that his pants sagged halfway down his legs. Then she reached under the skirt and dropped her panties to the ground.

He pushed a hand between her legs, groping and searching with his fingers as she stroked his erection.

"Stop teasing," he said, his voice deep and husky with passion. Bend over. You're killing me."

"Yes, I am."

It was a small knife, a blade of three inches in length and only half an inch wide. It might have been used to open letters or trim fingernails. Honed and sharpened each night for weeks now, it gleamed in the dim alley light, razor-sharp, its tip like a needle.

Lucia Pacheco took the blade from under the leather belt around her skirt and plunged it into Chiro Cordero's neck. She knew just where to place the blade, had studied it in books at night, sitting in the bed she had shared with her husband, Ignacio.

In a matter of seconds, she thrust the knife rapidly into his neck five times, first severing the carotid artery, then pushing it through and nearly severing the trachea so that the only sound he could make was a high-pitched wheezing grunt. She moved quickly, knowing she would have only seconds to do what she had come for.

Cordero's hands went to his throat, his eyes wide in surprise, then terror as he realized he was dying. Blood poured from the severed artery, and he tried to make his way to the alley door and summon his men, but he was weakening with every second.

Lucia shoved him hard against the bar's block wall. His pants halfway down his legs, he stumbled, and his knees buckled. With his back against the wall, he slid down, clutching his throat.

Lucia knelt beside him, using the knife between his legs, thrusting into his genitals. With each thrust, she whispered into Cordero's face.

"This is for my husband, Ignacio Pacheco, the love of my life."

"This is for Glauco Capilla, who was a friend to us."

"This is for the boy Naldo who will never have the chance to grow up and leave this place."

The light faded from Chiro Cordero's eyes, and, with the wheezing hiss of his last breaths, he died.

Lucia rose and walked, dazed and bloody, down the alley. She had done what she came for. Moving in the shadows, staying away from the main streets, zig-zagging through deserted alleys until she made her way to an old church.

Seated on a bench under a tree in the churchyard, she took deep breaths, fighting back the nausea that threatened to churn up from her stomach. After a minute, when her breathing slowed, she took out her rosary beads. For an hour, she prayed, recited her rosary, and made her confession directly to God, as there was no priest.

It was the priest who found her the next day, still seated on the bench, her head back against the tree trunk. The police officers who investigated her suicide had never seen anything quite like it.

This one truly wanted to die," one police officer said.

People often say they want to kill themselves by slitting their wrists, but few succeed. The officers nodded in appreciation at the expertise she showed, finding the radial artery in each arm and cutting them open lengthwise to make sure she bled out and died.

Why she did it was a mystery until the police put two and two together and realized that she matched the description of the prostitute who sliced up Chiro Cordero in an alley.

"Hmm. Probably figured it was better to do it herself than let Cordero's men get hold of her."

"Seems a shame," Another said. "She was a fine looking woman." He nodded at the rosary beads. "Religious too. Unusual for a whore."

Numbering in the tens of thousands, there were far too many victims to identify more than a comparative handful, but Valera organized a task force to find and rescue those he could. As *Los Salvajes'* command structure broke down, the cartel's contacts for its various enterprises were identified.

Valera led a series of raids, arresting those who had engaged in illegal activity with *Los Salvajes*. These included the captains of two fishing boats, one operating in the Gulf of Mexico and Caribbean, the other in the Pacific off the western coast of Mexico.

It was a monumental task, taking the reports of family members who claimed their loved ones had been heading to the border but then disappeared off the face of the earth. Valera's expanded investigative team, assisted by resources provided by the U.S. government, collated, sorted, and cross-matched information against the missing persons reports, searching for links that might lead them to the victims.

Over the years, the cartels had become experts at covering their tracks. In the same way that they laundered money, information about their victims was distorted through so many transactions that the success of Valera's team was minimal at best. When they were able to uncover a viable lead, they worked with local governments to find and recover victims. This happened far less frequently than Valera and the victims' families would have hoped, and even if they were successful, the results could be heartbreaking.

Francisca lay on her cot one night, blinking her eyes in the dark at the sound of heavy footsteps rushing through the building. She heard the voice of the black-haired man who had raped her on her first day there, followed by a gunshot, then a loud thud as a body hit the floor.

The door to the dingy closet that was her room burst open. Men dressed in black and carrying rifles rushed in. She cowered on the cot, pulling the stained sheet up to her chin to cover her naked body.

One of the men in black carried a blanket and covered her with it. "Come with us?"

"Please don't hurt me," Francisca sobbed, speaking in the Portuguese she had learned over the months of captivity.

"We are not going to harm you. We were sent to take you away from here," one of the men said.

Francisca began sobbing, unable to speak. The deliverance she had prayed for, and that her sister Gabriela promised would come, had finally arrived.

With the blanket draped around her, the men led her and several other girls from the back of the building through the dingy bar and into the humid night air. Francisca saw the black-haired man lying on the floor in the hallway, a pool of blood around his head.

Outside they stood beside a bus while another man—the others called him the lieutenant—also dressed in black, was making notes on a pad. Francisca could see now, under the street lights, that they were all police officers.

"What is your full name?" the lieutenant asked.

Francisca gave him her name.

The lieutenant looked up from his pad, "And there should be another … your sister, Gabriela." He looked around at the group of girls, most sobbing like Francisca, all staring terrified at the ground waiting for the next act of their personal nightmare to unfold. "Which one of you is Gabriela?"

"Gabriela …" Francisca fell to her knees, weeping. "My sister is dead."

"Dead?" The lieutenant counting the girls lowered the notepad. "Who killed her? We'll find that person and charge them with murder."

"No," Francisca said, shaking her head so that her tears fell to the alley's trash-strewn pavers. "She killed herself … three months ago." She looked up, her face contorted. "They all killed her … the men who came to do what they did!"

The policemen there stared at the ground as if ashamed

of what other men had done to the girls. When the lieutenant nodded, they loaded them onto the bus.

"Where are we going?" Francisca asked.

"Back to Mexico," the lieutenant said.

"To my family?" Francisca asked, her eyes brightening for the first time. "To my mother and father?"

"To Mexico, after that ..." the lieutenant stopped and nodded at the driver to close the door, not wanting to make promises that would not be kept.

Valera's team of investigators never located Francisca's parents. After temporarily relocating to Mexico, she was sent to Honduras to live with her aunt, her mother Marita's sister. The nightmare of her time as a sex slave would haunt her for the rest of her life. There were times when she thought that, perhaps, Gabriela had made the wisest decision by taking her own life.

On the same night that Francisca was rescued, a detachment of Chilean commandos conducted a raid on the mountain headquarters of *El Ejército de la Revolución Popular*—the Army of the People's Revolution. Funded by money from the U.S. government and funneled through Valera's team, this raid was far less successful than the one carried out by the Brazilian police.

Surrounding the camp before dawn, they set up loudspeakers and shouted orders for the occupants to surrender. They didn't expect anyone to comply, and no one did.

It was impossible to say who fired the first shots. The commando leader claimed his men were fired on from the camp. If so, then the occupants of the camp had a death wish.

Completely outnumbered and outgunned, illuminated by floodlights from helicopters circling overhead, the revolutionary fighters were easy targets for the camouflaged commandos. When the roar of gunfire stopped after fifteen minutes, no one inside the compound was standing, and most were dead. The few wounded, moaning on the ground, were soon put out of their misery by commandos walking through the camp, shooting bullets through their heads while they searched for the leader, the one they called simply *El Gallo*—The Rooster.

Among the bodies on the ground were the brothers, Manolo and Javier, sons of Paco and Lupe. Since they could no longer be questioned, identifying them was impossible. They lay side by side, their rifles still in their hands amid fifty other young fighters. The commando leader looked around, disappointed. "We didn't get fucking *Gallo*," he said, spitting on the ground, then shrugged. "But all in all, I suppose it's a good night's work."

Manolo and Javier were dumped in a common grave with the other fighters. The report of the raid sent back to Valera was simple enough. *Raid conducted on the revolutionary camp. The brothers, Manolo and Javier, were not found.*

Hector and Marita never knew what had happened to their daughters. They prayed they somehow found their way across the border as the coyotes had promised, but there were so many broken promises they held out little hope, and Francisca and Gabriela were gone to them forever, or at least for the duration of this life.

Paco and Lupe also prayed each day for their boys, sold and sent to fight in a war that meant nothing to them. As the years passed, they imagined them as young men growing up—working, living, perhaps marrying—in the United States. They whispered to each other in bed at night, wondering if their sons had given them grandchildren and if they would be named after the grandparents.

Hector and Marita, Paco and Lupe, and thousands of others sold into servitude by the cartels toiled their lives away, on farms and plantations, in factories and warehouses, wherever the cartels found a buyer. The red-faced coffee grower had told them that if they worked hard and saved, they could buy their freedom, but that, too, was a lie.

The meager wages he paid them were barely enough to buy the food he gladly sold them from his own pantry. They wore their clothes until they turned to rags on their backs and then scrounged through barns and trash heaps, looking for enough cloth to piece together a garment to cover themselves. No money was left to buy their freedom, pay for medical care, or decent housing. They lived solely to toil for their owner.

Governments worldwide were beginning to pay attention to the problem of human trafficking. Questions were being asked, and the more they asked, the more perilous the lives of the people purchased from the cartels became. Men like the red-faced coffee grower were not about to release them and run the risk of being prosecuted for engaging with the cartels in modern-day slavery. Instead, the slave owners worked them until there was no more work in them and then let them die.

Hector and Marita were dead within fifteen years, as were Paco, Lupe, and thousands of others. Lost and forgotten, their lives blinked out entirely unnoticed by the world.

What had begun as a dream for a better life became a nightmare. The great hope of America had lured them as it had generations of immigrants before, seeking better lives for themselves and their children.

But they hadn't understood that to come to America meant to become part of it, one with it, welcomed through the front door when invited, not sneaking through the back door like a trespasser. It was an honest mistake and an understandable one for desperate people, but for those trafficked by the cartels, it was a terrible one.

Lured to the back door to serve the purposes of politicians, they never had a chance to enter through the front door and see their dream realized. They never understood that they were only pawns in the politicians' games.

Sole stayed with the Valera family for several days, helping Enrique get them to a safe place in the tiny village in the southern Mexican state of Chiapas where Cedro had lived as a boy. The locals were mostly relatives or childhood friends, and it was as safe a place for them as could be found in Mexico. The threat to Valera's family had diminished as the wars between the cartels escalated and kept them occupied.

Then Sole got up early one sunny morning and packed up his backpack. He found Valera having coffee on the stoop of the small house in the village where his family would wait out the days ahead.

"Are you leaving?" Valera said, looking up from his coffee. He'd known this moment would come but still, there was a hint of surprise in his eyes.

"I am," Sole said. "It's time."

"I suppose so," Valera said and stood to shake his hand.

"Take care of yourself, Enrique." Sole hefted the backpack to his shoulder

"And you, my friend." Valera watched him drive away, a solitary man, anonymous and unknown. He would never be recognized for what he had done or given the honor he was due. His name would never appear in the papers or on television. But then, Valera knew that Sole preferred it that way.

"Come and eat," Josefina called from inside. "The children are hungry."

As Sole disappeared down the road, Valera stood, tossed the dregs at the bottom of his coffee cup into the grass, and went inside

---

He drove through Mexico from south to north toward the border for a day. Lovell called sometime around noon.

"How are things in Washington?" Sole asked.

"Going as well as can be expected," Lovell said. "Sylvia is a real ball-buster, though."

"I picked up on that," Sole said, smiling as he drove. "Sylvia, huh. Getting pretty chummy with her, then."

"Hah. Chummy is not a word I would ever use to describe a relationship with her," Lovell laughed.

"So, what's up?" Sole asked.

"She wants you to come here and go over plans. She has a few possible ops in the works." Lovell paused and added sardonically, "All of them designed to enhance the president's standing in the polls, of course."

"Of course."

"When can you get here for a sit-down with her. She says she wants to get to know you a little before the next op

... establish protocols, and firm up the chain of command. You know, the usual bureaucratic bullshit."

"I know."

"So, when can you get here?"

"I'm not coming."

Lovell was silent for a moment before he said, "I half expected you to say that ... hoping you wouldn't ... but yeah, I guess I'm not all that surprised." He paused and then asked, "Mind telling me why? After everything we went through down there, I was hoping we might be a team."

"I don't know," Sole said. "We were a team ... still are, I suppose." He shrugged as he drove. "I guess I just like to choose the team I'm playing on ... and what game I'm playing in. Seems to me that working for Sylvia Lostrum takes those options away."

"She's not going to be happy about this," Lovell said. "Probably go through the roof when I break the news to her."

"Sorry to put you in that position," Sole said.

"Oh, don't be sorry. I'm kind of looking forward to it." Lovell lowered his voice as if others might overhear and added, "She is an arrogant asshole, you know."

Sole laughed, "I picked up on that too."

"So, this is the end then. You go your way. I go mine," Lovell said and chuckled. "And never the twain shall meet again."

"We'll meet again," Sole said. "You have my number. If something interesting pops up, give me a call. If it's up my alley ... the kind of game I want to play ... maybe we can team up again."

"Well, that's something," Lovell said, and there was

genuine respect, mingled with regret, in his tone. "It's been an honor working with you."

"And with you," Sole said honestly and disconnected.

When night fell, he continued driving, stopping only for gas. It was a thirty-six-hour trek to Juarez, where he planned to cross the border into El Paso. After that, he wasn't sure.

The need to keep moving was on him, an urgent drumming in his brain compelling him to keep going until … what? John Sole couldn't say. For now, it was enough to keep moving.

More by Glenn Trust

vinci-books.com/authors/glenn-trust

Follow the link to stay up to date with Glenn Trust's new releases

About the Author

Glenn Trust is the author of the bestselling *Hunters, Sole Justice, and Journey Series* of mystery/thriller/suspense novels. He has also written standalone works, including *Dying Embers, Mojave Sun,* and short stories.

There are no superheroes or knights in shining armor in his stories. According to Trust, knights are for fairy tales. His books are gritty and based in the real world, with characters who face their frailties while dealing with their roles in the story. The heroes are average people doing the best they can.

The villains, as real villains often do, look like us. Trust's monsters hide behind the smiling faces that pass us on the street. They look like us, and this makes them more frightening.

He is a Georgia native but has lived in most regions of the country at one time or another. Varied experiences, from construction worker to police officer, corporate executive to city manager, color and provide insight into the characters he creates. His stories are known for detailed plots, solid research, and realism.

Today, he writes full-time and lives quietly with his wife and two dogs, Gunner and Charlie.